In the Tower of the Wizard King

An Age of Wizards Novel

MICHELLE MILES

This is a work of fiction. All characters, organizations and events portrayed in this novel are either products of the author's imagination or used fictitiously.

IN THE TOWER OF THE WIZARD KING

Cover Design by Erin Dameron-Hill

ISBN: 978-1-7333887-0-2

Praise for In the Tower of the Wizard King

"The book has a very strong and intriguing plotline as well as unforgettable characters. I liked the parallel narration of the present and the past as it made the story both more complicated and more involving…" —*5 stars, Amazon Reviewer*

"The mix of past and present stories brings the reader full circle and will keep you engrossed in the story. Beware though, you may not want to put the book down! …two thumbs up…!"
—*5 stars, Goodreads Reviewer*

"Michelle Miles brilliantly weaves twists and turns, love stories both past and present, secrets, betrayal and revenge, with multi-dimensional characters, two different timelines and two different worlds."
—*5 stars, Amazon Reviewer*

"I thoroughly enjoyed every aspect of this book, and highly recommend it. Filled with fantasy and three dimensional characters, I couldn't put it down." —*5 stars, Amazon Reviewer*

Dedication

For all those who believe in love, magic and happily ever after.
This book is for you.

Pronunciation Guide

PEOPLE:
Aoife (EE-fa) Burke
Sean O'Connell
Fiona (FEE-o-nuh) – Aoife's mother
Niall (NEE-ull) – the Wizard King and ruler of Illyria
Deaglan (deck-LAN) – Niall's father
Cian (KEE-an) – Ruler of Anatolia
Sunnie – Aoife's half-sister
Liam Burke – Fiona's human husband
Caleb O'Brien – Sean's partner and friend
Queen Siobhan (shiv-AWN) – Queen of Anatolia
King Ardan – King of Anatolia
Einin (a-NEEN) – Fiona's mother

PLACES:
Anatolia, Cian's kingdom
Illyria, Niall's kingdom
Cliffs of Mhothair – where the Towers of Illyria are located
Lambridge Castle – home of Prince Cian
Brookdale – Human realm, where Aoife hails from

Part One

Awakening

Chapter 1

Present Day in the Human Realm

An incessant buzzing pulled Aoife Burke out of a dreamy, heavenly sleep. Her hand fumbled on the nightstand trying to silence the thing when a pillow crashed against her face, jarring her from half-asleep to fully awake.

"Make that phone stop already," her dorm roommate growled. "It's been going crazy for the last ten minutes."

Still groggy and trying to wipe the sleep from her eyes, Aoife dropped the pillow to the floor and yanked the cell phone off the charger as it stopped buzzing. When the small screen lit up, she had four missed calls. All from her mother.

Her mother never called her, so to have four missed calls meant something terrible had happened.

She snapped to a sitting position, her fingers fumbling on the screen as she tried to get to the missed calls screen when it started to buzz again. She swiped the screen and answered.

"Mom?"

"Aoife, there you are at last. I've called to let you know that your father passed away." Fiona's even tone held no emotion whatsoever.

Aoife blinked, a sudden sickness piercing through her gut as her hand tightened on the phone. She hiccupped a breath and forced her mind to remember to inhale, exhale. "What do you mean he passed away? He's dead?"

Instant regret and guilt poured through her. She'd skipped going home for Christmas three months prior because she couldn't stand the thought of her mother giving her a frosty reception. When Aoife turned thirteen, her relationship with Fiona underwent a drastic change, something Aoife had never understood.

"Yes, I'm sorry. He's gone." Aoife detected a soft quiver in Fiona's voice as she answered.

Her parents' marriage had been rocky for a while too, but Aoife naively thought despite all that, they would always be together. Tears pooled in Aoife's eyes as she clutched the phone and gulped in air, desperate for breath. Her roommate, Jenna, moved to perch on the edge of the bed, putting a comforting arm around her shoulders.

"I'm sorry to have to break the news to you this way, but there's no time, really." Fiona sniffed so quiet Aoife almost missed it. "Your sister is in Shanghai filming a movie but I called to let her know. I thought you needed to know, too."

"Mom, wait—"

"I have to go before it's too late."

"Too late for what? Mom!"

But the line went dead.

Her insides had curled into a low, tight knot in the pit of her stomach. Aoife shrugged off Jenna's arm and scooted off the bed. A deep-seated ache settled in her chest and she was only thinking about one thing—getting home.

"What happened?" Jenna asked, her voice timid and high in the darkness.

"I don't know. My dad died. That's all I know." Aoife pulled her duffle bag out from under the bed and blindly shoved whatever clothes she could find inside, fighting back tears.

"I'll come with you," Jenna offered and rose.

"No." Aoife spun to face her as she stood and then froze. "You don't need to do that."

Her family dynamic was far from normal and she didn't know how she'd explain that to Jenna. Her mother was cold and distant, disappearing for sometimes days on end. Her sister, Sunnie, was the precious favorite child that always got her way. She'd gotten her big acting break and was off globetrotting and trendsetting. She landed in the tabloids more than once but despite that she was still the favorite. Aoife resented her for being the star daughter while she was pushed aside and ignored. They were never close emotionally and now she was across the globe. Aoife couldn't wait. She really needed to find out what happened.

Jenna blinked owlish eyes at her. "So you're going to drive all the way home tonight alone? It's one in the morning."

"Yes." Aoife went back to shoving clothes into the duffle bag. She wandered toward the bathroom to grab her toothbrush. "It's only a five hour drive from here. I can be there before the sun comes up."

"Are you sure you're okay to drive?" Jenna asked. "I mean, you just found out your dad died. You're emotional—"

"I'll be fine."

There's no time really. I have to go. Before it's too late.

Her hand tightened around the toothbrush as she shoved it into the bag. She stuck her feet in her red Keds, snatched her phone and bag and started for the door.

"Aoife?"

She paused as she reached for the door. "Yes?"

"You going to get dressed?"

Aoife glanced down and realized she still wore her rumpled t-shirt that proclaimed I RUN LIKE A GIRL, and shorts. She huffed and dropped her bag, rummaged through it until she found a pair of jeans. She kicked off her shoes, pulled them on over her shorts and then picked up the bag again, shoving her feet back into the sneakers.

"Be careful," Jenna said as Aoife flung open the door.

"I will."

But all she could think about was keeping it together and getting to her mother before something worse happened.

Before it's too late.

Seeing the SOLD sign in the front yard of her dilapidated childhood home was like a twisted nightmare from which Aoife could not wake. The grass was overrun with weeds and had patchy brown spots indicating it had been neglected for quite some time. The hedges needed a good trimming and the flowerbeds had long since been abandoned.

Wasn't it bad enough her father was dead? Now their house had been sold? It was like a knife in her gut had twisted, cutting through her internal organs and flaying her open.

Aoife stood on the cracked sidewalk at the end of the front walk looking up at chipped paint, shutters that needed to be replaced and a well-worn roof. But it had been her home. She had grown up there and she loved it.

When had they put the house up for sale? The strangest thing of all was her mother's car, still parked in the driveway. Like she was still there. Maybe up in the attic doing whatever it was she did up there. Aoife and her sister were never allowed. Sometimes she thought it was her mother's sanctuary, where she'd go when she was angry at them or Dad, or the world in general. Her mother seemed angry a lot.

She walked up to the front of the house and peered in through the windows. No one was about. It looked deserted. Pain shot up her arm and she glanced down, realizing she gripped the ring of keys so hard in her hand, the metal dug into her palm. She relaxed her grip and then picked out the door key. She stuck it in the lock and tried to turn it, but it wouldn't budge.

The locks had been changed.

Cold dread stretched through her chest as she realized the house was really sold and her father was really dead. Where was her mother? She'd somehow managed to disappear in the time it took Aoife to drive from the university in Austin to Brookdale, the tiny town on the eastern outskirts of Dallas.

There's no time really.

No time for what?

A truck rambled up the street and she turned to see a faded red Ford F-150 pick-up rattling its way toward the house. She shaded her eyes from the early morning sun to get a good look at the driver. He parked the truck, swung open the door, stepped out and paused.

Recognition hit her with the force of a straight-line wind. Sean O'Connell had been the object of her teenage crush. They stared at each other for a long, quiet moment. He looked exactly the same as he did when Aoife left home five years ago. The stiff breeze tousled his black hair and ruffled his white shirt.

She stepped off the porch as he started toward her, all confident masculinity.

"Aoife." The sound of her name on his tongue was pure honey. The dark brown eyes reminded her of melted chocolate and were set deep in his chiseled, rugged features. "You have my deepest condolences on the death of your father."

Grief punched her in the gut. She hadn't really dealt with her father's death yet. It was raw and new and she was still in shock. Her mother had been so odd about it when she'd phoned to tell her, and now her mother was missing. The only person who could give her answers was nowhere to be found.

"Thank you." She glanced back up at the house, as though she would find the answer to the mystery. "I can't find my mother."

"She's gone?" he asked, sounding astonished.

"Do you know where she went?"

He shook his head. "No. Aoife, do you know what happened to Liam?"

"All I know is Mom called me in the middle of the night but she didn't tell me much of anything," Aoife admitted. "Only that he was dead. I was hoping to find out more."

"You drove all night to get here?"

She suppressed the fatigue and grief pounding the backs of her eyes. "Most of it, yes."

Sean moved closer to her, reaching for her hand and grasping it. "Aoife, I'm so very sorry to be the one to tell you this…but your father was murdered."

She stared at him as though he'd grown a horn out of his forehead. "What do you mean? wnMurdered?"

"I mean he was found dead on the outskirts of town at his favorite fishing hole. I identified the body this morning at the county morgue."

That shortness of breath returned and pinpricks of light danced in her vision. The next thing she knew, she was staring up at the sky while Sean stood over her. A headache throbbed, radiating from the back of her head. He helped her to a sitting position, his reassuring hand on her back.

"Are you all right? You fainted."

She gripped his arm so hard, her fingers dug into his flesh. "Where is my mother? Why didn't she identify the body?"

"I don't know. That's why I came looking for her."

He tried to help her to her feet but she shoved him off and stood, brushing dirt from her jeans. She realized then she still wore the shirt that proclaimed she ran like a girl with no bra, and she blushed. Standing braless was the least of her worries.

Her mother was missing. Her father was dead.

A terrible thought crossed her mind as she inhaled a deep breath and looked up at Sean. "Do you think my mother had anything to do with it?"

"God, no. Why would you think that?"

"Because he's dead and she's missing. I know they had their differences but I don't think my mother is a killer. Do you?"

"No, of course not." He started to reach for her but dropped his arm. "Aoife, you've had a shock. You look exhausted. Maybe you should get some rest."

"I don't want to rest. I want to find out what happened to my parents. I have no place to go. My key doesn't work in the lock." She peered at him, her brow creasing. "Where is she? Do you know?"

Before he could Answer, Mrs. Jennings from next door came out of her house and approached, waving. Aoife suppressed a groan. Mrs. Jennings was the town gossip. God love Brookdale. The small town was a breeding ground for gossip and nosey townsfolk and she was the number one gossiper.

"Aoife, dear. I just heard," she called.

"I'll bet," Sean snorted.

"How does she know already?" Aoife frowned.

But the woman was upon them before he could answer. She had curlers in her hair and a housecoat hastily thrown on with slippers on her feet. Like she had seen them outside and rushed out to get the scoop. Aoife resisted rolling her eyes.

"Poor Liam. Whatever happened to him? Do you know?"

She clenched her keys into her fist, the metal biting her palm again. Her question cemented the only reason she was out of her house so early.

"And how is your mother, dear?"

Sean moved between them. "Fiona is devastated and Liam's cause of death is still being determined." He wrapped an arm around Aoife and turned her away. "Good day, Mrs. Jennings."

Her wide-eyed surprise was the last thing Aoife saw as she turned away, grateful Sean was there.

"We'll find her," he said low, so only Aoife could hear.

"I don't understand it. It's as though she disappeared in a puff of smoke." She looked back over the house, glaring at the SOLD sign, wishing she had some sort of super power to burn it down. "Do you know who bought the house?"

"I saw her yesterday," he said, ignoring her question.

She stiffened and wiggled out of his grasp. "You did? Where?"

"Downtown." Stubborn determination not to tell her too much, edged his voice.

Why? He sounded so vague. Like he wanted to tell her but didn't want to tell her. He shoved his hands into his pockets and shifted from one foot to the other. Next door, Mrs. Jennings pretended to water her flowers.

"And?" she prompted.

"You know your father hasn't lived here for months."

Another abrupt change of subject left her head spinning. She stared at him, dumbfounded. When had everything changed? Why hadn't her mother told her? Shame flooded her. She'd been so intent on staying away from home she hadn't a clue as to what was happening. She hadn't been home in a long time. What was the point? No one seemed to want her around. Fiona didn't care two figs about her. It was her sister who was the darling of the family.

A dull ache took up residence in her chest and she tried to rub it away.

"You didn't know, did you?" he asked.

"No." The word sliced through the still air like a knife stabbing through her heart.

"I'm sorry, Aoife." He sounded genuinely sad. "I didn't think you knew because I hadn't seen you around Brookdale since you left, after high school."

Yes, and her life had turned out so grand since she left. *Not.* Nothing she planned had turned out the way she wanted. Her father mostly ignored her and doted on Sunnie while her mother kept her at arm's length as much as possible. From the time she became a teenager, they hadn't got along so it seemed logical to leave for college.

She enrolled in classes at UT Austin. Since she had no financial help from her parents, she applied for grants, students loans and took on a job waiting tables.

"I didn't want to come back." Admitting that, was hard for her but it was the cold truth. She never wanted to come back.

"I can't say I blame you."

"My dad is lying on a cold slab of metal in a morgue, my mother is missing and I doubt my younger sister gives a shit about any of it. So why do I?" It was more of a rhetorical question. She didn't expect him to answer.

"Because you care about them, Aoife. You always have. Even when you hid how hurt your feelings were when Fiona brushed you aside. Even when Liam showered Sunnie with all his love and affection and ignored you."

She merely stared at him, her mind blank but amazed he'd

noticed. He flushed and turned away but she was on to him. She'd known Sean since she was a girl. He worked in the small grocery store and sacked groceries. At the time, he was working his way through college.

By the time she made it to high school, he had become a student teacher and she'd see him in the halls. He was her first official school girl crush. His black hair was different then. Long enough to brush his collar. If she didn't know any better Aoife would swear Sean had never aged.

"You said you saw my mother?" It was her turn to abruptly change the subject.

He shrugged. "Doesn't matter, does it?"

Aoife stiffened. "Yes, it kind of *does* matter, Sean. I have no idea what's going on. I don't want to think she had anything to do with Dad's death, but it's weird she's gone. If you saw her and she told you something—anything—I'd really like to know."

He pressed his lips together and looked away, gazing up at the house. "I saw her so she could give me this." He reached into his pocket and pulled out a copper key. "It's the new key to the house."

She gaped at him as he let the key ring dangle on his forefinger, the morning light winking off the shiny metal. "*You?* You bought the house? Why?"

He shrugged, gave her a lopsided smile. "It's a nice place."

She was far from amused. He cleared his throat and lost the grin.

The pain of loss burned through her. Even though she knew there was no way she could buy the house, she wished there had been some way for her to get it.

"So you bought it," she concluded.

"I didn't figure you could. And your sister wasn't interested since she's gallivanting across the globe making movies."

Three years her junior, Sunnie had moved to California at eighteen and was immediately discovered. The girl was under a lucky star or something. She'd landed several parts in smaller budget movies and then managed to get a starring role in an action flick.

And what sort of funds did Sean O'Connell have lying around that he could swoop in and buy her childhood home? She gave him a closer inspection but didn't notice anything different. He still wore the same scuffed cowboy boots, the same faded jeans. He drove a ten-year-old pickup that rattled down the street. He didn't *look* like he had money to spare.

"If it makes you feeling any better, I don't think Fiona had anything to do with Liam's death. You're right. She's not a cold-blooded killer."

"My parents were never a warm and fuzzy couple. They fought a lot but that was normal for them. I guess I expected them to go on forever. What are your plans for the house?"

"Why do you want to know?"

"Because it was *my* house. I spent my childhood here and the only happy memories I have from my childhood are *in* this house."

An emotion she tried hard to read flickered over his face. Regret? Sorrow? He covered it quickly and then shrugged.

"Nothing really. She sold it fully furnished. Said she didn't want to move anything."

Her brows drew together in confusion. She couldn't figure out what was going on, but she knew something was up. Why would her mother sell the house fully furnished? And why leave her car behind? She glanced at the sold sign, looking closer, but saw no realtor's name on it. Or even that it was for sale by owner. Did he know more about her mother and her disappearance than he let on?

"You had a lot of conversations with my mother, didn't you?" Her eyes narrowed with suspicion.

His response was another shrug. She folded her arms across her chest. "All right. What the hell is going on here?"

"What do you mean?"

"Don't give me that wide-eyed innocence, Sean. I'm not stupid. Something about this—" and she waved her hands toward the house, "—doesn't make sense. The house fully furnished with all our stuff. Her car still in the driveway. What aren't you telling me?"

His gaze slashed over to Fiona's abandoned car then back to her. "There's nothing to tell. I know you're worried about her but I'm sure she's all right wherever she is. What about your sister? Have you heard from her? Is she worried about her, too?"

She didn't know. She hadn't talked to Sunnie in years. She was the last person Aoife had considered calling. She hadn't thought of contacting Sean either, yet here he was. Proud new owner of her childhood home.

"I wouldn't know. Sunnie and I aren't on speaking terms. I *am* worried about my mother. Our relationship wasn't always roses and sunshine, but she's still my mother and I still care about her. Where is she, Sean?"

"I honestly don't know."

Scowling, Aoife changed the subject. "If my father wasn't living here, then where was he living?"

"They were separated," Sean said. "Fiona stayed here though it looks like she had trouble maintaining it."

Her head throbbed and she doubled-over, the shock of it all finally too much to bear. Pinpricks pierced the backs of her eyes again and she sucked in several large breaths, trying to keep from passing out a second time. Aoife braced her hands on her knees and stared down at a weed pushing its way through the crack in the sidewalk. Sean was at her side a second later though she hadn't seen him move and put his hand on her shoulder.

"You all right? Do you feel faint again?"

Tears stung her eyes and she blinked them away as fast as she could. Aoife didn't want him to see her cry. Hadn't she had enough bombs for one day?

Her parents were separated. BOOM!

Her childhood home was sold. BOOM!

Her dad was dead and her mother was missing. BOOM! BOOM!

"I'm fine."

"You don't look fine. Let me get you some water."

His hand was on her shoulder but she shrugged it off and stood straight. "No. I'll be all right. I'm just…I need to go."

"Aoife, don't be silly—"

"No. I'm leaving. I've got to get away from here." Though where she would go, she didn't know.

She stalked to the car and got in, slamming the door. As she stuck the key in the ignition, he came around to her open window and leaned in.

"If you need to talk…" His voice trailed off.

"I have nothing more to talk to you about."

He stepped away as she started the car and stomped on the gas, speeding down the street leaving burned rubber in her wake.

Chapter 2

In the Land of Faery Past

"'Tis your wedding day, milady!"

The high-pitched exclamation from Lady Fiona's handmaiden echoed off the stone walls. Thank the gods for the tapestries to absorb the banshee's shriek. Fiona pressed two fingers against her temple and rubbed at the headache forming. She hadn't yet managed to get out of bed but she knew the servants had been coming and going since before dawn.

Aye, indeed it was her wedding day. A day she had long been prepared for since she was but a girl. At age six, she was betrothed to the young prince, Cian, heir to the throne of Anatolia. She'd first met the prince on her ninth birthday, which her parents' thought was the perfect gift. Fiona wanted a pony or a unicorn. Even a dragon would be a better gift than a stupid boy.

Winnie shoved back the bed curtains letting the bright morning light burst inside Fiona's cocoon. The girl had opened every window covering to allow the sunbeams to slash across the floor. Fiona had to shield her eyes and blink back the sudden tears from the brilliance.

"'Tis no time for a lie in, my lady. We have to get you dressed and ready!"

The girl pulled back the coverlet and Fiona groaned. It wasn't that she didn't want to go to Lambridge Castle, the Anatolia royal family home. Cian was likeable in an unassuming sort of way. She liked him. He liked her.

But there had to be more to life than being someone's wife, even if she would be queen someday. There had to be passion and fire and intensity and…and…something more. She wanted adventure, not marriage to a boring prince. Mayhap that was other girls' dreams, but it wasn't hers.

She threw her arm across her eyes to shield them from the morning glare but Winnie was relentless.

"Come on, now." She pulled at her wrist, trying to force her to get up. "We have to get you in the bath."

Fiona groaned her reluctance. She was about to tell the girl to piss off—a most unladylike phrase—when the door to her chamber banged open. A rustle of skirts immediately followed and she knew she was in deep trouble. Fiona bolted upright as her mother came striding in, her cobalt silk and taffeta skirts swishing about her and her constant entourage following her. She halted near the bed, fists on hips.

"You're still abed? You lazy, good for nothing girl. Get up. Get up *now*."

Fiona was out of the sheets as fast as she could move and hustling across the bedchamber to her waiting bath. Her mother barked orders to everyone else to get Fiona packed and ready for her wedding. The wedding gown had been specially made with layers of beautiful Anatolian lace over a supple silk material that hugged her every curve.

While Fiona was in the bath getting her hair washed, her mother trotted over and perched on the edge. She looked over Fiona's naked body with a critical eye.

"You've been at the lemon cakes again, haven't you?"

"No, Mother," Fiona said.

Because she really hadn't. She'd been a good girl and pretended the lemon cakes didn't exist at all. She knew the lashing she'd take if she didn't fit into that gown.

"You're looking a bit pudgy. Mind your appetite. No man wants a woman who has too much weight on her," her mother said. And she reached down and pinched Fiona's stomach as if to indicate she was fat.

She was certainly nothing like her mother. Not thin and wiry and downright gorgeous. Her mother could eat whatever she wanted and maintain her perfect figure while Fiona had struggled with her weight most of her childhood. She blamed the lemon cakes and the strawberries and cream, and the peaches in syrup with cinnamon and nutmeg.

"Today is your wedding day, girl, and with that comes certain responsibilities you have to your new husband," her mother went on.

Fiona wanted to slide under the water and hide her mortification. The last thing she needed was a discussion about her "responsibilities" in front of her handmaiden and all the other servants. She was well aware she was expected to consummate the marriage that very night.

"Aye, Mother, I know."

"Do you? Do you really know?" her mother replied in that snide tone of hers.

"Aye, I do," Fiona shot back, her ire getting the best of her.

Her mother shoved Winnie out of the way and grabbed a handful of damp hair and jerked her head back. Fiona winced with the pain but knew better than to cry out.

"Don't take that insolent tone with me. You will listen, and listen well. You will do whatever it takes to produce an heir to the throne. I'll not have our good family named soiled because you couldn't conceive. I don't care if you have to fuck him standing on your head. Is that clear?"

A deathly silence fell over the room. Fiona stared up into the cold determined eyes of her mother. Not that she had any other choice.

"Perfectly clear."

"And stop eating lemon cakes or no man will want you." She clapped her hands in quick succession. "Donella, get those trunks. I want everything loaded in the carriage quickly."

She left in a swish of silk and taffeta. Donella motioned for the trunks to be removed while the others followed her mother out, leaving Winnie and Fiona alone. But Fiona knew the servants talked and there would be whispers circulating about how she had treated her by the time she was dressed and out the door.

Winnie reached for her hair and gently massaged her scalp where her mother had pulled the strands.

"My lady—"

"It's fine." Fiona drew her knees to her chest and bit her bottom lip to force the tears away. She would not cry over that bitch. "We'd better hurry, Winnie. We mustn't keep her waiting."

"Aye, my lady."

Fifteen minutes later, Fiona was out of the tub, dried off and began the long task of dressing. She had a traveling dress for the carriage ride to Lambridge Castle. She would change into her gown once they arrived. Winnie's enthusiasm waned after her mother's whirlwind appearance and for that Fiona was grateful. She couldn't take much more of the girl's gushing about her wedding day. It should be her happiest day. But Fiona was far from happy.

"You'll make a lovely bride," Winnie said as she finished braiding her long auburn hair and curling it around her head.

"Thank you." Fiona forced the words past her lips and tried to sound sincere.

"A pity I won't get to see you in that gown."

The thought of leaving Winnie behind sent a panic into Fiona's heart. Winnie may be an overzealous girl but she could overlook that if only to have someone with her that was familiar. Of course, her parents would be there but they were only there to make sure Fiona went through with the ceremony. Fiona turned to her and gripped her hands.

"You must come with me."

"My lady, I—"

"No excuses. You simply must. You can ride in my carriage. I can't face those people alone, Winnie. Please."

"But—"

"Pack your things quickly."

"What will your mother say?"

"My mother can hang for all I care. I will deal with her myself. But you're coming. I'll meet you at the carriage."

The girl's face lit up with such joy, Fiona thought she might burst. She squeezed her hands back and then dashed off to see to her packing.

She gave her bedchamber one final glance imprinting it in her mind's eye. She would likely never return when she took her place at Cian's side. He would eventually rule Anatolia and she would be his queen.

Why did that make her sad? Shouldn't she want to be queen of a vast and prosperous kingdom like Anatolia? She turned from the room, closed the door behind her and walked down the stairs for the last time. The bridal procession waited outside the front door of the manor. Prince Cian had sent several of his personal guards to escort them—men dressed in the royal colors of scarlet and gold. They were mounted on the biggest horses she'd ever seen. Two were in front and two in the back. Did she really need four men to escort her and her parents to the prince?

Winnie clutched her small knapsack, her face white and her eyes big and round as her mother was giving the girl a good lecture about why she wouldn't be going. She glanced her way, hoping

Fiona would rescue her from the tongue-lashing, but then that would get her in trouble as well. Instead, she waited for an opportune moment to intercede.

"…is very dangerous, my lord. Prince Cian wanted to ensure your safety."

Apparently, her father had the same question as she did about the guards. "Bah, the road is not so dangerous. I travel it myself with only my steel to safeguard me," he said.

"Begging your pardon, my lord, but there is rumor of the wizard king raiding local villages and attacking travelers on the road. Prince Cian felt it necessary we ride with you," the guard replied. "He wishes to see his bride and her family safe to Lambridge Castle."

The wizard king? Fiona had heard no such rumors but then she wouldn't. She was kept out most of those discussions since she was a woman.

"Very well then. Ah, Fiona, there you are, dearie. We must away, for your Prince Cian awaits." Her father noticed her standing there and gave her a polite nod then waved her toward the carriage.

When her mother saw her, she charged over and grabbed her arm.

"About time. What kept you? And what is this servant girl babbling on about? She's not going with us."

"My apologies, Mother. Actually she is going with us, I asked her to be my personal handmaiden. Winnie has been with me since we were girls, it seemed only fitting she help me dress for my wedding," Fiona said.

Her mother didn't like the response. Her lips thinned into a straight line as she glanced between the two of them.

"Come on, dearest. We can't dally around here all morning. It won't do for the bride to be late to her own wedding," her father said, waving her mother toward the carriage.

"Very well. She will ride—"

"With me, Mother. Thank you."

She wrenched her arm free from her mother's grasp and marched toward the carriage with a confident stride. That left her mother riding with her father. Fiona thanked the gods she wouldn't have to listen to her mother berate her for the entire ride. When she and Winnie were safely inside, the coachman closed the door after her.

Fiona peered out the small window and watched her mother stomp to the carriage behind them. A moment later, she heard the door slam shut and Fiona melted into the velvet cushion, expelling a breath. Winnie still clutched her small knapsack on her knees.

"Relax, Winnie," Fiona said on a chuckle. "My mother will take her anger out on me."

"That's what worries me, my lady. What will she do?"

"Give me a righteous tongue-lashing I'd imagine. But that's not for you to worry about, I can handle her."

But could she? She knew there would be wrath to come. She only hoped it would happen behind closed doors and not in front of Cian or his people.

It would be early afternoon when they arrived at the castle and Fiona had no doubts that the entire kingdom would turn out for the nuptials. She sighed, not looking forward to being on display.

Winnie reached into her knapsack and pulled out a deck of cards. "How about a game to pass the time?" She grinned as the held them up.

"Winnie, that is a marvelous idea."

The girl shuffled the cards and dealt. They played several hands, passing the time and chatting about inane things. Winnie didn't bring up the wedding again and for that Fiona was grateful.

"Do you suppose they'll have lemon cakes at Lambridge Castle?" Winnie asked as she shuffled the cards for their next game.

The girl knew of Fiona's penchant for the tasty cakes she was forbidden to eat. She started to reply when they heard a loud crack followed by a boom that shook the ground. There were shouts and then the horses whinnied as if in pain.

The carriage jerked violently as it moved forward and Fiona's stomach lifted. With some horror, she realized they were falling and everything moved into slow motion. It took some presence of mind to grasp the edge of the bench as cards scattered from Winnie's hand. The girl screamed as they crashed against the ground, the window in the door shattering as she smacked her head against the jagged glass.

Fiona did her best to control her fall but she couldn't stop from flinging out her hand to break it. Glass sliced through her palm as she landed on her shoulder. Blood striped Winnie's forehead. Fiona cradled her wounded hand against her chest and reached over to shake the girl.

"Winnie!" She dragged her body closer to her friend and listened to see if she was still breathing. Thankfully she was.

Before she could feel relieved that Winnie was still alive, she heard another screech of horses—her parents' carriage must have been attacked as well—and then more shouts from men. Swords clanged against each other in the distance, men fighting.

Above her, the door flew open and she squealed with fright. One of Cian's guards stood on top of the carriage and held his hand down to her.

"Come quickly, my lady."

"But Winnie—"

"There's no time. I must see you safely to—"

An arrow caught him in the neck and he toppled forward. Fiona shrieked again as half his body fell inside the carriage. She was trapped inside with an unconscious girl and a dead man with blood running grotesquely down his face. Before she could process that, someone landed on the carriage, making it rock. Another minute later, Cian's guard was heaved out of the doorway and thrown back as though he were nothing but a rag doll.

A second face appeared above her, gazing down at her with the blackest eyes she'd ever seen. His face was covered in a thick red beard. Fear twisted inside her gut as his face split into a smile, showing off black rotting teeth.

"There ye are. Stay put now." He straightened and called out to someone else. "I got 'er. Right the carriage so's we can get 'er out."

She could hear more men's voices as they neared and she knew what they meant to do. She scooted closer to Winnie and wrapped her arms around the unconscious girl, holding her close so she wouldn't sustain further injury. The men rocked the carriage and righted it. The opposite door banged several times. Gently, she put the girl on the cushioned seat.

One of the men behind her flung open the door and grabbed her, dragging her from the carriage. Her dress was torn and smudged with blood, her hand throbbed where she'd cut it, but all that was the least of her worries. Winnie was still unconscious. The carriage had been destroyed.

As the bearded giant of a man stepped in front of her, something cold and sinister shifted through her and for a moment, she could see her breath crystallize in the air. Even the man in front of her noticed and looked around, baffled by the sudden drop in temperature.

"Something ain't right here," the man behind her said.

But as soon as the words were out of his mouth, the coldness passed.

"Shut up." He glared at her captor and then refocused on her. He ran his hand over her face but she jerked to move away, causing her to get closer to the smelly man behind her.

"Ain't you a pretty thing. Yer a prize, a'right." Then he glanced to the man behind her. "Bring 'er. The wizard king's awaitin'.'"

Oh, gods. They were taking her to the wizard king? The man clamped his hand on her wrist and dragged her behind him. She did a quick count to see there were five men. As she was forced onto the horse in front of her captor, she saw the carnage around the two carriages. No one had been spared and she feared the worst. The driver was dead, face down in the mud.

As they galloped past the other carriage, she saw much to her horror, her mother and father were dead. Her mother's throat had been slit. Her father lay on his side, a pool of crimson around him. Next to him was a dead guard with an arrow in his forehead.

She barely had time to process that when the henchman to her right careened off his horse with an arrow in the side of his neck. His horse whinnied and reared back and narrowly missed stomping on the dead man.

"We're under attack!" the man in the lead shouted.

But who? They'd killed all the guards that were traveling with them. Another arrow breezed through the air and hit her captor's arm. He grunted, jerked the reins on the horse and changed direction. The henchman in the lead unsheathed his sword and turned toward the assailant—wherever he was. He made eye contact with first Fiona and then the man behind her.

"You two get her to the king. We'll take care of this brigand."

Her captor nodded and galloped off with the one who'd found her while the other two headed toward the attacker.

Chapter 3

Present Day in the Human Realm

Sean O'Connell stalked to his old pickup in long, fast strides. He slammed the car door shut and sat in silence for the longest time listening to the chirping birds and wondering why he had a boner.

Damn girl. He refused to be attracted to her. He *couldn't* be attracted to her.

She was three-hundred years his junior and far too young for him. That and he made a personal policy to not get involved with any of his charges or anyone related to one of his charges. He knew from experience it was a bad idea.

He remembered her as the nerdy girl who wore glasses and made goo-goo eyes at him when he'd taken the position of student teacher at her high school to keep an eye on her. He knew he was probably her first crush.

Aoife was a toddler when he was assigned to keep Fiona under surveillance. As an agent in the Inter-dimensional Portal Protection Agency, a sub-bureau of the Enchantment Enforcement Agency, his job was to keep humans out of portals to Faery or any other realm for that matter. He lacked the magical ability to open them and was only authorized to close them. But Fiona wasn't human— she was Fae—and he had been assigned to keep her *out* of Faery. The only explanation he received was because "she was a dangerous and powerful force" and she had to be kept from returning to "wreak havoc," though he couldn't imagine what havoc that could be. It couldn't be anything worse than what he'd done.

Even though Fiona knew who he was, he couldn't let anyone else know his true identity. He'd taken a liking to Aoife, though, and had an unyielding sense of needing to protect her. Now Aoife had returned to the small town, sans glasses. Gone was the nerdy girl, replaced by a petite, beautiful young woman with eyes so green they reminded him of the Woodland Forest in Faery after a spring rain, and lips so red they rivaled that of Snow White's.

Not that he'd noticed.

Aoife didn't even know how beautiful she was. As a Fae, he could see the flicker of the glamour spell shimmering around her. A glamour spell he could see through but was so powerful, Aoife couldn't. Sean knew that, too, was the work of Fiona. She kept Aoife's true visage hidden from the human eye.

He'd searched for Fiona everywhere he could think to search. He'd tested the portals he knew about to see if she'd gone back to Faery, but those tested negative for even a trace of her. Aoife was right when she said it was as though the woman had simply disappeared in a puff of smoke.

What the hell?

He knew she must have gone back to Faery but he couldn't find any proof and he knew if he stepped across the portal, he'd lose years in the human realm. Years he couldn't afford to lose leaving Aoife alone, unguarded, now that her mother was gone and Liam was dead.

There was some other wicked force at work and he suspected Liam's death was due to something Fae related, rather than human related. Likely Fiona knew that, too, which would explain her mysterious vanishing.

Sean gripped the steering wheel until his hands cramped. How was he supposed to keep his mind on the job when Aoife looked at him the way she did? And the way she smelled—like a cool spring morning after a thunderstorm, sharp and sweet.

His cell phone rang bursting into the silence and making him jump. He fumbled in his jeans pocket for the phone and finally answered on the third ring.

"What?" he barked.

"Geeze. Who pissed in your Cheerios?" The gravelly voice on the other end of the phone belonged to his partner, Caleb O'Brien.

Cal had been assigned to Fiona's case with him when the Fae woman slipped out of his grasp and made an unauthorized return trip to Faery several years ago, doing who-knew-what there.

"What do you want, Cal?"

"Man, you are seriously a grouch. That means you must have found the girl." He chuckled.

"I found her. She's here. Came back to the house."

"Did you tell her Fiona gave you the joint yet?"

He'd hedged the question as much as he could, letting her think he bought it. Knowing the truth might have sent her over the edge. How could he explain Fiona had entrusted the house to him, pressing the key into his palm and making him swear to never let Aoife step foot in it again? He wasn't sure where the For Sale sign came from though it was likely something Fiona conjured.

"I told her I bought it. Sort of." He'd lied to her face and hated it.

There was a pause. "And?"

"She wants to know what my plans are for it."

"And you said?"

"I said nothing, all right?" Sean practically growled the words. "I don't have all day to shoot the shit with you. What do you want?"

"I have some news if you'll chill out for a second." He laughed again, as if Sean's bad mood didn't bother him at all. And it didn't. They'd been working together awhile and Cal knew the difference between a bad attitude and a pissed off attitude. "We caught a blip of some residual energy. I think it's Fiona."

"Where?" He sat up straighter in his seat.

"You're not going to believe this, but it was in the house."

Sean looked through the driver's side window at the house, which was quiet and dark and empty. "*The* house? *Her* house?"

"Yep."

"Shit."

"Right. I'm on my way. Wait for me to go inside."

Ten minutes later, Caleb arrived in his sporty coupe. It was hard to be inconspicuous in this town when he insisted on driving around in a canary yellow sports car. Cal had 50-year-old single malt Scotch whisky taste, on a champagne budget and preferred his women hot and fast.

Cal wasted no time with greetings as he reached into his pocket and pulled out a folded piece of paper and handed it to Sean.

"Remember when we put those energy monitors in the house?" he asked.

That was ten years ago when they snuck inside while no one was home to install them. Nothing ever came of it. "Yeah?"

"Look." Cal pointed at the paper.

Sean unfolded it and peered at the readout with a spike in the readings shortly after two in the morning. "This was earlier today."

Cal nodded agreement. "And it came from somewhere *inside* the house."

"Where inside the house?"

"Couldn't pinpoint it. Now that you're a shiny new 'homeowner,'" he put air quotes around the word *homeowner*, "thought we could check it out."

Sean re-folded the paper and stuck it in his pocket then reached for the key. He started for the front door in long fast strides. Caleb followed, matching his gait step for step.

He unlocked the door and pushed it open. They split up, each one taking a room without even talking about who was going where. Years of working together meant they didn't need verbal communication much anymore. Caleb took the kitchen, Sean searched the living room.

If there was an energy spike somewhere in the house, that meant there was a portal somewhere in the house. A portal neither Sean nor Caleb knew about. They'd suspected several years ago Fiona may have opened one, but they'd never had proof and they never found it. The installation of the energy monitors was a way to catch her in the act if she'd tried to escape to Faery again.

She hadn't. She'd stayed put in the human realm.

Until two days ago when there was a spike in energy at one of the portals. That was someone entering the human realm not someone leaving. And whoever that someone was, Sean suspected he or she was responsible for Liam's death and Fiona's disappearance.

"Nothing in the kitchen," Caleb said. "Anything here?"

He shook his head. "No. Let's check upstairs."

A thorough search of the bedrooms turned up nothing. Sean tried not to linger too long in Aoife's room, even though he wanted to. She'd left it five years ago and Fiona had changed nothing. It seemed as though she merely closed the door when Aoife left. Had she secretly hoped her daughter would be back someday?

He met Caleb in the hallway.

"I don't get it," Cal said. "There was a definite spike in energy here."

"We're overlooking something, then."

"Is there a basement?" Cal asked.

He shook his head. "No." And then he caught sight of the string hanging from the ceiling. "But there's an attic."

Brushing past Caleb, he pulled down the attic stairs and unfolded them. They both peered up into the darkness for a long moment before Sean took the first rung and started up. He entered the musty attic and fumbled with his smartphone until he could get the flashlight app to work. As Caleb entered behind him, the room flooded in white light.

There was nothing unusual about the attic. It had the typical boxes and storage bins of holiday decorations, everything from Halloween to Christmas. A small writing desk was in one corner covered in dust, in another corner, an antique trunk.

"I don't get it," Caleb said.

"Me either."

"If there was a portal here, wouldn't we know it?"

"We should," Sean agreed. "Fiona was good about hiding things like that. She knew what we'd look for."

"Like energy spikes. Then she would know we'd find the portal if she used it."

"Maybe that's why she used it," Sean said.

He walked across the creaky planks of the wooden floor, searching. For what, he didn't know. He looked closely at the writing desk. Cobwebs clung to rolled up pieces of paper stuffed into the cubbies of the writing desk. They looked as though they'd been undisturbed for years. Decades even.

Sean reached for the scrolls, pulling them out. While most of them were parchment, one in particular had a smooth texture like oilskin. A faded red ribbon was tied around it. He pulled it open and let the material unfurl so slowly it reminded him of the unfurling of a sail. Someone had written something on the oilskin in a methodical hand. The perfect penmanship marched across the skin with precision and deftness in symmetrical straight lines. The language was not English but of something he couldn't read or understand except for two words written in pencil in a haphazard scribble across the top. *Eradication Spell.*

"What is it?" Caleb peered over Sean's shoulder at it.

"It's a spell scroll." With a gentle hand, he rolled it back up and tied the ribbon about it once again.

What was Fiona doing with an eradication spell and what did she intend to do with it?

He placed the scroll back in its place and went back to examining the contents of the desk, trying to forget about the spell scroll. Several books were stacked on the top also covered in a thick layer of dust. Sean blew off the grime, a white cloud puffing in the air. He turned his head to keep from inhaling it and then picked up the first book. It was still covered in a thick layer, so he brushed it off to reveal the faded gold embossed title, *Hidden Dimensions and Fae Time Travel.*

Cal peeked over his shoulder. "That can't be good."

Sean agreed with a nod as his partner wandered to another part of the attic. He put down the book and picked up the second one titled *A Hypothesis of Fae Magic in Other Realms.*

"What is your plan, Fiona?" he muttered.

"Sean, look at this."

Caleb stood at the antique steamer trunk and waved him over. On the lid of the square trunk was a circle of Celtic knotwork with a sword slicing vertically through the center. There was no lock on the latch. They exchanged a knowing look before Sean pushed open the lid.

Inside held nothing but musty dresses and boxes of antique jewelry.

"No portal," Caleb said.

But Sean thought he saw something glimmering around the edge of the trunk. He knelt down and peered closer. He flipped off the flashlight and in the darkness he could see the pale pink glow.

"There's residue here." He ran his finger over the edge and lifted up his hand. He could see the glittery pink substance on the tip of his finger.

"What is that?" Cal asked.

"Something magical Fiona used to open a portal."

"But where?"

"It has to be in the trunk," Sean said. "Somehow she figured out a way to keep it hidden. Even from us."

"How do we open it then?"

Sean shook his head. "No idea."

Below them, they heard the front door bang closed and then a muffled shout of hello.

"What the hell is *she* doing here?" Caleb asked.

"I have no idea. I'll get rid of her."

Sean pocketed his smartphone and made a dash for the attic stairs. He took the steps two at a time and then closed it up.

"Sean? Are you here?"

He bounded down the stairs as she started up them. "Aoife, what a pleasant surprise. I see you let yourself in."

She halted with one foot on the bottom step, looking up at him with question on her face as he descended in a hurry. He took her by the arm and led her away from the stairs and back to the front door. He saw her brows draw together in confusion and then annoyance as she pulled her arm out of his grasp.

"I knocked several times but there was no answer. I saw your truck outside, so I figured you were still here. Whose yellow sports car is that?"

"Mine." He flashed a grin. She cocked her head to one side, her expression perplexed with an "I don't buy it" look. "What can I do for you?"

He needed to shoo her out of the house before she discovered Caleb and, more importantly, the portal leading to Faery. He didn't need that kind of trouble on his hands.

She took a deep breath. "I came back because I…" Her voice faltered. She cleared it and went on. "I have a request." She glanced around the entryway into the living room and stared at it for a long moment. "I can't believe she sold it as is. It looks just like the day I left. Nothing has changed."

All the fight went out of him. This was still her home even though she didn't live there. She'd lost so much in the last few hours he needed to give her a break. She walked into the living room, stood in the center of it and eyed everything.

"Did my mother say why she wanted to sell it as is?"

He hesitated, remembering the last conversation he'd had with Fiona.

I need to you to take care of the house for me, Sean. Make sure Aoife never comes here.

Why?

It's not safe for her. Do you understand? She can never come here. Can you do that for me?

When he refused, she forced the house key into his hand.

Finally, he reluctantly agreed, though at the time he didn't understand what that was all about. It was only a few hours later when Liam turned up dead and Fiona had gone missing, he realized she must have known it was going to happen and she'd given him the house for safekeeping. But safekeeping from whom?

The police had already been through the house looking for

clues or anything that would lead to solving Liam's case. But Sean knew they wouldn't find anything here. At least not in the human realm.

"She didn't say," he replied at last.

"It's so odd. But then my mother was always odd."

He still had the issue of the portal and his partner upstairs and needed to move things along. "So what's your request?"

She picked up on the hard edge of his voice and shot him a glare. "I realize this is your house, Sean, but I lived here once." She glanced around again, a sad wistful look on her face. "It was my safe haven in some ways."

He recalled so much about her in a flash of memory. The high school bullies tormenting her because she was different, odd, nerdy. The same bullies he then tormented and threatened within an inch of their lives if they came near her again, though she never knew it. He'd been a sort of unseen guardian angel and he made sure she never found out.

She heaved a sigh and turned back to him, arms crossed. "There are some sentimental things I'd like to take if that's all right with you."

"Sure, sure. Whatever you want." He would give her the moon if that got her out of the house. A thump upstairs drew her attention to the ceiling.

"What was that?"

"That? Nothing. Must be squirrels on the roof or something." He clasped her elbow and ushered her toward the door. "Now isn't a great time. Come back tomorrow and I'll let you have whatever you want."

"Is there someone up there?"

"Nope. No one up there." He opened the front door and shoved her onto the porch. "See you tomorrow."

With that, he shut the door and clicked the lock. He watched her through the stained glass window in the door, waiting to make sure she left before going back upstairs. She stood on the porch for the longest time and then heaved a sigh and finally walked away.

Sean bounded back up the stairs and to the attic as soon as she was gone.

"What was that all about?" Caleb wanted to know.

"She wants some sentimental things from the house."

"And you're going to let her?"

"I told her to come back tomorrow, so we don't have a lot of time to figure this out."

"We can't seal the portal especially if Fiona intends to use it to come back through," Cal said.

"Then we better figure out a way to keep it secure from Aoife," Sean said.

"And how do you propose to do that? She has Fae blood. The portal has been activated, so it'll act like a homing beacon to her."

Sean knew Cal was right about that. She would sense the magic in the portal. Perhaps that was why she came back in the first place. While he and Cal had Fae blood, they didn't possess the same type of magic Aoife did. The portal wouldn't and didn't call to them as it would her.

"I know. I think that's why she came back. She just doesn't know it yet." Sean rolled up his sleeves. "Let's figure something out."

Aoife walked to her car still puzzling out the events with Sean. He'd acted like he was trying to keep her out of the house. He didn't want her anywhere near the stairs that much was clear. At her car, she halted and turned to look back.

She was baffled by why her mother would sell it to Sean in the first place. Complete with all the furnishings? Why would he want that? What did he intend to do with all that stuff? Sell it? Give it to a local charity? She didn't like the thought of either scenario so she had to get what she wanted before anything happened.

For the last five years, she'd relied on her friends to help her through making decisions like this and now she didn't know what to do or who to turn to. She'd driven away from the house dejected with no place to go and her life upside down. She'd stomped on the brake, turned the car around and gone back with anger burning in her gut. She had intended to demand Sean give the house back to her but she'd chickened out and asked for things of sentimental value.

She was such a weakling. She could never go anywhere and demand anything of anyone. It wasn't part of her DNA. But as she stood on the sidewalk looking up at the house, something shifted inside her. Like someone flipped on a light and she had the sudden urge to charge back into the house and make Sean tell her what he was doing there.

Her hands curled into fists. No, she wouldn't do that. Not yet. She'd come back at another time and when she did, she would find a way in and she would get the answers she sought with or without Sean.

Chapter 4

In the Land of Faery Past

Thick, lacy snowflakes cascaded from the darkened sky by the time Fiona's remaining captors arrived at the castle in the Cliffs of Mhothair. The Towers of Illyria were the home of the wizard king. All her life she'd heard tales of the tyrannical man and feared the worst. Why did he want her? She prayed to the gods Winnie was still alive. The girl was her last hope. They hadn't been far from Anatolia. When they failed to arrive, Prince Cian would send out a search party and they'd find Winnie and the others.

And then Fiona would be rescued.

But she had to worry about her present situation. The wizard king's fortress was on the top of the cliffs at the end of a winding cobblestone pathway. Some said the fortress was guarded by a sleeping dragon curled around the twin towers that would wake when unwanted visitors approached, breathe fire on them and roast them alive. Others said it was guarded by magic from the wizard king himself and he would draw down the lightning to strike anyone who dared enter.

Surely they were nothing more than rumors, for she neither saw a sleeping dragon nor the sight of the wizard king standing on the tallest tower to keep a watchful eye over his domain. Nay. What she saw were two stone towers against the cloudy late afternoon sky, the pointed spires stretching upward. So tall were they, she wondered if they touched the sky. The heraldry of the king flapped in the stiff breeze at the top of the ramparts. A dry moat surrounded the fortress, making it impassable save for the main road.

As they approached, the drawbridge lowered, a yawning black abyss greeted them. Dread washed over her as they trotted inside and the drawbridge closed with a finality she didn't like.

They relinquished their horses to a couple of stable boys. The bearded man and another led her through the castle walls, twisting and turning through the long hallways so that she could never find her way out again. She suspected that was on purpose. They headed up a winding stone staircase. At the top of one of the towers, they paused and the bearded man knocked on the door.

"Enter," came the muffled command.

The heavy oak door swung open and they entered a dimly lit chamber. She expected it to be a bedchamber, but it wasn't. A desk was under the one window, half-rolled parchment papers scattered across the top. Several candles burned, the flames flickering and wax dripping down the candleholders.

A man stood hunched over a table with his back to them, his hands busy with something that looked like a mortar and pestle. They waited while he continued doing whatever it was he was doing, the men silent at her side. The bearded man shifted from one foot to the other, then glanced at his fellow soldier who merely shrugged.

"Leave her and be gone," the man said.

The two men scurried from the chamber without a backward glance, closing the heavy door with a bang. Fiona was left standing in the center of the room alone, shivering and trying to control the fear that bubbled up her throat. She would not allow him to see her fright.

He continued at the table for long silent moments, crushing something in the mortar. He finally laid aside the pestle, straightened his back with a stretch and expelled a heavy sigh. He turned toward her, the light catching his face just so and she could see he was an old man.

Was this the wizard king? The one who had struck fear into the hearts of men and women across kingdoms? He didn't look so scary.

The corner of his mouth pulled up in a grin, crinkling the winkles on his face. "Lady Fiona, welcome."

She peered at him as he turned fully toward her. He reached for a gnarled walking staff and shuffled over to her.

"The tales are true then. You are quite beautiful."

"Who are you? What do you want of me?"

"All in good time, dearie." He smiled again, shuffling his ancient body in a wide circle around her. He reached for one of the candles and held it up between them, squinting at her as though to get a closer look. "Aye, quite beautiful."

"Are you the wizard king, then?"

His laugh turned into a barking cough before he finally got it under control. "Do I look like the wizard king to you? No, dearie. But I work for him and he doesn't take kindly to being called that. He wanted me to inspect you first."

"Inspect me?"

"Hold still, eh?" He set aside the candle and his walking staff and moved closer. "Won't hurt a bit."

When he reached for her, she shrank back. "What won't hurt? What are you doing? Why am I here?"

"Questions. Questions. So many questions." He clucked his tongue and shook his head. "His Majesty will answer them all soon enough. Now hold still."

He reached for her again but she was too frightened to move. His hand landed on her abdomen. He pushed into her stomach, gave her a quick squeeze and then grinned again.

"Fertile, are ya? He'll like that. Still a virgin?"

"That is none of your damn business," she replied.

"And sharp tongued. He'll like that, too."

"Am I to be raped then?" she wanted to know. "I demand answers."

"*Och*, my lady. You think the king is so cruel? He would never take a woman without her consent. And he'll have answers for you when he summons you," the man said.

"When will he summon me?"

"When he's ready." He laughed and then coughed again. "There is no rushing the king, dearie. What happened to your hand there?" He pointed to her wound.

The second she looked at the blood crusted along her palm, it started to throb. "I cut it when your men turned over the carriage."

"They turned over the carriage, did they?" He clucked his tongue. "Fools. His Majesty insists upon hiring these mercenaries, yet they are nothing but fools. Come. Let me clean and bandage it before infection sets in."

He reached for his walking staff and waved her toward his table, shuffling toward it with his slow gait. The man seemed harmless enough, so she moved to stand next to him. He struck a match and lit several more candles in candle holders. The corner of the musty room illuminated with yellow flickering light. She could see now, the bookshelf above the work table was crammed with books and small vials of substances she couldn't identify. One of the vials glowed pink and she could see sparkles dancing inside. Was it fluid? Or solid? She wished the light was better so she could see more things.

She stole a glance into the mortar and saw a black paste and she wondered what it was. There were water stains on the wooden table. A few small plants with green sprouts in various stages of growth were to one side. She could even smell the sweet scent of flowers but could not find any. She spied a long wooden stick, gnarled like his staff. Surely that wasn't a magic wand?

He hummed to himself as he reached for a clean rag and a small vial of a blue substance. He dabbed the blue liquid on the rag, reached for her hand and patted it across the wound, cleaning it of the dried blood with a gentle touch.

"I'm sorry you were brought here under such circumstances, my lady. I told His Majesty not to do it, but he wouldn't listen. He insisted it was the only way."

"They killed my family." She tried to keep the waver out of her voice, but she was unsuccessful. Hot tears burned the backs of her eyes. She tried to blink them away, but couldn't. One tracked down her cheek.

She may have hated her mother sometimes, but she certainly wished no ill will on her. She regretted the hateful things she thought about her only hours before her demise. Guilt slashed through her. She would miss her as she would miss her father's absent-mindedness.

He cursed under his breath. "Fools. You must tell His Majesty this, so he can punish the men. No one was to be harmed."

She worried about Winnie. Had the girl regained consciousness? Would Prince Cian find her still alive? Would she be able to tell him what had happened?

The man dabbed more liquid on her hand, cleansing the wound. She watched him, thinking of Cian and her parents and Winnie. He was a stranger to her but he was kind.

"What is your name?"

"My name does not matter, my lady." He flashed another grin as he reached for a bandage. "I'm no one of importance."

"You are to me. You could have let my wound fester. You didn't and for that I am most grateful, so I should very much like to know your name to thank you properly."

The man wound the bandage around her hand and tied it off. "Deaglan, my lady. My name is Deaglan."

"Well, Deaglan, thank you very much for cleansing my wound." She leaned toward him and kissed him on the cheek.

His eyes went wide for a moment and then he chuckled. "High spirited girl. Aye, His Majesty will like you quite a lot I should think."

Someone pounded on the door, then opened it before Deaglan could respond. A sentry entered, wearing full armor and a white cloak.

"Have you examined the girl?" He didn't even bother to look at her when he spoke.

"I have. His Majesty will be pleased. She is young and fertile, not to mention beautiful," Deaglan replied.

"Then he wishes to see her immediately." The sentry waved her toward him.

She remained rooted to her place. "I…I don't wish to go."

"Don't be frightened," Deaglan said. "He won't hurt you."

Fiona turned to Deaglan. "Please come with me."

He shook his head. "I cannot. My place is here in the tower, by His Majesty's command."

"Come on, girl," the sentry urged. "The king does not wish to be kept waiting."

Deaglan gripped her shoulders and squeezed a little, giving her a small smile. "You'll be fine. I promise."

Taking a deep breath, Fiona turned and stepped toward the sentry. He led her from Deaglan's tower, down the spiral stone steps and through the castle.

They left behind that tower and climbed steps to another. This one had more light, more torches lining the walls. Two more sentries flanked a wooden door with heavy wrought iron hinges. They paused and her guard rapped. There was a muffled "come in" behind the door. The sentry on the left reached for the door and pushed it open.

Her guard led her inside the chamber which was large, palatial. It seemed bigger than the first floor of her manor. Open windows lined one wall with gossamer curtains billowing in the cold breeze. It was well-furnished. A desk on one side with a high-backed cushioned chair. A table in the center surrounded by four low chairs. A marble pedestal with a bronze bust of someone she didn't know, and luxurious rugs lined the stone floors. A large fireplace hosted a bright fire while every candle in the room was lit, giving it a warm inviting glow.

But there was no sign of His Majesty. The sentry beside her stood at rigid attention.

Despite the open windows, the room was cozy.

It seemed forever before they heard footsteps coming from somewhere in the depths of the room. The king emerged from the shadows with a catlike grace. He was tall, fine-boned, pale-haired, blue-eyed and nothing like Fiona had expected. He had a long slender nose in a beautiful yet masculine face with high cheekbones and a small dimple in his square chin. He paused several feet away, his gaze on her.

"Leave us." His voice was a low timbre that reverberated around the room and through her. She shuddered to the balls of her slippered feet.

The guards hurried out, closing the door behind them. She and the king stared at each other a long silent moment, sizing each other up.

"You are quite lovely, though I would not expect any less of Prince Cian. He has exceptional taste in all things, especially ladies."

She remained silent, trying to decide if he was insulting her or not. Or was he merely stating that Prince Cian had other interests where ladies were concerned?

"I apologize, my lady, for kidnapping you in such a manner, but it was the only way to get the attention of His Highness." He took a step closer to her, inspecting her up and down as though she were his prize. And mayhap she was. "My wizard tells me you are fertile. Good."

So Deaglan was the true wizard, not this king. Yet he hid behind the title wizard king with alarming alacrity. Everyone knew the wizard king lived in the Towers of Illyria. King Niall was nothing more than an immortal Fae man.

She idly wondered how Deaglan had gotten the message she was fertile to the king so quickly.

"What do you want with me?" She whisper-shouted her words, lifting her chin and giving him her best intimidating look.

He wasn't intimidated by her and why should he be? He was the one in control.

"What I want is for that miserable lump of a man, Prince Cian, and his kingdom to suffer endlessly. The only way I knew to do that was to steal his bride."

"He will come for me," she said.

"Oh, I'm counting on that, my lady. I look forward to him coming to the gates of the Towers backed by his army."

She blinked. "And that's what you want?"

"It is."

"What do you hope to accomplish?" she demanded.

"I thought that obvious, my lady." He walked to the highboard table and poured a glass of wine. "I hope to accomplish a war and wipe out the bloody kingdom of Anatolia once and for all."

Her brows drew together as she watched him sip his wine. "But why?"

"There is no reason for me to give you my family history, my lady, so suffice it to stay we have a long-standing blood feud, he and I. Only now I have the means to destroy him."

"With your wizard?" she asked.

"Precisely."

She found it difficult to believe the kind old man who cleaned her wound was a callous killer and someone who would do the bidding of this cold-hearted king. She couldn't allow this man to destroy Anatolia.

"And what does my fertility have to do with all this?" she asked.

He held his glass of wine and peered at her over the rim. "In time, you will come to love me. We will wed and you will produce an heir for me. A strong boy who one will day rule Illyria and Anatolia as one."

"You intend to marry me?" She couldn't hide the surprise skittering through her.

"I do. I'm pleased to have you as my honored guest."

"There is no need to coat it in a decorative phrase, Your Majesty. We both know I am a prisoner here. Furthermore, I will never love you. I *could* never love you. And I refuse to marry you."

"We shall see, won't we?" He sipped his wine again, smirking. "You cannot tell me you love that simpering fool, Cian."

She clenched her fist and immediately regretted it when the pain lanced up her arm. "I do. He is my betrothed. At least *he* didn't kill my family."

A dark look came over his face. He set aside the glass. "My men did that?"

"Aye, they did. My parents are dead, my handmaiden was severely injured and likely dead by now. They killed all the guards, the coachmen, the drivers. I suppose I shouldn't be surprised by your plan, since senseless killing seems to be your method." She tilted her head back up, looking down her nose.

His eyes narrowed as he stalked by her and pulled open the heavy door as though it weighed nothing. "Arrest the mercenaries at once and take them to the dungeon."

The sentries at the door went off to do his bidding. King Niall walked to her, took her hands in his. "You have my heartfelt condolences, my lady. It was not to be that way. They were instructed to bring me you and only you and leave the others." His finger brushed over the bandage on her hand. "And I see you were injured during the ordeal."

"It's fine." She tried to pull free, but he held fast.

He turned over her hand and kissed her uninjured palm. "I will take you to your chamber next to mine. I should like to get to know you, my lady. Over time, mayhap you will come to forgive me."

She didn't want to forgive him anything. He killed her family. He had plans to kill Prince Cian and destroy Anatolia. She had to find a way out and warn Cian. The old wizard seemed to have befriended her. Mayhap she could talk to him, get his help. Mayhap she could talk him out of doing the king's bidding.

"I'll have a bath brought to you and some clean clothes. If there is anything you need, please ask. I will grant your wish."

"Release me," she said.

"Anything but that, I'm afraid." He paused outside the door to the chamber next to his. "You must be famished. Dine with me tonight and you will see I am not a heartless man."

She didn't believe him. She had no choice but to cooperate and if she did, then mayhap she could win her freedom.

"Very well. I will dine with you."

He kissed her hand again. "I will see you again soon, my lady."

True to his word, he sent his servants with a bath and clean clothes. Her room was not as palatial as his but it was large enough for her with a bed, a wardrobe and a fireplace tall enough for her to stand in. The servants stoked the fire and lit the candelabras which gave the room a rich warm glow.

Two girls brought heated water and filled the copper tub near the fire. When the pots were empty, they waited a moment and then they filled up again with steaming water. She watched with suppressed awe at the magic at work. When it was done, Fiona stripped and stepped in and sat, drawing her knees up to her chin and pressing her forehead against them. She dangled her injured hand outside the tub to keep it from getting wet.

"Leave me. I can bathe myself," she said, her voice thin and hollow.

"But, my lady, His Majesty said—"

Her head snapped up. "I don't care what he said. Get out. I wish to be alone."

The girls scurried from the room. When the door clicked shut, her head dropped to her knees once more. It took only a few seconds for the tears to burn her eyes and slide down her cheeks. She allowed the grief to come, to pulse through her. She would never forget that image of her mother and father dead, blood everywhere. She wished now she hadn't looked. But she had to know, didn't she? She had to see what had happened to them.

And what of Winnie? Did she live? How severe were her injuries? And who was the unknown assailant that killed one of her captors and injured another? Had the mysterious person tried to save her? And if so, why? She didn't know what had happened to the other two—mayhap they had been killed.

When she'd cried all the tears she could, she rubbed the sponge against the sweet-smelling soap and scrubbed her skin until it was pink and raw. Not an easy task one handed. Like it or not, she was stuck there. But for how long? There had to be a way out. A way to free herself.

Angry that she'd been captured and her family had been killed, she squeezed the sponge in her good hand until her fingers ached. Water dripped from it, splashing in the bath. In a fit of rage, she flung it at the wall beside the fireplace. It hissed as it hit the wall and then landed on the floor with a splat. She glared at it, hating it and everything about it.

Still not satisfied with her outburst, she punched the water with such a force it sloshed from the tub and splattered across the floor.

The fire sizzled and went out. Great. She stared at the darkened fireplace. She hadn't even realized the scream of frustration had built up in her lungs until she flung her hand out and a pop of light brightened the entire room. The fireplace lit back up and a fire roared even bigger than before.

Fiona emitted a small gasp as she stared at it and then looked down at her hand. She had done that? But she didn't have magic, did she? Her magic had never manifested—something that disappointed her mother. She was Fae, after all. And though she had never exhibited any signs of magic, she knew it was entirely possible. Her mother had always told her that sometimes it skipped a generation or two and since her mother didn't have it…well, it seemed as though she did after all.

She had been running on high emotions all day. Could that have somehow triggered the magic inside her? If her magic had finally manifested, then there was hope yet. Hope she could free herself from Niall's prison. She would have to plan her revenge accordingly. Slowly. Methodically. For King Niall would one day pay for all he'd taken from her.

There was a timid knock on the door. It cracked open and one of the girls stuck in her head.

"My lady? Do you need assistance?"

She folded her arms over her naked chest. "I…I seem to be having some difficulty since I'm one handed."

"Would you like help, my lady?"

Fiona peered at the girl with blonde curls framing her small round face and softened. She reminded her of Winnie. "Aye, but only you may help me. No one else."

The girl came in and closed the door. She dried her off and helped her into a fresh gown.

"What is your name?" Fiona asked.

"Elspeth, my lady."

"That's a lovely name. Thank you for helping me."

Elspeth dipped a curtsy as there was a knock on the door. She scurried to open it and King Niall stood on the other side. His deep blue eyes sparkled as he looked at Fiona, took her hand and kissed it.

"You look ravishing, my lady. Shall we dine?" He placed her hand in the crook of his elbow and led her away from her chamber.

They descended the stone spiral stairs in silence. All she could hear was the echo of their footsteps and the pounding of her heart. But now Fiona was no longer as afraid. She had something Niall didn't know about—magic. She planned to learn to use it and she knew who to ask for help.

Chapter 5

Present Day in the Human Realm

After a restless night in a cheap motel, Aoife decided to do some investigating on her own before returning to the house. Her plan was to arrive ahead of Sean. She had a hunch he wasn't living in the house yet since she didn't see any of his personal effects. There had been too many things still belonging to her and her family. She intended to snoop.

Early that morning, she went to the creek where they'd found her father's body. As she exited the car and stood on the embankment, staring down at the crushed grass, a strange sense overcame her. Her ragged breath was loud in her ears and her skin tingled and prickled as though she had walked through cold air. She doubled-over, her hands on her knees. Her stomach cramped with sickness as it coursed through her and she bit her bottom lip to stop from retching. It took several moments for her to get it under control but the wave of nausea finally subsided.

When she was fully composed, she stood straight again and peered at the trampled grass. She slid down the embankment to the crime scene and knelt down next to it. Waving her hand over the place where her father was found she got that same strange tingling sensation making all the hairs on her body stand on end.

Did it mean something? And if it did, what?

She noticed something black on a few blades of grass. When she touched it, a black sludge came off on her skin. She rubbed her fingers together and then brought them closer to her nose to sniff it. It smelled like…sulfur?

Puzzled, she searched for other clues, but found nothing. Only the black sludge that stank.

Aoife returned to her car. Taking a deep breath, she started it and headed for the house. Sean's demeanor the day before had been so odd, like he didn't want her anywhere near the stairs. Or maybe he didn't want her in the house at all. Either way, she intended to figure out what he was hiding.

At the house, his old truck was gone as well as the yellow flashy sports car. She took that as a good sign. She walked to the front door and rang the bell. No answer. She knocked several times. Still no answer. She glanced around the silent street but saw no one out and about. Not even nosey Mrs. Jennings. It was shortly after sunrise and still too early for the neighbors to be stirring.

A black limo came down the street and parked then the driver got out to open the back door. The second the honey-blonde stepped out of the car, Aoife's heart went into overdrive. Sunnie Burke, her younger sister, paused on the sidewalk staring at her through round-rimmed, designer sunglasses, wearing a turquoise dress that clung to her curves and matching strappy sandals with a red sole. Her oversized designer handbag hung from her forearm as she slowly dipped her shades down her slender nose with her free hand and pinpointed Aoife with her lethal blue gaze.

Oh, how she hated her sister.

Sunnie was the exact opposite of Aoife. Tall, lithe, golden-skinned, soft wavy blonde hair and blue-eyed. Whereas Aoife had mousy brown hair that had the texture of straw, and dull green eyes. For the better part of her childhood, she wore glasses to correct her nearsighted vision. Now at least she could wear contact lenses to get away from that nerdy part of her. She never really got her growth spurt like she hoped and remained horizontally challenged at five-foot-four, a whopping six inches shorter than Sunnie.

What was Sunnie doing in Brookdale anyway? She was supposed to be in Shanghai filming a movie.

Her sister sauntered up the front walk, her heels clicking in a rhythmic clack against the pavement, paused at the foot of the rickety wood steps and looked up at her, then the house, then back at her.

"I'm surprised to see you here, Aoife." Her voice hinted with the slow Southern drawl that was impossible to get rid of after living in a small Texas town all her life.

"What are you doing here?" Aoife asked. Not a great comeback but it was all she could muster.

"Because my daddy is dead. I came on the first flight I could get. I've been traveling for over fifteen hours straight. I'm tired. I'm hungry. I want answers. Where's Mom?" She pulled her shades all the way off her face and Aoife could see the bags under her eyes.

For whatever she was, her sister did love their father. She should, after all she was the favorite. She was the one that was constantly in the spotlight, the apple of Dad's eye.

"Newsflash. Mom is missing and did you even bother to notice the sold sign in the yard?"

Aoife delighted in the shock that registered on her sister's face. So she hadn't known either. Sunnie snapped her head around and stared at the sold sign for a long moment before turning back. Her eyes narrowed into sharpened daggers.

"Where is Mother?" Sunnie's tone was glacier cold, almost accusatory.

Aoife was taken aback, her breath catching in her throat. She hated confrontations but she knew the one with her sister was inevitable. She didn't think it would be so soon though, since she was lulled into a false sense of security believing that Sunnie was in another country.

"How should I know? I got here yesterday morning and she was gone. I haven't been able to find her." It took great effort to keep her voice level.

Worry creased Sunnie's brow. "What happened to Dad?"

"Dad was murdered. That's all I know."

Her face drained of color and her shoulders slumped and for the first time Aoife saw genuine distress in her sister. Sunnie pressed a hand against her stomach. "Murdered?"

"All I know is he was found dead by the creek."

"How did he die?" Her voice lifted an octave at the end of the sentence.

"I don't know." Aoife was ashamed to admit it.

Anger replaced the worry on Sunnie's face. "Haven't you gone to the police to find out? What are they doing about it? Are they investigating? What are *you* doing about trying to find Mother?"

All good questions. The truth of the matter was Aoife had no idea what to do about it and going to the police hadn't crossed her mind, though it should have. All she could think about was getting inside the house because for whatever reason, something drew her there. Like it was where she was supposed to be and nowhere else.

Sunnie huffed. "As usual you're useless."

Something else niggled at Aoife as she ignored the barb. "Did you know they were separated?"

"Of course, I did. They split before Christmas. You would know that if you ever bothered to come home."

Aoife stared in stunned silence at her perfect sister, with her perfect hair and her perfect career. The words hit her like an arrow through the heart and she hated that she was right. She should have come home more often. Regret burned through her.

"Dad wanted a divorce but Mom wouldn't agree," Sunnie went on in a sour tone. "He left her anyway. The divorce was final two days ago."

Two days before he was found dead.

The unexpected news sent hot pinpricks all over Aoife. She sat hard on the front steps and stared down at the ancient wood. She wasn't sure how she was supposed to feel or what she was supposed to think. The damning evidence surrounding her father's mysterious death and her mother's disappearance told the story. A story Aoife didn't want to really acknowledge as fear prickled her. She refused to believe her mother was capable of killing anyone. Aoife had to find her mother now more than ever. She needed answers to all the questions swimming around in her tired brain.

"So, what? You don't have anything to say to that?" she demanded.

Aoife could only shake her head, her lip quivering and tears threatening. Sunnie huffed out a breath.

"Do you think Mother had anything to do with his death?" She sounded cold and distant.

Aoife drew up straight, the fury pulsing through her. "No. And you shouldn't either," she snapped.

Sunnie drew in a long slow breath then let it shudder out of her. "I don't think so, either. I'm glad you don't." Something about her tone softened. Aoife watched as she took a tentative step toward her, closing the gap between them. "I never hated you, you know. I wanted to be smart like you."

Shock rolled through her as she stared at her younger sister, unsure what to make of her words. There had always been a rivalry between them. Sunnie got all the attention while Aoife studied hard to make the honor roll, to make it out of town and into a good college.

"That's all I wanted to say." She turned on her heel and clicked back up the sidewalk.

"Where are you going?" Aoife asked.

"To the cops. I'm going to find out what happened to Dad."

Aoife listened to the click-clack of her sister's heels down the pavement, the slam of the car door and then acceleration of the limo as it pulled away from the house.

Her heart hurt.

"Mom, where are you?" she whispered to the wind.

The trunk, the wind seemed to answer back.

The fine hairs on her arms stood at attention. A pulling sensation yanked at her gut as if there were an invisible rope tethering her to something. Something behind her and above her. Aoife uncurled her petite form from the steps and stared at the house, unable to shake the feeling that something called to her. Sean had promised her she could get things out of the house that day, yet he hadn't arrived.

She was alone.

It was time to do a little breaking and entering.

Standing on the front porch, the wind whispering across her bare arms, she knew what she had to do. Before she lost her nerve, she bounded down the front steps and hurried around the side of the house to the back. She knew there was a window with a broken lock. She could get in that way.

Moments later, she had the screen off, the window open and crawled inside. She dropped to the living room floor and peered around, holding her breath and listening. She heard no movement and knew the house was empty.

Aoife took a few moments to scan the living room. Nothing had changed. The kitchen still had all the pots and pans and dinnerware. The pantry was still fully stocked. So were the refrigerator and freezer. There was enough food to last a month or maybe two.

She headed for the stairs and halted at the bottom when she got that familiar tingling sensation. It was similar to what she'd felt at the crime scene but different. It seemed as though something pulled her, forcing her up the stairs. Before she knew it her feet were moving and she stood at the top of the steps.

Once again, all the hairs on her body stood on end. Her heart pounded a furious beat. Her nerves jangled on a sharp edge. Something called to her. Something wanted her to reach up and open the attic stairs.

She halted mid-reach, gasping for breath and shoving back

against the wall. She couldn't. She'd been forbidden her entire life to go into the attic. Her mother made that painfully clear. She was not allowed and neither was Sunnie.

So why then did she have the uncontrollable urge to pull down the attic stairs and go up?

Do it, Aoife. Go up into the attic.

The voice whispered inside her skull. She had no idea whose voice it was. She didn't think it was her own. She was compelled to open the attic and take that first upward step.

So she did. With her heart pounding in her throat, she ascended and paused in the darkness listening to her ragged breathing. She stood on forbidden ground.

Now what?

The trunk.

Again that voice. She scanned the darkened room, only barely able to make out shapes. There were the holiday decorations on one side. An old desk on another. She headed for the desk.

The trunk. The trunk.

She pressed her palm against the side of her head and rubbed. She was hearing things.

The desk was coated in a thick layer of dust that had been disturbed not so long ago. There were several cubbies with papers sticking out of them in a chaotic and untidy way and two books that had finger and handprints left behind in the dust.

"Hidden Dimensions and Fae Time Travel," she read aloud.

She picked up the second book, *A Hypothesis of Fae Magic in Other Realms*, and flipped through it. She understood none of it as it was written in a language she couldn't comprehend. She dropped the book and reached for one of the scrolls when her fingers brushed one that felt different than paper. Curious, she pulled it out and untied the faded red ribbon, letting it roll open. Despite the flawless handwriting, the words were of a language she couldn't understand. Except for the two words in English scrawled across the top.

"Eradication spell?"

She dropped the scroll and shoved it away as something dark gripped her. Like she'd touched something forbidden or evil. With her heart pattering a quick beat, she reached for another scroll. The parchment fell open on the desk revealing a drawing of an ancient map. The ink had faded. When she peered at it closer she couldn't make out the words, which were in the same language as the book. Something flowery with lots of squiggles and she had no idea what it said. A small compass was drawn in the lower left hand corner with north pointing to the right.

Aoife reached for a second piece of paper. It had been folded and looked as though it was a page that had been ripped out of a book. Again, the language was strange. Like nothing she'd ever seen before. As she stared at the faded ink, the words and letters re-arranged and morphed into words she could read.

A wizard of both Fae and Wizard blood will come into power and rule from a silver throne.

"A wizard of both Fae and Wizard blood…?" Her voice was quiet in the darkness.

Something behind her glowed. She dropped the paper and turned to see a symbol on the top of the trunk had lit up, like a beacon in the darkness.

The trunk. The trunk. The trunk.

It called to her. She was certain she had heard her name coming from it. In a fog, she walked toward it and dropped to her knees. It was an old steamer trunk. She had never seen it before in the house. Where did it come from? Was it her mother's?

The glowing symbol on the top was an intricate Celtic knotwork circle with a sword through it. The light pulsed, beckoning her.

The trunk, Aoife.

"Yes," she heard herself say. "The trunk. Of course."

Her fingers brushed over the Celtic knotwork and suddenly the interior illuminated. Light pushed out around the lid. She gasped and opened it. When the blinding light faded, there in the trunk was a stone staircase leading down into darkness.

"What the heck…?"

Downstairs, she heard a door slam and then Sean's voice. "Aoife? Are you here?"

Step into the trunk, Aoife.

"Yes, I must."

She stood and stepped onto the first stone step. Her racing heart thumped a wild beat and the next thing she knew she was on the second step. Then the third.

"Aoife, wait!"

Glancing up, Sean appeared at the top of the attic stairs. She sucked in a sharp breath, grasped the lid and slammed it closed above her head. She was instantly plunged into total darkness and hunched down on the step, waiting for Sean to open the lid and come after her. She heard nothing. No sounds above.

Panic seized her. She reached above and her hand brushed against smooth, cool stone. She pushed and pushed and pushed but the stone would not give. She flattened her trembling hands against where she thought the lid was but again met cold stone instead of smooth wood. The lid had disappeared. Where did it go?

A cold tingling sensation went through her as she realized she was trapped. Gasping for air, she banged the side of her hand against the stone until it hurt, shouting Sean's name as hot tears stung her eyes. Her voice bounced off the stone walls around her, echoing through the shadows. It was useless. He couldn't hear her. Sean didn't follow her because Sean couldn't follow her. She was trapped.

There was no going back and there was no way she could get out. Her only option was to go down. With her pulse racing, she descended into the shadows.

Sean met Aoife's gaze as she hunched down inside the trunk. He didn't mistake the surprise on her face when she saw him. Surprise quickly turned into panic and fear and her flight instinct kicked in.

"Aoife, wait!"

He dove toward the trunk as she closed it with a snap. By the time he skidded to a halt, he shoved open the lid to see nothing but old clothes inside.

"Shit!"

Aoife must have found the portal. It was in the trunk as he'd suspected. But how did she activate it? Had Fiona left her some way to trigger it? He snatched his phone and was about to dial Caleb when it started to ring. It was his partner.

"There was an energy spike in the house," Caleb said before Sean could answer.

"I know. Aoife found the portal. Get over here."

Minutes later, Sean and Caleb stood in the middle of the attic, trying to figure out how to make the portal work for them. Neither had any luck.

"What did you see?" Cal asked.

"She was standing in the trunk, but it was almost as if she were standing on something inside it. Because all I could see of her was from the shoulders up. When she saw me, she panicked and closed the lid. By the time I'd gotten to it, it was that." He pointed to the musty contents.

"Anything unusual about the trunk or the lid after it closed?"

"Not that I remember." Sean scanned the room and noticed the papers scattered on the desk. "She found something."

He stomped over, Cal on his heels, and picked up the page. "*A wizard of both Fae and Wizard blood will come into power and rule from a silver throne.*"

"What does that even mean? That doesn't sound good." Cal reached for the map. "This is a partial map of Faery."

Sean peered down at the crude hand-drawn map. He saw mountains, forests, rivers and a faint drawing of an arrow pointing to the middle of the forest. "What's that?"

Caleb brought it closer to his face. "Looks like an arrow to the center of those woods."

"Where?"

"It was labeled but the ink is too faded to read now."

"We need to figure out where that is. Odds are that's where Fiona is headed. Wait a second." Sean reached for the book titled *Hidden Dimensions and Fae Time Travel.* He flipped through it quickly until he halted on one particular page that had been marked.

"What is it?" Cal asked.

Sean read aloud. "*Time travel in Faery is possible but only when used in conjunction with the Time Sphere. This mystical orb has innumerable powers, one of which is the ability to transport the user to any other time period within the Fae realm. But be warned, time is a constant and anything you do in that span of time could change the future. Even your own.*"

There were two Time Spheres in Faery. One was in the Ivory Wood. The location of the other one had remained a mystery. It was an enchanted sphere that could not only show past and present events, but when used in conjunction with magic, could allow someone to time travel to the past or even see into other realms. It could also show the future, though it was mostly a blur and travel to the future could be deadly. Not many attempted it and lived to tell about it.

Cal emitted a low whistle. "Do you think that's where she's headed?"

"Not sure."

He noticed the spell scroll had been moved and opened. Aoife found that, too, and likely wondered what an eradication spell was, like he had. He tried to think like Fiona. If she were going back to Faery and looking for the Time Sphere with an eradication spell memorized, then who did she plan to eradicate?

His partner snapped a picture of the map with his smartphone. "I'm sending this to HQ. They'll be able to cross-reference it with the archives and figure it out. We should call Bryant. See if he can help us get the portal open."

Bryant was their boss and the deputy director in the Inter-dimensional Portal Protection Agency. Now that Aoife and Fiona were actually in Faery, how was he going to explain that to his director?

The damage was done, though, and there was no going back. They had to get the portal open and find Fiona and Aoife before…well, before what? He wasn't sure. He never knew the reasons why Fiona wasn't allowed in Faery. He'd never questioned an order from his superior. He only followed them.

"I'll call," Sean said, reaching for his phone.

"Already on it." Cal had already dialed and had it on speaker as it rang.

Sean ran his hand over his chin, the stubble whispering against his palm. His boss was not going to be pleased with the new developments.

"Cal, I got your map and message. We're on it," Bryant answered. "What about the portal?"

"We think Fiona opened it, sir," Cal said. "And Aoife followed her through."

There was a long, dead silence on the other end and for a moment, Sean thought his boss had disconnected.

"What do you mean?" he asked at last.

"Just what I said."

"Is Sean with you?"

Shit. Sean cleared his throat. "Yes, sir."

"Your order was to keep Fiona out of Faery. Under no circumstances was she to enter."

"Yes, sir," Sean agreed.

"And you failed. How'd they get there?" Bryant demanded.

Cal flung him a questioning glance. Sean ignored it.

"Through a portal hidden in a trunk. I'm not sure how Fiona opened it or how Aoife managed to activate it. We don't know where Fiona is headed but we think the map may be a clue." Sean shifted from one foot to the other.

"Stand by."

There was more silence and a shuffle of paper, muffled voices and then Bryant was back on the line. "The map is of the Ivory Wood. Do you boys know what's inside the Ivory Wood?"

"No, sir," Cal answered.

But Sean knew and he cringed, realizing with some horror why Fiona was headed there.

"The Time Sphere," Bryant said, his tone flat.

Another pause and silence as they both digested that information. Dread washed over Sean, leaving a knot in the pit of his stomach. He looked at Cal, whose eyes widened with understanding.

"Why would Fiona want to go to the Time Sphere?" Cal asked.

"Likely because she's interested in altering the past." Bryant's voice was unemotional and Sean could imagine the straight-line of his lips as he said it. "It won't be easy for her to get to it with the protection spell around it."

"Then how will she get to it?" Sean asked.

"I'm sure she has the magical resourcefulness to figure that out. Whatever she's planning to do my guess is there's a specific event she wants to change."

No one knew much of Fiona's history other than she had been the daughter of a noble lord and lady betrothed to Prince Cian of Anatolia. In a tragic twist of fate, her parents had been murdered by highwaymen on the day of their wedding and she never made it. Lady Fiona had disappeared without a trace.

Until she turned up in the human realm.

"You boys better find her before she does something we can't reverse," Bryant said.

"We'd like to, sir, but there's the matter of getting back to Faery," Sean pointed out. "And finding the women."

"On the off chance Fiona slipped by you, Sean, we had Cal put a tracking device on her." Sean gave Cal a quizzical look but he feigned innocence. "I'm not happy they *both* managed to get into

Faery. I'm sending you the coordinates of a portal. Use that one. Find the women and get them out of Faery and back to the human realm. I trust that order is clear, gentlemen?"

"Abundantly," Sean said.

Cal clicked off the phone. They stared at each other in cold silence.

"Why didn't you tell me about the tracking device?" Sean asked.

Cal raised his hands in surrender. "It was top secret. I couldn't. I swear."

"Why?" he demanded.

"Bryant wanted to make sure Fiona wouldn't try to take Aoife back to Faery before her powers manifested. So he had me put a tracker on Fiona as a failsafe measure," Cal said.

"Why didn't he ask me to do it? Fiona and Aoife are under my watch."

Cal shrugged. Sean didn't like it. If Bryant had something against him, then he needed to know. He had a sneaking suspicion he knew why Bryant didn't have him do it. The Agency must still not trust him after his mishaps back in Faery. Even though he no longer had magic, the implications were loud and clear to Sean.

"How do you track her?" Sean asked.

"She has a tattoo on her left shoulder blade. She chose the same symbol that's on the top of the trunk." Cal reached into his pants pocket. He brought out a small box and handed it to Sean. "It's a compass that tracks the magic in the tattoo."

Sean flipped open the box to see the needle inside pointing southwest. "She went along with it?"

"She didn't have a choice. She'd been caught coming back through the portal for the third time."

"When was that?"

"Aoife was young. Nine or ten, I'd guess. I cornered Fiona because I was ordered to and told her she had to have the tattoo. She didn't fight me."

Sean recalled the incident well. He and Cal found Fiona in a field north of Brookdale. She had somehow perfected the ability to leave and return the human realm at precisely the same time. Not even the Agency knew how she did it.

Odd that Fiona didn't resist the tattoo. That had been the last time she left the human realm for Faery before her most recent disappearance. Sean mulled that over, thinking about what he knew about Fiona. Maybe the woman had procured whatever she needed in Faery and waited to act until Aoife was grown. Or maybe it was for another reason altogether.

"Why did Fiona give you the house?" Cal asked, breaking into his thoughts.

"She figured out who I was a few years ago and knew the Agency sent me. She put the fake sold sign in the yard and then gave me the key the day before she disappeared. She told me to keep Aoife away from it."

"How'd that work out for you, buddy?"

Sean glared at him. "The point is she didn't want Aoife in Faery either because she knew the portal was in the house. But now they're both there and we have a real problem. If Fiona is headed to the Time Sphere, then we don't have much time."

"Why? Isn't time infinite at the Time Sphere?"

"No. It can only be activated every five hundred years. That's five hundred Fae years, not human years. Fiona is more powerful than you realize, Cal. I'm told she's one of the strongest Fae there is."

"That's why you had to keep her out. Why we had to make sure all the portals were closed."

"Right and now we have to get them out. I suspect Fiona is headed to the Time Sphere for a very specific reason."

"Then let's get on with it and stop her," Cal said and waved him toward the attic stairs.

Sean couldn't agree more but he hoped stepping back into Faery wouldn't be a mistake.

Chapter 6

In the Land of Faery Past

The day after Fiona's arrival, King Niall entered the wizard's chamber without knocking. He never knocked. As his wizard, Deaglan was bound to him by blood and had helped him gain control of the kingdom of Illyria. He would also help him squash Prince Cian once and for all.

"Your Majesty, how may I serve you?" Deaglan bowed low to him as he entered the room.

"Tell me what you've learned of the girl."

"She has untapped power within, Your Majesty. She doesn't even know she has it."

"But Prince Cian knew, didn't he?" He folded his arms across his chest. Niall knew the prince well enough to know that the girl was more than highborn. She was special and he sensed it from the first moment she'd stepped into the castle. It had to be the reason Cian wanted her.

"It's possible. But I must wonder why, since he has such a hate for magic users. She and the prince were betrothed at a young age. The king of Anatolia still lives, Your Majesty, Prince Cian has not been crowned as yet."

"But he will be soon because, as we know, the king is dying. 'Tis why he moved up the wedding. What about the girl's untapped power? Is there anything you can do to bring it to the surface?"

"I can work with her, but she may not be such a willing participant. She's lost her family and freedom all in one day, sire."

"I made it clear to her she is a guest. Not a prisoner."

"Even so, you must go out of your way to make sure she is comforted while she's here."

"What do you suggest? Clearly you have something in mind."

"Allow her to move freely about the castle, sire. Have a guard or two trail her if you feel she may try to escape, though I doubt she will. The terrain below the towers is quite treacherous,"

Deaglan said.

Niall nodded in agreement before he even finished. "Aye, I agree with you. I must not treat her as though she were a prisoner." Niall ran his hand over his chin. "What news of Prince Cian?"

"He has not yet mobilized his army but I don't think he's discovered the carnage left behind by your mercenaries. When he learns they slaughtered all but the lady, he *will* come after her."

"Of that I am quite aware, Father. It will be weeks before he could even hope to reach the Towers, though, which will give me all the time I need. What of her magic?"

Deaglan sighed. "With her cooperation, she will be one of the most powerful in Faery. More so than…" He halted and pressed his lips together.

Niall lifted a brow. "Than me, you mean?"

The wizard smiled. "What are your plans for the girl?"

"I intend to seduce the lady and win her heart. And then I mean to marry her as soon as possible. There is not much time before Cian comes for the girl. And once that sniveling prince realizes he's lost his bride and his advantage I will conquer Anatolia with her help and yours. But first you have to awaken the magic inside her."

"I will do my best, Your Majesty. But know this—if you marry the girl and conceive a child…I believe that child will become more powerful than any wizard or Fae in the entire realm."

Niall stared at him for a long quiet moment. A child more powerful than anyone? Than Deaglan? Niall raked his hand through his pale blond hair and then turned away from the wizard. He knew the possibility existed but he didn't realize it would actually work.

"Are you certain of this, Father?"

"It is only my conjecture," Deaglan said. "A child born with Fae and wizard blood has only been recorded one other time. Imagine the possibilities, my son, for I know well your capabilities. Her magic trembles below the surface, just out of reach."

"And you can bring it to the surface?" he asked.

"Aye, much like I did yours."

Niall turned to face him. "Then do it. Teach her as you taught me."

"As you say, Your Majesty," Deaglan said with a nod of his head. "I swear it will be done."

That afternoon, Fiona perched on the window seat and stared out the window. Far down below, she could see the rocky cliffs of the mountain as snow swirled in the cold wind. Even if she wanted to escape, how could she? She knew not how far Lambridge Castle was from the Towers of Illyria. She would never make it on foot and she was nothing more than a prisoner in the castle.

A knock on the door and then it opened. Niall entered, standing in the open doorway.

"I hope I'm not disturbing you?"

Dinner the previous night with him had been awkward. He had offered his sincerest condolences on the death of her parents, as though that would bring them back from the dead. She had refused to speak much when he asked her questions about her family and her life in Anatolia. He even had the nerve to ask her about her betrothal to Prince Cian.

"What do you want?"

Irritation flashed across his face before he controlled his emotions. "You are not confined to your bedchamber, my lady. I hope you know that."

"As you say." She turned back to the window, watching snowflakes dance in the wind.

He stepped into the room, his footsteps quiet against the stone floor and over the thick rug in front of the hearth. She was aware of his movement toward her and stiffened. When his hand landed on her shoulder, his fingers were warm against her skin.

"I would like for you to treat this as your home." He paused, and then dropped his voice. "Fiona."

Hearing her name on his lips startled her and she looked up, meeting his level gaze. The warmth of his smile echoed in his voice. "I do hope it's all right if I call you that."

Her body tensed with his touch and the way he asked her permission to use her given name. It did not displease her, though she supposed it should have. His hand hadn't moved from her shoulder and yet he hadn't made a move to do anything else. When she spoke, her frail voice was foreign to her ears.

"Aye, it is."

"Good. And you must call me Niall. Let us drop all formality between us."

"If that's what you wish, Your Majesty."

"Ah, it is. There is no need to call me Your Majesty, I must insist." He brushed the back of his hand along her cheek, giving her a smile before he lifted his gaze and looked out the window at the snowy landscape. "'Tis a shame the snow moved in so quickly this season. Otherwise, I would take you for a ride along the cliffs. The scenery is quite breathtaking. Instead would you care to join me for afternoon tea?"

"Tea?" Mayhap he was sincere about telling her to treat this as her home.

"Aye, tea. My baker makes tiny lemon cakes that are the best in all of Illyria. But then I am quite partial to her lemon cakes so I'll let you judge for yourself."

"Lemon cakes, you say?" Now he managed to get her attention. Her mouth watered at the mere thought of lemon cakes. She hadn't had one in so long.

He grinned and stuck out his arm. "Aye, lemon cakes."

Together, they descended the winding staircase and crossed the great hall. They entered a large library with a twenty-foot high ceiling and soaring windows overlooking a courtyard and beyond, to more mountains. A fire blazed to warm the cavernous room, plush chairs and settees were scattered throughout and the floor was covered in a thick and richly designed rug from one end to the other. Braziers burned in every corner giving the room a warm and inviting glow. She could not hide her smile.

"I can tell by the look on your face this room delights you." He led her to one of the chairs and motioned for her to sit. "You are, of course, welcome to the library any time you like."

"Truly?" She perched on the edge of an oversized chair, her hands in her lap.

"Aye, truly." He poured tea from a silver pot into a china cup with intricate scrollwork along the edge in silver. "Cream?"

"Aye, thank you."

He added a dollop of cream to her tea and handed her the cup then poured one for himself. Dainty cakes were stacked upon a tray on the nearby table and she spotted the lemony ones right away. She clasped her hands in her lap in an effort not to seem overeager.

"No servants?" she asked, glancing around the room looking for the others.

"I prefer to take my tea in solitude in the library. And serve myself." He smiled again, a genuine smile that warmed her. He placed one of the lemon cakes on a plate and passed it to her.

"You're a bit of an enigma," she said.

Niall chuckled. "And why is that, my dear?"

"Yesterday you seemed different. Harder. Cold. Today…" She paused, searching for the right words.

"More even-tempered? Calmer?"

"Something like that."

He sipped his tea. "I realize you have lost much and I once again apologize for that. I am attempting to show you kindness, though I promise there is no underlying motive to my actions. I merely want you to be at ease here. I want you to be happy."

"You don't intend to release me, do you?" It was something she'd come to grips with while staring out her window. "I'm to remain here indefinitely."

He pressed his lips together. He didn't want to answer, she could tell. And by that, she knew the truth of it. She placed the tea cup on the table in front of her.

"Prince Cian will come for me, you know."

"I know."

"And when he does, he will do whatever it takes to get me back."

"I'm counting on that."

The coldness in his voice pressed into her. She knew he intended to kill the prince but it was only then she realized she was the bait. "You may try to appease me by allowing me to roam the castle at will, Your Majesty, but my feelings for you will not change."

"And what feelings are those?" He lounged back in the chair, the cup in his hand, looking far too relaxed for her comfort.

She rose and looked down on him. "One day I will seek revenge for all that you've taken from me. I will avenge the deaths of my parents. And my heart will be glad of it."

"You may try, my lady. You may try."

Fiona shuddered. Her appetite lost, she stalked from the room.

She could feel sorry for herself and continue to be a victim or she could take control of her situation and do something about it. She managed to find her way to the tower where Deaglan resided. By the time she climbed the stairs and made it to the top, her legs burned and she was out of breath. But no less angry. She pounded on the door.

"Enter," came Deaglan's muffled voice.

She shoved open the door and found him pouring clear drops of liquid into a small vial of a pink powdery substance. She halted and watched as the white drops twinkled and the powder turned into a thick gel-like substance. She glanced at the bookshelf over his table and saw another vial like it—the same vial she'd seen when she first came to him. It mesmerized her.

He corked the bottle, placed it on his shelf and then turned to her with a smile.

"The lovely Fiona. What brings you to me this fine afternoon?"

"Deaglan, I want you to teach me."

One thick black brow rose. "Teach you what, dearie?"

"Magic. You *are* a wizard, are you not?"

"Aye," he answered slowly and with caution.

She clutched her hand into a fist, wondering how she could show him what she'd done in her chamber the night before. "I know I have magic. I can feel it swirling around inside me, but I don't know how to use it. Will you help me learn to use it? To control it?"

His eyes widened ever so slightly as he regarded her. "You have magic?"

"Aye. Is that so hard to believe? I am Fae, after all." Before he could answer, she rushed on. "Deaglan, last night in my chamber I was able to light the fire in my fireplace with nothing more than my hand." She held up her good hand for him to see.

"And how did you do that?"

"I don't know, truthfully. I was emotional and angry. When I threw my hand out like this, a burst of light emitted from it and lit the fire. I hoped you could teach me to control it. I could be your apprentice."

He looked thoughtful, though a little sad, as he turned from her and walked to the one window in his room, his hands clasped behind his back. "You do not know what you ask of me."

"I do know. There have been Fae apprentices to wizards." She wasn't quite sure if that were true but she had to try anything to get him to agree. She added softly, "Deaglan, you cannot expect me to stay here against my will. Can you?"

"It is not for me to say, dearie. All of us who reside within the Towers of Illyria obey His Majesty. Even me." He turned back to her, his face drawn and sad. She didn't understand why. "He has a reputation as the wizard king to uphold. He will do whatever he can to maintain that."

"But you said yourself he doesn't like to be called that."

He nodded. "Aye, I did. And it is not something I would ever say to him or you if you know what's good for you. He has a power all his own and has no qualms about wielding it. He takes great pleasure in that those who do call him that name fear him."

"Why do they fear him?"

Deaglan looked sad again and his mouth drew down in a grimace. "Because of what he did to gain his crown."

"He murdered the king and queen in cold blood."

She'd heard the story. She knew he used a dark army conjured by magic to storm the tower walls, killing anyone in their path. They were unstoppable. They were ruthless. They were malevolent.

Something clicked inside her head and it occurred to her that Deaglan must have helped Niall gain his crown with that dark army. As the wizard, he would be the one to use his magic—along with Niall's—to conquer the people of Illyria. And what of the blood feud with Prince Cian?

"Why does he hate Cian so much? Why does he wish to destroy him?"

Fatigue creased his face and he expelled a breath. "Must I tell you?"

"I must know," she said with a nod.

"They are brothers." Deaglan turned again to the window, hands still clasped behind his back as he stared out. "They have different fathers, but the same maternal blood runs through their veins."

Fiona pressed cold fingertips to her lips to keep from gasping aloud. Queen Siobhan of Anatolia was Niall's mother? *And* Cian's? It didn't seem possible. "Go on."

"Niall was the elder. Abandoned at an early age by his father." His voice cracked as he spoke, as though telling the tale pained him. He paused and Fiona waited until he cleared his throat, trying to get his emotions in check. "Eventually, Siobhan married Ardan, then crown prince of Anatolia. He was willing to raise Niall as his own despite the threat of scandal that he married a woman with a child born out of wedlock. A year later, Cian was born and Ardan sat on the throne as king. The boys were raised together, though there was a distinct favoritism Ardan showed his own son, Cian. Niall was pushed aside and ignored, and the queen did nothing to stop it."

He paused again and Fiona thought she knew where Deaglan was going with the story. Yet she remained silent and let him continue.

"Niall was noticeably different, not only in appearance but also in other ways." He turned to face her, dropping his hands to his side. "In his magical abilities. It was said the boy could conjure any manner of thing he liked including things his brother hated, spiders, snakes, the like. When he bored of torturing his brother he used his magic in other ways. The servants in the castle and the commoners alike feared him. In time, the tales reached the ears of his absent father who at last returned, forcing the queen to give up the boy to him."

"And she agreed?" Fiona could not imagine under what circumstances a woman would give up her child, any child. It baffled her.

Deaglan nodded. "She knew it would be for the best. By then, Cian and Niall had developed a strong hate for each other. Cian knew he was the rightful heir of Anatolia and Niall was not, since he was nothing more than a bastard."

The wizard poured a glass of water and handed it to her. "Then what happened?"

"Then Niall's father taught him how to control his magic but the boy had been tainted. An insatiable desire for power and revenge had been infused inside him. Niall's father, wanting to make up for lost time and to make the boy happy, did anything he asked."

"And Niall's father is the one who helped him conquer Illyria?" she asked.

He nodded, still unable to hide his sadness. As if the tale he told really affected him. "Do not think to escape him, dearie. He will never stop hunting you if you do."

She placed the goblet of water on a nearby table and went to him, grasping his hand. "I cannot stay here. I don't belong here. His men killed my parents. Please help me learn the ways of magic, Deaglan."

His mouth thinned into a straight line as he looked her over. He rested his aged palm on her cheek. "You are young with a pretty face and don't deserve to die here under his rule. I do sense the power within you and it is strong."

She nodded, the hope welling inside her.

He dropped his hand and heaved a sigh. "I will teach you."

As the days passed, Cian had not made a rescue attempt and Fiona couldn't help but feel abandoned in the towers with Niall and his wizard. All she could do was pray to the gods that Cian found Winnie alive and prepared an invasion and rescue. She knew those things took time to plan and so she would bide her time.

Her training began immediately, much to her delight. Deaglan started her with a simple glamour spell. When she wasn't with the wizard, she spent her free time in the library, flipping through books to find something useful she could use with her newfound magic.

It was vast and had more books than she'd ever seen. There were fairy tales and histories and stories of the legendary heroes who once roamed the land. One hefty book told the tale of Queen Maeve, once ruler of the Otherworld, who had given up her powers and immortality for the love of a human man. To this, Fiona snorted. How could anyone with magic and immortality want to give that up for a *human*?

As she flipped through the pages, reading passages here and there, a burst of iciness passed through her. Gooseflesh rose on her arms and her breath puffed out in white plumes. She'd had that sensation before when she was standing at the carriage as the men kidnapped her. Even the mercenary behind her said something didn't feel right about that. She shivered as she glanced around but saw nothing and no one was about.

She replaced the book on the shelf. "Hello? Is anyone there?"

She moved around to the other side of the shelf, peering through the shadows and for a moment, she thought she saw movement. She hurried toward it as a book slid off the shelf and landed with a loud bang against the tile floor at her feet. Fright skittered through her as she came to a halt.

"Hello?"

Her voice echoed through the empty library. She stood still, not even daring to breathe, as the temperature returned to normal and she could hear no movement. When she was satisfied she was indeed alone, she glanced down at the book at her feet.

It was a particularly crumbling tome titled *A Hypothesis of Fae Magic in Other Realms*. She picked it up and hurried back through the shelves gently placing it on a table. The pages were yellowed and musty and she delighted in turning them and reading the careful script that had been handwritten. She had a hard time reading most of it as the words were faded, but what she came to understand was that it was a book about how to safeguard magic and use it.

As she continued to read, she stumbled across a whole section about portals. She'd had no idea there were portals in Faery. Portals that could be opened and closed at will. Her heart tripped in her chest as she stared down at the faded words. The more she read the more excitement skittered through her veins. The more she realized this could be her way out of Niall's towers.

There were two different kinds of magic—magic within and spellcasting. With the magic within, one could create and do almost anything within reason. One could not make another fall in love with someone, nor could they use the light magic to do harm or bring others back from the dead. Dark magic, however, had its own rules. Rules Fiona knew nothing about. Rules she preferred not to know.

Spellcasting was inherent with wizards. There were only a handful in the realm of Faery. And one happened to reside within the walls of Niall's tower.

Opening a portal, according to the book, was a form of spellcasting. She hoped Deaglan would teach her how to do it. She could escape from Niall and get back to Cian.

Fiona almost ripped the page from the book, but the thought of doing that sent a pang through her. She couldn't deface a book, any book, so she ran her hand over the writing and memorized the page number then replaced it with care back on the shelf.

As she did so, Niall entered the library. "Ah, my lady. What a pleasant surprise to find you here. I trust you're enjoying my books?"

She clasped her hands in front of her. "I am."

"I've been looking for you." He closed the distance between them and did what he always did. He took her hand and kissed it. Her wound had finally healed, leaving a pink scar. "I'm glad to see your hand is much better."

"Thanks to Deaglan."

"He is quite good at healing," he said with a nod. His thumb brushed over the scar, sending tingles through her.

"You were looking for me?"

She tugged her hand free and again clasped them in front of her. Something about him unnerved her. Every time he was near, her heart fluttered and her stomach flickered with something she didn't know how to describe.

"I was. You've been here several weeks now and the time has come."

"For what?" She didn't hide the suspicion in her voice.

"My lady, I am formally asking for your hand in marriage." He reached for her again but she drew back.

"I believe you know I'm promised to another," she snapped.

"Aye, I know. But Prince Cian has no love for you," he said. "Do you not know this? You were betrothed to him because of your impeccable pedigree. Your noble birth will give him the royal heir he needs to carry on the bloodline. You are nothing but a pawn to him."

"And what am I to you?" she countered. "I am nothing more than bait to lure Prince Cian here so you can kill him."

"I saved you from a life of misery with him. He has an insatiable taste for women and is never satisfied with one. He will only want you to produce a successor and then he will discard you as though you were rubbish." Niall's voice was hard as steel and she could hear the hatred he harbored for his brother in his words.

"You only say that to turn me against him."

"Do I?"

She nodded.

"Come with me."

Without waiting for her to respond, he took her by the hand and led her to the center of the library, past shelves of books to the opposite side. He paused at a crystal globe mounted in a circular stone stand. Without releasing her, he waved his hand over the sphere.

"What is it?" she asked.

"A Time Sphere. It can do many things. It can show the past or the present, sometimes the future though it is often not in focus. Watch, my lady, as it shows you the present."

The interior glowed and turned translucent so she could see

inside it as it filled with smoke and then an image. She peered at it closely and saw Prince Cian. He lay in a bed, his lean and muscular chest bare and his hands tucked behind his head. Her cheeks flamed when she realized there was a woman sucking on his shaft and he smiled with rapt enjoyment. The scene changed. He was with a different woman who was on her hands and knees while he took her from behind.

Fiona had seen enough and turned away. Her stomach cramped with the horror of knowing Niall was right.

"I'm sorry you had to see that but you had to know the truth. Do not think for a moment he loves you and will be true to you."

Mayhap not but did he deserve to die?

"I will never hurt you." His words came out on a breath and he stood so close, they fanned her cheek. Her eyes fluttered closed. "I will remain true to you as your lord husband and king."

"That is your vow to me?" she asked.

"Indeed. I offer you the protection of my kingdom, my crown and my body." He trailed warm fingers across her cheek. "You don't have to decide today. I urge you to consider it, my lady. Will you do that for me?"

She turned her head and met his cool gaze. Pinpricks of heat went over her as she looked at him and something inside her seemed to melt a little. If she agreed to cooperate and become his wife, it would allow her more freedom about the castle. He would, mayhap, even trust her. She could feign happiness and all the while plot her escape.

"I will consider it," she said.

"I'm glad."

He cupped her chin in his hand and tipped her head back. His lips brushed hers in a soft kiss but before she could even respond, he had released her and was gone.

Chapter 7

Present Day in the Human Realm

The stone staircase that Aoife descended narrowed the farther down she went. She put her hands on the wall to steady her feet. The steps were so small she had trouble keeping her balance. She could see nothing ahead, nothing behind, not even her hand in front of her face. She whimpered, sniffled. Maybe this had been a mistake, what was she thinking? Why had stepping into the trunk been a good idea?

It called to me. It spoke to me. It beckoned me.

It was unlike anything she'd ever experienced, as though something pulled at her, tingling under the skin and heating her blood. Drawing her closer and closer to the thing she wanted most which was something she couldn't even describe or acknowledge. All she knew was that she had to step into the trunk.

The cadence of her heart throbbed loudly in her ears, the air around her seemed to thin and she felt as though the walls closed in on her. She'd never been claustrophobic before but it was something she could easily develop if she didn't get out of this place soon.

Aoife took another step. Her sneaker slipped off the stone. She gasped as she lost her footing and a second later her balance. She plunged downward at an alarming rate and there was nothing she could do to slow her descent. Her hands raked down the rough stone walls, the jagged edges scraping her delicate palms.

Below her she could see a blinding light, an opening, and her heart climbed into her throat as she realized she was plunging directly into it. The stone walls had disappeared and she flailed her arms, thinking it might slow her down but it did nothing to help her fate.

She thought for sure she could see ground beneath her. A flash of green and pink and orange. It flew upward toward her and all she could think to do was bend her knees and try to turn her body to absorb most of the impact in a way that she wouldn't break every bone.

That was her last coherent thought before she landed, the wind knocked out of her, her head smacking on the ground.

She awoke some time later to a bright light pressing the backs of her eyelids. The same bright light she'd seen while falling? She was too afraid to open her eyes yet. She opened her senses and listened. The sound of running water trickling nearby. Birdsong. Voices in the distance, so far away she could only make out their muffled sound. She lay on something cool that had the texture of grass.

She did a quick mental inventory of her body but nothing seemed to be broken, or sore for that matter. Like she'd landed in a soft bed. Aoife wiggled her fingers and then her toes and rolled to her back with a groan.

Relieved she wasn't dead, she blinked her eyes open. Her vision was blurry. Even though she blinked to try to clear her contacts, she couldn't. She sat up and glanced around but everything was a colorful blur. Orange and red and yellow and blue and purple all blended into one mass of color. Perhaps she'd gotten something in her contacts? She wasn't sure. And she didn't want to take them out for fear of being unable to get them back in without contact solution.

Aoife could still hear the trickling water nearby but she couldn't see a damn thing. She was faced with no other choice and popped the one contact out of her right eye. Blinking, she squeezed her left eye closed and looked around. She was shocked to discover she could see clearly out of her right eye. And the colors were so vibrant. She removed her left contact and held them both in her palm.

Looking down at her hands, she could see the abrasions where she'd dragged her palms along the rough stone wall. Dried blood caked both hands. She would have to clean them later.

At the moment she was in awe of the wonder around her. Aoife climbed to her feet and stood in the middle of a garden with flowers taller than her, in brilliant colors. Colors she had never seen so dazzling at home. Bright red and orange tulips that soared toward the sky. Gorgeous sunflowers waving in the slight breeze. Marigolds dotted along the edge of the sidewalk in red, orange and yellow. In front of her was an elaborate fountain with a sculpture of a flower spewing water. The source of the trickling sound.

Where was she? Had she imagined the whole trunk episode? No, she couldn't have imagined it for she had the scrapes on her hands to prove it. Had she landed in Wonderland? She reached out and touched the nearest flower, feeling the smooth leaves and smelling the sweet scent of the petals. It certainly felt real and it smelled real, too.

She stepped to the fountain, still holding her contacts in her hand as she looked over the edge and gazed down at her reflection. A strangled gasp escaped her throat as she peered down at a face she hardly recognized. She jumped back, shaking her head to clear it and rubbing her eyes. She took a tentative step again to the fountain. The face that wavered back up at her remained the same as before.

Aoife lifted several locks of her thick wavy auburn hair, fingering the soft strands between her thumb and forefinger. It was thicker, fuller, softer. Not the straw to which she was so accustomed. She ran her hand through the long locks, marveling at how luxurious they were between her fingers.

She peered into the crystal clear water again, staring at the face that stared back at her. She was beautiful. Her lips were full and red. Her cheeks were sharp and accentuated. Her chin came to a delicate point with a dimple in the center. Her wide eyes were the color of emeralds, not that dull sheen she knew, and fringed in long lashes. Even her boobs were perkier and bigger.

Whatever this place was that made her look this way, she liked it. She wanted to stay forever.

"Look out!"

Aoife glanced up to see a young girl running full speed straight for her. She tried to move out of the way but she wasn't fast enough and the girl collided with her. They toppled to the ground, knocking the wind out of her. Before she could move, though, the girl was up on her feet a second later.

"Sorry! Sorry!"

"Wait!"

Aoife caught a glimpse of golden blonde hair bouncing behind a tall girl as she bounded away on slender muscular legs, something tightly grasped in her hand. She halted when Aoife called and turned back, but she bounced from one foot to the other.

"Hurry. Hurry. Gotta go. Time is wasting."

"I need help."

There was a commotion behind Aoife. She turned to see several guards brandishing swords heading their way. Oh, crap. Who were they? The rest of the area came into focus and she realized she stood in the middle of a castle garden. The two towers stretched toward the pinkish-blue sky and were so tall, the spires disappeared into the clouds.

"No time. Come on!"

The girl grabbed Aoife by the hand and tugged hard enough to make her stumble. They took off together running through the garden, leaves of trees and plants slapping her in the face. Aoife followed, unsure what else to do. She didn't think asking the castle guards questions was a good idea, especially if she were trespassing.

They left the flower garden behind and passed hedge after hedge, the girl's cloak fluttering behind her like a cape. Aoife realized with some horror they were winding through a hedge maze, cementing her lost sense of direction completely. She also realized she'd lost her contacts somewhere along the way. Probably when the girl smacked into her at the fountain.

The girl turned right, left and right again and then halted at a dead end. They could hear the shouting guards coming after them. Sweat beaded the girl's forehead and her damp hair plastered against her head. Her chest rose and fell with the breath she tried to catch as she stood staring into the leaves of the hedge.

"Now what?" Aoife asked.

"Shh. I'm thinking."

The guards neared. She could hear them on the other side of their dead end. "Well think faster."

The girl shoved whatever she had grasped tightly in her hand into a knapsack that crisscrossed her body. Even as she did so, she never took her keen eyes off the hedge in front of her.

"There it is!" she exclaimed and shoved a hand into the hedge.

Aoife heard a click and then a whoosh and a second later, the girl pulled open a hidden door that materialized out of the middle of the greenery. She stepped in and then beckoned for Aoife to follow.

"Come on. You don't want to get caught by the wizard king."

A wizard of both Fae and Wizard blood will come into power and rule from a silver throne.

The words burst into her mind as she recalled reading them on the torn out page.

"The wizard?"

"There they are!"

Guards had come into sight now and charged toward them. The girl emitted a high-pitched squeal. She launched out of the doorway, grabbed Aoife and dragged her inside, yanking the door closed. They were plunged into shadows and it took several minutes for Aoife's eyes to adjust. When they finally did, they stood on a dirt path surrounded by trees. Pale sunlight slashed through the branches, splashing on the ground in front of them.

The girl spun towards Aoife, her hands on her hips and her breath see-sawing in and out of her. Her face was bright red and for the first time Aoife noticed the girl had pointed ears. She dressed like a boy in a brown tunic, soft green padded pants and tall suede boots. Aoife didn't miss the dagger at her side either.

"Are you mad? You could have got us caught!"

"I'm sorry. I—"

"I should have let them capture you. You good for nothing." And then she kicked Aoife in the shin.

"Ow! That wasn't very nice."

"Ari, stop it. Oh…*hey*. Who's this?"

A tall boy stepped out of the shadows and made his way to them. He sidled up close to Aoife, a goofy grin on his face. He looked a lot like Ari. So much so, Aoife was certain they were twins. They were the exact same height, had the same golden hair and bright blue eyes. Ari shoved him away from Aoife.

"Don't start, Orrin. She nearly got me caught!"

"Oh, calm down, you're so dramatic. The guards probably weren't even close," he said.

"They *were* close. They saw us enter!"

"Who cares? It's not like they can catch us. They don't know how to open the gate." He turned his attention back to Aoife. "What's your name, lady?"

"Don't you even want to know if I got it?" Ari stamped her foot like a petulant child.

He sighed and turned his attention back to his sister. "Of course you got it. That's why the guards were chasing you."

"But you didn't even *ask*."

"All right. Let's see it." He held out his hand and wiggled his fingers.

Ari, all smiles, reached into her pouch and brought out two small pink crystals that sparkled even in the half light. She handed them to her brother, who took them, held them up to the light and nodded approval.

"Perfect. This is what we needed."

Something clicked for Aoife. "She's a thief. You're both thieves."

"For a good cause." Orrin grinned as he palmed the crystals and then slipped them into a pocket out of sight.

"What cause?" Aoife asked.

"We gotta eat somehow," Orrin replied. "What's your name?"

"Aoife," she said.

He bowed with a flourish. "Orrin the Great, at your service, my Lady Aoife. And this is my sister, Ari the Drama Queen." Aoife chuckled when Ari stuck out her tongue at her brother.

"There's nothing great about you." Ari rolled her eyes as she said it. "And anyway I'm Ari the Stealthy, not the Drama Queen."

"Of course I'm great. I knew where the hidden gate was, didn't I?" He turned his attention back to Aoife. "What were you doing in the tower of the wizard king, my lady?"

"Ah…" Aoife wasn't quite sure how to respond to that. "The tower of the wizard king?"

"She's lost, you dolt," Ari said and punched her brother on the shoulder. "We should open the gate and shove her back into the hedge maze. Let the guards have her."

"No, we shouldn't. And anyway we can't. The gate has already been locked. I can't open it again," Orrin said. "I agree with you, though, sis. She *does* look lost. What manner of dress is that? Are you a foreigner?"

He looked her up and down. Aoife pulled her cardigan closer to her frame, trying to hide her huge boobs. She'd dressed for summer that day because it was hot back home. She wore a thin white T-shirt, an even thinner cardigan for fashion not function and khaki shorts that hit her mid-thigh. The only sensible thing she happened to wear was her red Keds.

"I guess you could say that," she said. "Where am I?"

"The kingdom of Illyria," Orrin said, as though she should know where that was.

Aoife's brows drew together in confusion. She had never heard of Illyria. "And where is that exactly?"

Orrin took a step back and looked at his sister, thumbing back at her. "Where did you find this one, Ari?"

"In the castle garden. She was standing there in the middle of the path. I bet she's an escaped prisoner. I bet the wizard king is looking for her right now and we could get a ransom for her if we took her back."

"No, no, he's not, I swear it," Aoife said, holding up her hands in surrender. "Please. I'm lost and could really use some help. I'm looking for someone, though I don't know if she's here and I really need to know where *here* is."

"She doesn't even know she's in Faery!" Ari exclaimed, exasperated. She flung her hands in the air and paced in a small circle around her. "Look at her, Orrin. She dresses weird. She smells weird. She even has weird hair."

Self-conscious, Aoife smoothed her luxurious new tresses.

Ari halted in front of her, fists on her waist. "I know what she is now. She's a Changeling. That explains her weird clothes."

Aoife's gut knotted. Ari looked at her with such disgust she feared the worst. There were two words that stuck out in her mind the most, though—*Faery* and *Changeling*. Faery was a mythical place that only existed in the imagination. And a Changeling, as far as she knew, was a Fae child switched with a human child. She doubted she was that. She also doubted she was standing in Faery.

Could she have conked her head harder than she thought when she landed?

"I'm not a Changeling, I swear."

"Oh, yeah? Then how'd you end up here?" Ari demanded, her eyes narrowing.

"Cut it out, Ari." Orrin shoved his sister aside and regarded her with interest. "Can't you see she's scared? You're not helping. She's not a Changeling, that's for sure. She doesn't smell human."

She *was* scared and—back up, what did he mean she didn't smell human? What did she smell like? This was all too much for her. Worry gnawed at her gut. What would they do to her? Turn her in to the wizard king? She didn't know these kids. How did she know she could trust them? The answer was she couldn't.

She backed up a few steps, but had no idea where she was or where she would go or even how to get back home. And if her mother was here—in Faery?—how was she going to find her? How was she going to get back to that staircase in the trunk?

"If we aren't taking her to the wizard king, then we should take her to the marquis. He'll know what to do with her," Ari said.

"We're not turning her in to anyone." He sounded exasperated and looked unconvinced, for which Aoife was grateful. He tapped the tip of his forefinger against his smooth chin. "I think she needs our help, sis. Who is it you're looking for?"

Aoife considered telling him the truth and then changed her mind. What if her mother was wanted by the wizard king, too? "A friend."

"Does your friend have a name?"

How likely would the kids know her mother? She decided the odds were against it. "Fiona."

"All right then," Orrin said with a nod. "We'll help you find your friend, Fiona, but first we have to see a merchant. The village isn't far from here. Come on."

Orrin started up the path. Ari flashed a glare that told Aoife everything she needed to know—the girl disliked her and quite a lot.

"We should get you some proper clothes, too," Orrin said over his shoulder. Yes, they should. But Aoife didn't have any money. She didn't even have her purse since she'd left it in the car parked outside the house. Her stomach fluttered as she thought back to the house which made her think of Sean. He saw her enter the trunk. Had he tried to come after her and couldn't? Would she be stuck here forever?

"I'll pay you back somehow," Aoife said.

"You're going to spend our money on clothes for her?" Ari complained. "Why are you helping her?"

"Hush up, sis."

"Why *are* you helping me?" Aoife asked.

Orrin halted to give her a thoughtful onceover. "We had a mother once. You remind me a little of her."

The gut-wrenching admission made Aoife even more grateful than she was moments ago. It was hard to imagine being orphaned. Orrin, though, was doing his best to take care of his sister. She admired that about him and patted his shoulder.

"Thank you."

As she followed the twin thieves, she heard Ari whisper, "She doesn't look anything like our mother." Orrin admonished her with a loud shush. Which made Aoife grin all the more.

Chapter 8

In the Land of Faery Past

Every day since she arrived in the towers, Fiona and Niall shared their morning meal in the relative peace of the castle. She had come to look forward to their time together when he would tell her what he had planned for the day. He ran his domain with quiet efficiency and all the people within the towers seemed to like and respect him. They did not fear him as she'd heard in so many stories. She had come to believe those were merely fables meant to scare children. But she wondered, too, about the story of how he gained his crown. He did not seem like the cruel man that Deaglan described.

Sometimes he would invite her along on his morning rounds, from the gardens to the stables, to the armory. That morning, he asked her to join him in the greenhouse.

"You have a greenhouse on the cliffs?"

"It's rather rudimentary but, aye, I do. It's on the edge of the gardens. I visit it once a week." He spooned the remaining porridge from his bowl and took the last bite.

"What do you grow there?" she asked.

"Fruits and vegetables mostly and some herbs. We are far away from any village and the trek down the cliffs can be quite treacherous, especially during the winter months. The greenhouse allows us to have a constant supply of food. So will you join me?"

She sipped her morning tea, considering. She had an appointment later with Deaglan and she wasn't going miss it for anything.

Well, mayhap for Niall.

She placed her cup back on the table. "I'd love to."

The joy at her acceptance was evident on his face. He tossed his napkin on the table and rose, holding his hand out to her. "Shall we then?"

Fiona gripped his hand, his warm fingers closing around hers. It was far from erotic but something about his touch sent tendrils of heat through her. The attraction to Niall grew daily, making it more and more difficult for her to resist him. Such an attraction could be perilous for her. Once she had fallen for him she would never be able to break free. Even now her desire to return home dwindled as she began to think of the Towers of Illyria as her home.

They walked through the castle into the gardens and past fragrant roses and other flowers. The cobblestone pathways were covered in a dusting of fresh snow and she shivered.

"You're chilled," he said. "Let me get you a cloak."

Before she could reply, he snapped his fingers and conjured her fur-lined cloak. He wrapped it around her shoulders, slipping his arm around her and leading her farther into the gardens.

"That's a handy trick," she said and smiled.

"You'll find I have all sorts of handy tricks."

The greenhouse was at the edge of the gardens and much larger than she had imagined. The glass enclosure was also dusted with snow, giving it a frosted appearance. He opened the door for her and motioned for her to go inside.

The greenhouse was redolent with the smells of fresh herbs and vegetables. There were vine ripened tomatoes, peppers, chilies, cucumbers, beans, squash, leafy greens including spinach and lettuce. One side of the greenhouse was solely devoted to herbs. Basil, rosemary, thyme, watercress and cilantro.

"You grow all this here?" She didn't bother to hide the surprise in her voice. "I thought you said this was rudimentary."

He chuckled. "It's rather a small greenhouse but fits our purposes quite well."

"I'm impressed."

"I don't have much of a green thumb," he said. "I have excellent greenhouse keepers to thank for this. Come see the citrus trees."

"You have citrus trees?"

He laughed at her genuine surprise as he took her hand and led her past all the greenery and into what could only be called a wing in the greenhouse devoted to the orange trees. She could smell them the moment she turned the corner.

"Ah, they look as though they're ready for picking." He plucked one from a nearby tree and smelled it. Pleased with it, he held it out to her. "Smell."

She sniffed. The scent of the orange peel punctured through to the back of her throat and she could swear she could taste the succulent sweetness of the orange. Her mouth watered.

"It smells wonderful."

Pleased with her response, he peeled back the rind, dropping it on the ground, and then broke off a piece of the orange for her and held it to her lips. Flushing to the tips of her ears, she took the slice into her mouth. The juices burst through her mouth as she chewed.

"It's delicious," she said around her mouthful.

"As I said, I have excellent greenhouse keepers."

"What do you do with the surplus food? Surely you don't eat all this here." She waved her hand to encompass the citrus trees.

"In the winter, we store it and use up as much as we can. By the time the spring thaw comes and the cliffs are navigable again, we send some of the food to the local villages on pack mules. We keep them well stocked through the summer."

Fiona had to admit she loved that about him. That he was so willing to give up most of his crops to the peasants who needed the food much more than he or anyone in his castle did. It endeared him to her.

"That's very generous of you," she said.

"I'm glad you think so. You see, I'm not such a tyrant." He popped a slice of orange in his mouth and then peeled off another one for her. She waved him off though. He dropped it in nearby waste receptacle. She gave him a questioning glance. "We'll use the waste for mulch and other things."

"I have to say I'm impressed."

He looked well pleased. "I knew you would be."

Niall turned, moving close to her. His body heat radiated over her and suddenly she forgot everything. When his hands cupped her face, she could smell the sweet citrus tang on his fingers. Her heart quickened as he looked her over with that sensual light in the depths of his eyes.

He was going to kiss her.

She was going to let him.

When Niall's lips met hers, her knees weakened. She tasted the orange on his lips and his tongue. His velvet mouth slanted over hers in a perfect fit of dreamy intimacy, as though he was always meant to kiss her. The sweet tenderness of his kiss made her quiver.

Feeling her shudder, he pulled back. When his lips left hers, they left a void behind.

"You're cold. I should take you back to the castle."

But even as he took her hand and led her away, she could no longer deny the desire burning within her, the pleasure radiating outward nor the quixotic sweetness he left behind. She was falling hard and fast for Niall.

"Good. Good!" Deaglan's praise made Fiona smile.

The harder Fiona worked, the more she wanted Deaglan's accolades. He was a tough teacher, not allowing her to be lazy. With his guidance, she mastered casting a glamour, first on herself and then on Deaglan. He was surprised though not displeased at how quickly she managed to become proficient.

She had even learned how to control the light pulsing through her—the light she realized was her magic. Deaglan taught her how to find the silvery thread of magic residing within her, dormant. He helped her learn how to uncoil it and harbor it. It had exhilarated her.

Her current lesson was how to create and control fire in her hand. It took considerable concentration, but she managed to do it. She held the flickering ember in her palm, marveling at how she brought it to fruition. The emotion she had felt when she lit her own fire had been part of her magical awakening, so Deaglan said, and she recognized that now.

"Now what?" she asked, breathlessly.

"That is a lesson for tomorrow, dearie." He pushed her fingers closed over the fire, snuffing it out as though snuffing out a candle flame.

"Why tomorrow?"

"Because you need rest. Your cheeks are flushed."

She cupped her face and could feel the warmth there. "But I'm not tired."

"More tomorrow," he said, his voice firm.

He sat at his desk, reaching for his quill and a fresh piece of parchment. A ritual she'd seen him do every day after their lessons. She had a sneaking suspicion he kept notes on her progress.

"No reason to hang around here, dearie."

But she was reluctant to leave yet. Instead, she walked to his work bench and peered at all the bottles and jars and books lining the shelves above it. Her eye was drawn once more to the pink sparkly substance in the bottle with a cork.

"What are all these things, Deaglan?" She ran her finger along one shelf, pausing at the pink one. At one time, he'd had two vials, but now only the one.

He scooted his chair back and shuffled over. He stood next to her, looking over the items. "These are items a wizard needs for all sorts of things."

"What kind of things?"

"Nothing to worry your pretty head about."

"But I'm curious," she pressed, her mind on the portal. How could she ask him about it? "Especially about this one. It caught my eye the first day I was here." She pointed to the bottle.

"That. Oh, aye, that." He reached for it, rolling the small bottle in the palm of his hand. "'Tis very special indeed."

She peered at it. "What is it?"

He closed his hand around it. "So inquisitive. I don't think I've known anyone quite like you, my lady."

"I have a curious mind," she said with a bright smile. She leaned back against the table and fluttered her lashes at him. "The sparkles are dazzling. I can't quite take my eyes off them." And she glanced at his closed hand for good measure.

His fingers opened one by one. "Aye, they are something magical these…sparkles…as you call them." He paused then held up the bottle to the candlelight. She could see them dancing around in the pink solution, bobbing back and forth. "They are not sparkles, though. They are Tears of the Dryad."

Fiona blinked. She had never heard of such a thing but now she was mesmerized and had to know more. "Where does one get tears of a dryad?"

He chuckled. "From a dryad, of course. The tears from this particular tree nymph came from the Woodland Forest."

"Home of the Elves," Fiona said and he nodded.

"This species of tree nymphs are tied to the trees. You may remember a great fire there some eons ago. Their queen wept for the death of the trees and those tiny creatures that lived in them."

"So these tears are from the queen of the dryads?"

"Aye. They are quite powerful when mixed with…well, they are quite powerful."

She waited, hoping he would continue without being prompted. He studied her with a contemplative look on his aged face. Then he uncorked the bottle.

"I will trust you with this, dearie," he said. "There are very few who know how to make what I have created here."

Her heart thudded in anticipation. Was he going to tell her his magical secrets?

"Are you familiar with crystals?" he asked.

She shook her head.

"There are magical crystals in all colors. They have different uses but the pink is one of the most powerful. When ground down into a powder and mixed with…" he paused again, choosing his words carefully, "…with other ingredients, this is the result."

Although he didn't say it, she understood he meant mixing the crystal with the tears created whatever was in that bottle. He waved the open bottle under her nose, but she smelled nothing.

"Odorless, aye?" he asked.

"Aye."

He turned to the center of the room, tipped the bottle until one drop slid out and plopped on the floor. For a long quiet moment, nothing happened and then a pop of light burst from the drop and exploded into a round hole in front of them. The edges shimmered with pale pink light. Fiona gasped with her delight and wonder.

"What is it, Deaglan?"

"A portal."

Excitement skittered through her. This was what she'd been so desperate to learn. And all the while he'd had the substance in a bottle in his workroom. She peered through the gap in the air, trying to discern what was on the other side.

"Where does it go?"

"Step inside and see for yourself." There was a smile in his voice.

Her breath quickened as she stepped toward the hole, then paused. "Are you sure it's safe?"

He chuckled. "Perfectly. Come back and tell me what you find."

Taking a deep breath, Fiona stepped into the portal. It was as though she stepped into an icy wind as it cut through her. She shuddered and saw the opening on the other side. Another step and she was through…and in her own chambers.

She turned back around in time to see the portal close and disappear. But Deaglan, the sly old dog, had sent her to the other tower. She giggled, pressing her cold fingers against her mouth. How wonderful!

Out of the corner of her eye, she saw movement and spun toward it. A figure emerged from the corner of the room wearing a long black cloak with edges shimmering in gold and a hood shadowing most of the face. Alarm sliced through her and she started to shake.

"Who are you?"

"Who I am does not matter. I mean you no harm." Fiona could tell by the chin and lips and voice that it was a woman. She hovered near the shadows, refusing to move closer.

"Show yourself."

"I cannot. Lady Fiona, I come to tell you that you must marry King Niall. It is imperative you go through with the vows." Her voice was rough and weak. It wavered, as though the woman was on the brink of tears.

"What? Why?" Fiona squinted as though that would make the woman's face come into focus through the shadows. She could only see the lower half, with her dimpled chin.

The woman reached for her and clasped her wrist, her icy fingers digging into her flesh. "You have doubts, I know, but he loves you. And somewhere, deep down, you love him. Marry him, Fiona. Say yes."

"I-I do have doubts." A knock on the door made Fiona jump and she turned towards it. "One minute!"

But when she turned back, the woman had released her wrist and was gone. Who was she? How had she gotten in here? Fiona ran to the window but it was locked tight. Aside from that, her chamber was at the top of the tower. Scaling an outside wall would never work because there were no footholds or handholds.

The knock sounded again. "Fiona, dearest, are you in there?"

It was Niall. Still shaking, she tried to calm her nerves. She smoothed her hair back and opened the door. He bowed to her with a flourish and then reached for her hand, kissing it.

"Dearest, your hands are cold. Are you well?"

She tugged it out of his grasp. "I'm fine. What brings you here?"

"May I?" He waved his hand toward her room asking for an invitation. She nodded. He stepped inside. "Your fire is out. No wonder you're so chilled." He snapped his fingers and a second later, fire ignited in the hearth, warming the room. "There. That's better."

"Did you want something, Niall?" she asked.

She knew he was trying to impress her with the way he doted on her. But all she could think about was what the woman said to her. She looked him over and for the first time really saw him. He was tall, slender with the hint of muscles in his fine-boned physique. The kiss under the orange tree came back to her, making her lips tingle in anticipation. She admitted she was attracted to him, that she could marry him and quite possibly be happy the remainder of her days.

"Aye, I do." He stepped to her, taking her hands once again in his. "The time for our wedding has come. We cannot delay any longer. Have you decided?"

She'd allowed him to court her. Woo her. It was hard to deny how much she liked the attention. She'd never received such from her parents or even Prince Cian. The prince had never really taken to her. They were friends and friendly but they hadn't shared any intimacy at all. A sweet kiss here. A hug there. A caress or two. But there was no passion, no fire, no intensity.

Niall was different. Niall made her feel as though she were special, as though she were something worth worshipping. He'd seen to her every need, her every wish, her every whim. The only thing he didn't allow her to do was leave the castle. For that, she could forgive him. He'd no more treated her as though she were a prisoner, or even an honored guest. He treated her as though he truly wanted to win her favor. As though he might love her. As though she already belonged here.

The woman's words came back to her. *He loves you. Deep down, you love him. Say yes.*

"I have decided," she said, looking into his cool blue eyes. "And I agree to marry you."

His eyes sparked with delight at her answer, and a hint of desire. His smile was genuine as he kissed her hand again. "It makes me happy to hear you say that, dearest."

Fiona delighted in the sensual feel of his lips on her palm. With her decision made to stay with Niall, to marry him and let him love her, she knew what she had to do. She couldn't allow Niall and Cian to go to war over her. She had to warn off Cian. She had to break the betrothal between the two of them and tell him she had made her decision of her own free will to remain with the King of Illyria.

Her heart fluttered up to her throat. Mayhap there was also another way to keep Niall from going to war.

"I require one thing. A wedding present if you will." It was an impulse. A last-ditch effort to save her kingdom.

That seemed to stop him cold. "And what is that?"

"Cease your attack on Anatolia."

He released her hands and stepped away, moving toward the fire. He turned from her and clasped his hands behind his back, something she'd seen Deaglan do numerous times. It struck her then how oddly similar they were. How much they seemed to resemble each other in mannerisms and other things.

"I cannot promise you that, my dear."

It was what she expected him to say. Even if he promised, she didn't believe he would keep his word. She knew how much he hated Cian.

"It is my condition for marrying you," she said, sounding stronger than she felt. "Anatolia was my home. My family lived there for generations. There are innocent men, women and children who live there and are not a part of your fight with the prince. And despite whatever feud you have with Cian—"

"It is not for you to discuss with me," he snapped. "Anatolia is my concern. And mine only."

"Then I cannot marry you." It was a gamble, she knew, because she knew how desperate he was to destroy all that Cian had.

Niall turned slowly from the fire and pinned her with his pale glittering gaze. The firelight danced upon his face, shadowing it and making it seem almost frightening. Though he'd promised her he would never take her against her will, he still could and that terrified her.

"It means so much to you?" he asked.

"It does."

He stepped toward her, his gaze never leaving her face. "All right, then. It shall be done. You have my solemn vow the people of Anatolia will not be harmed." He took her hands again in his. His finger ran over the silvery scar on her palm. "Does that satisfy you, dearest?"

Her heart thudded. "Aye, it does."

"Good. I'm glad to hear that. Then you'll marry me?"

"I will."

He cupped her face. "A kiss to seal the agreement?"

All she could do was nod. The pad of his thumb brushed over her lower lip before his head dipped and their lips met. She thought her heart would beat out of her chest. His mouth closed on hers, his tongue dipped inside and tasted hers and her body reacted with such violent need she would have let him take her then and there. This kiss had more desire than the one in the greenhouse.

She shuddered against him as he wrapped her in his arms, never breaking the connection. Their breath mingled and for a moment she thought their souls touched. It shook her to the core, turned everything she ever thought she knew about him upside down.

And yet it was right and real. She belonged with him and believed he told her the truth when he promised he would not attack Anatolia. He had promised he would spare Anatolia and for that she was forever grateful.

When they broke, her breathing came in gasps though she tried hard to hide it. Even so, he noticed. He brushed his fingertips over her face, caressing her.

"Preparations are already underway for our wedding. I hope you don't find that presumptuous."

She shook her head for she feared if she gave him a verbal response, her quivering voice would give away how deeply he affected her.

"I look forward to you being my wife, my lady."

"As do I," she said and was well pleased that she spoke the truth.

He kissed her again, holding her so close she thought he would never let her go. Warmth and need spread outward from her center, curling into a tight coil in her lower abdomen. His mouth left hers and trailed kissed over her face, down her neck.

"I would take you here, now," he said, his words coming out in a warm breath over her skin, "but I wish to wait until we are properly wed. I would never dishonor you."

"You would not dishonor me." She clung to him, her pulse fluttering in a wild beat against her throat. Wanting him as much as he wanted her.

He planted a kiss behind her earlobe. "Only a little while longer to wait, my sweet. I will send servants to help you prepare."

With that he released her and bowed before leaving her alone in the room. Her pent-up need boiled inside her.

Fiona returned to the window, leaning her forehead on the cool glass and blowing out a breath, watching as it fogged the pane. She sensed some sort of movement behind her and spun around in time to see what she thought was a portal closing. A prickly sensation went over her. Had the woman remained in the room while she spoke to Niall? And if so, who was she? Why had she come to urge her to marry Niall? Had she been one of his spies? One of Cian's? It didn't make sense. She didn't have time to ponder the thought though, when the servants arrived to dress her for her wedding.

Niall took the steps down the tower two at a time and walked with a hurried long gait toward Deaglan's tower. By the time he reached the old man's workroom he was out of breath. He pushed open the door, not bothering to knock.

Deaglan was at his desk, scratching again with his quill on that damned parchment.

"What news of Cian?" Niall asked without preamble.

Deaglan put down his quill and leaned back in his chair, lacing his fingers on top of the parchment. "His army has been arriving in waves while the prince himself makes his way here even now. He thinks to overtake the Towers and breach the castle walls."

"He will never make it past the outer defenses. Nor will he make it up the cliffs." Niall balled his fists.

"Nay," Deaglan agreed. "But something vexes you anyway."

"I promised my bride the people of Anatolia would not be harmed, as it is her home kingdom."

"So she has agreed to marry you after all. You intend to go through with this plan, I see."

Niall nodded. "I do. I did not promise her I wouldn't kill Cian."

"Have your feelings for her changed at all?" When Niall responded with a glare, Deaglan nodded understanding. "I see. You love her. You think killing Cian will erase his threat."

"It will erase my hatred and assuage the need to see him dead," Niall replied.

"Well, as it is, you're in luck. You will have your chance with the prince, Your Majesty, when he comes to reclaim the girl," Deaglan said. "You will have your opportunity to destroy him then, I'm sure."

"He will never get her. We marry tonight and will consummate the vows immediately after. She's now mine and Cian no longer lays claim to her once she is my wife."

"As you wish, Your Majesty. The girl's potential for magic has come a long way but she still requires training. She begins to control it but it's still wild and unpredictable."

"Which you will help her with, no doubt."

"Indeed. And what do you require of me in the case of Cian?" Deaglan asked.

"I require you to help me defeat him when his forces decide to attack."

"Our defenses are already prepared, Your Majesty."

Niall walked toward the door but Deaglan called after him. He paused, turned.

"Love is not a weak emotion. Tell her. Tell her before it's too late," the wizard urged.

"I will consider it."

Niall left his father to see to the final preparations for his upcoming nuptials.

After Niall left, the whirlwind of activity began immediately. Servants showed up to bathe her. She hadn't realized he meant to marry her that very night. As one of the girls finished coiling her hair about her head, a large red-cheeked woman bustled into the chamber. She carried a pile of fabric in her short stubby arms and when she entered the room, put it with care on the bed as though it were precious cargo. She puffed out a breath and turned, her face dotted with sweat.

"There are too many stairs in this godforsaken place," she huffed and then pushed back a lock of hair from her face. "I've brought your gown, my lady." She motioned to the pile she'd deposited then clapped her hands as her face broke into a broad grin. "Let's get you into it!"

Fiona was only dressed in a shift as she walked over to inspect the gown. It was nothing like the one she was to wear when she married Cian. That gown had been white and covered in exquisite Anatolian lace. This gown was pewter with beautiful roses and thistles embroidered along the neckline and the skirt. It took her breath away. She fingered the delicate stitches.

"It's lovely."

"And you'll look lovely in it with that red hair of yours. Turn, turn. His Majesty awaits."

Fiona complied as the rustle of material was behind her. The woman slipped the lovely pewter silk gown over her head and smoothed it down over her body. She cinched her so tight into the gown she could scarcely breathe. One of the serving girls helped slide her slippers on her feet.

"Oh, but aren't you a sight. The king will be well pleased, I'm sure." She waved her over to the mirror on the other side of the room. "Come have a look."

Fiona followed the woman to the mirror and was stunned at her transformation. The gown was fit for a princess—nay, a queen. And it hit her with such force she pressed her hand against her stomach. She was going to be a queen.

The woman stood behind her, her hands on her shoulders as she smiled at her reflection. "Aye, he'll be well pleased indeed."

She turned and shooed the girls out of the chamber.

"Where are you going?" Fiona asked, afraid to be left alone. "What happens next?"

"Wait here, my lady. You'll be escorted to His Majesty shortly."

And with that she closed the door with a snap. Now that the traffic had cleared and she was left alone in her chamber, she had time to mull over everything that had happened.

Images of the Time Sphere haunted her. Had Niall conjured them to make her believe it? Was Cian planning her rescue? It had been weeks and he had not showed, which reinforced her decision to forget him and remain here with Niall.

Remembering his kisses, she pressed her fingers against her lips. His mouth had burned against hers and she liked it. Her body burned with desire and need, even still. Even now thinking of the kiss made her want to kiss him more. And more than kiss him.

She knew she did not love Cian, but she had hoped to come to love him one day. Niall had made her feel things she thought would only come after a time. He had given her hope of a future with him. She could not forget the way his lips felt against hers, or the way he had treated her as though she were a delicate flower, something to hold and cherish.

Cian had ignored her when she went for a visit. Could it be he had refused to come for her when he learned her fate? Or mayhap he never even knew what had happened to her?

Fiona also could not get the words of the woman out of her mind. The voice had sounded eerily familiar. Even the face seemed a bit familiar though she couldn't figure out why. How could she refuse him? If she did, he would marry her anyway and perhaps torture her into compliance. She didn't trust that he was not a cruel man, deep down. If only she could get Deaglan to tell her how the portal worked, she would be free of all this madness.

A knock on her door interrupted her interior monologue and halted her worry. She could do nothing but wait now and take her fate into own her hands.

Deaglan opened the door and peeked inside. It was as though her thoughts of him conjured his presence. When he saw her, he pushed the door open wide and smiled at her.

"Lady Fiona, you look positively radiant. I'm to escort you to your wedding." He stuck out his arm.

She ignored it. "Are you? Before we go, Deaglan, I need to know something."

"And what is that, my lady?"

"Earlier you told me to come back to you to tell you what I found when I stepped through the portal," she said.

The smile faded from his aged face as he nodded. "That I did. And what did you find?"

"I stepped through and came here. I found a woman urging me to marry Niall. I tried to talk to her but she disappeared. Do you know who she was?"

"Portals are strange things, dearie. Are you sure there was a woman here?" He grinned, as though it were all a farce.

"I'm sure. She spoke to me quite clearly. Why would she urge me to marry the king? Did he send an emissary to convince me?"

"That I cannot say. Nor do I know of any such emissary, as you call it, sent by the king. He wanted you to make up your mind for yourself."

"You think I'm making this up?" she asked, trying not to sound defensive.

"Of course not." He took her hands in his, kissed one of them. "I think you have wedding jitters."

She tugged her hands free. "Tell me how the portal works."

"Ah, 'tis a secret. I'm afraid I cannot. Come, before you're late to your own wedding." He held out his arm again.

She waved him off. "I shan't leave until I know more about the portal."

Deaglan's bushy brows drew together, knitting a long thick line over his eyes. "Why do you wish to know so badly?"

He didn't bother to hide the suspicion in his voice. Her heart kicked into a full gallop and she knew she would have to be careful not to raise his suspicions further. She clasped her hands together and gave him her best innocent look.

"Oh, Deaglan. You know I always have questions about how things work. The portal is no exception." She grinned broadly and fluttered her lashes, giving him her best performance.

He seemed to relax then as he expelled a puff of air. "I'll tell you but you must promise never to share the secret."

"You have my word."

He seemed unconvinced as evidenced by his lengthy pause of consideration. Then he gave her a quick nod. "All right, then. You think of the place you most want to go before releasing a drop of the tears."

"And when it opens it opens to that place?" she asked.

He nodded.

"And you thought of my chamber before you released the drop?"

"I did." He extended his arm to her once more. "Now, shall we go?"

"Tell me one more thing." She ignored the perturbed look he gave her. "Niall showed me the Time Sphere in the library."

He stiffened, his face guarded. "Dangerous magic that. What did he show you?"

"Images of Cian." She swallowed hard, her mouth bone dry. "With other women. Is it the truth? Does the Time Sphere show the past and the present as he said?"

"You think Niall tricked you with conjured images?" She nodded. "I'm afraid, dearie, what you saw in the Time Sphere was the truth. Not even Niall's magic is powerful enough to concoct a lie."

She expected to be crestfallen at the news, but instead relief spread through her. To think she would have been saddled with Cian her entire life. He was an unfaithful rogue but yet he did not deserve to die. Nor did anyone deserve to die because of her. She would have to find a way to get a message to him, to send him back to Anatolia unscathed.

"I am sorry, my lady," Deaglan said.

She waved away his concern. "'Tis all right. Shall we?"

Fiona took his arm and faced her fate.

Chapter 9

Present Day in the Human Realm

Sean and Caleb drove to the specified coordinates of the portal, which turned out to be an abandoned warehouse in the heart of downtown Dallas. It was mid-morning and while the traffic into town was a nightmare, getting to the warehouse hadn't been too difficult. It was in a part of downtown normal people generally avoided. There were the few homeless scattered around the street. A couple of thugs here and there who gave them a cursory glance as they exited Sean's old pick-up.

"Glad I didn't drive my car down here," Cal muttered.

Sean knew the area well. He also knew the warehouse was owned by the Agency. One he had come through himself when he was first assigned to the human realm to track Fiona. There was a numbered keypad on the door and Sean punched in the code to unlock it. Caleb swung open the door.

The three-thousand-square-foot warehouse was not inviting. Dirt smudged the windows along the top, blocking out most of the sunlight. Still, slashes of light tried to press through the muck, dust particles danced in what little light there was and the place smelled musty and dank. It was empty save for the stone dolman standing alone and quiet in the center.

It looked so odd there surrounded by greenery and flowering vines. Like it belonged in a castle garden instead, or maybe some rich Dallasite's backyard. It was beautifully strange.

Sean had no idea how the flora managed to stay alive in this stuffy, lightless place. One could walk around the entire dolman and see nothing but an empty space between the stones. And yet he could see the shimmer of light around the inside edge of it and knew HQ had activated the portal. It was ready for them to step through. Both of them stood in front of the doorway, staring at it. Neither wanted to take that fateful first step.

"How long has it been since you've been back?" Caleb asked.

There was an unwritten rule between the two of them not to ask personal questions. Before they knew each other and he was first recruited into the Enchantment Enforcement Agency, Sean had a very different life. He had been the son of a noble once, with powerful yet deadly magic.

For Sean, it had been many years since he'd been back to Faery. After the tragic accident that killed his family, the EEA recruited him as a guardian to keep rogue terrorists from other realms out of Faery. They had trained him to be a weapon—a killer—the last line of defense between a portal to Faery and the human realm. He had no desire to step foot into Faery again.

Time in Faery moved at a much different pace than the human realm. It could have been centuries in Fae time since he'd been back. He'd never planned to return. He never *wanted* to return. Much like Aoife never wanted to return to Brookdale.

"That long, eh?" Caleb asked, his voice echoing in the silence.

Sean wondered why Caleb hesitated, why he didn't seem so eager to return. But then he decided he really didn't want to know. And, more importantly, he didn't want Cal to know anything about his past. The only way to keep that from him, really, was to keep him from going with him. He wasn't sure how he was going to pull that off yet.

"Well, no sense in hanging around here. Let's go." Caleb took a step but Sean caught his arm.

"Wait," Sean said. "We should talk about this first."

"There's nothing to talk about," Cal said. "Bryant wants us in to find the women."

"I know. But I think…" He paused, choosing his words carefully. "I think I should go alone."

Cal was silent a long moment as he peered at him with sharp assessing eyes. "Why?"

"I may need you here," Sean said, thinking quickly. "You're the only one I trust on this side."

"And what would you have me do?"

Sean hesitated, trying to come up with a reasonable excuse. "I need you here in case."

"In case what?"

Sean growled low in his throat. "In case I need you here, that's all. This is just something I need to do alone."

"Ah, I see. Because of Aoife? You want to get to her before

Fiona does?" Caleb asked and folded his thick forearms over his chest.

"That, yes." And he had no idea what to expect when he stepped back into the realm after being absent for so long.

"Why are you so spooked about going back to Faery? What'd you do? Kill somebody?"

Cal said it in jest, yet it hit far closer to home than he knew. But Sean couldn't worry about the past. He had to focus on the future, on finding Aoife and Fiona and getting them back to the human realm.

"Just wait for me here. If I'm not back soon then you can follow."

He raised a brow. "You expect me to sit here and wait around?"

Cal was not the passive type. He preferred to go in guns blazing. Sean could tell he was annoyed with the thought of sitting idly by while he played the hero. But he wasn't trying to be a hero. He was trying to save the women and get back. He had no idea what it would do to him when he stepped into the magical land again. Would being back in Faery recharge his dead magic? No one knew the answer to that when he'd posed the question long ago. He wasn't all that keen in finding out but he really had no choice.

"For now, yes."

"And you can't tell me why, I guess." Cal's lips thinned in annoyance. When Sean failed to answer he sighed. "All right. I'll wait here. I'll give you forty-eight human hours to get your shit together and then I'm coming in after you. Here. You'll need this." He handed Sean the compass.

"Thanks. I'll be right back. Hopefully with the ladies." Sean pocketed the compass. Forty-eight hours would be plenty of time.

"Let's hope so."

He turned to the dolman and stepped through the portal.

The twins led Aoife through the thick underbrush and into a clearing. Ahead, she could see a small village surrounded by a tall stone wall and a gate guarded by sentries. At the edge of the woods, they paused and Orrin gave Aoife a once over.

"Ari, give her your cloak."

She pouted. "Why?"

"Because we can't take her in looking like that. Give her your cloak so she can cover up."

Orrin was right. She'd stick out like a sore thumb in that place without the proper attire. It wasn't like she was a tourist and could blend in. With a huff, Ari handed over her cloak. Aoife wrapped it around her shoulders. The girl was shorter than she was so the edge of the cloak hit her mid-calf.

They resumed their walk toward the village and were soon at the gates. The sentries didn't try to stop them but Aoife could see their eyes following them as they entered. Orrin and Ari seemed unconcerned by the attention and so Aoife continued to follow them through the village.

It was a bustle of activity. The people were dressed in bright colors. The air was redolent with smells that made her stomach rumble in response. In the center of town was a pole that soared high above the people, covered in ribbons and flowers. Young girls with flowers in their hair danced around it, their cheeks pink and rosy and their giggles light and lilting.

Shops lined both sides of the cobblestone street. There was a dressmaker, a candlestick maker, a baker, a grocer, a butcher. Jewelry and bath salts and a weapons shop. An apothecary named Fine Herbs and Potions. To her surprise, that's where the twins headed.

A bell tinkled their arrival. The store looked like something out a storybook or movie. Shelves lined the walls and were full of dried herbs on one side, books on another. There were bottles and baskets and jars all labeled with a precise yet ancient hand. She paused to read through the labels. There was mugwort, anise, yarrow root, angelica.

Behind the counter—and the man sitting on the counter—a rainbow of crystals glittered against the flickering candlelight of the store.

The man perched on the counter could only be called an imp. He was short, stocky, with a head full of curly brown hair and a thick beard. He had a smashed in face, though that looked to be quite normal for him, and a bulbous nose. He was, by all accounts, rather ugly.

"Well, well. If it ain't the good for nothin' twins. What are you trying to peddle today? More counterfeit items?"

"This isn't counterfeit, Morgrim." Orrin reached into his pocket and pulled out the pink crystal.

"This time," the little man said.

He pulled a monocle from the small pocket on his vest and held it up to his left eye. He held out his hand for the crystal and Orrin dropped it into his palm. The man was silent for a long moment before looking back up at Orrin. His eyes narrowed with suspicion.

"Where'd you get this?"

Orrin shrugged. "Found it."

"Did ya now?" Morgrim looked unconvinced. "This all you happened to 'find' then?"

The boy kept his face impassive. "That's all."

Aoife peered at Orrin and knew the boy lied. Ari had given him two crystals. His youthful stoic face gave away nothing, though, as he stared back at the dwarf. He must have had something in mind for the second one, but she had no idea what was special about the crystal.

"Uh huh." Though he sounded unconvinced. "And how much will you be wanting for this little trinket?"

"Fifty gold."

He balked at that. "Ha. Not likely. Think again."

"It's a fair price. Besides, you don't have any of those, do you?" Orrin nodded toward the shelves of glittering colorful crystals behind him.

Morgrim looked over his shoulder and gave the crystals a brief inspection before peering back at the boy. "So it would seem. I'll give you twenty-five then."

Ari emitted a low whimper and shifted from one foot to the other.

"Forty-five," Orrin countered.

He peered at him with annoyance. "Thirty."

"Thirty-five and you throw in a bottle of angelica," Orrin replied.

He considered and then groused, "Fine." He closed his meaty hand on the crystal. He jumped down behind the counter, his head bobbing along as he walked to the back, then returned a moment later. He counted out the thirty-five gold pieces into Orrin's hand and then handed him a bottle of dried purple leaves.

"Pleasure doing business with you." Morgrim tipped his head at the boy.

Orrin pocketed the coins. "As always, Morgrim."

They left the shop and stepped back into the busy street. Ari huffed out a breath.

"You should have asked for more."

"I couldn't ask for more. You know why. Besides, it'll be enough," Orrin said. Then he looked at Aoife. "Let's get you some clothes."

"With our money?" the girl complained.

"Hush, Ari," he groaned.

They headed down the street to a local clothing shop. It wasn't exactly the mall but it would do. Aoife wasn't sure how she would repay their kindness but she'd find a way. They stepped into Sybil's House of Cloth. Perhaps in Faery, this was akin to a Gap or maybe even Old Navy.

A woman greeted them with a bright smile. "Welcome. How may I assist you today?"

"My sister needs a new gown." Orrin thumbed at her.

The woman, whom Aoife assumed was Sybil since her name was on the door, gave her a cursory glance. "We don't have much stock but I'll check to see what we have."

She disappeared behind a curtain which gave Aoife a chance to browse. She found soft suede brown pants and an oversized tunic. Then she found a dark green vest and stifled a giggle. It was like something out of a fantasy book or movie.

Sybil returned with a gown over her arm. She held it up for them to see. "I'm afraid this is all we have."

It looked like a potato sack with arm and head holes. Even the material looked rough and uncomfortable. Aoife cringed. She refused to parade around Faery in that.

"How much for this?" She held up the clothes.

"Those are not for ladies." Sybil sniffed indignation.

"How much?" Aoife asked again.

"Five gold for the lot."

Ari balked. Orrin opened his mouth to say something.

"He'll give you two," Aoife countered before he could reply. "And you'll throw in these." She held up soft suede, knee-high boots. They were her size and probably didn't offer much protection from the elements but she didn't care. She didn't plan to be in Faery long.

Sybil pressed her lips together in disdain. "Three and it's a deal."

Aoife looked at Orrin who didn't hide the surprise on his face. He grinned and pulled out three gold pieces and handed them over. "Deal."

"You have a place I can change?" she asked the woman.

Sybil pointed to a small room off to the side. Not much different than a dressing room in a department store. She quickly changed, rolling up her street clothes and tucking them under her arm. She wished she had a mirror to survey her new outfit.

When she emerged from the dressing room, she handed Ari back her cloak.

"Well? What do you think?"

"You'll do." Orrin said.

"She looks like a guy," Ari said.

Aoife resisted the cutting remark that Ari's outfit was similar.

"I'm comfortable. That's all that matters to me," she replied.

They filed out of the shop and headed down the main thoroughfare. Now that she had clothes, she wasn't certain what she should do next. Where would she find her mother? More importantly, *how* would she find her mother? She had no idea where she'd gone.

As the thought passed through her mind, she saw a woman emerge from a weapons shop. She was dressed in a similar fashion to Aoife—tall black boots, padded pants, tunic, padded vest. She had a quiver of arrows over one shoulder and carried a bow. Her auburn hair was pulled into a long braid and there was something eerily familiar about her face. She strode down the street with a purposeful stride, her head held high and her eyes sharp as she kept her gaze on everything and everyone around her.

Aoife couldn't believe her eyes. Or her incredible luck.

"Mom?"

Orrin and Ari both followed her gaze to the woman…her mother.

"It's her! It's my mother."

But the crowd was too thick to push their way through. And then they caught sight of royal guards coming up the street heading directly toward them. Ari halted, frozen in place. Orrin wrapped his hand around his sister's upper arm and spun her around. But Aoife wasn't willing to let her mother go that easily.

"Come on, Aoife," Orrin said, urgency in his voice.

"I found her and I'm going after her. Thank you for what you did for me and good luck," Aoife said.

"Are you mad?" Ari's high-pitched voice broke over the din of the crowd. "You'll be caught."

But Aoife wasn't listening. She shoved past several women, keeping her eyes fixed on her mother. Fiona saw the guards heading up the street and ducked into a shop out of sight. Aoife cursed under her breath.

Behind her there were shouts and she stole a glance over her shoulder. More guards and they'd caught and arrested Orrin and Ari, their hands bound. One of the guards took note of her, then, and pointed in her direction. Her heart jumped into overdrive. When she looked back in front of her, the second group of guards had eyes on her and headed right for her.

Shit.

She glanced to her left and to her right but the throngs were too thick and she had no place to go. It didn't help that people made a path for the guards to get to her. With her heart in her throat, she took off to her left. Maybe she could duck into one of the shops and hide, like her mother had. It was the wrong thing to do. The guards shouted for someone to stop her. She only took a few running steps when a tall man blocked her path.

"You wouldn't be running from the guards now, would you?" He grasped her by the arm and dragged her to the nearest one. Damn him. Then he shouted, "I got her!"

When the guards caught up, he handed her over. They gave him two silver coins. As though she were a prize.

"Your reward, good sir."

He grinned at her with triumph as he pocketed the coins.

As her hands were bound and she was led away, Aoife managed to steal once last glance at the town but her mother was nowhere to be seen.

Sean stepped through the portal and found himself in the woods near the outskirts of town. The tracking device must have gotten him close to Fiona. She must be somewhere in the village. He hoped Aoife was nearby as well. He could see the walled village was a bustle of activity. Two sentries guarded the north gate just as two sentries guarded the south gate. Those were the only ways in or out.

He kneeled at the base of a tree and felt around under a pile of leaves, looking for the pack the Agency left for him. He pulled open the large burlap sack and found clothes, money and weapons. Stepping behind the tree so he wouldn't be in the open, he quickly changed into the tunic, vest, padded pants and tall black boots. The boots were scuffed and well-used but that was fine by him. It'd help him blend in. There were two daggers. He attached one sheath to his belt, stuffed the spare clothes and his own, along with the weapon for Caleb, back in the sack and hid it again under the leaves.

He pulled the compass from his pocket and checked it. The needle bounced toward the village ahead. That's where he'd find Fiona.

As Sean made his way from the wooded area, he halted. Royal guards had entered both the north and south gates and headed right for a young couple in the center who seemed frantic to get out. But they'd been caught, their wrists tied. Another girl was spotted trying to outrun them, but she was caught too by the guards coming through the south gate. He recognized that auburn hair immediately.

"Aw, shit, Aoife."

The last thing he needed was her taken by the royal guards to the Towers of Illyria. They led their prisoners to the north gate. There were four guards, one on each side of the duo and one on each side of Aoife. The others remained behind as they filtered through the village, as though looking for something or maybe someone else.

He had to get her away from them but it had been too long since he'd been a man of action. He wondered if he still had the stealth that he had before he transferred to the Inter-Dimensional Portal Protection Agency. All he could do was try and the worst that could happen…well, he'd be dead. Or captured. And then they'd all be in the hands of the wizard king.

He watched as they made their way north, putting distance between them and the village. They were in a hurry for whatever reason. Sean moved down the slope, keeping his footsteps as quiet as possible as he got behind them. Now that he was closer, he could see the other two prisoners were nothing more than children.

He pulled the dagger before he came upon Aoife and her

guards, matching them step for step. She had her head down, keeping her eyes on her feet. But he watched her as she tried to get her hands free of the rope. Her wrists were already red and raw.

Sean knew he would have to move quickly. Clutching the dagger, he held his breath as he moved closer to one of the guards and then pounced. He stuck the dagger into the man's kidneys, wrapped an arm around him and eased him to the ground. The other guard next to Aoife didn't even notice.

But Aoife did. Her head snapped around, her eyes wide as she met his gaze. When she saw him, she stifled a little gasp of surprise. He put his finger to his lips to keep her quiet. She clamped her mouth shut and gave a slight nod as he circled behind her. He killed the second guard just as swiftly but this time he didn't go unnoticed.

The other pair of guards saw what had happened, spun and drew their swords. The two children stumbled backward, watching with wide eyes as the guards charged Sean who was armed with only a useless dagger.

"Drop your weapon and we'll let you live," one of the guards said.

"Release the girl and I'll let you live," he countered.

"You have a death wish. Very well."

He charged while the other guard realized the two children were getting away with Aoife on their heels. He ran after them but Sean lost sight of them as he dealt with his own problem. He ducked the first blow and lunged, sticking the man in the ribs. He slashed upward, gutting him. As he dropped to the ground, bleeding out, Sean snatched his sword and turned to head after the other one.

He charged toward the guard, not waiting for him to turn around. It had been too long since he'd held a sword in his hand, but it felt like old times and he had no problem using it. He flung the dagger end over end at the remaining guard. It landed in his back between his shoulder blades. He dropped to the ground and tried to roll over but Sean was there before he could move. He stabbed the guard quickly before he could get up again.

Ahead, the trio halted. Aoife stared at him with bright green eyes. The boy broke into a wide grin while the girl did her best not to look at the dead men.

"That was wicked," the boy said. "How'd you do that?"

"Sean. How did you find me? How did you get here?" Aoife

looked him up and down and her cheeks turned a rosy color before she quickly looked away. Was she *blushing*? At him?

"There's no time to explain." He dropped the sword on the dead man and retrieved his dagger. "We've got to get out of here before the guards are discovered." He cut the rope around their wrists.

"Thank you, my lord," the boy said. "You saved our life."

"I'm no lord," Sean said. "Today was your lucky day. You two better run on home."

"We haven't got a home," the girl said and the boy glared at her and shushed her.

"Sean, this is Ari and Orrin. They're twins."

A shout from the village behind them got their attention. Sean motioned them toward the trees.

"We can't stay out in the open. Once the guards discover the dead, they'll launch a manhunt for us. Get to the trees."

They ran toward the woods. Sean urged them to keep going until they were as far from the village as they could get and they'd put as much distance between them and the dead guards as possible. All panting, they stopped in a cluster of trees and dropped to the ground.

"My mother is here, Sean. I have to go after her."

"You're not going anywhere without me," he said. "Besides, I know where she's headed." He didn't need the compass to show Fiona's direction. Now that he had his bearings and knew they were near the Towers of Illyria, he knew which way to the Ivory Wood.

She blinked surprise. "You do? How? And how did you get here? I came through a…" She halted and gave a cursory glance at Ari and Orrin. "I entered in the castle gardens."

"Fiona left clues behind in the attic. One was a map of the Ivory Wood with an arrow drawn to the center of it. She's heading there, we can intercept her. I came through a portal, too."

"A portal?" Orrin said. "I knew there was such a thing. I *knew* it. Didn't I tell you, Ari?"

"Yeah, yeah but you didn't know for sure." She rolled her eyes at her brother.

"Where is the portal? We can use it. We can get away from the wizard king and his guards," Orrin said.

"It's not that easy," Sean said. "There are only certain people who know how to open them." He met Aoife's gaze. "Fiona is one of them. And so are you, Aoife."

"Me? I don't know how to open a portal. I don't know anything about that."

"But you do. You opened the one in the trunk and it led you here."

She dragged her bottom lip through her teeth, thinking. Did she even realize how sexy it was when she did that? Probably not. Just as she probably didn't know how gorgeous she was with her hair flowing down around her shoulders. His fingers itched to run through those thick locks. He clamped his hand into a fist.

"But I don't know how to open it."

He grasped her by the shoulders. "Think, Aoife. *Think*. Tell me how you found it in the trunk."

"I…broke into the house. I thought you were hiding something from me." She paused, meeting his gaze.

He nodded to urge her on. He *was* hiding something from her—the portal. But that was now a moot point.

"I thought maybe my mother had left some clue behind as to where she went. But something…called to me. I felt…drawn to the trunk, like it wanted me to come up to the attic. My mother had always forbidden me and my sister from going up there."

She broke his gaze, remembering. He could see the distance in her eyes, knew she recalled the details of how she entered Faery.

"And then what happened?"

"I saw the map. And the page ripped out that said something about a wizard king. There was a glowing symbol on top of the trunk. It…beckoned me. So I opened it and saw a stone staircase leading down." She blinked and met his gaze again. "That's when you found me. I panicked and closed the lid, but then I couldn't open it again because it had turned to stone. I had to go down and I fell but woke up in a garden."

"The magic in it acted as a homing beacon to you. That's why you felt it call to you. You have Fae blood, Aoife."

She stared at him, mute. The color drained from her face and her eyes went wide with shock. "I don't understand. My mother…"

"She's a Fae, Aoife. She's from Faery, but was forbidden to return. That's why I'm here. I have to get her back to the human realm." He halted, unwilling to add *before she does something she can't undo*. He didn't think she could handle the news about the Time

Sphere, so he'd keep that under wraps until he had to tell her.

"If she's from Faery…" She faltered.

"So are you," he finished for her.

"I knew she didn't smell human," Orrin piped.

Sean flashed a look to silence him.

She bit her thumbnail. "How? How did I end up in Brookdale? And what about my father? Was he a Fae, too?"

"I don't know. You'll have to ask Fiona how she ended up in Brookdale because I don't know the answer to that, either," he said. "But we've got to get to her."

He moved to stand but she caught his arm to stop him. He could see the questions lining her face and knew she needed more of an explanation but he didn't have the answers she wanted. He could hear her erratic breathing, knew she had trouble trying to catch her breath and that quite possibly she was on the very edge of hyperventilating.

"Sean, if Liam wasn't my father then *who* was my father? Or is?"

"I wish I knew but I don't."

Her shoulders slumped, as though the wind had been knocked out of her. Anguish was written all over her pretty face as she surged to her feet.

"Then I have a lot of questions for her," Aoife said in a confident tone laced with distress.

"We're coming, too," Orrin said.

"No. You're staying here. Both of you." Sean shook his head.

"Mister, we got no place else to go," Ari said. "And anyway sounds like a grand adventure. We can help."

"You don't understand. Once we find her mother the next stop is the human realm."

Ari pouted, Orrin crossed his arms over his chest looking indignant. Aoife slipped her hand into his and it startled him, shook him to the core. He delighted in the softness of her hand, the way her fingers laced with his.

"Let them come, Sean. I'll keep an eye on them."

The last thing he needed was two children underfoot. But he could tell this wasn't a battle he would win with Aoife judging by the determined set of her jaw. He'd figure out what to do with them once they arrived at the Time Sphere.

"Fine. But daylight burns. Let's get moving."

Chapter 10

In the Land of the Faery Past

Fiona and King Niall were married in a brief ceremony in the main hall of the castle. The faces that surrounded them were unfamiliar to her. The more steps she took toward her groom, the more her nerves gripped her. There was no going back now, not that she would. Her path was set. Her decision made. However, she did not consider the future consequences of her actions until she stood at the altar, her hand in his as the cleric wrapped their joined hands with a band of silk.

Only when they were joined and their vows had been taken did she recall something her mother had said about the wedding night. Those certain responsibilities were more pleasurable to think of now that she had married Niall.

They sealed their bond with a kiss, their first as man and wife, a king and his bride. The spectators applauded with apt approval. Their hands still bound, Niall led her from the main hall to the banquet room where a grand feast had been prepared for the wedding couple. They were seated at a high table at the end of the room while everyone else entered and took a seat.

"Are you happy, my queen?" he asked. Servants filed through the room with steaming dishes to dole out.

Was she happy? Did she know true happiness? She hadn't been happy about going to Anatolia to marry Cian, she knew that. And it had devastated her when her parents had been murdered in cold blood. She certainly wasn't happy to be kidnapped and taken to the Towers of Illyria. However, what could have been horrible for her turned out to be quite all right after all. She turned to him and smiled and answered with absolute honesty.

"I am happy."

"We are only here for a short while to make an appearance."

His eyes scanned the large room, pausing on a few people here and there. She, too, eyed the room to see what caught Niall's attention. Her gaze landed on a man standing behind several seated women. He was dressed as a guard but looked out of place as he fidgeted with the sword at his side. She couldn't make out his face under the hood which she found rather odd as the other guards wore no hood.

A woman was hunched over her trencher, a hooded cloak hiding most of her face. A young girl sat ram-rod straight in the seat next to her, her eyes wide and round as she took in her surroundings. Something about the girl sent a ping of familiarity through Fiona, something that made her wonder who she was and why she looked scared out of her wits. Another hooded woman sitting on the other side of the girl patted her hand, said something to make her have a sudden vested interest in the trencher in front of her. The man behind them continued to fidget.

It was a puzzle for sure.

But Niall seemed unconcerned with them as he turned his attention back to her. He lifted their bound hands and kissed her fingertips.

"I have waited a lifetime for this moment. For you."

Pinpricks of heat went over her. His scorching gaze sent her senses reeling. She knew what he wanted. She wanted that as well. She would give herself to him willingly.

"Have you?" Her voice came out on a breath.

"You have nothing to fear from me, my queen." His warm breath went over her fingers and he kissed them again. "I will never force you. Though I do hope it is something you want as I do."

Her mouth went bone dry and she could not stop the pounding of her heart. He smiled and it reached all the way to his eyes, making them sparkle with delight. With his free hand, he trailed his fingers over her cheek, down her throat and over the pulse pounding a wild beat there.

"Do you want me as I want you?"

"Oh, aye, I do."

Again that smile, that devastating smile that seemed to make her come undone at the seams. She was acutely aware of her shallow breathing and yet there was nothing she could do to stop it.

"We will eat first. You must be famished."

In response, her stomach rumbled. They were served roasted duck with potatoes and leeks in a cream sauce. Despite her hunger, she didn't have much of an appetite but she knew she would need her strength. She ate as much as her nervous stomach would allow.

When Niall finally rose, she had to as well since they were still bound together. He turned to his people, who had fallen quiet. The room was still and all she could hear was the wild beat of her heart and the flutter of her pulse in her ears.

"Honored guests, my queen and I bid you good night. Please stay as long as you like to enjoy more food and entertainments."

Blood rushed to Fiona's head and all she could think about with every step back to his chamber, was what was to come. She stole a glance at him and couldn't help but admire the high cheekbones and strong jaw, or the way a wisp of golden hair fell across his forehead. How warm and strong his hand felt. It did nothing to tame the wild beat of her heart.

As they passed through the castle, a cold ripple of air went through Fiona and she shuddered. It had happened before. Once at the carriage, once in the library and now a third time. She wondered if there was a ghost stalking her. She moved closer to Niall, her breath pluming.

"Did you feel that?"

"Feel what, my dear?"

"That sudden coldness in the air." But even as she said it, the cold air was gone.

"The towers are cold this time of year," he said, reassuring her. "I'm sure we merely passed through a draft."

Even though she was satisfied with his answer, it still niggled at her. It hadn't been the first time she'd felt the distinctive cold pressing through her. In fact, she'd felt it on the way to the wedding with Deaglan. But she brushed it away. After all, she had more important matters to consider like her wedding night.

They made their way up the long curved stone stairs to his chamber. Inside, only a few candles blazed to light the cavernous room, giving it a warm romantic glow. He led her to the bedchamber where the bed had already been prepared in anticipation of their night together.

As they stood in the chamber, he unbound their wrists, letting the silken cord fall away. He reached for her hair then, pulling the pins out one by one. When her hair was free, he ran his fingers through the locks.

"You are a beautiful woman," he said. "I see why Cian wanted you for his own. But now you belong to me and only me."

She trembled.

"Are you chilled?"

He didn't wait for her to answer as he snapped his fingers and the fire in the hearth increased to a tall blaze, throwing heat into the room.

"Better?" he asked.

She could only nod. He cupped her face, peering into her eyes.

"Do you fear me?" he asked.

"No."

"Good. I don't wish for you to fear me. I know you do not love me. Yet. But I believe in time you will come to love me."

"You do not love me," she countered.

He chuckled. "Insightful as well as beautiful. I find you attractive in every way. I have since the day you were brought to me. And I have wanted you."

"You knew you were kidnapping Cian's intended. Did you expect me to be a troll then?" she asked, unable to resist the barb.

Again he chuckled, a low rumble deep in his chest. "I did not. I know the types of women Cian prefers and you are not one of them."

Her brows knit. "I don't understand."

"He prefers women who are not as high-spirited and vivacious as you. Brainless twits, if you will."

She understood and she should have realized. Those were the women he tended to pay more attention to when she was at court. She had ignored that, pretended they didn't exist because she had been betrothed to him. He only acknowledged her presence and their betrothal when he had to. She knew, ultimately, she would be his wife and future queen. Their betrothal, however, had not stopped him from being with other women.

Now, she *was* a queen. Queen of Illyria. Mayhap Niall didn't love her, but he *did* want her as his own. She should put Cian out of her mind, and yet she couldn't. She knew he had come to reclaim her and she had to get him to leave, willingly.

"Let us not discuss that any longer. He is no one of consequence here. The only one that matters is you," he said.

With her heart pounding, she stepped into his embrace, slid her arms around his waist and kissed him. She gave herself to the kiss letting him take his time with her, taste her, as she tasted him. It was much like the first kiss they'd shared.

His warm body pressed against hers. His hands tangled in her hair as he gently tugged her head back to deepen the kiss. It stole her breath, robbed her of any coherent thought and she knew she would never be the same. He'd branded his taste into her mouth. He'd melted a little more of her resolve.

When they broke apart, he took her hand and led her to the bed. He circled her, stood behind her. Heat erupted over her body when she realized he tugged at the laces of her dress, pulling them slowly from the tiny eyelets one by one. When he'd finished, he slipped his hand under her overdress and pushed the garment off her body. It fluttered to her feet in a pool of delicate satin.

Niall tugged the shift off her shoulder, baring her flesh. He kissed her there, his mouth hot, warm and soft. He then moved up her neck to her earlobe.

She should hate him. She should hate this. But something about the way he kissed her made her knees weak and pushed all thoughts of revenge for killing her parents out of her head. Fiona turned and fell into his arms, her mouth hungry against his. He was surprised though not displeased by her actions and backed her toward the bed.

He gathered the material of her shift in his hands and pulled it up, up, up over her head. He tossed it aside and then she stood naked before him. Goose flesh erupted over her skin, her nipples peaked, her breath grew ragged. He took a step back, his heated gaze moving over her.

"Lovely. As I imagined."

Niall kicked off his boots, pulled off his tunic and shoved his pants to the floor but she was too shy to look. She had never seen a naked man before. Her cheeks enflamed, she let him push her back onto the bed and nudge her legs apart with a gentle hand. Her knees fell open, exposing her damp center shrouded by dark curls.

"I promise not to hurt you."

His voice whispered over her as he leaned down, kissing first one nipple then the next. A bright flash of heat pulsed through her as he made his way down her ribcage and kissed the flat plane of her belly. His hands caressed her inner thighs, moving closer and closer to that part of her that throbbed, wanting his touch. Needing his touch.

He planted a kiss on each hip bone, as though he paid homage to each and every part of her. Every brush of his lip was an erotic sensation.

He kissed one inner thigh and then the other. He pulled apart her female lips with his fingers and then did something she never expected when he kissed her there on her warm, wet center.

Fiona cried out with the pleasure searing through her. His tongue moved into her wet seam, her hips rocking in concert with every stroke. She lost complete and utter control as her hands fisted the bed sheets. She felt a different kind of pressure as he inserted a finger inside her, sliding through her wet channel back and forth.

When he lifted his head, his eyes met hers and she could see the glint of desire burning in the blue depths.

"Did you like that, my love?"

She bit her lower lip and nodded. Her voice had left her it seemed and all she could do was whimper. His finger still slid in and out of her and then between her female lips.

"Your body is tight here." He pushed two fingers inside her but this time didn't move them away so quickly. He moved them inside her. "I want you to be ready."

Her body was tight everywhere. She felt as taut as a harp string, every muscle ached for more. She had never known such need before. She rocked against his palm, trying to assuage the pleasure-pain erupting from her center.

"Are you ready?" he asked.

She whimpered an acknowledgement and he removed his fingers. He settled between her legs, pushing them up and out a little more. She tensed when he used the head of his shaft to rub between her female lips, moving it back and forth and back and forth.

"You're so wet." His voice was full of awe as he continued to stroke her, increasing pressure and speed. "I'm ready to take you, my love."

"Take me."

The words burst from her without thinking. She wanted this. She wanted *him*. He pushed his shaft inside her with a quick thrust that broke her maidenhead. She cried out with the momentary pain. He immediately moved out and back in again, pumping inside her until the pain was replaced with pleasure.

The orgasm erupted, pulsing outward from her center and bursting from every pore. It lit up the room with such fantastical light, he halted. When she cracked her eyes open, she saw he gazed down at her with awe and wonderment.

"Don't stop," she begged. "Please, Niall."

So he started again, increasing the pace of every thrust and covering her with his long body. Their mouths fused in a passionate kiss of desire and need, and she thought for a moment she could stay there with him forever.

Her hands fisted in his thick hair, their tongues dueled with each other in an oral battle for dominance. She could feel a second orgasm building, her legs latched around his hips. They came together, the light once again bursting from her as he spilled his seed inside her.

When it was all over, he gathered her against him, holding her close.

"Your magic has fully manifested," he said.

"How do you know?" She traced a line across his chest.

"You're glowing." There was a smile in his voice.

Aye, her skin held a faint golden glow and now she understood why. Their intimacy had fully awakened the magic inside her. It was something she hadn't expected. Nor had she expected to feel so completely happy in Niall's arms. Still, she must go through with her plan to get rid of Cian once and for all.

Fiona startled awake and sat up. The candles had long since been extinguished and moonlight slashed through the windows onto the floor in slats of silvery white. Her new husband slept next to her, snoring softly.

A stab of guilt buried in her chest and then she was assailed by a terrible sense of bitterness. Ice spread through her gut as she clutched the sheets to her naked chest. They had made love again and again. She had allowed him to take her body, mind and soul. She had allowed herself to fall into those depthless cool blue eyes. How could she have let him suck her in? How could she have fallen for him so hard and fast? He was her enemy, wasn't he? He had sent men to kidnap her and intended to destroy her kingdom, killing the prince.

Pushed on by thoughts of warning Cian, she slid from the bed. Now was her chance. If she had any hope of pulling off her plan, she had to act quickly. She pulled on the shift over her head and walked on silent bare feet through his bedchamber, leaving behind things she didn't need.

In the bed, Niall stirred as he rolled to his side. She halted, her heart pounding in her throat, and waited. He didn't wake. She hurried through the chamber and out the door to slip to her own room next door. Once there, she dressed in a thick woolen gown and pulled on soft suede boots. She threw on a fur-lined cloak and then cracked open the door.

No one was about, the castle was silent and still. Closing the door behind her, she picked up her thick skirts and descended the stone staircase as quickly as possible. Her heart still ramming in her chest, she made her way to the west tower. She took the stairs two at a time until her thighs burned from the exertion. She had to settle for going up one at a time until she finally made it to the top.

Exhausted, her breath see-sawed in and out as she pressed her ear against the door to listen. But the oak was so thick, it was impossible to hear anything on the other side. She would have to take her chances that Deaglan wasn't inside.

She pushed open the door, the hinges creaking with the effort. She cringed, praying no one heard. But things remained still, dark and quiet inside. She closed the door with a snap and leaned against the wood her hands shaking and her knees quivering. She couldn't tell if that was from her mad dash across the castle and up the tower or if it was solely from nerves.

She decided it was both.

Fiona could only make out shapes in the darkness but she knew the room well enough to know the placement of all the furniture and objects. She made her way to his writing desk, fumbling with the items on top of it until she found a matchbox. She struck it and lit a candle, making a small circle of light.

On the desk, she could see his perfect penmanship scratched on the parchment. She held the candle down closer to it and moved the parchment around so she could read it.

It pains me she asked me to help her learn magic. I wanted to refuse, oh, how I wanted to deny her that. But seeing the look of hope on her lovely face, it was hard to tell her no. Niall, however, was quite pleased with the development. More so because she had come to me of her own accord and I did not have to convince her myself as Niall had asked me to do.

Teaching her has been easy. She is quite capable, though she hasn't even realized it yet. Her magic is strong yet unwieldy. She knows not yet how to control it. It will be her undoing if she doesn't learn to manage it better. And yet I believe she will be stronger than even Niall, who has wizard and Fae blood alike, and should she conceive the child will have formidable power.

Fiona stared at the words in astonishment. Niall had Fae and wizard blood? Could that mean Deaglan was his father? And…Cian his…half-brother? The story Deaglan told her of the rivalry between the two siblings came rushing back and she recalled the sadness in his voice, the sorrow on his face. Deaglan was the wizard who took the boy away. All this time and she had no idea.

She shuffled the pages and moved to another piece.

Her power grows daily, yet I believe she suppresses it. She keeps it from expanding, from consuming her. Mayhap she fears it. If she would only embrace it, no one would dare oppose her. Not even Niall. I think part of him is troubled by the force of her magic, though he never speaks of it. He comes to me daily to check her progress. He tries to hide that he loves her but I can see through him. A father knows his son, after all.

Her body stiffened in shock as she gasped, covering her mouth with her free hand.

A father knows his son. So Deaglan *was* Niall's father. Why hadn't she seen it before? By the gods, what would happen if they *did* conceive a child? How powerful would that child be? And she had allowed him to take her more than once, spilling his seed inside her.

And Deaglan knew Niall was in love with her. True, he had treated her with reverence, like she was the most beautiful and beloved woman in the world. The only one who mattered to him. She admitted she had feelings for him, too. Her stomach clenched. She shuffled the pages once again and peered down at the scrawl.

Cian the Cruel. My spies have sent a raven to notify me he is on the move and heads toward the Towers of Illyria even now, on Niall's and Fiona's wedding day. He lays in wait at the foot of the cliffs to make his move. He will do whatever he can to get the girl back. He has brought his entire army. He hopes to flush out Niall and his men but I have advised His Majesty to wait him out. Winter is upon us and the coming snows will no doubt bury the prince and his men in good time.

The prince was nearby. He had come for her with his army. He intended to take her back by force if necessary. Her heart pounded harder as she kept reading, mesmerized by Deaglan's ancient scribble.

I warned Niall not to go through with it but he is stubborn as the day is long. He intends to kill Cian despite his promise to his bride. And once the prince is dead and there is no one left to lay claim to the throne of Anatolia, he will send his men in to attack. His men who, even now, wait for the signal and, by the gods, I am to help him. Death is my reward for defying him. I dare not refuse him.

Tears sprang to her eyes. So Niall had never intended to call off his attack. The bastard! And he threatened Deaglan's life should he refuse to help him. Her hatred for him resurfaced. How could she have been so stupid? How could she have allowed herself to feel anything for him other than abhorrence? She had to save herself and warn Cian.

Sickened with the knowledge she had been a pawn all along in both Cian's and Niall's blood feud, she placed the candle on the nearby table and went to the bookshelf. She peered up at the sparkling pink substance known as Tears of the Dryad. Next to it, another vial that looked similar but had a bluish glow. For a moment she considered taking it as well but decided against it. All she really needed was the Tears of the Dryad and reached for it. It was her salvation and once she had properly warned Cian, she would use it again to transport herself to a new realm. She would flee this place forever.

She uncorked the bottle, her hand shaking. Deaglan had called him Cian the Cruel. On what grounds? She thought of the prince and tipped the bottle, watching as the glittery substance made its way toward the mouth of the bottle. The drop landed on the floor with a silent splash and the portal appeared just as the door behind her opened.

"Fiona, wait!"

Deaglan. She gasped and hurried through the portal turning in time to watch it close before he could follow her. The bottle was still tightly clamped in her hand as the icy wind whipped through her. She fumbled with the cork but finally got it firmly in place, then stuck the bottle in the pocket of her cloak.

She stood in the middle of an encampment, all around her, tents flapped wildly in the wind. It was silent save for that, and there were no men about. She heard the distant whinny of a horse and shivered. She turned toward the tent behind her and, with her heart in her throat, stepped inside.

Candles blazed, lighting up the small interior in a warm yellow-orange glow. It was a large tent and she could hear men's voices coming from somewhere to the left. She followed them and halted inside the canvas doorway. There, Cian sat at small wood table with three other men. Maps were scattered about the table top and goblets full of wine or some other drink. She froze, watching him and remembering the images from the Time Sphere and listening to their talk.

His devastating good-looks had not changed since the last time she'd seen him in person. That was nearly a year ago. He sported a three-day growth of whiskers on his chin and cheeks and looked tired with dark circles under his eyes. He had marched across the kingdoms to find her. There was nothing about him that told her he was cruel.

"Do you have a plan on how to get my betrothed out of the towers?" Cian asked. "Time is running out. Soon, Niall will send his forces to attack."

"I do not believe he will, Your Highness. The snow continues to fall thicker and thicker and the temperature has dropped. The men are freezing."

"I intend to go to war with the wizard king. Get me a battle plan for infiltrating the towers."

So he *had* come for her. How long had he been here at the foot of the cliffs trying to get to her? Even so, she had a plan and she intended to stick with it.

"Cian." Her soft voice broke through the men's.

He looked up to meet her gaze as the others turned to stare at her in surprise and shock.

"By the gods! Fiona!" He stood so quickly, everything on the table jostled. He hurried around it, ignoring the gapes of his men and took her into his arms, hugging her tightly. "How did you get here? Did you escape? Never mind. Thank the gods you're here. You're safe."

"I'm safe," she said with a nod. "There is much I need to tell you."

"Of course. I'm so relieved to see you here. Men, leave us. I wish to be alone with my betrothed." He wrapped an arm around her shoulders and walked her to the opposite side of the tent as his men filed out. He paused at his bed and sat her down. "Your hands are freezing. Let me get you some mulled wine."

He poured a cup of wine and handed it to her, then poured one for himself. "I've been terribly worried about you. When you failed to arrive at the castle, I led a search party to find you. We found Winnie—"

"Winnie! Is she all right? Does she live?"

"She's fine and thanks to her, she was able to tell us who had kidnapped you. She heard the men say they were taking you to the wizard king."

Instant relief sputtered through her so sharply, she couldn't stop the tears from falling. The girl must have been conscious when Fiona was taken.

"Thank the gods she's all right. I thought she was dead."

"She's perfectly fine. She's at Lambridge. She'll be there when we return. I am sorry about your parents, Fiona. We found the fresh graves."

The stabbing pain returned to her chest. She nodded. "Thank you for your condolences. But I don't understand. There were fresh graves? Someone buried them?"

"Aye, but let's not discuss that now. I want you to know I will avenge them. Did that monster hurt you?" She shook her head. "Good. Tell me everything that happened."

She took a deep drink of the wine then set it aside. She began with the attack on the carriage and how the men had taken her to Niall. She did not, however, tell him that she had married him, consummated those marriage vows or even that her magic had manifested. Those were things better left unsaid.

"I managed to escape from the Towers." She left out the part about the portal as well. She had the Tears of the Dryad safely tucked into her pocket. She didn't want Cian to know she had it. "Niall means to kill you and take over Anatolia."

"I know what he intends to do." A dark look of hate came over his handsome face. He took a healthy swig of his wine. "And I'll not let him kill me or take control of my kingdom so easily. He may have that wizard, but that doesn't mean he can defeat me."

"I'm glad to hear you say that." She rose. "There is one more thing I wish to tell you."

He moved to her, took her by the shoulders, smiling. "And what is that, my darling?"

"I...I don't think we should marry. That is, I think we should break off our betrothal."

A hard glint came into his eyes. "And why is that?"

"In light of everything that's happened I need some time, Cian. I need to go home. And…" She paused, choosing her words carefully. "I know about the other women."

His fingers tightened on her shoulders. "Do you?"

"Aye, I do."

His brows drew together, that dark look once again coming over his face. "That is unfortunate. However, I'm not letting you go."

The harsh edge of his voice surprised her. She stared at him. "But I don't understand. I am releasing you from the betrothal. You are free to marry whomever you wish."

He clamped a hand on her wrist, his fingers biting into the sensitive flesh. "I'm afraid it's not that simple. You are bought and paid for. Your mother assured me I was getting a woman of noble blood that would produce the heir I needed. So you see, she sold you to me and I paid her dearly for it. So much gold, in fact, she was prepared to leave your father and move to a little country estate I had set up for her."

"B-but…we were betrothed when I was a child."

"Aye, we were. Your father had it arranged. But when you were older and it was plain you were of no interest to other men, your mother came to me. Your family, you see, was broke due to your father's excessive gambling habits. When my father's health began to fail, she brokered a deal with me. I heartily agreed since you have the proper breeding to continue the royal line."

A lump formed in her throat. She stared at him, wordless, as the rush of blood drained from her head. Her own mother had sold her as some bride slave to this man? And for what? Gold? No wonder she was so adamant she consummate the marriage with him the night of their wedding.

Fiona had a difficult time believing her father had been a heavy gambler, yet it made so much sense now why her mother hated him. Why she despised everything about him.

All Cian wanted her for were her female parts to make sure his line continued, that he had an heir. How *dare* he treat her as nothing more than a brood mare? How *dare* they all treat her as nothing but stock, as nothing but a pawn?

"I can see the dawning of truth in your eyes, my darling. Did you fail to realize your family estate continued to prosper despite your father's failed business dealings?"

She hadn't noticed, but then why would she? She was never allowed to be present when business was discussed and she had no clue to the condition of their estate. She tried to jerk her hand out of his vice grip.

"Let go of me."

"I don't think so."

Fiona tried to push past him, but he was quicker, stronger. He moved in front of her, his hands on her upper arms as he shoved her back. The back of her legs hit the side of the bed, pinning her. One hand closed around her throat as he shoved her down with the other.

"You will stay with me. Marry me and do what I tell you to do."

She gasped, trying to catch her breath. Fear knotted inside her. She tried to push him off her as she flailed against him. He backhanded her and she tasted blood on the inside of her mouth. Putting all his weight on her he kicked her feet apart, and then tore at the bosom of her dress. She jarred her mind free of the fear long enough to hit him across the cheek but that only served to anger him more. His fist met her eye socket. A shower of pain exploded in her face and she faltered, weakening her attempts to fight back.

Without releasing his chokehold on her, he lifted her up by the neck, spun her and flung her face down. He pressed a hand into the middle of her back, shoving her into the coverlet.

"Bitch. You're mine and I'll take what's mine."

Again he kicked her feet apart as he pushed up her skirts. Tears flowed freely and she cried out when he entered her, pushing roughly inside her, pounding against her.

No. No. No. She couldn't allow him to continue to force himself on her. Deaglan's words came back to her in a rush. *Her magic is strong yet unwieldy. She knows not yet how to control it.*

She needed her magic now more than ever. She flexed her fingers as the anger burst through her and then fire formed in her palm. She jerked her arm in an awkward motion, flinging the fire ball to her left. It hit the back of the tent, sending it up in blue-white flames.

Cian cursed and let her go, fumbling for his pants. She rolled off the bed, her hands balled at her sides. She could no longer contain the hate within her as she flung out her hand and a bright white light burst from her, hitting Cian in the chest. He never saw it coming.

He flew backward, landing on the floor and skidding a few more inches. Was he dead? Had she killed him? She had to get out of there before his men were alerted to the fire in the tent. Numbly, she fumbled in her pocket for the bottle. Her fingers landed on it as she heard the first of men's voices coming into the tent.

Quickly, she pulled off the cork and froze. Where would she go? She whispered words, the only words she could think of.

"Take me far, far away from this realm."

She released a drop of the Tears and stepped into the portal, the black opening closing up the moment she stepped to the other side.

Part Two

Fractured

Chapter 11

In the Past in the Human Realm

Frosty air sliced through Fiona as she stepped through the portal. For a moment, she was shrouded in ice crystals and darkness and her breath halted, nearly freezing in her nose and throat. The cold pressed into her so deeply it was as though ice crystals were shoved through her. It made her numb and hardly able to think but somehow she managed to make her feet walk forward and move into the light on the other side of the portal.

She lost her balance and tumbled, free-falling into oblivion. She threw out her arms to catch herself but there was no way to stop her descent into nothingness. She cried out when she landed, her eyes squeezed shut and her body shivered with such violence her teeth clacked together. She clutched her elbows and tried to regain control but she couldn't stop shivering and she was unable to shake off the cold.

Where had she gone? Stepping through that portal had been quite unlike the one she'd gone through from Deaglan's room to hers.

Warm arms wrapped around her and scooped her up, cradling her closer. She was aware of the musky male scent enveloping her and tried to open an eye but couldn't.

"There, there. I've got you, miss."

There was something reassuring and comforting about the strong male voice next to her ear. She felt safe and secure and protected. His body rocked against hers jostling her in his arms as he walked at a brisk pace. Even though she couldn't stop shivering, she somehow knew she would be all right. Once she released her fear and a sense of calm passed over her she fainted.

A soft hum surrounded Fiona when she came to and she

realized she was snuggled under several layers of blankets. She wasn't cold anymore. Languorous warmth spread through her body and she exhaled a contented sigh. It was still an effort to open her eyes. Her eyelids felt as though they had lead weights on them. She eventually managed to open her eyes and focus.

She was in a strange room. The man's house? She didn't know. She wanted to fling off the bedcovers and make for an escape but her arms and legs wouldn't cooperate. They, too, felt as though they were filled with lead. Fiona glanced around the room and halted when she saw the man sitting upright in a chair next to the bed, dozing.

He was human.

She had heard the stories when she was a child about the human realm. How Fae would walk through the dimensions and switch a Fae child for a human one. Changelings, they were called. According to one legend, some Fae stole the prettiest human babies to rear as their own, replacing them with a more troublesome fairy baby. Folklore and bedtime stories meant to entertain and nothing more. It had often been a favorite threat of her mother's when she thought Fiona misbehaved, which was often.

This man sitting before her did not resemble one of the fairy folk.

His ears were rounded. His sandy blond hair cut short. His handsome face looked as though it'd been chiseled from the finest marble. His cheeks and chin were shadowed with stubble, as though he hadn't shaved in a few days. He wore a red plaid shirt with the sleeves rolled to the elbows, unbuttoned at the top.

Gods, had she made it all the way to the human realm? When she wished to be taken far away from her realm, she hadn't any idea she would walk through another dimension into another world.

Perhaps sensing that she looked at him, he started awake. When the man opened his eyes, his sharp blue gaze landed on hers. Once the sleep had been blinked away, he realized she was awake and jumped to his feet.

"You're up." He stood stiff, as though he didn't know what else to do or what to say next.

His voice was deep and rumbling and definitely the voice she heard earlier. He must have been the one who picked her up.

"I'm up," she replied.

"You had me worried. I'd never seen anything like that before. What happened to you? Did someone hit you?"

She didn't know how to respond because she didn't know what she looked like. She recalled Cian punching her and the pain radiating through her face. She must have bruises on her cheek and perhaps even her throat where he'd held her in a choke hold.

And then the bastard had raped her. A silent vow went through her mind. She would have her vengeance one way or another. She would make him pay for what he did to her.

She had stepped through the portal and then fell. What had she looked like when she landed in the human realm? Had she fallen out of the sky? It must have looked odd and fearful to the man who rescued her.

"I'm not sure," she said at last. "What's your name?"

"Liam," he said. "Liam Burke. What's yours?"

"I'm Fiona."

He took a cautious step toward the bed. "I didn't know what else to do, so I brought you here."

"Where's here?"

"My home. Do you mind if I sit?" He indicated the edge of the bed.

"No."

He perched next to her and placed a hand on her forehead. His hand was warm and gentle. "Your color has returned. And you no longer feel like an ice cube."

"An ice cube?" She wasn't sure what that meant and her brows drew together in question.

"When I found you, you were covered in frost and ice. Like you'd been inside a deep freeze. You were white as a ghost and you couldn't stop shivering." He dropped his hand, his gaze landing on hers again offering a smile.

That explained a lot. She'd been terribly cold. Moving through the dimensions must have done something to her. It was as though she'd stepped through a blizzard when she crossed. It was so cold she thought for certain her innards had frozen solid. But she couldn't tell him that.

"How did you end up there by the lake?"

"What lake?" she asked.

"I was fishing at the small lake on the outskirts of town when there was a bright flash of light and suddenly you were there. Do you remember that?"

"I…no. I don't remember." Because she wasn't sure how to explain it to him, she lied.

"It's all right. Maybe it'll come to you soon enough. Your face is looking better," he said, peering at her with an intensity that made her shift in the bed. "Did someone hurt you?"

"Aye, but he is no longer relevant," she said. "He can no longer hurt me here."

Liam seemed satisfied with that answer but she could tell he still had questions. "I've got some soup if you're hungry. You've been out for a couple of days."

A couple of days? Had she lost that much time in the human realm already? At the mere mention of food, her stomach rumbled. "That would be nice."

"I'll bring you some." He rose and started for the door.

"Liam?" He turned back at the sound of his name. "Thank you for helping me."

"You're welcome. I'll be back with the food."

When he left the room, Fiona struggled to a sitting position. Despite her leaden state, she was able to prop up on the pillows and give the room a good once-over. There was minimal furniture and it looked tidy and well-cared for. Lace curtains covered the one window and late afternoon light filtered in through them, giving the room a warming glow.

She had no idea where his home was nor had she any idea what she was going to do next. She had only thought as far ahead as leaving her realm. What was she going to do now? Where would she go? She couldn't stay here.

She ran her hands through her hair, pulling out tangles and then tucked the locks behind her ears. Liam returned with a tray and a bowl of steaming soup, some bread and a mug with a hot liquid. He halted in the doorway, shock registering on his face for a brief moment before he recovered and moved into the room. He placed it on the bed over her.

"I made some tea, too," he said.

"Thank you. That's very kind of you."

She picked up the spoon as he settled back on the chair, watching her. Making her feel awkward. She paused and glanced his way.

"Do I owe you money for the room and food? I haven't any money."

"No, of course not." He continued to regard her.

"Then is there something else?" she asked, trying to gently prod him away from her.

He blinked, realizing he stared. "Oh, no. I'm sorry. I don't mean to stare. I've never seen anyone like you before."

Unsure what that meant, she stuck her spoon into the soup and took a sip. It warmed her from the inside out. "I'm like anyone else."

He shook his head. "No, you're not. You're probably the most beautiful woman I've ever seen."

Fiona blushed. "Then you must not have seen many women."

"I haven't seen many Faeries, if that's what you mean."

She nearly choked on her soup. The spoon fell from her hand and clattered against the bowl. Her appetite disappeared as her heart quickened and she realized then her mistake. She had failed to hide her true appearance behind glamour. She knew why he stared then. Her pointed ears were quite obvious to him, especially with her hair tucked neatly behind her ears.

"Your ears gave it away," he said.

She pulled her hair back over them, trying to hide them again but the damage had already been done. Even if she'd managed to hide her face upon waking, he would have seen when he rescued her. He didn't sound surprised. Rather, his voice held an edge of awe and wonder.

"I thought Faeries were only in folklore," he continued. "I'd heard the stories from my granny for many years."

"Your granny?" she asked, her voice weak and soft.

"She's Irish. She still lives in County Cork and she's still kicking at the age of ninety-three. My dad moved to America when he was a lad and married my mother some years later. Granny was unhappy she was a yank," he said and chuckled. "We moved around a lot when I was a kid but we finally settled here."

She cleared her throat. "Where's here?"

"Brookdale. Just outside of Dallas."

She had no idea where that was but it was nice to know she had a locale to place her arrival. She also had no idea what a 'yank' was but she didn't question him.

"Don't worry, though. I won't give you up." He gave her a

reassuring smile, sounding sincere.

"Give me up?" Her brow furrowed.

"Give you away. Tell anyone who you really are. I can keep a secret."

She peered at him, her mouth dry. She wasn't sure what to make of Liam Burke. He seemed rather at ease with her being a Fae. Yet she wasn't sure she could fully trust him.

"Why would you do that for me?" she asked.

"It seems like the thing to do. Besides, people are nosey enough around here. The neighbors have been by several times trying to get a look at you but I ran them off."

"I appreciate you taking good care of me," she said. "As soon as I'm able, I'll leave."

"Take your time. It's not often I get to take care of a beautiful woman." He unfolded his long lean form from the chair and stretched. "When you're done, don't worry about the dishes. You can set them aside. I'll be back later to pick them up."

"Where are you going?"

"I've kept watch over you for the last few days. If you don't mind, I'd like to get some sleep." He stifled a yawn.

"Oh." She flushed again, her cheeks warming at the thought of this man watching over her while she was out cold. She wasn't sure how she felt about that. "Of course."

He ambled out of the room. Fiona went back to eating and devoured the soup, the bread and drank every drop of tea. With her stomach full, she put aside the tray on the table by the bed and leaned back into the pillows, pulling the blankets to her chin. A sense of melancholy washed over her in the silence. It gave her ample time to think about Niall and Cian and everything that had happened to her.

Fiona knew she should have never left Niall. He had been kind to her, despite his insistence on marrying her. He seemed to really love her. Yet she had been foolish enough to think she needed to warn off Cian, to break off their betrothal. What had it gotten her? Nothing.

She remembered the vial then and wondered where it had gone. She still wore the same gown she had when she left the Fae realm and slipped her hand under the covers to her dress pocket. Her heart stumbled when her fingers brushed over the small glass vial and she pulled it out of her pocket.

She still had the Tears of the Dryad. She could open another portal. She could return home and leave the human realm behind.

The only question that remained, truly, was did she want to return to her old life or make a new one here?

Three months had passed and yet Fiona could not bring herself to leave Liam's home. He had been kind, caring and far too happy to allow her to stay for as long as she wanted. Knowing she wasn't of the human realm, he went out of his way to make sure she understood she could stay for as long as she liked.

She knew she was pregnant almost immediately after arriving in the human realm. Her constant fatigue and voracious appetite was her first indication something about her body had changed. That and she hadn't menstruated since arriving.

Mixed emotions spread through her when she came to the realization she was carrying a child. Whose, she didn't know but she prayed to the gods it was not Cian's. She hoped beyond hope the babe belonged to Niall, for he was the man she truly loved. If a child came of their one night together, she made a vow she would love and cherish him or her until the day she died.

But how would she know who the father was until the child was born and aged?

She had been keeping the secret since shortly after her arrival but now she knew she had to tell Liam. She had to be honest with him. She'd made her decision—if he threw her out of the house, she would find someplace to go, to have her child and raise the babe alone. And someday she would use the Tears of the Dryad to return to Faery, taking the baby with her.

Fiona found Liam in the kitchen early that morning cooking a hearty breakfast for the two of them. He often did that on Saturday mornings and she found she quite liked when he made bacon, eggs, sausage and pancakes. Despite the rudimentary fare of the human realm, she had quickly grown accustomed to it.

"Good morning," he greeted when she entered the kitchen. He reached for a cup and poured her a steaming mug of freshly brewed breakfast tea. Despite his love of coffee, she had never quite acquired the taste for it. "You're looking well this morning."

Fiona took the cup from him and set it aside on the counter.

She had to get this out before she lost her nerve. "Liam, there's something I need to tell you."

"That sounds serious." He grinned as he flipped pancakes.

"It is serious. Quite."

His hands stilled over the pan as he peered at her. He removed the pancakes to a plate and shut off the burner before turning to her and giving her his full attention.

"What is it? What's the matter?"

"I've known this for a while now, but I wasn't sure how to tell you." Her stomach clenched tight, fearful of his reaction. She hiccupped a breath.

He reached for her, taking her hands in his. "Whatever it is, you can tell me."

"It's just that…I didn't know for sure until recently. And if you want me to go, then I will."

"I don't want you to go, Fiona. I want you to stay. I want you here with me." He squeezed her hands in reassurance.

His kindness was almost too much to bear. Hot tears flooded her eyes. She blinked them back. "Liam, you shouldn't say that until you know what it is I have to say."

He kissed her cheek. "Whatever it is, I want to help. Tell me."

She took a deep breath. "I'm pregnant."

His hands never faltered on hers. His gaze never left hers. He stood steady and strong as though it made no difference to him that she was pregnant with someone else's baby. Liam pulled her into a fierce hug, squeezing her tight and holding her for a long moment before releasing her and holding her by the hands again.

"Are you very angry with me?" she asked, her voice weak.

"No." He kissed her cheek again and went back to preparing breakfast. She watched as he plated food for her and then handed it to her. "I suspected."

"How?" she asked, taking the plate absently.

"You sleep and eat a lot." He grinned, as though proud of himself for noticing. "Do you know who the father is?"

Fiona sat down hard on the chair, the plate clattering on the table in front of her. She stared down at the bacon, the eggs, the pancakes and tried to decide how to answer. She hoped the father was Niall.

"Yes," she said at least. "He's dead, though."

She didn't know what made her tell the lie that the father was dead. Something deep inside her wanted to believe Niall would come looking for her yet at the same time, she hoped to stay hidden in the human realm for however long it took to realize who the baby belonged to—Niall or Cian.

Liam took the seat next to her, his coffee cup in his hand. "So there's no one to provide for the baby?"

"No."

A harsh truth to admit. Fiona was no more capable of taking care of herself in the human realm than she was a babe.

"Then it seems to me there is only one thing we can do." He reached for her hand. "I'll marry you. Give the baby a name and we'll raise it together. That is, if you'll have me."

A wave of apprehension swept through her. She met his gaze. "Liam, you would…do that for me?"

"I know you don't love me and I'm okay with that," he said. "Hopefully we can find some happiness together. The truth is, Fiona, I've been alone most of my life here. Since my parents died over a decade ago, I've no other family."

"What about your granny?"

"She's far away in Ireland and has dementia. She wouldn't know me even if I showed up to visit her."

Hearing that twisted her heart for him and she couldn't help but feel an acute sense of loss. While she had never really gotten along with her mother and her father was mostly absentminded, she could understand how the loneliness was palpable.

"Since that day you landed here when you were beat up, covered in sheets of ice and nearly dead, I've enjoyed taking care of you. I couldn't turn you out of the house, especially in your condition," he continued. "So will you stay and be my wife, Fiona?"

Her belly fluttered with the sudden idea that all would be right if she just said yes. She looked him over and saw the sincerity in his face and knew his offer was a genuine one. He meant what he said and he was willing to take care of her and make sure she and the baby were well cared for. For the first time since coming into the human realm and leaving behind her world, she was willing to believe everything would be all right.

"Yes, Liam. I will be your wife."

Chapter 12

In the Land of Faery Past

Niall greeted the dawn alone in his bedchamber. Disappointment went over him as he realized Fiona was nowhere about. He'd hoped to spend the morning with her abed. He padded through the room, looking for her but she wasn't there. Perplexed, he glanced around but saw her wedding clothes still in a heap where they'd been left. Grinning, he thought the little minx was somewhere in the other room, naked and waiting for him.

He hoped so. He had to tell her his true feelings for her. He intended to profess his love for her, tell her how much she had come to mean to him and promise her his heart. He would cherish and honor her all the days they were wed. He had even decided to let Prince Cian go, to allow him to return to Anatolia unscathed and resume his repulsive royal life there. He would give up waging war against the prince or his wife's homeland.

An urgent knock on the door pulled him from his thoughts. He grabbed a robe and flung it around his shoulders as he pulled open the door. Deaglan stood on the other side with a grave look on his face. Indeed, he looked as though something dreadful had happened.

"Father, what is it?"

"Fiona…she…she's gone."

Niall stiffened. "What do you mean she's gone? Gone where?"

"There's a vial of Tears of the Dryad missing from my workroom. I am almost certain she took it." He raked a shaking hand through his hair.

Niall's shoulders slumped. "You think she used the Tears to open a portal and escape from me."

"I believe she did, aye." He nodded slowly. "There is more I must tell you. A fire broke out in Cian's camp. It killed most of his men, horses and destroyed provisions. The prince is retreating to Anatolia, my king."

"Is Fiona with him?"

"I couldn't say."

"Then I have to find out."

He shoved his father aside, not caring he hadn't bothered to dress. He had to get to the library and use the Time Sphere to see if Fiona had made it back to Cian. Deaglan fell in step with him, his hurried gait matching Niall's.

"And if she's with him, what will you do, Your Majesty?"

"I will kill them both." He said it like a vow.

"Has your love for her fizzled so completely and so soon, my son?" Deaglan's words were soft and low.

Niall spun to his father and shoved him back against the wall with his arm. "Do not speak to me of love when she betrayed me on the very day of our wedding. I gave her a crown to this kingdom."

"But did you not betray her, too, Your Majesty?" he asked, his eyes sharp as he stared down his son. "She found my journal. She read the notes. Likely she knew what you intended to do with the child you created together yet you never told her."

Niall dropped his arm, defeated. "If she had stayed, she would have known my feelings for her were true. She would have known I'd changed my mind about Cian."

"Yet you would still use your own child for magical means?" he asked.

"No," Niall said, the word sharp and quick. "I couldn't. Wouldn't." He blew out a heated breath. "I was but no longer. Her disappearance changes everything, though."

"Her disappearance comes from self-preservation. I know it's difficult for you to hear but you must. You kidnapped Lady Fiona and brought her here against her will. And while she agreed to marry you, she did not agree to sacrifice her first born."

Niall scowled, hating that his father was the voice of reason. He spun on his bare heel and continued through the hallways toward the library, ignoring his father who insisted on coming along with him. He pushed open the doors and went to the Time Sphere.

"Show me Lady Fiona."

Smoke filled the orb but yet it showed him nothing. Niall pressed his hands against the cool glass.

"Fiona. Show me Fiona."

Again it showed him nothing but the smoke.

"Prince Cian, then."

An image flickered through the orb, showing him the defeated prince retreating from the foot of the cliffs back to Anatolia with his men. No Fiona.

"She's not with him," Niall said. "Could she be his prisoner?"

"Not likely. The Time Sphere would have showed her if she was."

"Then where is she?" Niall peered at the orb, as if he could conjure an image of her.

"It appears, my son, she is no longer in Faery."

Days passed. Despite Niall's determination to find his love, he could not. Deaglan's suspicions that she was no longer within their realm were confirmed when they received a message from Prince Cian demanding the return of his betrothed.

If she was no longer in Faery, then where was she? How had she managed to open a portal to another realm? Niall's frustration and anger over her disappearance had left him bereft and desperate to find her. He visited Deaglan often, helping him comb through his dusty spellbooks looking for something—anything—that would help them find her.

"You must remember, my son, Fiona's magic was strong and growing stronger every day. She was more powerful than either of us realized. If she used the Tears in precisely the correct way, she could have transported herself anywhere." Deaglan leaned back in his chair, his hand resting on a particularly thick tome with yellow-aged pages.

Niall paced the length of the small room, his hands clasped behind his back. "How am I to find her then? We've found no spell or incantation or anything that can cross realms or worlds."

"There is…one thing we could try. But it will have to be from someone with immense power."

Niall halted mid-pace, his booted foot scraping along the stone floor. "What is that?"

"An old myth about the Time Sphere states it can open other times, realms, dimensions, whatever you wish to call it." He tapped the book in front of him.

Niall moved closer to peer over his father's shoulder at the words written in an ancient careful hand. The passage described a wizard of immense power invoking an incantation in conjunction with the Time Sphere. Once the words were spoken, the Time Sphere would be able to look across realms to find the person one sought.

"Neither you nor I have that much power," Deaglan said.

"We can combine our power and open the Time Sphere together."

But his father was already shaking his head. "It can only be one person. One wizard. The incantation is very specific about that."

"Then who does have that much power?" he asked.

"No one in this world."

An idea formed. Something he had seen in another one of his father's old books came to mind. Niall placed a hand on his father's shoulder. "You mean no one in this world *yet*."

Deaglan's brows drew together in question. "What do you mean?"

"You give all your power to me."

His father clenched his jaw. "It's never been done. It's dark magic."

"But it *can* be done. Can it not?"

"In theory, aye. The spell has never been tried."

"Then we try it. If it works, then I can find Fiona and bring her back." Hope filtered through him, rising to his breast. He would go after her and bring her back to Illyria. And he would never let her go.

"It's not wise to invoke dark magic. You know the price is steep, as well as I," Deaglan said.

Niall did and he knew his father referred to his conquering of Illyria. He had been consumed by his hate and the dark magic swirling inside him. He also knew his father went to great lengths to remove that dark magic.

"I have to try," Niall said.

Deaglan looked up at his son, understanding softened his features. "You love her that much? You would go to all these great lengths to find her?"

"I love her, aye. And if she loves me too then she will come home with me."

His father rose from his chair. "All right then. Let's find that spell."

Niall stared at him. "You would give up your power for her?"

"I will give it to you for your happiness."

"Your sacrifice will not be made in vain."

It took weeks to find the spell. Precious days that put more and more distance between Niall and Fiona. His frustration mounted to interminable levels. So much so he had turned angry and nasty. Though he tried to hide it, it was clear to all that resided in the towers he was falling into a deep depression.

"Have faith," Deaglan said. "The book is here somewhere."

"And yet you haven't found it. Are you hiding it from me? Do you not want me to save Fiona from whatever fate she's befallen?"

"Of course I want you to save her. You must have patience, Your Majesty."

"I'm out of patience!" He banged his hand against the table in Deaglan's work room, rattling the contents and making the candles flicker.

Deaglan stared at him from across the room, the silence stretching between them. Niall drew up tight and stiff, exhaling a heated breath.

"Forgive me," Niall said. "I'll continue to look." He moved deeper into the room to search the dusty bookshelves on the far wall.

"Perhaps we are going about this in the wrong way," Deaglan suggested.

"What do you mean?"

"The spell would not be in a book. Rather, it would be a scroll." He stroked his chin, looking thoughtful. "Aye, a scroll. I recall that now."

Niall watched as Deaglan went about opening drawers, pulling out scroll after scroll until he found one that gave him pause. He lifted it slowly out of the drawer and placed it on the table in front of him. It was tied with a faded red ribbon. When he untied it, the oilskin scroll unfurled.

"The Eradication Spell," Deaglan said. He glanced up at Niall. "Are you still certain about this?"

"If you're still willing then aye I'm still certain."

"There will be a price to pay," he warned.

"What is it?"

"You know that is never revealed until the spell is complete."

Niall thought it over, wondered what horrors would he have to endure to find Fiona. If he had her back, he would be able to face any price. She was worth it.

"I want you to be prepared for that," Deaglan said.

"I am. Let's proceed."

With a nod and a grimace, Deaglan gathered several black pillar candles. He lit them one by one and then placed it on the floor between them. Then he reached for a vial of salt and drew a large circle around the candles and Niall. He set aside the empty vial and stepped inside the circle, then outstretched his hands.

"Give me your hands," Deaglan said.

Niall clasped his hands. "Now what?"

"Now you say the incantation written on the scroll. It's in the olde tongue. I taught you that many moons ago. Do you still remember it?" his father asked.

He nodded. "I do."

"Then say the words and once you are finished, release my hands and blow out the candles."

"Why?"

"'Tis the dark arts, my boy, and this is ritualistic magic. It must be done just so or it will not work."

Niall nodded and took a deep breath. He glanced at the oilskin and committed the words to memory and then began the incantation. He said the words carefully, slowly so as not to miss anything. Once he finished, he released Deaglan's hands and blew out the candles as he instructed.

And then they waited.

Nothing happened.

Niall started to say the spell had failed when Deaglan sucked in a sharp breath, his back bowing and his head tossed backward. He emitted such a howl it sent Niall into a panic. Deaglan pitched forward. Niall lunged to catch him before he crashed against the floor.

"Deaglan, what is it? What's happening?"

His father grasped a handful of his tunic and looked up at him. His face had drained of color. Deep lines that were not there moments ago etched into his face as though he had aged a hundred years in a matter of seconds. As Niall held him, he watched a white plume lift from Deaglan's body as though it were a vapor. It curled upward in lazy tendrils before spinning into a mini cyclone and then plunged back down. The smoke slammed into Niall's chest so hard, his grip loosened on Deaglan. His father slipped from his arms and landed on the floor with a crash.

The smoke that had curled above Deaglan's body pushed inside Niall and he knew the spell had succeeded and the transfer of power was complete. He rose to his full height, aware of the energy pulsing through him, igniting and strengthening his own tendrils of magic.

"Father, it worked. We did it."

When Deaglan didn't reply, he glanced down to see him curled on his side on the floor. Niall kneeled beside him. "Father?"

He didn't answer. Niall gave him a nudge and Deaglan rolled to his side.

The spell had killed him.

Niall buried his father on the Cliff of Mhothair, his guilt and grief an ever present companion. In his desperation to find his wife, his father had sacrificed himself. He preferred to remain in solitude, away from the servants or anyone that would look upon him with baleful eyes. He did not want their pity or their sorrow but he knew their whisperings. How sad they were for him after losing first Fiona and then his father.

A tightness had settled permanently in his chest. He had not been able to eat and refused food, even when the servants delivered it to his chamber. Over and over, he relived that day in Deaglan's workroom. Holding his father's hands, chanting the incantation, blowing out the candles. He should have never gone through with it. Deaglan should have never allowed it. Niall wondered if Deaglan knew the true effects of the Eradication Spell. Had he known it would kill him? Did he willingly sacrifice himself to help Niall find Fiona?

Regardless of whether or not Deaglan knew the steep price for the transfer of power, it was done and Niall had killed him. He would forever carry that horrible memory with him and regret the decision to use the damned spell. The only thing he had left of his father was his magic now residing inside him. If he could go back and change the past, he would. He had that power with the Time Sphere.

The Time Sphere that Niall swore he would never use to time travel. When Deaglan brought it to the towers to keep it from falling into the wrong hands, his father made him promise he would never use it in such a way. Niall intended to keep that promise.

He had even abandoned hope of finding Fiona through it.

Almost.

His feet carried him to the library, despite his wish to return to his bedchamber. If Deaglan had truly sacrificed his life for Niall to find Fiona, then mayhap he should at least try. He stood staring at the offending orb in the deathly silence for a long while. He had contemplated destroying the sphere. But that wouldn't give him the answer he sought.

And he needed to know where she was so he could return her to her rightful place in Faery. Deaglan had given his life and his magic for him and Fiona. He would find her. He had to.

Niall placed his hands on the Time Sphere and captured that magic inside him. Part Fae and part wizard, he had the best of both magical worlds. He could invoke spells and he could control the wild Fae magic inside him with a mere thought.

Now he thought of Fiona as he channeled that magic into the sphere.

"Show me where to find my wife."

The mystical orb sparked to life and flickered and a moment later fuzzy images appeared. But as they moved, they became clearer and Niall could see Fiona with a young girl whose hair was the same color as hers. With eyes like his and a cleft in her chin. Like his.

A flush of adrenaline surged through him as he stared at the girl in shock. Another much younger girl came into the scene. This one with long blonde locks but still resembling Fiona.

A man who joined them, picked up the blonde girl and spun her around while she giggled. Then he greeted Fiona with a hug and kiss that was far from just friendly. He was human.

And Niall knew instantly where to find Fiona.

She was alive and well in the human realm and she was the mother of his daughter.

Part Three

Convergence

Chapter 13

In the Land of Faery Present

King Niall stood in his chamber, his hands clasped behind his back as he gazed out at the cliffs below. The long cold years had made him bitter and even though he had everything he desired, he could not deny the palpable emptiness pounding through him.

He regretted nothing. Nay, that wasn't true. He *did* regret killing his father for his power. Deaglan understood all too well how desperate he was to find his lost love. The guilt and shame of that day still burned within his soul.

It had enraged him when Fiona disappeared from his bed and his life. Being with her had changed him and if only she had stayed until morning, she would have learned he had decided to forego attacking Anatolia allow Cian to live and forsake all plans to use their child for personal magical means. He knew all too well the steep price for that. He wanted them to live in peace as a family. All because he had *her*.

His discovery sent him into a rage and he had destroyed Anatolia anyway. No one knew to this day if Cian lived or not. Niall didn't care either way.

It had taken him quite some time to pinpoint her exact location within the human realm and had crushed him when he found her living with some pitiful mortal. The man had to die, didn't he? He didn't deserve her. No one did. He sent his men to capture her and bring her back and when she refused, the mortal stepped in to rescue her. He got in the way, sacrificing himself to save her like some noble lord. Even now Fiona's anguished scream echoed in his mind.

And now she had slipped through his fingers yet again.

A knock on the door interrupted his brooding and he turned from the window.

"Your Majesty." His man bowed with the greeting. Niall waved him inside. "I have news."

When the man paused, Niall scowled. "Well? What is it?"

"The woman has entered Faery. She's been spotted in the village. Would you like us to apprehend her, sire?"

Niall smiled. At last, Fiona had returned to her realm. After all these years, he would finally be able to capture her, to bring her back home to the Towers of Illyria where she belonged. Where she would understand what it meant to leave him.

"Nay, I will go with a small group of men. It has been many years since I have looked upon her face. I wish to see hers when I capture her."

"As you wish, sire. Will you need horses?"

He shook his head. "I will sift us there to her location. Ready four of your best men and have them meet me in the library."

"By your command, Your Majesty." He strode out of the room.

Niall turned back to the window and looked out once again at the cliffs. "You will be mine again, Fiona. I have missed you these long years but you will be mine and you will pay for what you did."

He spoke the words as a vow then left his chamber. The Time Sphere in the library would tell him her exact location. He pushed open the doors and halted. The room was dark and silent. It had not been used since that fateful night when he found Fiona hiding in the human realm.

He stood in front of the Time Sphere. Now she was within his grasp. He waved his hand over the orb.

"Show me the girl."

It flickered to life and moments later her image was within the sphere. She wasn't far from the village. But she headed somewhere with purpose. She hadn't changed in the years since he'd seen her. And despite his loathing for her, he still desired her.

The four guards entered the library. He joined them in the center of the room. "Gentlemen, my queen has returned to Faery. It's time we persuade her to return to the Towers and take her rightful place with her king."

Fiona knew she had to make haste. The Time Sphere in the Ivory Wood would be active soon and she needed to be there when it was. She had been planning this for years but it had taken Liam's untimely death to push her into making her move. She had never been more certain about anything in her life.

It had taken her numerous trips to Faery in secret to find all the information she needed to go back in time using the Time Sphere. She had methodically planned what she would do once she returned. There were many past mistakes she wanted to rectify. The first one allowing Prince Cian to rape her. The second was marrying Niall. And if all that failed, then mayhap she could, at least, save Deaglan's life.

The miserable bastard had killed his own father and for what? Power? Magic? He had absorbed the wizard's magic, taking it into himself and rising into the monster he was now. He destroyed all that she knew in Anatolia, wiping out the entire kingdom with his powerful magic.

She had gone back to Anatolia once. To see the destruction, the crumbling castle had left her bereft. No one could have survived that. The kingdom had been left in tatters with no one to rule. Prince Cian was presumed dead though his remains had never been found among the charred earth the wizard left behind. Niall even robbed her of the pleasure of killing Cian.

She had a chance now to restore order to Anatolia by saving the destruction of the realm. She hated the thought of Cian surviving but at least she would have her vengeance. She would take her revenge on both Niall and Cian.

She was grateful Aoife and Sunnie were safe in the human realm. The magic here could not touch them there. And even if she did manage to erase her one night with Niall, she was confident her two daughters would remain alive in the human realm. So the tomes she'd read claimed.

The only thing she hadn't worked out yet was how to return to the present once she'd finished her to do list in the past. But that was something she'd worry about later. She had her priorities, after all.

She made a quick stop in the village to pick up provisions and weapons. She'd procured a bow and arrow. It had been years since she had her hands on one but she knew she could still shoot, though perhaps not as straight as she once did. Once she had the bow and quiver of arrows, she headed through town to find the farrier. He would know where she could buy a horse. But as she made her way down the main thoroughfare, she saw several of Niall's royal guards enter the south gate.

Fiona couldn't chance getting captured, so she ducked into a nearby shop, pretending to peruse several of the vases until the danger had passed. As she stepped out onto the street again and looked north, she saw them apprehending two young Faes. She hustled toward the south gate to get out of town before they noticed her. She may not have been in Faery for years, but her face was still recognizable. She knew from her past experiences she was still wanted by Niall in this realm.

She stopped at the farrier and waved to get his attention. She knew this man, knew he was honorable and reputable, though they each pretended they were not well acquainted. He gave her a nod of greeting as he put down his tools. He was tall, thick-boned, with a mop of curly red hair. His face was covered in a thick red-gold beard and he peered at her with green eyes. His hands were dirty, his forehead beaded with sweat.

"Can I help ye?"

"I'm in need of a horse," she said.

"It'll cost ye." He glanced around the bustling town square.

"I'm prepared to pay." She patted her hip indicating her small purse of coins.

He nodded. "See the stable boy. Name's Roan. Ask for the gray gelding. Ten gold pieces."

"You have my thanks."

The farrier went back to his horseshoes, ignoring her. She hurried to the stable and asked for Roan. When the boy appeared, he was the spitting image of the farrier only smaller and younger. They shared the same color eyes and the same mop of curly red hair. His face and clothes were streaked with dirt. He'd been mucking the stables when she arrived. The man was selling her his own horse?

"The farrier said to ask for the gray gelding. I'm to give you ten gold pieces for it," she said.

The boy's eyes widened. "Ten gold?"

"Aye, ten. If you give me a saddle and tack and make it quick, there's another five gold in it for you."

He scurried off and moments later returned with the gray horse, saddled and ready to go. She counted out the fifteen gold pieces into the boy's hand and then ruffled his hair.

"Tell the farrier he has my undying thanks."

She mounted the horse, gave him a wave and rode off at a

gallop without turning back. She could finally make it to the Time Sphere before it was too late. If she could sift she would but she'd lost that ability some time ago. She never discerned exactly why that was. She suspected going through so many portals had damaged some of her magic. And the only person she could think to ask was dead.

If she didn't stop, the Ivory Wood was a half a day's ride from the village at the foot of the Towers. She knew she took an awful risk entering the realm so close to Niall's domain but the village had everything she needed. That she knew for certain. Aside from that, she'd taken other risks before and not been caught. She was confident she could make it to the Ivory Wood with no problems.

Fiona maintained the gallop for as long as she could. She didn't want to push the old horse too much. Glancing up at the sky, the sun descended toward the horizon and she knew it was past midday. She would be in the wood by nightfall.

A creek ran through a meadow and she halted, dismounted to give the horse a rest. He drank at the creek while she bent down at the edge and splashed cold water on her face. She'd forgotten how tiring it was to ride for long periods of time without stopping.

"Hello, Fiona, my dear."

The familiar voice behind her made her freeze. She could reach for the dagger at her side, but then Niall would anticipate that and could easily counter-attack. She straightened to her full height and turned slowly to face him. By the gods, he was still as handsome as ever. He wore his pale hair longer now, brushing the collar of his high-necked tunic. He was dressed in fine linens with a cobalt crushed velvet vest that brought out the blue of his eyes. The same eyes that had so ensnared her long ago.

A myriad of emotions skittered through her and it was hard for her to decipher them all. Everything from desire and joy, to revulsion and hate. She wanted to kiss him. She wanted to stab him. She didn't know which order to put them all in and she had no idea how to feel as she stood there looking into him and he looking into her.

He stood several feet away with four guards, two flanking him on each side. He came more than prepared. He came to capture her.

Over her dead body.

She gave him her sweetest smile. "Hello, Niall. What an

*un*pleasant surprise to see you here."

"I could say the same to you. How long has it been, my dear?"

By human time, twenty-three years. By Faery time? Nearly a century. "Too long, I'm afraid."

"Aye, indeed, too long," he said with a nod. "But you came back, didn't you? You finally returned to Faery and I've missed you so."

Niall hadn't realized she'd been back numerous times in those years. Once even to filch from his own library. It was how she found the location of the second Time Sphere in the Ivory Wood—she dare not use the one in his library—and how she discovered the way to break the protection spell. It was the same day she'd stumbled upon the book, *Divinations*. It contained all sorts of wild prophecies, but the one that caught her eye was the one about the wizard king. The one which foresaw that the time of the wizard king would come. *A wizard of both Fae and Wizard blood will come into power and rule from a silver throne.*

She knew then it was about Niall, just as she knew she had to stop him.

That day had been most stressful for her when her energy and adrenaline had run so high it had taken days for her to recover. When she returned to the human realm, her body had literally crashed and she'd slept for nearly four days. She'd feigned a sickness and Liam had, thankfully, believed her. At the time, Sunnie had been two and Aoife was five.

"Have you missed me?" she asked. "Somehow I doubt that."

He clicked his tongue. "A pity you doubt my love for you."

"I find it difficult to believe you love me, Niall."

"You will address me as Your Majesty."

His face went impassive and darkened. He looked frightful and beautiful all at the same time. She'd seen that look many a time. She recalled it specifically when he'd learned the mercenaries had killed her parents and he ordered their arrest. She discovered later he'd had them executed.

"Ah, so we're back to our formal titles, are we? Then I must insist you address me as Your Majesty, for am I not still your queen?"

A cold smile that didn't quite reach his eyes. "You are. And as my lady wife and queen, you must be punished for your feral behavior. A woman's place is with her husband."

"Must I be punished, Niall? I think not." She refused to call him by his royal title.

His jaw clenched. "You will come back to the Towers with me, willingly…or not."

"Once again you think to control me, to capture me. I am not the same fool as I was years ago. I'm much stronger in both my mind and my magic." Fiona fingered the dagger, trying to decide if it was worth using or not.

Niall's gaze flickered to her hand and then back to her face, narrowing into icy blue slits. "Nor am I a fool as you once played me. You earned my trust. You gave yourself willingly to me. You told me you were happy and that you wanted me. Was that, too, a lie?"

A pang of guilt went through her. Aye, she had told him those things. At the time, they hadn't been a lie. It had been the truth and what she truly wanted. Now things were different. Though in another place, another time, she believed she could love him as he loved her. She believed she could be with him and remain his queen and raise Aoife together. Taught by both of them, Aoife would wield stronger magic than either of them possessed. And, Fiona believed, she would mayhap even help him destroy Prince Cian.

But at the time, she had in her stubborn mind to warn Cian of Niall's impending attack, of his determination to destroy Anatolia and the kingdom with it, of his intent to rule both. She had been hurt by his deceit to control her, to wield the magic Deaglan willingly pulled out of her. The magic she had discovered for herself and thought she could use to escape from Niall's grasp.

It had all been her undoing.

She had been a pawn for both Cian and Niall. She hated them both.

'Tis' why she had to go back, why she had to change things to make them right. To set her path on the way it should have been and erase the scars of the past.

"Tell me true, Fiona."

She had to do it, much like she did on their wedding night, when she looked him in the eye and told him she was happy. That had been the truth then. "I lied to you."

Though a little piece of her *did* want him, she could never admit that to him now. She could never tell him she had wanted him so desperately she gave herself to him to seal their marriage vows and allowed him to make love to her more than once. Nor that they had conceived a child that very night.

For years, she feared Aoife had been Cian's. But as she grew, she could see how much she favored Niall. She had the same nose, the same cheekbones, the same dimple in her chin as he. But she'd taken some of Fiona's traits as well. Her eye color and her beautiful auburn hair. Her smile. Her red, full lips.

And at the age of four, when her ears began to change into delicate points at the tips, Fiona knew she would have to hide her true appearance, just as she hid her own. Humans would never understand. So she placed the glamour spell over Aoife, altering it to make sure not even Aoife would know her real visage. Only those who had Fae blood could see through it.

She regretted that, too, but it was ultimately for Aoife's protection.

His pupils expanded and his eyes turned black, a shadow of rage creasing his features and changing him from handsome to frightening. Her hand landed on her dagger as she whipped it out as quickly as he gave the signal to his men to charge her. She flung the dagger at the first one on her left. It hit him square in the chest. He staggered backward, his hand clasping around the hilt.

The other three had drawn their swords but she was much faster than they could even hope to be. It was something she had taught herself over the years—a way to control her magic and fuel her body with it. She had discovered, quite by accident, she could speed up her movements which certainly came in handy when faced by three royal guards who meant business.

In a second, she had the bow in her hand and an arrow nocked against it. She fired the first round then reloaded. She killed the third guard. One more and the fourth one was dead at her feet. She nocked another arrow and this time pointed it at Niall, holding the string taut.

Niall hadn't even moved from his position.

He stood ten feet from her, rigid and at attention and a gamine grin on his face. He applauded slowly, clapping his hands together in mock appreciation. Yet she could see a hint of alarm flicker across his features.

"Impressive, my dear. Wherever did you learn that?"

"Wouldn't you like to know?" She couldn't keep the snappish

tone out of her voice.

She had learned much in the years since leaving Faery. She had taught herself the ways of magic, the magic Deaglan, may he rest in peace, had begun to teach her. She wondered how powerful she would be had he continued to teach her.

"I would, actually." He held up his hands in surrender. "Put down the bow and arrow, dearie, will you?"

The rage storming through her caught her by surprise.

"Don't ever call me that again." Deaglan had called her that. Niall wasn't fit to use the same term of endearment. "You will return to your tower and leave me be."

"Will I?" A pale brow quirked upward toward his hairline.

"Aye, you will." She'd yet to lower the bow.

"Wherever you're headed, I will find you. We have unfinished business, you and I," he said.

"I agree we have unfinished business. But not here." Not in this time anyway. She didn't want to give away where she intended to go.

"Then where?"

She didn't have an answer. She didn't want to answer. She remained where she was, weapon at the ready and pointing at his heart. Her muscles started to quake and she knew she couldn't keep up the façade much longer. One of them had to relent. But, by the gods, it would not be her first.

Niall dropped his hands and walked toward her. She couldn't help but notice he still walked with that catlike grace.

"Stop," she growled and pulled the arrow tighter.

"You won't hurt me, Fiona. You can't hurt me."

"I mean it. Stop."

He was in front of her now, at the end of her arrow. Daring her. "Go ahead. Shoot me. Put me out of my misery because I am tired of feeling as though my heart is missing."

Ouch. She hadn't expected that at all. What was he saying? That he missed her? That he truly loved her? She didn't believe him. She *couldn't* believe him. He was nothing to her. He was her enemy and he had to be destroyed.

She hadn't even realized she had tears in her eyes when she lowered the weapon, releasing the arrow and holding it at her side. Niall moved closer, standing only a breath away from her. His eyes lowered, his lips parted, his breathing was irregular. For a wild moment she was certain he intended to kiss her.

He could kill her as easily. He could grab her, throw her to the ground and do to her what Cian did. When his hand came up toward her face, she flinched, jerked back. Confusion creased his brow as she quickly stepped away.

"Don't touch me." Her words were an icy whisper.

His eyes blazed with fire, regret, anger. "I didn't know how I would feel when I saw you again, Fiona. I didn't expect to want you again. I wanted you to suffer for leaving me. For making me search for you all these long years."

Her heart rammed against her breastbone, a sudden burn of more tears in the backs of her eyes. By the gods, Deaglan had been right. Niall *was* in love with her yet he was still unable to say the words, for whatever reason. He turned and walked away, still with that fluid elegance. Anxiety spurted through her as she watched him walking away from her in defeat.

"We have a daughter."

She wasn't sure what made her say it, what made her blurt out those words. She shouldn't have. It was what he sought, after all. What he wanted most. She would hand it to him before ripping it away in the most hideous way possible. She wanted him to suffer. Despite his love for her, she needed him to suffer.

Niall halted, turned his head to look at her over his shoulder. She could see understanding in his eyes almost as though he already knew. "A daughter?"

"We conceived her the night we were married. She looks like you. She has your nose and your chin."

"What's her name?"

Her heart was in her throat as she built up the courage to tell him what she'd long wanted to tell him. "I'll not share that now. I know what you intend to do to her should you find her. I know you intend to steal her magic. I won't let you do that, Niall. I won't."

Again that dark shadowy look came over his face. "How did you find out about that?"

She had her ways and more secrets than she was willing to part with. One of her trips back to Faery had been to Deaglan's workroom where he'd kept an extensive journal of his teachings and how he and Niall might use the child they would make together. She had been appalled and horrified to learn Niall would not only steal his father's magic—killing him in the process—but also his daughter's to gain more power, more magic.

"It doesn't matter how I found out only that I did. I make this promise to you here, now. Before I leave this realm, I will make sure every thought of a child we might conceive together is thoroughly and completely wiped from your mind."

He chuckled, clearly amused at the notion of her threat. "And how do you intend to do that?"

She grinned, well pleased with the sudden solution that leapt into her mind. "I intend to kill you before she's ever born."

His eyes narrowed with suspicion. "Not even you have that much power, Fiona."

"No?" She cocked her head to the side, smiling. He had no idea of what she was capable. "Have you forgotten who my tutor was?"

Niall stiffened. "I have forgotten nothing. I find it difficult to believe you would wipe our child from existence. Not even you are that heartless."

She merely grinned. She had taken that into consideration when she first concocted the scheme. It was why she insisted to Sean that Aoife stay in the human realm. The research and information from sources across Faery she found confirmed as long as Aoife remained in the human realm, the magic in Faery would not touch her. Even if Fiona changed past events through magical means, Aoife would still remain alive and well.

But that was not up for discussion with the man who had betrayed her. She wasted no more time with words as she formed a light ball in both palms. In a lightning quick move, she flung them both at Niall. He had been unprepared. When the light hit him in the chest, he stumbled backward several steps, his tunic smoking. The hit had left behind material scorched black.

Fiona formed more power in her hands but before she could act, he sifted. Even so, she didn't miss the flash of pain and regret on his face before he disappeared.

Chapter 14

In the Land of Faery Present

The four travelers made their way south, putting the Towers of Illyria and the little village behind them. However, they had to give the village a wide berth to avoid any further royal entanglements. Aoife could tell Sean was annoyed with adding time to their trek by the way he huffed, the way he shoved branches out of the way with a mighty exasperation she had never before seen. She didn't know what to say to him.

She didn't know what to feel either. Since getting that fateful late night call from her mother telling her Liam was dead, her life had unraveled at the seams. It was the thread holding everything together and now it had been yanked. If Liam was a mortal and he wasn't her true father, then who *was* her biological father? And if Fiona was Fae, didn't that then mean Sunnie had Fae blood, too?

Pain throbbed at the base of Aoife's skull as she tried to make sense of everything. She thought back over her childhood, trying to piece together fragments of memories. Her mother had once disappeared for days, infuriating her father. They'd had a horrible shouting match. She was nine at the time. Another time her mother had been so ill, Liam took care of her and her sister for days. But he'd seemed annoyed and angry and she'd tried so hard to be good. But being good at age five when all she wanted was a Happy Meal and her mommy, was hard.

They emerged onto what looked like a main road. Ahead they could see a stone cottage with gray smoke curling from a chimney. Sean halted, glanced up at the sky.

"We're running out of time. We'll never make it on foot. We need horses," he said.

"What do you suggest?" Aoife asked. "I don't see a horse dealership anywhere nearby."

"Funny."

He shot her a straight face before a thoughtful look came over his features. He gave the boy a glance. Aoife could see the wheels in his head turning and knew he concocted a plan.

"Orrin, you come with me. Aoife, I want you and Ari to walk past the cottage and wait for us on the other side."

"Why? What are you doing?"

"The boy and I are going to procure horses. You're going to wait for us while we do it."

Realization hit her. "You're going to steal them?"

"Liberate. Totally different." He flashed a grin. "Come on, kid."

Orrin didn't bother to hide his wide smile as the two of them broke into a run toward the cottage. Aoife sighed. Next to her, Ari bounced from foot to foot and then gave her an imploring look. She knew immediately what the girl was thinking.

"No way. You're coming with me and we're going to do what he says. Come on."

She stuck out her lip in a mighty pout.

"No arguments," Aoife said.

They hurried down the road past the cottage. But she made sure to get a good look at the place as they passed by. There were chickens in the yard and a few cats lazing in the late afternoon sun. Beyond the cottage, she could see the stable and a stab of guilt speared her. She didn't like the idea of stealing, but Sean was likely right in that it was the only way they were going to find Fiona.

Ari fidgeted, paced a few steps away, then back. She bit her fingernails. It had been way too long and Aoife began to wonder if something happened, if they got caught. And if so, then what? She had no clue where she was or where they were going.

"What's taking so long?"

No sooner had the words left Ari's lips when the two of them galloped down the road. Sean reined to a halt long enough to hold a hand down to her. She didn't hesitate as she grabbed it and hoisted herself up into the saddle in front of him. Ari was already on the horse behind her brother and they galloped away as the sun dipped toward the horizon.

Practically sitting in Sean's lap distracted her to the point she had a hard time thinking. His body was warm and hard. She bit her lower lip as she looked down at his strong arms and his tight, confident grip on the reins. She had never been on a horse and had no idea how to ride. It wouldn't do anyone any good for her to be distracted. She had to keep thoughts of Sean, his powerful hands and strong arms in check. She forced her derailed thoughts back on track.

"I don't like the stealing, Sean," she said.

"Relax. I left something behind so they could buy another pair."

She exhaled a heavy breath, relieved he didn't outright steal them. "How far to the Ivory Wood?"

"Not far now."

Her heart thudded in anticipation. What would she say when she saw her mother? How would she react? How would they stop her from doing whatever it was she was going to do? A million things went through her mind.

The road they were on narrowed and then turned a sharp left but Sean didn't ease up on the horse. They galloped on, covering as much ground as they could as the sun dipped closer to the horizon. The trees thickened and only when it was impossible to keep up the frantic pace did he slow.

Aoife understood now why it was called the Ivory Wood. The bark was white and the trees were tall and straight, reaching high into the early evening sky. Even the leaves were white as they bushed out at the top, creating a thick canopy overhead. But the ground was probably the most spectacular as it was covered with a thick carpet of yellow, orange and red leaves. She had never seen such contrast. It was a feast for her eyes.

They heard the whinny of a horse and Sean came to a complete halt, cocked his head and listened. They heard it again coming from somewhere off to the left. He turned the horse and walked it toward the sound. As they neared, Aoife could make out a clearing and another contrast in color that was so odd it looked out of place.

Greenery, lush and beautiful, spilled into the white trees and fiery-red leaves. And in the center, they could see a sphere glowing in the late afternoon sunlight sitting atop a circular stone platform. A gray horse whinnied and trotted away from the green oasis, passing by them. Sean stopped again, slid off the horse and then reached up to help Aoife down. Orrin grasped the reins of both horses, holding them tight in his small hand.

"Stay here, all of you. I'm going to check it out," Sean said.

"But—"

He put a finger over her lips and shook his head. "Stay and be quiet. If it's your mother, I'll get her and bring her back here."

She relented. For now. "All right."

Sean crept from them, his feet silent on the bracken. Aoife marveled at how stealthy he could be and wondered how it was possible he didn't make a sound as he moved closer to the silent sanctuary before them. When he was out of sight—and earshot— she turned to the twins.

"Stay with the horses," she whispered.

"Where are you going?" Ari demanded.

"With him." She thumbed in his direction.

"Sean wants us to wait right here." Orrin pointed at the ground, a defiant look on his face.

"Keep your voice down. I know what he wants but I'm not good at following orders. Stay here with the horses. We'll be right back."

"But Aoife—"

"She's my mother, Orrin. You may not understand but I have to be there. I have to see her. Now stay put."

Aoife tried to follow his path but wasn't nearly as good at keeping silent as Sean. She would have to learn how he did that. She crept closer and then halted when she heard Sean's voice, loud and strong.

"Stop right there, Fiona."

And then her mother's fluid, snooty reply. "You're too late, Sean."

"Am I? The protection spell is still in place."

Aoife moved closer so she could see the two of them and crouched between two trees. Her knees crunched on the leaves but neither seemed to notice. She could see her mother's face now. Her expression was one full of strength and ironclad control. She stood straight and tall and unflappable.

"Not for long."

She lifted her arms outward from her body, palms up. Aoife watched in awe as light formed at her fingertips, and then a ball of bright white light danced in both palms.

"Don't do this, Fiona. You can't change the past."

Change the past? What was he talking about?

"What do you know?" she said. "You don't know my life. You don't know what I've had to endure to get to this point. I spent more than twenty human years with a man who never understood me or what I was. I accepted that because it's what I had to do to protect my child. I have to go back to keep her safe. It's the only way."

"It's not the only way," Sean said.

Aoife didn't mistake the flick of his hand as he rested it on the hilt of his dagger. Her gaze cut to her mother, but she hadn't seen. Her mouth went dry and it was hard to swallow.

"It is," she insisted. "The only person I can trust is myself."

Her blood red lips thinned into a determined line as she turned and flung the two balls of light toward the sphere. They smacked against a force field and burst against it in a wild starburst. The force field fractured, cracking all around it before exploding in a flash and disappearing.

Fiona didn't hide the triumph in her smile as she stalked toward the sphere.

"Fiona, no. Don't do this." Sean followed her, his steps longer, and closed the gap between them.

"I can do this and I will."

"What about Aoife?" Sean asked.

That stopped Fiona. She halted, dropped her head and rubbed her forehead. "Aoife will be fine. She's safe in the human realm. The magic here can't touch her."

Well, that wasn't exactly true was it? She was right here in Faery, staring at her mother's back and wondering what was so important about that sphere.

"But you can't be sure of that."

"I must believe everything I've read and learned is true." She looked over her shoulder at Sean, her emerald green eyes so much like Aoife's glittering with determination. "I have dedicated my life to this very moment. I'm going back, Sean. And you're not going to stop me."

Aoife chose that moment to bolt to her feet and step out of her hiding spot. "What about me, Mother? Can I stop you?"

Sean's head snapped around. "I told you to stay put." He practically growled the words.

Fiona's wide-eyed gaze landed on her. First shock and then fury as she whirled on Sean. "You were supposed to keep her out of the house. I trusted you with that. That's why I gave you the keys."

"You *gave* him the key? He didn't buy the house?" Aoife asked.

"Take her back, Sean. Get her back to the human realm. Get her out of here." Desperation laced her voice, her hands clenched at her sides.

"I can't. Not without you," he said. "You and Aoife have to come back with me. Orders."

"To hell with your orders. Get her back before it's too late."

The sphere started to buzz a low-pitched hum. The sun had dipped below the horizon but the globe emitted a mesmerizing golden glow, pulsing outward toward the three of them.

"It's time. I can't wait any longer."

"Too late for what, Mother?" She didn't like the sound of this. Whatever her mother was planning, it scared her, shook her to the core. She had never seen such determination as she held her body rigid and took another step closer to the sphere.

"What do you mean to do, Fiona?"

"I mean to save a life and correct a past mistake."

She lifted her hands, ready to place them on the orb but before she could, men materialized all around them. Men that were royal guards. And one man in particular who appeared next to Fiona and clasped her wrists, pulling her away. She shrieked in frustration.

He was tall with pale blond hair and the coolest blue eyes Aoife had ever seen. His chiseled jaw was set with solid resolve as he clamped his arms around her mother and dragged her away from the still humming sphere.

"Let me go, Niall!"

"I know what you mean to do, Fiona, and I'll not let you. You cannot erase what we had together. You cannot erase our child."

"Aw, shit," Sean said under his breath.

Comprehension smashed into Aoife with such force, she took a quick sharp breath.

Fiona struggled against him, trying to wiggle her way free and kicking her feet. But the man, Niall, held tight. He was stronger than she and Aoife couldn't help but stare in awe at the two of them. Seeing her mother fight like a wild cat was unlike anything she had ever witnessed.

Aoife moved closer to Sean and slipped her hand in his. "What's happening? Who is that man?"

Sean expelled a breath as though he'd been deflated. "That's the Wizard King. We are so screwed."

Chapter 15

A wizard of both Fae and Wizard blood will come into power and rule from a silver throne.

The words echoed back to Aoife in a flood. She could see it typed on the ripped out page in her mind's eye. There were other passages around it but she couldn't recall any of them now. She wished like hell she'd read the entire page but that damn trunk had distracted her.

"You're not getting away this time, Fiona," Niall said. "Arrest them all and keep them under guard until I get back."

He disappeared with Fiona in a blink.

Aoife refused to release Sean's hand even as they were surrounded. She thought of the twins and prayed they would stay hidden. If they were smart, they would. And she knew Orrin was no idiot.

Guards pointed their swords at them to keep them from doing anything stupid. By now, night had fallen and the only light was that of the sphere's pulsing light. She would question Sean on that later because he seemed to know what that was but she sure didn't have a clue.

A second later, Niall returned without her mother. He examined the sphere with a contemplative look, waved his hand over it. Nothing happened. The state of the sphere had not changed. He turned away from it and fixed his cool blue gaze on first Sean and then Aoife. Her heart kicked into overdrive. His jaw was clamped tight in a hard rigid line.

When he looked at her, he softened. There was a spark of joy in his eyes and the corners of his mouth relaxed into almost a smile.

"You are Fiona's daughter?" he asked, as though desperate to know the answer.

She gave a cursory glance to Sean who peered down at her. She hoped to get some help from him but he was utterly useless. He gave a stiff shake of his head. Should she not answer him? And if she didn't then what? She looked back at the king, met the hard cold blue stare and she shivered.

"And don't lie to me. I'm done with lies," he said.

Sean squeezed her hand. Either in reassurance or support, she wasn't sure.

"I…I am."

"You favor her. You have the same eyes. The same mouth. But you also favor your father." He ran a hand over his square chin and looked sort of sad.

That's when she saw the indention there in the middle of his chin. An indention much like hers. A lump formed in her throat as she peered at him, recognized the slender nose, like hers. The high cheekbones, like hers. She had only seen her revised face once in the fountain but she knew for sure she had the dimple in the middle of her chin.

The wizard king must be her father.

You cannot erase our child.

She tried desperately to connect the dots between him and her mother, but there was a whole lot of white space in between and she had no idea where dot one led to dot two and so on. They obviously had a history together. They knew each other well. But she couldn't figure out how Fiona ended up in the human realm married to Liam. There was a large chunk of her mother's history that was nothing more than a black hole.

"I cannot let you go," he said. "I'm taking you back to the Towers."

Before either of them could utter a word, Niall closed his eyes and a second later they blinked through space. Aoife's stomach flipped and bottomed out, her heart pounded with such pain she wanted to curl up and die. They ended up in some type of jail cell. Niall stood on the other side of the bars and peered back at the two of them.

"You two will stay here while I decide what to do with you and Fiona."

And then he was gone.

Aoife released Sean's hand and dropped to the floor, groaning. He kneeled next to her, his hand on her back.

"Are you all right?"

"What did he do to us? I feel sick," she said.

"He sifted us." He patted her back with a gentle hand. "It'll pass. Just give it a minute."

"What does sifting mean?"

"Some Fae 'sift' through time and space to get where they want. It's a form of magic. Your mother rode a horse to the Time Sphere so she doesn't or can't sift. I'm not sure which."

At least she had a name for the orb now—the Time Sphere. And she understood some of the things Fiona and Sean had said. That she was going back to correct a past mistake, that she wanted a life of freedom.

You cannot erase our child.

Her stomach cramped again as the memories and thoughts and feelings swirled within her and she somehow knew…*knew*…what her mother meant to do.

She lifted her head, met his dark brown gaze. "Can you sift?"

"I can but only myself. I can't transport others with me like the wizard king."

That explained why he didn't sift them to the sphere. She scooted against the wall and drew up her knees, hugging them to her chest. Hot tears burned at the backs of her eyes and she blinked them back.

"Sean, what is the Time Sphere?"

He cleared his throat, uneasy, and moved to sit next to her. One knee was up, his forearm resting on it. "It can be used to move forward or backward in time."

"And my mother was going back in time to correct a past mistake." Her voice was thin, hollow, wavering. She knew she was going to cry.

"Aoife—"

"I get it now. Why she hates me. She doesn't want me to be born." Her voice hitched and she gulped in a huge gasp of air before dropping her forehead on her knees. She didn't want him to see her cry.

"She doesn't."

"She does. She told you to take me back to the human realm. That the magic here wouldn't touch me there. But I am here, Sean. I'm in Faery. If she'd succeeded, then I would never exist."

Her muffled voice sounded pathetic to even her own ears. Sean must think she was a total weakling.

Sean wrapped his arms around her and dragged her into his lap, holding her against his chest and letting her bury her face in his tunic. He smelled like the earth—like the woods and sunshine. He also smelled of leather and horse. She got a grip on her emotions, refusing to even let one tear drop because she was stronger than that. All her life, her parents had brushed her aside as though she were a nuisance. She may not understand all of it, but she understood more of it.

Her father was not her father. Liam wanted nothing to do with her, naturally, because Sunnie was his daughter and he adored her. Her mother was a Fae who wanted to exact revenge on her father, who happened to be the dreaded wizard king. He hadn't known she was his daughter. Why? Why had Fiona kept it from him? Two days ago, all she ever worried about was getting orders right at the greasy spoon where she worked and passing her classes. Now she worried about being wiped out of existence forever.

"I'm not going to let her do that. Do you hear me?" His arms tightened around her as he whispered into her hair.

"What if—"

"Fiona is likely in a cell of the dungeon like we are. She can't get to the Time Sphere now. And it's only going to work for a limited amount of time. Once that light flickers out it won't work for another five hundred years."

Surprise flashed through her. He seemed to know a lot about this Time Sphere. She didn't understand why and, frankly, she didn't care. She was glad he knew and was willing to share the information with her. For years she felt like she lived in the dark. For the first time she was finally getting answers. For the first time, the light was on.

She craned her neck to gaze up at him and her heart tripped in her chest. His milk chocolate eyes met hers with such heartfelt tenderness, an ache formed where her heart was. Her throat closed up and her mouth had gone desert dry. His lips parted and she could hear a ragged breath escape him. She flattened her hand on his chest and was startled at the erratic beat of his heart against her fingers.

When she was fourteen, she'd had a mad crush on him. She'd pined for him for years. When he showed up in her high school as a student teacher she had been ecstatic. Her excitement was quickly squelched when he avoided her as though she had some sort of communicable disease. She had long dreamed of kissing him but once high school was over and she headed to college, she tried to forget him.

Tried. But she never really did.

She could admit she never had a steady boyfriend because no one measured up to Sean. And the worst part was she didn't even know why. All she knew was she wanted to belong to him.

"Aoife?"

"Yes?"

"I'm going to kiss you now."

Her pulse fluttered and heat pounded through her the moment his mouth landed on hers. His lips, so soft, caressed hers. His tongue, so wet, tasted hers. Fireworks exploded. Confetti tossed. Balloons released. Every nerve-ending stood up and cheered. It was everything she ever imagined and more. It was everything she ever dreamed and more. It was everything she ever wanted and more.

As his mouth moved over hers, it was slow and thoughtful as he took his time. As though they had all the time in the world. His tongue parted her lips once again in a soul-touching stroke, causing the pit of her stomach to churn in a wild swirl. It was a kiss to assuage her aching soul.

And when he raised his mouth from hers, she yearned for him to kiss her again.

"We'll find a way to stop her." He brushed hair back from her face. "I promise you that. I'll protect you as I've always protected you."

More truths clicked into place. "You've always protected me?"

"There's something I want to tell you." He brushed her forehead with light kisses.

"You're my guardian angel?" She said it to tease him and even punctuated it with a half-hearted giggle.

"In a way. I've been watching over you since you were a toddler. When you were in high school, I made sure those bullies never bothered you again."

Warmth cascaded through her as she squeezed her eyes shut against the rush of emotion that went through her. She knew there was something strange about that but she could never figure it out. She'd been bullied by a group of mean girls when she was fourteen. They'd made fun of the way she looked, told her how ugly she was and that she would never have a boyfriend or get a date to prom. They'd pushed her around, slapped her books out of her arms in the middle of the hallway between classes. Her papers had scattered everywhere.

The bell rang and they ran off to class, giggling and calling her horrid names. Sean, the student teacher, had helped her pick up her papers as he consoled her. He seemed to have come out of nowhere.

Don't listen to those girls, Aoife. They're just petty and jealous.

Jealous of what? They're right. I'm a troll and I'm late for class.

She'd snatched the last paper out of his hand. But instead of going to class, she hid in the girls' bathroom and cried.

"You did that. For me." It took everything she had left in her to keep her voice from wavering.

"I made sure they never bothered you again."

She wondered what he did to them but she thought better than to ask. Some things were best left to the unknown. Though thinking of Sean scaring the pants off those girls did make her smile. They gave her a wide birth after that day. So had Sean. She never knew why but she thought it was because he thought her weak. Now she understood so much more.

He was a Fae, she knew that now. That explained why he never aged and why he looked the same as he did when she was in high school.

"You were never a troll to me. I could see through the glamour spell to your true visage."

"Glamour spell?" That got her attention and she sat upright, peering into his eyes.

"Your mother placed a glamour spell to hide your true features from the human world. Likely to hide these," he traced the tips of her ears with his fingers, "from those who would never understand."

She gasped at the sensual sensation it sparked through her. Her fingers collided with his and she suddenly understood. Her ears had points. She hadn't noticed that in the reflection of the fountain, but then she hadn't had time to really study her new face.

"Why'd she make me so ugly then?"

"To hide you, most likely. You're far more beautiful than any of those girls who tormented you. You have a light inside you that beams so bright, anyone can see it. They did. That's why they picked on you. They didn't get it. But I did."

She blushed and looked away, her blood warming.

"Psst. Aoife."

Standing at the cell door with a key in her hand was Ari. Aoife and Sean got to their feet.

"Ari, how did you get in here?" Aoife asked.

"Thief, remember? I know a secret way in and out." She held up the key with a triumphant smile on her youthful face, then unlocked the door. "Orrin is waiting outside the dungeon."

"You shouldn't have come after us. It's too dangerous," Aoife said.

"Hardly." The girl rolled her eyes. "No one saw us."

"I agree with Aoife," Sean said. "It's too dangerous and you shouldn't have come."

"Do you want out of here or not?" Ari demanded as she unlocked the cell door.

They exchanged a glance before bolting for the door. Ari started for the exit, Aoife right behind her followed by Sean. But Aoife stopped at the next cell and peered in.

"What about my mother?" she asked. "We should get her out, too."

"There's no one else," Ari said. "I checked."

"Are you certain?" Sean peered into the empty cell next to them, then moved to the next.

"Duh. Like I checked all the cells. I'm not an idiot, you know. There's no one else here."

"But there was."

Aoife stared at the open cell door at the end of the corridor. She hurried toward it, the others on her heels. When she arrived, she saw the lock had been melted.

"She escaped. It was foolish of Niall to not have wards around her," Sean said.

"Then we have to find her," Aoife said.

"She'll be heading back to the Ivory Wood."

"Actually, no, she won't."

Niall's voice at the opposite end startled them. He stood next to their open cell, the firelight from one of the torches flickering over his face. Sean stepped in front of Aoife and Ari like a shield.

"She's gone," Niall said.

"Gone? Where?" Sean asked.

"Mayhap you should come with me. It would be better if I could show you, rather than tell you."

"Where's Orrin?" Aoife asked.

"The boy is safe. Come with me."

He motioned for them to follow and turned to leave the dungeon. Aoife and Sean exchanged a curious glance. He took her hand as they hurried after Niall. His footsteps echoed back to them as he made his way up a winding staircase and through a heavy wood door.

Aoife wished she had time to examine her surroundings as they made their way through the castle. She saw portraits and tapestries on the walls and thick, plush rugs and ornate furniture. Torches gave way to elaborate candelabras lighting the way, reflecting on the stone walls and giving the place a warm and inviting glow. It was nothing like she imaged a castle would look. She expected cold and drafty and musty and this was warm and inviting and bright.

They rounded a corner and entered two giant wooden doors that had to be at least twenty feet tall. The stone floor gave way to marble that sparkled from a fire blazing in the oversized hearth. Aoife gasped when she realized they were in one of the biggest libraries she had ever seen. Books stretched from floor to ceiling.

She craned her neck to get a look at all the shelves lining the walls and extending for what seemed like forever. Soaring windows on the opposite wall showed nothing but nighttime and she wished she could see out. She thought she could see the outline of snowcapped mountains.

They went past shelves which reminded her of a public library to the center of the room. There, Orrin stood at a crystal globe mounted in a circular stand that looked much like the one in the Ivory Wood. It, too, hummed and emitted a golden glow.

Ari hurried to her brother and hugged him, relieved he was safe. Niall had, at least, made good on that statement.

"You have the second Time Sphere. I thought it had been lost for centuries." Sean's voice held a note of awe and wonderment.

"It was lost until my father found it. He brought it here when I claimed the throne of Illyria and it's been here ever since. There are only a few people in this realm who know of the existence of the second Time Sphere," Niall said.

"My mother was here, wasn't she?" Aoife asked. "She used the Time Sphere and escaped to the past."

"I'm afraid she did," Niall said with a sad nod.

A wave of sickness went through her. She pressed her hand against her stomach. Sean squeezed the hand he still held.

"We have to go after her." Aoife looked at Sean with an

imploring gaze.

"What do you know of her plan?" Niall asked, glancing between the two of them and ignoring Aoife's desperation.

"Only that she intended to go back in time to correct a past mistake," Sean said.

Niall paced the short length of the area, his hands clasped behind his back. "I, unfortunately, know what her end game is. I saw her earlier today and tried to stop her but she's grown more powerful than I and tried to kill me. I narrowly escaped. I had to sift back here."

They were silent as he gathered his thoughts, halted. He rubbed at a place in the middle of his chest as he contemplated his next words. He stepped toward Aoife, looking her over with a critical eye.

"Do you have magic?"

"I…I don't know."

"Aoife's magic has not yet manifested," Sean said.

He nodded in understanding. "Fiona's did not manifest until she was older. About your age, I should think. That's when she first came to me. You *will* go after her and stop her. I'm quite fond of living. But first you must know the past to understand the future."

Apprehension sparked through Aoife. At last, she was going to learn how her parents met and what happened so long ago to set Fiona on this path of destruction. It terrified her.

"Tell me."

He gave her a small smile. "I was a fool then. Aye, I probably still am. At the time, Fiona was betrothed to Prince Cian, heir to the throne of Anatolia and my half-brother. We shared a mother, you see. We loathed each other with a fierce hatred. Despite being older, I was nothing more than a bastard child who would never inherit the throne. I was able to create magic at a young age. I admit I wreaked havoc on the kingdom and my brother because I was consumed with jealousy and rage. My mother must have sent for my wizard father because I was so unruly. When he returned, I was a boy and she willingly gave me up. Let me go with him to learn to control my magic." He clasped his hands behind his back and paced again. "Cian was to ascend to the throne and I knew he would marry before then, so to hurt him and to show him I was still stronger and more powerful, I stole his bride." His gaze pierced Aoife. "Your mother."

"You kidnapped her?" she asked, wide-eyed.

"I did. My father, Deaglan, taught her magic. He could sense the power within her. He also knew a child from us would be more powerful than either of us. Because that child would have both Fae and wizard magic." He stopped pacing and walked to her, staring at her with those piercing blue eyes until she shivered. "You are that child, Aoife."

"But…but…I have no magic."

"Not yet." His gave her a knowing smile. "I trusted Fiona a little too much. Gave her free reign of the castle as my father suggested. I made the fatal error of falling in love with her. She betrayed me. Left me after our wedding vows were consummated."

Aoife shifted from one foot to the other as she tried to come to grips with the story Niall told. She stared at him with a certain wonder and calm. He was her father—her real father. Not Liam. Part of her was overjoyed at the thought of knowing. Another part of her feared him and what was inside her. Could she wield magic like her mother? Would she even want to?

"How did she betray you?" she asked. She could not help but think Fiona betrayed her, too.

"I deserved it." He put his hands behind his back and paced several steps away, guilt on his face. "So determined was I to destroy Cian and Anatolia, I intended to use any means necessary. I knew creating a child with Fiona could help me with that end goal." He glanced at her over his shoulder, the pain evident in his crystal-clear blue eyes. "I intended to steal the magic of our child and use it for myself."

Aoife emitted a strangled gasp while Sean stiffened and went rigid next to her. Niall turned toward her and closed the gap between them in two steps. When he reached for her she flinched. Sean stepped between them, unwilling to let him get close to her and pushed his hands away. Niall looked at Sean and then back to Aoife, his expression imploring.

"I swear to you I've abandoned that idea, Aoife. I want you to know that. I need you to know that. I know too well the consequences of taking another's magic. It's how I killed my father."

"Your father?" She pressed cold shaking fingertips against her lips.

"Aye. When Fiona stole the Tears of the Dryad and used the potion to make a portal, I was so desperate to find her I talked my father into using the Eradication Spell. His magic came into me but it took his life in the process. I regret that now and have spent these long years harboring that guilt deep inside me." He rubbed at the middle of his chest, as though trying to lessen the pain.

As he spoke, Aoife saw sudden pinpricks of light and her knees turned to water and buckled. Sean lunged for her and caught her in his arms, holding her upright. She clutched his tunic in her fist, her mother's words haunting her. *I mean to save a life and correct a past mistake.* She knew what her mother meant to do when she went back in time.

"Aoife?" Niall tried to move toward her, concern etched on his face, but Sean gave him a warning glare. He stepped back.

"The Eradication Spell was in the attic. We have to stop her," she whispered. Then to Niall, "I'm all right."

Sean gave her a nod of understanding and helped her stand upright again. He turned to Niall.

"What is this Tears of the Dryad?" he asked.

"A potion. One drop can open a portal," Niall said. "To anywhere. She stole it from my father's workroom and used it to escape."

"Is that when she went to the human realm?" Aoife asked.

Niall nodded. "I believe so. Prince Cian had come to reclaim her that same night. He and his army waited at the foot of the cliffs. But it was snowing heavily and it was too risky for him to ascend to attack. He eventually returned to Anatolia. At the time, I thought with Fiona. But when I received a message demanding her return, I knew she had gone elsewhere. It took me a while to track her down in the human realm. I found her living with a mortal."

Aoife didn't miss the look of distaste on his face. "Liam. He was the man who raised me. My step-father."

"My condolences on your loss."

"You killed him." She balled her free hand. The mystery of Liam's death had been solved.

"I sent my men to capture Fiona. A fight ensued. I made the error of misjudging the strength of her power. They attacked her and she fought back. Liam was a casualty in that fight. He got in the way. Damn fool tried to save her. I am sorry he was killed."

Anguish squeezed her heart and she closed her eyes to stop the tears that wanted to erupt. Her parents had fought a lot and even though they appeared to hate each other, in the end, Liam had sacrificed himself to save Fiona. Maybe a little piece of him had still loved her.

"And now she's returned to Faery with vengeance on her mind," Niall said.

"You think she's going back in time to stop the wedding from happening," Sean said.

"I know she is. She told me she intended to kill me before Aoife was even born." Niall reached for her, squeezed her upper arm in a gesture of comfort. "That must be difficult for you to hear, my dear, and for that I am truly sorry. I know why she thinks to get away with it. She's found some lore that says the magic of Faery will not affect those in the human realm."

"That's why she insisted I take Aoife back to the human realm," Sean said. "She thinks she'll be safe there when she alters the timeline."

Niall nodded. "It's me she wants to hurt. Not you. If she had stayed with me, she would have learned I'd decided to give up my quest to kill Cian and wipe Anatolia from the map."

As if that was some consolation. Though it may be true, it still cut her to the bone.

"So you want us to go back in time and stop her from killing you," Sean said. "That's not going to be easy."

"No, I don't expect it will." The wizard king gave him a good-natured grin. "You will have to tread carefully in the past so as not to make too many alterations. However, if you could be so kind as to make sure Fiona doesn't murder me that would be much appreciated."

"And I would like to be born. So why are we standing here? Let's go," Aoife said.

"You should go home, Aoife, where it's safe. If the lore is true—"

"No," she said with a snap, cutting off Sean. "I'm going." She had never been so sure in a decision before.

"But—"

"No, Sean. I have as much at stake here as anyone. I'm going and no one is going to talk me out of it."

"If you're sure."

"I am."

"There is something else you should know. Faery time moves differently than human time."

Sean's brow wrinkled in confusion. "Yeah, I know that already. It moves faster in Faery."

He nodded agreement. "Aye, there is that. But regarding the Time Sphere…there is a reason why my father put a protection spell over it in the Ivory Wood and why he brought this one here to keep hidden." He waved toward the one before them.

"And what is that?" Aoife didn't like the ominous tone of his voice.

"Moving forward or backward in time alters the timeline. Fiona has already altered the past merely by stepping through time with her younger self. When you go back, it will further alter the timeline because you don't belong there anymore than Fiona does."

"I don't understand," Sean said.

"What once was will not be," Niall replied. "Even if you try not to interfere, know this. The one event that cannot change is Fiona and I must marry on the second moon of her captivity and consummate those vows that night. Otherwise, Aoife will never be conceived."

She and Sean exchanged a look of concern. She didn't like tampering with the past but they had no choice if they were to make sure she survived.

"Understood." He turned to her. "You ready?"

"We're going, too!" Orrin stepped forward. They'd been so quiet, Aoife forgot they were there.

"No. You're staying here where you belong." Sean shook his head.

"We can help," Ari said. "We know how to get in and out of places unseen."

Sean gave Niall a questioning glance. "Your Majesty?"

"The fewer people who go through the Time Sphere, the better. They best stay here."

"Sorry, kid," Sean said. "You two will be safer here."

Orrin's face fell as though he'd been told his puppy had died. Aoife went to him and hugged him. "They're probably right. You will be safe and we'll be back before you know it." She gave him a smile.

"All right. We'll stay. But not because we want to. I want to give you something." Orrin reached into his knapsack and pulled out the pink crystal, pressing it into Aoife's palm. "Take that. You might need it."

"You're giving her the crystal?" Ari burst out.

"Where did you get that?" Niall asked at the same time.

Aoife peered down at the pink crystal. "Are you sure, Orrin?"

He nodded. "I'm sure."

She tucked the crystal into her pocket for safekeeping.

"You thieving little monkeys," Niall said. "You stole that from me. How did you know how to get into the castle? It's well guarded." The twins kept silent. "I see, then. I'll have to find out how you snuck in and make sure it doesn't happen again."

Orrin flushed. "I'm sorry, Your Majesty."

Niall gave them both a stony look and then softened. "Where are your parents?"

"We don't have any," Ari said and Orrin flashed a look that made her gulp and shrink back.

"Our parents were killed by a highwayman," Orrin said.

"Well, then, mayhap penance for your crime is to stay here and do chores. I'll provide you with a place to stay and food and clothing. Do you agree?"

The twins' faces lit up as though it were the best news ever. Aoife admired that about Niall—allowing the kids to stay even though they'd stolen from him. Though she knew he'd be teaching them a life lesson.

"Very well then." He ruffled the boy's hair and turned back to Sean. "Are you armed?"

Sean patted the dagger at his side. Niall didn't seem satisfied with that. He pulled his hand down through the air and a sword materialized. He handed it to Sean who strapped it onto his belt with a broad smile. He looked at Aoife.

"Have you ever used a weapon, my dear?" She shook her head. "I can't send you back unarmed. Sean will show you how to use it." He repeated the gesture and handed her a dagger, then ushered them toward the still-glowing sphere. "You only have a limited amount of time. The sphere will only work for three more days."

"How do we get back?" Sean asked.

Niall reached into his pocket and brought out a gold coin. The markings were worn and smooth yet they could still see the profile of a king stamped on one side and two towers on the other. It was a coin from Old Illyria. He pressed it into Sean's palm.

"Give that to me in the past. That coin is your passage back to the future."

"And you're certain your past self will help us?"

"I am. When I see it, I will know what it is." He put his hand on Sean's shoulder. "Please bring back my beloved. I bid you good luck and pray to the gods you do not fail."

"As do I," Sean said.

Aoife had never released his hand and now held on with an even tighter grip.

"And so it begins."

Niall positioned them next to the sphere. He moved to stand opposite them and met Aoife's gaze. He gave her a reassuring smile.

"When you come back, I should like to get to know you, Aoife."

She didn't know why that surprised her, but it did. And she didn't have a response other than a small nod. *She had a father.* A living, breathing father that actually wanted to get to know her. That was more than Liam had ever wanted from her.

Niall raised his arms, palm up, and closed his eyes. A mist trickled from the orb and surrounded them. She could hear him chanting something but she couldn't make out the words. She glanced up at Sean, but his jaw was set and his gaze hadn't left Niall.

Her heart pounded a wild riot in her chest. She inhaled a deep breath and watched as the world around her spun. Slowly at first and then faster and faster until the library was nothing but a blur. She concentrated on how Sean's hand felt next to hers, the way his fingers tightened and his body stiffened. She heard his sharp intake of breath.

"Don't let go of each other."

It was the last thing she heard Niall say before she blacked out.

Part Four

Deviations

Chapter 16

In the Land of Faery Past

Fiona crouched behind the fallen log and watched the road, waiting with a fiery impatience. All her years of planning had finally come to fruition. She had calculated her arrival in the past to coincide with the day she and her parents traveled to Lambridge Castle for her wedding. If she could stop the mercenaries from kidnapping her, then she would hide her true self behind glamour and tell her past self to change her fate.

It sounded plausible in her head when she concocted the scheme.

She checked the angle of the sun. It was still early in the day and the caravan had not yet passed by. She hoped by now Sean had returned Aoife to the human realm. It had never occurred to her to have second thoughts until she saw her daughter standing there with that wounded look on her face.

What about me, Mother. Can I stop you?

Her wavering voice sent a shudder of guilt through Fiona. For a moment she considered calling everything off and returning to the human realm, going with Sean like he wanted. But she had come too far to turn back now. Determination settled through her when she begged Sean to take Aoife back. She hoped he had made it by now.

How had Aoife ended up in Faery? Had she underestimated her own daughter so much that the girl found the portal she left behind in the trunk? Surely not. But then how else? Unless Sean brought her and Fiona knew that couldn't be true. She'd trusted him to keep her out. And yet he hadn't. He had instead been ordered by that wretched portal protection agency he worked for to return her to the human realm. They'd been trying to keep her out of Faery for years but she always found a way around them.

She knew she should have deactivated the portal when she left but she thought it would be a quick way to get back to the human realm if she needed it. She had been sloppy and it was inexcusable.

And what if Aoife hadn't made it back to the human realm? Even if she did make it back, what if I'm wrong and the magic can *touch her there?*

Fiona shoved away the thoughts and turned her mind back to the task at hand. She had to trust that the information she found in the tomes in Deaglan's workroom and Niall's library were correct. She trusted Deaglan and everything he taught her despite the way Niall made him use her to get to Cian. She could forgive Deaglan for that because she knew what manner of man Niall was. She knew he forced the old wizard to do his bidding.

In the distance, she heard the distinct clop of hooves and the rattle of carriages. Her heart leapt into her throat. Now was the time. She nocked an arrow against her bow and waited, still crouched, her breath a ragged exhale and her muscles quivering.

Her plan was simple. When she saw the mercenaries attack the carriages, she would then launch her own attack. She would pick them off one by one. As she recalled, there were six of them, four of Cian's guardsmen, two coachmen and two drivers. She would have to be quick.

In the distance, she could see the first carriage round the bend. A drop of sweat rolled down her back but she did her best to ignore it. Her muscles quaked and she wasn't sure how much longer she could hold the bow at the ready.

Not far from her, she heard a shout and then a loud crack. A tree fell in the path of the first carriage, spooking the horses. A man jumped out of the underbrush and leaped up to the driver before he could even react and killed him and the footman. The horses reared and the carriage shook. Fiona froze, watching in stricken horror as the carriage—the one she and Winnie rode in— turned over. She distinctly remembered the terror that had coursed through her. Seeing and hearing the screams from inside renewed that terror and she froze.

Cian's guardsmen drew their swords but they were already too late. Two more mercenaries emerged from the woods. Arrows flew and killed them, knocking them from their mounts. One of the attackers rifled through the pockets of the dead men.

Meanwhile, the second carriage rounded the bend. A squeal of horses startled her and then she heard a horrifying screech followed by shouts and screams. It spurred her into action. Fiona bolted to her feet, knowing what was to come next.

She broke into a run, branches smacking her in the face as she made her way through the bracken. One guardsman was already dead as was the second coachman and driver. The caustic tang of blood wafted to her nose and she halted at the edge of the road, peering through the leaves to see the attacker drag her mother by her hair out of the carriage. She kicked and screamed and called for her father who was on his knees with a sword at the nape of his neck.

"Give them the money, Hugh," her mother pleaded. She must have thought they were highwayman and this was a simple robbery.

Her father reached for the purse at his side and tossed it to the ground. The one holding her mother bent at an odd angle and scooped up the purse of coins and tucked it away in a pocket.

"We thank ye, but we don't want yer money. We want yer daughter."

This from the bearded man Fiona clearly recalled yanking her out of the carriage. Her mother's eyes went wide as she grasped the man's forearm around her throat.

"Not my daughter. Leave her alone."

A stab of guilt went through Fiona. Her mother had pled for her life. Or tried to. Fiona readied another arrow, about to let it fly when the mercenary laughed and slit her throat, shoving her to the ground. Fiona had missed her chance. She covered her mouth with her hand to keep from crying out. Tears spilled down her cheeks and her grief was fresh all over again. Knowing her mother died at the hands of the mercenaries was one thing. Seeing it happen was quite another and it cut her to the core, causing her carefully laid plans to begin to crumble.

The one who killed her mother gave the go-ahead nod to the other man holding the sword point at her father's neck. He didn't wait to make sure the deed was done as he turned and walked back toward the second carriage, the coins jingling at this side.

Bastard.

Anger flaring, Fiona nocked an arrow and let it fly, hitting the man about to kill her father. He tumbled to the ground, the arrow sticking out of his head. She hurried toward her father who stared down at the dead man in shock.

"Wh-who are you?"

"I'm here to save your life. Now be quiet and play dead until I return for you."

"Play dead?"

"If you want to live, then do as I tell you. Stay down."

Her father needed no more encouragement. He lay down on the ground next to her mother. She hurried back through the brush to get to the first carriage but she was too late. The one remaining guardsman was there, leaning in to order her out. An arrow struck him in the neck and he fell dead in the opening. The bearded attacker shoved the dead man out of the way and peered down at her.

"There ye are. Stay put now." He straightened and called out to someone else. "I got 'er. Right the carriage so's we can get 'er out."

Three of the mercenaries came to help and shoved the carriage over with such force it was as though it weighed nothing. That's when she saw the man fling open the door and drag her out. It was an odd thing, seeing a past event happen before her eyes. And she wasn't sure how to react or what to do. She notched an arrow, ready to let it fly as soon as she got a clear shot.

As the bearded giant of a man stepped in front of her past self, the cold air punched her in the gut. It nearly stole her breath. She glanced up and could see their breath pluming in the air as well.

"Something ain't right here," her captor said.

Fiona realized *why* that had happened now. It had been because of her. She stood too close to her past self. She dropped the weapon and quickly moved back into the underbrush, putting more distance between them. She was too far away to get off a clean shot.

The bearded man said, "Shut up."

And then he ran his hand over her face. The girl she was in the past jerked her head away and backed into the man holding her.

"Ain't you a pretty thing. Yer a prize, a'right. Bring 'er. The wizard king's awaitin'."

With everyone left for dead, they herded her onto the back of a horse, trotting away from the scene and leaving behind the carnage. Numb with grief and anger, Fiona notched an arrow against her bow and ran after the mercenaries.

She loosed her arrow and was pleased when it found the neck of the henchman riding to the right of past Fiona. He fell off his horse landing next to her captor, whose horse whinnied and reared back. The horse narrowly missed stomping on the dead man.

"We're under attack!" The attacker on the lead horse turned his head and shouted back to the others.

Fiona released another arrow. She'd been aiming for her kidnapper, but it missed his neck and buried itself in his arm. He jerked the reins and changed direction. The henchman in the lead unsheathed his sword and turned his horse, heading straight for her.

"You two get her to the king. We'll take care of this brigand."

She noticed two of the men had turned their horse and trotted back toward her. She cursed under her breath, nocked another arrow and waited as they approached. She knew she could kill them both with ease but they had to get closer. When the first one halted his horse only a few feet from her, she released the arrow. It found its mark right in the center of his chest. He grunted and slouched forward.

The second man drew his sword. She readied a second arrow. She could see the panic lining his face as he spun the horse to and fro, searching for the attacker—her.

"Come out now," he called. "And you'll be spared."

She suppressed a snort as she released the arrow. This one missed only by a few inches. The mercenary flinched as the fletching grazed his cheek. He turned toward her and that's when he saw her.

"Bitch."

He kicked the horse into a gallop. Fiona quickly released another arrow. It hit him right between the eyes. The horse reared backward and they both tumbled to the ground. The beast landed on the poor sap, crushing the lower half of his body.

Not that he would have survived her brutal arrow through the brain.

She dropped her bow and stood a moment, looking over the massacre. She could smell the death in the air and see the blood turning the ground red. Her first instinct was to leave and hunt down the mercenaries. But she couldn't leave the dead here for the crows to pick over. There would be time for her to get to the towers before the wedding.

Fiona walked to where her mother lay dead. She stared out of sightless eyes. Years ago when the kidnapper took her away, she had seen both her parents dead but she had not realized the violence of their deaths until witnessing it firsthand. Now, at least, her father would live. Fiona carefully put her glamour into place to keep her father from recognizing her. It would confuse him to see her because he knew the past Fiona had been taken away.

He moved to stand next to her, staring down at them. Tears dampened his face. "She's gone." Then he looked up, around. "They're all gone. My daughter—"

"Will be fine," Fiona said. "Stay here while I check on Winnie."

She left him there and headed back to the other carriage. She pulled open the door to see the girl on the floor. It looked as though the bleeding from her head wound had stopped.

The girl mewled as Fiona grasped her under her arms and pulled her up to the seat. Her eyes fluttered open.

"Wh-what happened?"

"Shh. You're safe now," Fiona said. "You have a nasty bump on the head. I need something to use as a bandage."

"My petticoat?" she suggested.

Fiona nodded and reached down, ripping the edge of the girl's petticoat. It was, at least, clean. She folded it and pressed it against Winnie's head, then put her hand up to it.

"Hold that. And don't move. I'll be back."

"Where are you going? What about the others? They took Lady Fiona, didn't they?"

"Don't worry your head about them, now," Fiona said. She tried to ignore the knot of emotion clotting her throat. "I'll be back and then we'll get you to safety."

Winnie nodded and leaned her head back, still holding the cloth to staunch the bleeding.

When Fiona went back to bury the others, her father had already started digging a grave with his bare hands.

"I will not leave them to the crows," he said through pants, sweat dripping down his forehead.

The realization struck her. She'd altered the past by saving her father. What, then, would change in her future? Granted, it had been her intention all along to save her parents from being killed, but she hadn't really thought about the consequences of such actions and she didn't know what to expect in her now altered future.

It broke her heart to watch her father digging the grave barehanded. She knelt beside him.

"Hugh, let me help."

Hearing his name, he blinked at her in surprise. "You know me?

Who are you?"

"I'll tell you soon. But first, let me take care of this. Rest in the carriage and I'll bury them all."

"You will? Alone?"

"I'm quite capable." She gave him a reassuring smile.

He nodded and trudged away.

It took Fiona some time to use her magic to dig the graves for all the dead. The exertion had depleted most of her magic. The only magic she could still wield was to keep her glamour in place, and only because the simple spell didn't require a lot of her magical energy. She would need rest and a lot of it but at least her mother, the guards, the footmen and the drivers were all buried.

More than once she had to stop and force away the tears. As she covered the last grave with dirt, she heard the gallop of horses and fear sliced through her. Her father popped his head out of the carriage but she motioned for him to stay put. She hurried back to Winnie as the group of three men came into view. One she recognized immediately as Prince Cian. Her stomach knotted as an icy finger scraped down her spine. The last thing she needed was to get captured by Cian and his men. She stepped into the carriage and put a finger to her lips to signal to Winnie to remain silent. Together, they hunched down on the floor.

"They're all dead, Your Highness," one said. "And someone buried them. There are makeshift graves."

"It appears someone beat your men to it, Your Highness," the second man said.

Someone beat him to it? Fiona stifled a gasp that wanted to erupt. If she understood the man correctly, Cian had intended to kill her while en route to the castle. Why? What would he gain by that?

"My lady, it's Prince Cian, Lady Fiona's betrothed," Winnie whispered. "He can help us."

Fiona gave an emphatic shake of her head and held her finger up again to quiet her. Through the broken window she could see the prince dismount, his boots crunching on the leaves. His expression was hard as he walked behind the carriage and halted near the graves.

"Are there reports of highwayman in the area?" the prince asked.

"No, Your Highness," the first man answered.

"Dammed peculiar, wouldn't you agree? Could it be King Niall is more savvy than I give him credit?" There was an uncomfortable silence. "Or have I been betrayed?"

"Not by us, Your Highness." This from the second man, who sounded sure and strong. "If there is a snitch, it was someone else."

"You are the man I trust most, Finnegan. I will give you the benefit of the doubt this time." Cian's voice was hard, cold. "You are correct in that the graves are fresh. Whoever dug them must still be nearby. Spread out. Find them."

Winnie broke away from Fiona and shoved open the door. She tried to grab the girl by the sleeve, but she slipped away from her. Winnie stumbled out, still holding her head. "Here. We're here."

Cian's expression changed from hardened to surprise. He hurried toward Winnie, catching her as she pitched forward when she stumbled out of the carriage.

"Winnie? By the gods, what are you doing here? Where's Fiona?"

"We were attacked. I heard something about the wizard king before I passed out. I think they kidnapped her. They killed everyone, Your Highness."

"They took my betrothed?"

"Aye, Your Highness. This woman…she buried the dead." Winnie thumbed toward the carriage.

Fiona tried to scurry out the opposite door but the other two men were behind her. One grasped her by the arm. Cian peered at her through the broken down carriage.

"And you are?" he asked.

"Merely passing through. I saw the wreckage and thought I'd help," Fiona answered.

Cian gave a brisk nod of his head for them to bring her toward him. They gave her a shove and she had no choice but to walk to the prince. He looked up her up and down with a critical eye.

"You buried them?"

"I did."

"Then why isn't there dirt on your clothes? Or under your nails? How did you manage to dig ten graves without any help? Or without a shovel for that matter." He didn't hide the disdain in his voice and she knew he found it difficult to comprehend that a mere girl would have been able to dig the graves alone.

All good questions. She dare not tell him she used magic yet she couldn't come up with another plausible explanation so she remained silent.

"Was it magic you used?" he asked. "I despise magic users. Take her weapons. Bind her hands. She's coming back with us for questioning," Cian said.

His man stripped her of her quiver. She'd left the bow on the ground behind her, damn the luck. He then took the dagger at her waist rendering her defenseless.

Cian turned to Winnie, holding her by the shoulders. "You can ride with me. We'll get you back to the castle. I'll have my healer look at your head. You're safe now, Winnie."

"Thank you. Oh, thank you, Your Highness." The girl practically melted in his arms as he led her to his horse.

His man bound her hands in front of her. As he did, she glanced at the other carriage but saw no sign of her father. She was glad he stayed out of sight, but didn't count on him to be able to get her out of this jam. He was a tired, old man. At least, though, she managed to save his life. She sent a silent prayer to the gods he would be safe.

She mounted the horse behind her captor as they rode away. Even if she wanted to get away, she couldn't since her magic was still depleted. She would have no choice but to go with them. Despite that, she saw this as an unforeseen opportunity. She would have her chance to do away with the cruel prince once and for all.

Chapter 17

When Aoife awoke, her first awareness was of lying on something hard and jagged. It took a moment to realize her body was draped across Sean's and his elbow jabbed her in the side. She groaned and lifted her head to see where they were but recognized nothing. They looked to be in a forest.

For a moment, she was completely stymied by her position on top of Sean. He was all hard angles and thick muscles and yet his face was calm, serene. She brushed back a lock of black hair that had fallen over his forehead. His fingers clamped tightly around her wrist and his eyes opened.

They peered at each other a long moment, his dark brown eyes softening when he realized she was on top of him. One corner of his mouth lifted in a smile.

"I like waking up to you," he said. "It's a beautiful sight."

She flushed and pulled her wrist free, then rolled off him, landing in a pile of soft leaves. "And you have a bony elbow. That sifting gave me a headache and it kind of sucked."

"I'm afraid we'll have to do it again to get back home," Sean said, checking his weapons "Come on. We'd better get going."

"How do you know where to find my mother?" Aoife asked.

"I can track her."

"How?"

He stared at her with a look of consideration, as if trying to decide whether or not to tell her. He reached into his pocket and pulled out a small square box, flipping it open and handing it to her. It was a compass, but it didn't point north.

"A compass that doesn't work?" she asked, peering down at it.

"A compass that *does* work. It follows Fiona's path. At least, the Fiona from our time."

"How does it work? Is it magic?" she asked, genuinely curious.

"It's complicated." She blinked and waited. Sean took a deep breath. "I work for the Inter-dimensional Portal Protection Agency, Aoife. My job is to make sure portals between the human realm and Faery remain closed at all times. I was assigned to your case when you were two. When you were nine, your mother left the human realm and went into Faery. She's perfected a way to enter and exit the human realm on or about the same time she left making it seem like she was never gone. We still don't know how she did it. When she returned from that trip, my boss insisted she be marked so we could keep track of her."

"Marked how?" Aoife asked.

"She has a small tattoo above her left shoulder blade. It's a Celtic circle with a sword through it."

Aoife gasped. She knew that symbol. It was the same one on the trunk. The very one that lit up and beckoned her into the portal.

"You've seen it, haven't you?" he asked.

She nodded. "On the trunk in the attic."

"It's the symbol she chose for her tattoo," Sean said. "At the time, we didn't know about the trunk. We're not sure how long she's had it."

"Nor am I," Aoife said. "We were never allowed in the attic. I guess I know why now."

With a nod, Sean said, "Let's go. We have to find her before she alters the past." He consulted the compass and then pointed toward the west. "This way."

As they headed toward the sunset, Aoife's stomach rumbled with a mighty growl. She pressed her hand against it to silence it but Sean noticed. He grinned at her.

"We'll stop at the first inn we find for the night. They'll have food and drink there."

"Good."

She bit her lip as the flood of emotion inundated her. Here she was in the past, before she was even conceived, to try to save her own life. It was odd, that. She couldn't help but think of her sister, Sunnie, back in the human realm. If they failed and Fiona somehow managed to stop her wedding to Niall, how would that affect Sunnie?

Aoife had a devil of a time trying to wrap her mind around the conundrum of altering time. There were too many what-if scenarios. And too many things that could go horribly, horribly wrong. Like never being born.

Would the Fiona of this time still go through to the human realm to meet and marry Liam Burke? He was the man who raised her. He was the man who fathered Sunnie. What would happen to her now?

She hiccupped and realized a lump had formed in the back of her throat. She was on the verge of tears. She bit her lip harder.

Sean glanced at her. She blinked quickly to keep them at bay, but her eyes watered nonetheless. He took her by the hand, lacing their fingers.

"Don't worry, Aoife. We'll figure it out."

"Are you sure?" Damn it, her voice wavered. She was stronger than that. Wasn't she?

"I told you. I'm not going to let her wipe you out of existence."

"But what if you can't stop her? What if she gets there before we do? What if—"

He halted, turned to her and pressed a finger against her lips. "Stop. It's not worth worrying about right now."

"How do you know?"

He heaved a sigh. "Aoife. You're going to have to trust me. Can you do that?"

She met his dark gaze, saw the agonizing look on his face. Was he as tormented as she was about the whole ordeal? Slowly, she gave him a nod.

"I can."

"Good."

They resumed their walk as the sun dipped closer to the horizon. Ahead, they could see a small village inn that was two stories tall. Several horses were tied up outside. Gray smoke curled in lazy spirals from a chimney. They could smell the mouth-watering aroma of roasted meat and it made Aoife's stomach grumble again.

"All right. We'll stop here for the night," Sean said. "I'll do the talking to procure us a room."

"You have money?" Aoife asked.

He rolled his eyes. "Yes, so don't you worry about that, either, sweetheart."

She scowled at him. They entered and were greeted with a surly, snarling innkeeper with a shiny pate. Sean nudged Aoife behind him while he haggled for a good price on the room. There was a common room through a doorway and Aoife could hear chortles from drunken men.

"We'll take our food in our rooms," Sean said.

"Whatever." The innkeeper shrugged indifference.

Sean counted out a handful of coins in silver and bronze. Satisfied, the gruff man shuffled off, disappearing through the door into the common room. Sean turned to her and pressed a key into her palm.

"Upstairs. Last room on the left at the end of the hall. Wait for me there," he said.

"Where are you going?" she asked.

"I'll bring up some food."

"Why can't we eat in there?" She nodded toward the common room as a loud guffaw erupted.

"Not safe for ladies. There are too many unsavory characters in there. Trust me on this." He gave her shoulder a reassuring squeeze. "This is not a place for you. Now go and I'll be right there."

He trotted off and Aoife hustled up the stairs. She made her way down the hall and into the room Sean indicated. Sparse décor greeted her. There was a grimy window…and one bed pushed up against the wall. Her heart rammed against her chest. How was she supposed to share a bed with Sean? She couldn't. She wouldn't. She'd rather sleep on the floor on the threadbare rug.

Granted he'd kissed her and it had been spectacular but she suspected he did it more to comfort her than for any other reason. She doubted Sean was attracted to her.

Sean opened the door and entered with steaming trenchers and a jug on a tray. He also carried a bundle of something in a drawstring bag slung over one shoulder.

"Thank goodness. I'm starving," Aoife said.

She perched on the edge of the bed and took one of the trenchers. It was full of a hearty stew that smelled so good her mouth watered in response. He placed the tray on the bed next to her and then dumped the bundle. Sean seized the jug, popped the cork and took a healthy draft. Aoife gazed down at the trencher with a dubious expression. How was she supposed to eat without a spoon?

"It's not the Ritz, Aoife," Sean said, his tone flat. He sat cross-legged on the floor and slurped the stew out of the trencher.

She was not fond of eating with her hands. In fact, she wasn't fond of getting her hands dirty at all. But Sean was right. It wasn't the Ritz—not that she'd ever stayed there—so she lifted the trencher to her mouth and slurped in the hot stew.

It was delicious but so hot she burned her mouth. In a most unladylike manner, she spat most of the stew back into the trencher and waved at her mouth, trying to cool it off. Sean handed her the jug but she gave it a skeptical glance. She wasn't too keen on drinking after someone.

"I don't have cooties, you know," he said. "Besides, it'll help your mouth."

She took the jug and held it a moment. But her mouth was still burning, so she gave in and took a swig. The liquid was cool and sweet. When she finished, she handed the jug back to him.

"Thanks. What's in the bundle?" She nodded toward the drawstring bag.

"Provisions for the road. Oat cakes, bread and dried beef."

"You bought it from the surly innkeeper?"

"He gave me a fair price but I had to bargain with him. At least we won't go hungry trying to get to Lambridge."

"How far is that?"

"Too far to walk. We'll need horses."

Great. More riding. Now would be the time to confess. "Um, Sean. I don't know how to ride a horse."

He stared at her in disbelief for a long moment. "Then you can ride with me. We'll only need one horse in that case." He took another drag from the jug and then passed it to her.

She swallowed the sweetness, liking the way it heated her blood and relaxed her. She was warm from head to toe. "So how long have you been with this Portal Protection Agency?"

Sean cocked his head and looked at her. "How old are you?"

Her brows knit. "Twenty-three."

"About that long."

"And you've known me since I was two."

"That's right."

Aoife thought back over her life, trying to understand the timeline of events and to remember the first time she'd met Sean. She must have been five. Her mother had become very ill and Liam was the sole provider while she recovered. She remembered a man coming to the door, talking to Liam and questioning him about Fiona's whereabouts. They had conversed in low tones while Sunnie, who was two, played in her play-pen and Aoife sat at the kitchen table with French fries.

The pieces clicked into place.

"Oh, my god. You were the one who came to the door that day. My mother wasn't sick. She was missing. Wasn't she?"

"You were five."

She didn't have to explain further for Sean to understand what she was talking about.

"Yes. And Sunnie was two. Dad…Liam…took us to the playground that day and then bought us burgers and ice cream afterward. I thought it was the best day ever."

"But it wasn't?"

"At the time, yes. Looking back, no. Liam was angry about something. I know that now. I dropped my ice cream on the floor at the restaurant and he yelled at me." She flushed, remembering the incident. "And then he spanked me."

"Idiot," Sean muttered.

Aoife pretended not to hear. He may have been a horrible father, but he was the only father she ever had. "Why were you there that day?"

"The Agency sent me to find the portal Fiona had used. We thought it was in the house, but Liam wouldn't let me inside to look around. He was afraid you would remember and tell Fiona."

"Where was she?"

"In Faery. She'd managed a trip back more than once. I think now she was gathering information and figuring out a way to go back in time."

The food soured in her mouth. "To erase me."

She took another swallow from the jug, letting the sweetness burn away the sourness of truth. After their bellies were full, Sean tucked the provisions in his knapsack and Aoife tried not to think about being alone with him.

Actually, all she wanted to do was think about being alone with him. She had waited a lifetime for this moment and gave him a surreptitious glance from under lashes, watching as he moved about the room, checking the door to make sure it was secured and then checking the window. He peered through the grime but couldn't see out. He rubbed his hand through the dirt and smudged it, still unable to see anything.

"Are we safe?" she asked, suddenly curious why he checked the door and the window.

He glanced down at her. "Yes. Why?"

She lifted a shoulder in a half shrug. "I don't know. You checked the door. You check the window. I thought maybe you thought there was something or someone out there."

"I'm head of security. It's what I do." He rested his hand on the hilt of his dagger.

She grinned. "Good to know."

Their eyes locked and in that moment, warm delicious heat washed through her. He seemed to be peering at her intently, shredding her senses. She tried to assess his unreadable features, but could find no hint of anything buried in that ruggedly handsome face of his. One thing she was certain about, though, was the sensuous light passing between them. He must have felt it too because he looked away quickly, back at the window even though he could see nothing but darkness.

She turned her mind to other things. Remembering the crystal Orrin gave her, Aoife pulled it out of her pocket and turned it over in the light, looking at the way it sparkled.

"Why would King Niall..." She paused, smiled. "My father...why would he have a pink crystal?"

"It's magic."

"Magic. Of course." She didn't know why, but she found that hilarious and snickered. "I should have known. What kind of magic?"

He rolled his eyes at her. "They can be ground down and made into powders and used in potions, charms, spells and the like."

"And hexes?" she asked, still giddy.

He gave her that straight face again. "Yes, I suppose."

Aoife stuck the crystal back in her pocket. She tore off another edge of the bread and then reached for the tankard. She'd quickly gotten over sharing when she was so parched her mouth was dry as dirt. But the stuff in the jug was sweet tasting and she quaffed another large swig. It was a grave mistake as the drink went straight to her head in a hurry. She groaned and pressed her fingers against her temple, wishing like hell she'd not been so overzealous with the jug. Sean cut her a glance and pulled the jug away from her.

"That's enough drink, I should think." He put it far out of her reach.

Aoife was both glad and sad he'd taken it away. Sean looked her over, his eyes twinkling in the half-light.

"I think you've had plenty to eat, too." He pulled her fingers out of the remaining trencher and set aside the bread bowl.

"I was…going to eat that." Her words slurred, even though she tried hard to keep them steady.

"No, you're done." When he couldn't find anything to wipe her hands on, he used the edge of his tunic. "You should get some sleep. We have a long day ahead of us tomorrow."

"Pshaw." She waved away the comment as if it were nothing more than a gnat. "I'm not tired." Yet she yawned so wide, her jaw cracked.

But Sean gave her a gentle nudge to lie back on the bed. He pulled off her boots and then covered her with the scratchy blanket. He blew out the one candle, plunging the room into darkness with only the moonlight slashing through the grubby window. She could hear him heave a heavy sigh as he settled on the floor under the window facing the door.

But she wasn't finished talking. She still had more questions and she needed answers. Despite the fact the room seemed to waver under her. She blinked and tried hard to focus on what she wanted to ask him.

"Sean?"

"Yes?"

"Where did you learn to kill like that?"

There was a long silence and she thought for a moment he wasn't going to answer. Maybe even feign sleep. But she heard him breathe in deeply and then exhale.

"It's a long story."

"We have all night." She giggled again.

"No, we don't. We have to find Fiona tomorrow."

"That's tomorrow. I want you to answer my question now. You *owe* me that."

She shoved her upper body up and leaned on one elbow, squinting across the room to see him. He sat perfectly still staring up at the door with his hands behind his head and his feet crossed at the ankles.

"You're so cute, Sean. Why did you kiss me?" She'd blurted the words before he could answer.

In the darkness, she could see him drop his arms and turn his head but his eyes were nothing more than black orbs in the shadows.

"Because I wanted to."

"But *why?* I'm a troll."

"You are not," he said on a sigh. "Go to sleep, Aoife."

"My mother purposefully…" She slurred the word then hiccupped and tried again. "She made me ugly on purpose. And you liked me anyway."

"I could see through the glamour. I told you that."

"What did you see?" she whispered.

"A beautiful, lonely girl."

His words stabbed her right through the heart. She flopped to the bed and stared up at the cracked ceiling. God, he was right. She had been lonely her entire life. Never quite fitting in with anyone.

Now she discovered her entire life had been a lie. Nothing but a farce. She didn't even know her own face because it had been hidden from her ever since she could remember. Aoife reached up and ran the tips of her fingers over the slight points of her ears. They were *real.* Sean hadn't lied to her. He had told her the truth.

Her mother, though, had lied to her all her life. Did Liam know what Fiona was? Did Sunnie know she was half-Fae? Would the portal in the trunk call to her as it called to Aoife? Would she also end up in Faery? They were questions only Fiona could answer, so there was no use thinking about them now. Her thoughts went back to Sean and his mad killing skills. He never answered her question.

"Sean?"

A pause, then, "Yes, Aoife?"

"How did you know to kill those men?" She got back to her original question.

"Back to that, are we?"

"Yes. I really want to know."

"Part of my job in the Inter-Dimensional Portal Protection Agency is to keep out those who would destroy Faery. I am trained to kill and to defend the realm at all cost. Because it's my job and what I have to do."

Aoife stilled, her breathing halted. His voice was quiet in the darkness as he spoke, revealing things about himself she never knew. She turned her head to look at him and saw he still gazed at her. In the shadows she couldn't make out his expression. Despite knowing him all her life, she didn't really know him. He was practically a stranger to her. She wanted to know more, was happy she finally had a little insight into his past, and she wanted to ask more questions but she was unsure. So she waited.

"It was a long time ago." He exhaled a shaky breath. "I was recruited because I had special talents."

"What sort of special talents?"

He paused so long she thought he'd decided to keep it to himself. Then he said, "Magic." His voice was hollow, thin. "Deadly magic."

"You said you didn't have magic."

"That's true. I don't anymore. But once I was powerful. I was the youngest son of a noble many years ago. My magic manifested when I was young. Too young to understand or control it. I didn't know then I controlled it with my mind, a simple thought."

She shivered at how empty he sounded. How lost and lonely. She remained silent as he continued.

"There was an accident. My brother angered me and I reacted. I never meant to hurt anyone but the magic inside me was raw, violent. With one thought I could never take back, I killed my parents, my brother and my sister. I leveled the house. There was nothing left but soot and ash."

She pressed her cold fingers against her lips, her stomach cramping with the horror of it. "Sean, I'm so sorry."

"I'm not sure why I'm telling you this. I've never told anyone. The tragedy attracted the attention of the Agency and they took me in, saw me as an asset. They trained me and conditioned me to become an agent with a promising future."

Aoife knew there was more to the story. "That's how you learned to kill like that?"

"It is. They turned me into a weapon but when my magic was out of control and I could no longer be contained…" He paused, the silence settling between them. "I killed other agents. It took several of them to capture me. They…tortured me. They removed my magic, leaving me with only the ability to sift. I had to learn to fight with weapons. They retrained me and assigned me to you and Fiona. They thought I would be less of a threat there."

"I had no idea."

"You wouldn't. No one does except for the man who broke me." His voice was flat and full of disdain.

Despite the awful circumstances of how Sean came to the human realm, Aoife was really glad he had. She decided not to probe further. He'd told her enough of his dark past. She scooted to the very edge of the bed near the wall and patted the straw mattress.

"Come up here with me. The floor is no place to sleep."

"I best stay here." He sounded determined to stay put.

But Aoife was determined to have him next to her. "Come on, Sean. The floor is too drafty and hard."

He looked up at her, his eyes meeting hers. A heartbeat passed between them and for a moment she thought he wasn't going to move. But then he uncurled his body from the floor and stepped over to the bed. He lifted the edge of the blanket and climbed onto the bed next to her. They faced each other and she could, at last, see the contours of his face. Her fingertips fluttered over his cheekbones, making his eyes close.

"Aoife."

"Shh. Let me look at you."

"You can't see me in the dark." But he smiled as he said it.

"I can see you just fine, thank you."

"Aoife—"

"Shut it, will you? I'm thinking."

"Does it burn?"

She punched him on the arm, though she liked his playful tone. "I think I've always known you were there for me. Watching over me." She traced his strong, square jaw. "What did you do to those bullies?"

"Your train of thought is hard to follow." He grinned, eyes still closed. "And you don't want to know."

"Yes, I do. I really do."

"Your breath smells like mead."

"Is that what that stuff is called?" She giggled. "Tasted like juice to me. And I'm losing my buzz."

"I don't think you need any more."

"No, I don't need any more," she agreed. "I'll just get drunk on you."

That made his eyes pop open. "Aoife, you shouldn't say things like that."

"Why not? It's true. When I was fourteen, I had a mad crush on you but I didn't think you knew I existed."

"Oh, I knew." His hand landed on her hip and then slid upward to caress her back. "I knew you existed. I knew where you were at all times. I also knew those girls made you cry."

She bit her lip. "They were mean to me."

"They were. That's why I told them if they ever came near you again, I'd curse them and they would have bad luck the rest of their lives."

"You used magic on them?"

"I used the power of suggestion on them." He grinned. "And then I slipped Brad Roberts a twenty to make sure that Chastity tripped and fell in the middle of the hallway where everyone could see."

"She broke her nose." Aoife remembered well how the others made fun of her black eyes and her bandaged nose.

"She did. They left you alone after that, didn't they?"

Chastity was the popular girl. The one who picked on Aoife the most, called her four eyes and told her she was a troll. Brad Roberts was one of the jocks on the lacrosse team and had no love for the girl at all. Aoife had renewed respect for Sean.

"They did. Thank you for doing that for me."

"You're welcome." His arm tightened around her and he slid closer. "Do you still have a crush on me?"

"Still? I'm afraid I never stopped having a crush on you."

"I'm glad to hear that."

Before she could respond, his lips captured hers in a searing kiss. She melted against his hard body instantly, allowing her mind to clear. All she wanted was to concentrate on the way Sean's lips brushed against hers, the way he tasted her, the way his tongue delved into her mouth. All she wanted to think about was kissing him back. She could think of no other place she'd rather be than in his arms at this very moment.

She only wished it could last forever.

When they broke apart, he pulled her closer so her head could pillow on his chest. He held her so tight, she thought he would never let go.

"Aoife, I checked the compass. You mother is headed west toward Lambridge Castle."

"What's Lambridge Castle?" She toyed with the tie on his tunic, pulled it and then pushed open the laces. Her hand slipped inside, landing on warm skin covered in a sprinkling of dark hair. It was heaven. She didn't care what Lambridge Castle was, truly. All she cared about was touching him.

"Home of Prince Cian." He caught her hand, held it steady. "It will be dangerous. The castle is well-guarded and a large place and Cian is not that welcoming."

Reality kicked her and she stilled, trying to make her addled brain understand what he was saying. "So how do we find my mother then?"

He pulled her fingertips up to his lips, kissed the tips. "We'll figure that out when we get there. You should get some sleep."

"I don't want to sleep, Sean."

Her body pounded with need as she pressed against him. She knew what she wanted and she knew what he wanted, too. She could feel his hardened length press against her. She tugged the laces of her tunic and pushed it open in invitation. His gaze lingered on her cleavage. His hand caressing her back slipped under the material and smoothed over her skin.

"I don't think we should do this," he said.

"Why not?" She ran her tongue over her lower lip. Desire pricked through her nerves, making every inch of her sensitive to his touch. She relished the warmth of his hand on her back.

"Because…" He halted, his gaze lingering on her lips. "I can think of a thousand reasons why we shouldn't but only one good reason why we should."

Her breath caught, halting in her throat. She found the hem of his tunic and slid her hand under it, over his muscled chest, over every hard curve. "And that is?"

Sean pushed her to her back and cupped her breast, squeezed, then slid her nipple between thumb and forefinger making the hard bud pucker to a painful peak. She gasped with her delight and the need pounded to her warm wet center.

His mouth hovered over hers, his eyes gazed into hers. "I want you."

His lips captured hers before she could reply. She mewled deep in her throat as he continued to knead her breast. Her fingers fumbled with the laces on the waistband of his pants but he was way ahead of her. He shoved her hand out of the way and undid them, then went to work on hers.

His mouth never left hers as he pushed his hand under her waistband while her hand landed on his erection through the soft material of his pants. He halted before even touching her and waited. His mouth came away from hers when her palm slid down his length. He groaned deep and low in his throat as she stroked him there with the pads of her fingers.

"Touch me," she whispered. "I want you to touch me."

And, oh God, she had waited a lifetime for this moment. She had dreamed of it. She had wanted him forever, it seemed.

His fingers burned into her tingling skin as they slid down her body into to her damp curls, gently pushing against her swollen nub. A strangled gasp caught in her throat the same time he emitted a tormented groan. The sensual sensation went through her like a spark and she couldn't think. She couldn't move. Her hand halted stroking him but he didn't seem to notice or care as he continued to touch her, pushing deep and deeper.

Annoyance and impatience trickled through Aoife when she couldn't open her legs any wider to give him more access. She nipped his lower lip in her frustration. He seemed to understand as he pushed and shoved at her pants to get them out of the way. She kicked out her leg to help him and suddenly she had one leg out. Her knees fell open as he pressed his face against her neck and gave her a lick before pushing his fingers inside her.

She wrapped her arms around his neck, burying her hands in his hair and inhaling the deep scent of him. That bright smell of earth and sunshine that tingled her olfactory nerves and made her want him even more. His mouth was on her neck, tasting her while he continued to slide his fingers in and out of her and she rocked her hips against his hand in perfect tempo.

It was beautiful. It was perfect. It was everything she had ever imagined but she needed more. Her tangled fingers in his hair pulled his head back so their eyes could meet. She could see nothing of his expression other than his damp lips and yet a silent wave of communication passed between them.

Sean freed his erection from his pants and rolled on top of her. She opened her legs wider, allowing him to anchor his body between them and lower himself to her. She shivered in the delicious heat that rippled over her when he shoved up her tunic, exposing her pink peaks.

He hesitated and for a moment it seemed as though he had second thoughts. She reached for him, her hand colliding with his as she grasped his shaft and pumped him, tugging him closer and closer to her opening. His head went back, his eyes fluttered closed and then he slid home.

Aoife bit her lower lip to stop the cry that wanted to erupt. She had never felt anything more perfect than when she welcomed Sean into her body, mind and soul. Passion pounded through heart and head. In that moment, she'd forgotten everything and everyone. All that mattered was Sean.

He thrust into her over and over, his gaze never leaving her face. She reached for him, pulled him down on top of her and their mouths met in a fiery explosion. She clung to him, never wanting to release him and, it seemed, he clung to her. Holding her as close as he could get, keeping their bodies connected.

The orgasm built inside her at a rapid pace. She hadn't even thought about protection like she had with other guys. She somehow didn't care. She was with Sean. No matter what happened from now on, she could die happy.

He broke from her and buried his face again in the side of her neck. "I want to come." He whispered it against her skin, his breath hot and damp.

"Come. Come with me, Sean."

She closed her eyes and held on to him, focusing as all her muscles tensed as the orgasm built to an unstoppable peak. The wave of pleasure swelled and crested and a light pulsed through her, exploding against her closed eyes as Sean thrust one final time and halted, holding it there as he let his own climax subside. There was only the sound of their rasped breath.

"Aoife…you're…glowing."

"What?" Her eyes blinked open and, sure enough, a faint glow pulsed from her body. "I…don't understand."

"When you…" He paused, swallowed hard. "When you came, there was a bright light that pulsed out of you."

"You saw that?" She couldn't stop the flush that erupted over her cheeks. She thought that was something she'd imagined. Something only she saw behind her closed eyes.

In the darkness, she could see him nod. "It was unlike anything I'd ever seen."

"I'm sorry." She wanted to hide under the covers.

"Don't be sorry. It was beautiful."

She flushed again. "That's never happened before."

"It hasn't?" She shook her head. "Then I'm glad it happened with me. It was more beautiful than anything I've ever seen."

She could hear the smile in his voice and, oh how her heart squeezed. He gathered her to him, cuddling her against him.

"What do you think it means?" She nuzzled the base of his throat, delighting in the heady scent of him. Her hand landed on his chest and she could feel the fierce beat of his heart.

"I don't know. Do you feel any different?"

"No," she said around a wide yawn. "Do you still like me?"

He chuckled as he ran his fingers through her long thick locks. "I like you, Aoife. I like you a lot."

"Good." She yawned again. "Because I like you back."

Actually, she was madly in love with him but she couldn't say it to him. Not yet.

In the wee hours of the morning, long before dawn, Sean blinked awake and stared at the ceiling while Aoife slept in his arms. It gave him way too much time to think.

He should have never kissed her while they were in the dungeon in the tower of the wizard king. He should have kept his lips to himself and tamped down those amorous urges. But she had looked so fragile and upset when she learned the truth about her mother's trip back to Faery. The only thing he could think to do was kiss her.

He no longer thought of Aoife as that little girl with the big eyes and the fluttering eyelashes that blushed at him whenever she saw him. No. She was nothing like that girl anymore. She was luscious and a perfect fit against his frame. Whenever he held her against him, it was like he'd found that missing puzzle piece to complete him.

No, he shouldn't have kissed her. It had given him that first taste of her. It had drugged him and now that he'd experienced it, he was completely hooked. Addicted. Like an addict, he needed his next hit. He needed to taste her again but he needed more. One kiss would never be enough.

When Aoife invited him to climb into bed with her, his resolve not to fall for her weakened to the point of nonexistence. Resistance was futile. He was sucked in. He had to have her. And when she climaxed…

He smiled, glancing down at the perfect woman in his arms. Even hours later, her skin still held a golden glow. She stirred, coming awake slowly. Her eyes fluttered open and she peered up at him.

"Good morning." He brushed hair off her face.

Her smile faded as she sat up, color staining her high cheekbones. "We should get going."

With the absence of her from his arms, a coldness settled over him. He didn't like it. But she was right. They needed to find Fiona. He pushed up, bracing his weight on one elbow as he watched her flit around the room, gathering her clothes and dressing in a hurry. Her auburn hair was a mess about her face and she looked frazzled.

So beautiful. He couldn't help but smile.

She halted as she reached for a boot. "Why are you looking at me like that?"

"Because you're beautiful."

She flushed again and snatched the boot off the floor. "I don't know what came over me last night. I think I had too much to drink."

He scowled, disliking her excuses for their intimacy. He slid out of the bed, letting the blankets fall to the floor and expose his nakedness. She halted and stared at him with those big green eyes fringed in dark lashes. He stalked toward her but she matched him step for step as she backed up. She only stopped when she bumped into the wall. He braced one hand by her head and cupped her chin with the other.

"Let's get one thing straight, sweetheart. I don't regret anything that's happened between us. I especially don't regret last night."

She blinked those wide eyes and swallowed hard. "You don't?"

"No, I don't. You shouldn't either." To press his point, he leaned against her, naked body and all. Much to his delight she shivered.

A breath shuddered out of her and she dragged her lower lip through her teeth. Oh, he loved when she did that. It drove him mad. He focused on her lips—perfect, red lips—before looking back into her eyes. Her mouth parted as if to say something then clamped closed again.

"Tell me."

"I…" But she broke off and clamped her mouth shut.

"Tell me what you're thinking, damn it, Aoife. I'm not going to get angry. I *will* get angry if you don't tell me."

She swallowed hard again. "I don't want anything to change between us." She hiccupped as if that was the hardest thing she'd ever admitted.

The fight went out of him as he relaxed but remained pressed against her. He caressed her face. "I don't either."

"No?"

He really wished she would stop batting those lashes at him. It made him want to throw her on the bed and ravish her again. "No. I meant it when I told you I liked you."

"So did I," she whispered.

"Good. Since that's settled, let's get on the road."

He punctuated it with a quick kiss then turned and started to dress. But when he glanced her way, she still had a dreamy look on her face. She hadn't made a move to dress. She still stood there with clothes balled in her arms.

"Aoife?"

She blinked, coming out of her trance. "There's…something else I want to tell you."

She paused and he could see the wheels turning in her head as she considered her next words.

"And what is that?"

Her gaze focused on his face. "I…I don't want you to think you have to say it, too. It's something I've wanted to tell you for a long time." She worried her bottom lip again.

Sean stiffened, his nerve-endings on high alert. He suspected he knew what she was getting at and he wasn't sure he was ready to hear it. He knew he wasn't ready to say it but the way she looked at him, the way stains of scarlet appeared on the apples of her cheeks made desire flood his system. God, she was beautiful and he wanted her. He was glad he managed to pull on his trousers to hide his erection.

"Go on, Aoife." His voice was soft, encouraging.

Her eyes fluttered downward and she took an interest in the pile of clothes she still held. "I love you, Sean. I've loved you all my life. I've wanted you all my life and now…" The clothes slipped from her hands, spilling on the floor at her feet. "Now everything *will* change."

He knew what she meant. They could never go back to being just friends. Or pretending there was nothing more between them. He wasn't sure he could tell her he loved her back. He wanted to, but their situation was complicated enough without adding their feelings to the mix.

"Aoife—"

Her eyes lifted and she met his gaze. "No matter what we say or what promises we make to each other, things will change, Sean. I know that. You know that. But I think I can live for the rest of my days now because I got to spend the night with you. No matter what happens from now on, I will always cherish that."

He was stunned to silence as she picked up her clothes, turned and quickly finished dressing. With a sort of numbness, he pulled on his tunic and boots. As they left the inn, Sean knew one thing was for certain. He would always love Aoife.

Chapter 18

All the way to Lambridge Castle, Fiona shot Prince Cian dagger eyes. Not that he could see her. He was too busy fawning all over Winnie. He'd tucked the girl in front of him, holding her close whispering to her so only she could hear. She would smile at him in a girlish, flirty way and then her cheeks would redden with a comely blush.

Fiona seethed, watching as the man shamelessly tried to seduce the girl. Not that he knew she was there. She'd managed to keep the glamour spell in place since it didn't take as much power. Even so, it enraged her to see him do what he'd always done with the ladies.

And it enraged her Niall had been right about him. The images he'd shown her oh-so-long ago in the Time Sphere had been true. Not that she'd truly doubted them but to see him actively pursuing the girl in person was a slap in the face.

When they arrived, Cian and Winnie trotted off toward the stables. He helped the girl from the horse while his men took Fiona and led her directly to the dungeon. That was the last she'd seen of the prince and her handmaiden. She'd been dumped in a cell and mostly forgotten. Oh, she'd been fed and watered like some farm animal but no one else knew of her existence.

She paced the small confines of the cell as agitation clawed through her. Not only had the guards taken her weapons, but also her cloak which also meant they had the Tears of the Dryad. Which also meant she was stuck in the cell until her magic returned.

Somewhere in the dungeon, a door creaked open and then footsteps echoed. She halted her pacing and leaned against the wall, trying her best to act casual. She expected it was the guard bringing her food. To her surprise, Prince Cian and two guards arrived outside her cell.

His handsome face was impassive. She'd seen that look enough times to know he was hiding behind his cool demeanor ready to pounce.

"Do you wish to confess?" he asked.

"Confess what?"

"You were part of the conspiracy to kidnap my betrothed, weren't you?"

She blinked surprise. This is what he'd surmised from capturing her at the gruesome location? What else had Winnie told him? "I was not."

"I don't believe you." His sharp voice sliced through the dead air.

Frustration bubbled through her and her hands clenched. She'd had plenty of time to think about what was said at the carriage site. Cian intended to kill her and her family. There wasn't to be a wedding after all. What would killing her accomplish? War with Niall? Mayhap that's what they both wanted.

"Your Highness, do you think I would have buried the dead and stuck around to help Winnie if I was involved in the conspiracy to kidnap the girl?"

"That still doesn't explain why you were there." He folded his arms over his chest.

She huffed out a breath. "I told you. I was passing through."

"That road is not so well-traveled these days with so many highwaymen on the prowl. I find it difficult to believe you were merely passing through." He took a step closer to the bars. So close she could almost reach for him and lamented her low magic. "Now why don't you tell me the truth."

Something sparked in her past memory of the guards telling her father Prince Cian wished to make sure she was safe on the road to the castle, that the wizard king had been raiding local villages and attacking travelers along the road. But that wasn't true at all.

When Cian and his men had come upon the scene, one of the guards had said someone *beat his men to it*. Had the guards assigned to escort them to the castle been tasked with killing the entire traveling party before arriving? It seemed ludicrous and yet at the same time there could be no other explanation.

Fiona steeled herself, lifted her chin and looked down at Cian.

"That is the truth." Which of course was a lie. She could not divulge her true appearance. He would never understand she was from the future.

"It seems to me the only explanation for a weakling girl such as yourself to dig all those graves would be that she used magic. Did you use magic?" One eyebrow quirked. "I despise magic users."

"You said as much already and I used my hands." Not an outright lie, but not the truth either.

Prince Cian gave her a crucial piece of the puzzle—another reason why he hated Niall so much. Perhaps Cian could not wield magic and therefore, he hated everyone who could. Especially his half-brother who also happened to have wizard blood.

His gaze landed on her hands and narrowed. He was still unconvinced. "You were there when Lady Winnie awoke. She told me she overhead a man saying he was taking Lady Fiona to the wizard king. Are you working for King Niall?"

"No."

Lady Winnie? The girl was nothing more than a servant. How had she been elevated to a lady in so short a time? Everything Niall told her about Cian was true—he was nothing but a womanizer.

"So you had no hand in the kidnapping of my betrothed?"

"I did not."

A pause as he considered her answer, though it was clear he was still unconvinced. "If you will not willingly tell me the truth, then you give me no other choice."

Her stomach clenched. "And what is that?"

"If you choose not to confess the truth by the morrow, then I shall force you." He leaned toward her and they were only separated by the bars of the cell. "That won't be pleasant for either of us."

Cian strode away with a confident gait. Fiona balled her fists, allowing the anger to punch through her. She lifted her hand, palm upward but nothing happened. She was unable to produce any sort of magic. It must still be depleted. She had never lost her magic for so long before but using it to dig all the graves plus her emotional state exhausted her.

All she needed was a little magic, a little spark to melt the lock on the door like she had in Niall's dungeon. She leaned against the cool stone wall and closed her eyes, remembering lessons from long ago with Deaglan.

When she tired, he would tell her to find her center. To concentrate on that silvery thread of her magic. To allow it to replenish itself by meditation. She put her palms together and held her hands against her chest over her heart and quieted her mind.

How long she stood there, she knew not. But she thought she

heard footsteps, a guard slipping a tray of food into the cell and then leaving again. She had let her body relax and her mind shut down and when she finally opened her eyes, renewed strength coursed through her.

There were two uneaten meals in her cell. A rat gnawed on the loaf of bread the guard brought. She kicked it aside and the thing squealed and scurried back to the shadows. She would not die here.

Standing in front of the cell door, she closed her hand into a fist. It took several moments for the light to flicker in her palm but she felt it at last and then opened her hand. A blue-white glow danced in her hand. Smiling, she directed it to the lock of the cell. It hit the metal with a sizzle and then melted it. She pushed open the door and stepped into the corridor.

It had been many years since she'd been in Lambridge Castle but she recalled the layout as though it had been yesterday. The only place she could think to start was in the prince's chamber—a risk, she knew.

As she stepped out of the dungeon, she changed her glamour to one that was of a lady so she would be less conspicuous. She needed the Tears of the Dryad to escape using a portal and she had no idea what had happened to her cloak or her dagger.

She neared the dining hall and heard boisterous laughter. It gave her pause. One would think with his betrothed kidnapped, the prince would be moving heaven and earth to get her back. But, nay. Music floated from the room and she slipped inside and halted near the doorway to take in the sight.

She couldn't believe what she saw. The prince had Winnie seated next to him at the high table at a place of honor. He fed her slices of juicy meat, nuzzled her neck making the girl blush to the roots of her hair. A small group played cheerful music on one side of the room and the crowd laughed as though it was a joyous occasion.

It did nothing but ignite the rage all over again. She balled her fists, felt the heat pulsing in her palms and took a deep breath. It wouldn't do to attack him with her magic here in front of all to see. She would be arrested and tossed back into the dungeon. Or—worse—killed.

A messenger scurried into the dining hall and made straight for Prince Cian. The prince spotted him, placed a hand on Winnie's and waited as he approached the high table. The boy spoke to the prince, who nodded and fixed a grave expression on his face.

He rose then and waited for the music to stop and all those in the dining hall to turn their attention to him. He commanded that sort of interest whenever he stood and the people of his court obeyed.

"I have received word about my betrothed, your future queen. She has been kidnapped by the wizard king."

A collective gasp went around the room. Fiona pushed off the wall and stood straighter, peering at him and wondering what game he was playing. He already knew. This was not news. But the kingdom didn't know and now he wanted to make a good show of it.

"I shall mobilize my army straightaway and bring her back forthwith."

He made a motion to the messenger who bowed and scurried out. Fiona watched the boy hurry to one side of the room where the prince's advisor, Finnegan, pressed a small bag of coins into the boy's hand.

So, that's the way it was to be, then. Prince Cian would look like a hero. His assassination attempt had failed but now he had a greater cause—her own kidnapping.

"Please, pray continue the banquet. Let this be a feast of preparation for the morrow when we shall go to war against Illyria and her king!"

A shout of triumph rippled through the crowd. Fiona sank back against the wall, hating him even more. The music started up again, the dancers went back to dancing and the rest of the nobles went back to feasting. In that moment, it was clear to her the people of Anatolia had no love for her whatsoever. A wave of relief went through her. Relief that she hadn't married him after all. That she had never come to the kingdom. That she had ended up with Niall.

What a fool she'd been to think Cian wanted anything to do with her.

He took Winnie by the hand and led her out of the dining hall. Fiona spun and turned her back to him so he wouldn't see her, not that he would recognize her. But she didn't want to take any chances. They walked from the dining hall and into the main corridor. Fiona slipped in behind them, watching as they made their way to the castle gardens.

She followed on silent feet. She had spent many an hour in the castle gardens with Cian but he had never held her hand or slipped an arm around her as he did with Winnie. They made their way to a stone bench under a tree, the late afternoon sun casting long shadows along the pathway. Fiona paused, hiding behind a rosebush fragrant with yellow and white roses. With her heart pounding in her ears, she held her breath and waited.

"But what about Lady Fiona?" Winnie asked.

"I've sent my men to march to the Towers of Illyria," he said. "They march toward the towers now. On the morrow I will follow to reclaim my bride."

Fiona shook her head in disgust. Even if he was telling the girl the truth, he didn't seem to be in much of a hurry.

"Your help has been invaluable," he went on. "And for that I wish to give you a small token of my thanks."

He took her hands in his, kissed each palm. When he released one of her hands, he reached into his pocket. He placed the small bottle of glittery pink Tears of the Dryad into Winnie's hand. Fiona covered her mouth with her hand to stifle the gasp. He had no idea the power he had given over to the girl. If he did, surely he would have used it to get to Niall. The fool.

"Oh, it's lovely. What is it?" She shook it up, watching as the sparkles danced inside the gel liquid.

"Fairy dust," Cian said.

What a smooth liar he was. Or did he truly not know what he possessed? Had he never seen a magical potion? Likely, he hadn't. Niall's magic was not due to potions and hexes. He was a spellcaster.

"Really?" She moved to open it and Fiona stiffened. But Cian put his hand over hers and stopped her.

"You must never open it."

"Why not?"

"Because it will never sparkle again."

Fiona stifled a gag. She had no idea where he'd gotten that idea. At least Winnie hadn't opened it. Should the girl spill a drop of the substance, it could be disastrous.

"So it's merely to look at?" she asked.

"Aye."

He smiled at her before leaning over and kissing her cheek. But he didn't stop there. His kisses trailed down her neck. He pulled aside the material of her gown and kissed her shoulder, too. If there was a definition of a heaving bosom, Winnie's was it at that moment. Fiona rolled her eyes.

Cian whispered something to make her blush.

"I don't think I should," she said. "Lady Fiona—"

"Is your friend?"

She nodded.

"Your loyalty is endearing which is quite attractive," he said.

Realization dawned and Winnie gave him a nudge and scooted away from him. "My apologies, Your Highness, but I never meant to lead you on. Lady Fiona is my mistress. I don't wish to betray her."

Prince Cian stiffened and tugged down his tunic. Fiona wanted to erupt in a cheer but instead tamped it down.

"I see, then. Mayhap I should walk you back to your chamber."

"I am quite tired. It's been a trying time."

They stood and headed out of the castle gardens. Prince Cian tried to seduce the girl and she'd rebuffed him. With her heart in her throat, Fiona followed, keeping far enough back to make sure neither would suspect. He led her up the stairs to the second level. He opened the door to the chamber, bid her goodnight and waited until she was inside and the door closed before he turned.

Fiona pressed her back against the wall, trying her best to hide in the shadows. The rage and annoyance on the man's face startled her. When he stomped away, oblivious to her presence, she hurried to Winnie's door. Now was her chance to get the Tears of the Dryad from the girl and get out of the castle before her disappearance from the dungeon was discovered.

She didn't even knock before pushing open the door. The girl jumped, startled at Fiona's sudden intrusion. The large room had a wardrobe on the far wall with the one window and a canopied four-poster bed draped with thick velvet curtains. The curtains nearest the window had been drawn to block out the chill since there was no fireplace.

"Who are you?"

"I've come to…" She paused, then dipped a curtsey. "I've come to assist you."

Relief spread on her face. "Oh, thank you. I'm so out of sorts here, I don't know what to do with myself." She reached into the pocket on her gown and brought out the vial of Tears of the Dryad. Fiona's heart skipped a beat.

"That's lovely. What is it?" she asked nodding to it.

"Faery dust." The girl grinned and shook it up. "Isn't it beautiful?"

"Quite. May I see it?" She held out her hand.

Winnie was about to place it in her palm when there was a sharp knock on the door. She put it back in her pocket. Damn the luck.

When the girl opened the door, she heard her uncertain voice. "Your Highness?"

Fiona melted behind the bed, hiding behind the velvet curtains. Even though she had her true appearance hidden behind a glamour, she didn't want to take any chances. She heard the door slam.

"You think to refuse me," Cian said.

Fiona recognized that horrible tone of voice. It reminded her of the night he'd raped her. Her heart kicked into a fast beat as she pressed against the wall, hidden in the corner next to the wardrobe.

"Your Highness, please—"

But her words were cut off by a whimper.

"I take what I want, when I want."

There was a rustle of material and the muffled voice of the girl and Fiona knew, without a doubt, what was happening. She had to do something. She couldn't stand there and allow him to rape her, too. She glanced around, looking for a weapon but found nothing. If she was going to act, she had to act quickly.

Steeling her nerves, she rounded the bed and saw the horror unfolding. He had pushed the girl down on the bed face first. Her skirts were up over her hips while he fumbled with the tie on his pants. With the adrenaline pumping in a mad rush through her, she lunged. She wrapped her arm around his neck from behind and jerked as hard as she could.

Startled, he released the girl as he choked and gasped for air. Winnie flipped over, shock on her tear-stained face. It took all of Fiona's strength to hang on to him but he was stronger. He elbowed her in the side, jabbing her in the ribs. She loosened her grip enough for him to turn. He grabbed her, flung her to the stone floor. She cracked her elbow against it. Before she could recover from that, he kicked her in the stomach. That's when she felt the magic of her glamour flicker. She had to get out of here before she lost the spell altogether.

Winnie scurried off the bed and tried to make a break for it but it did nothing but enrage him further. He caught her by the arm, pulled her to him in a ferocious yank and palmed her breast.

"I'm not finished with you." Then he looked down at Fiona. "I'll have my guards deal with you."

Fiona, though, in one last defiance, climbed to her hands and knees and looked up at him. "You're a disgrace to the crown."

His boot met her cheek. Pain exploded across her face as she fell back against the cold floor. Tears stung her eyes. Cian dragging a whimpering Winnie away was the last thing she saw before she fainted.

Chapter 19

It took two days to get to Lambridge Castle. After they left the inn, Sean bargained for a horse to cut down on the travel time. Aoife knew he could have sifted, but she also knew that she would have been left behind. The last thing she wanted was to be left behind. Not that Sean even suggested that. He knew how important it was to her to get to her mother.

They didn't speak about their night together or her confession afterward. She secretly hoped Sean would profess his love for her in return but he hadn't. He looked as if someone had hit him with a two-by-four upside the head. She didn't think his face could drain of any more color by the way he had looked at her.

She hated herself for saying it. She should have kept her mouth shut and her feelings bottled up. But she thought if she took the chance, he would declare mutual feelings for her. He seemed as though he had mutual feelings for her by the way he talked to her about her past. He had always been there for her, after all. When he hadn't reciprocated, her chest constricted to the point she thought she would stop breathing. The ache hadn't totally gone away either. It still remained.

The glow of her skin faded to a dull shimmer, like someone hit a mute button. It was a constant reminder of their lovemaking. If she could have scrubbed it away with a bar of soap, she would have.

She rode in front of him on the horse, his warm body pressed against hers. It did nothing to soothe her bruised ego and everything to ignite the desire within her. How she could still want him after being rejected, she didn't know.

No, that wasn't true. He hadn't rejected her. He merely failed to fall on his knees and profess his undying love for her. It hadn't gone at all as she imagined.

They galloped at full speed so there wasn't a lot of chitchat. Otherwise things would really be awkward.

On the second day of their travels, as the castle came into view on the hilltop, Sean pulled the horse to a stop. Lambridge was like something out of a fairytale with its peaked turrets and heraldry flapping in the stiff wind to signal to whom the castle belonged. Behind her, he fumbled with the compass to open it and held it in front of her so they could both see the needle bouncing toward the castle.

"There it is." Sean's voice was soft in her ear, his heated breath tickling her skin. It made her shudder in delight.

"My mother is there?"

"She is."

"How do we get in?"

"That, my dear, is going to be the real trick."

He kicked the horse back into a gallop. The closer they got, the more she realized there was a lot of activity outside the walls. There was an encampment. The hillside was dotted with white canvas tents. Laughter and music and the whinny of horses could be heard on the wind. Scents of roasted meats and campfires were in the air. Sean slowed the horse to a trot.

"What's going on? Is that normal?" she asked.

"It's not normal," he replied. "It looks to me like he's preparing for battle."

He turned the horse into a copse of trees and dismounted, then held his hands up to Aoife. She hesitated only a moment before she reached for him. His hands landed on her waist as he helped her from the horse. When she landed in front of him, they were nose to nose. She could easily get lost on those dreamy brown eyes.

"Do you suppose he's heading to the Towers of Illyria to rescue the Fiona of the past?" she asked, remembering Niall's tale. It was odd to think of her mother in two separate tenses—one past, one present. Or was that future? It was all too confusing.

He nodded. "Possibly. With such a large army, it seems as though he's prepared to fight for her."

"But he doesn't get her," Aoife reminded him. "If Niall told us the truth he will return here without her."

"And past Fiona is still at the Towers of Illyria while our Fiona is here." He looked toward the castle and took a deep breath. "I hope she had the sense to use a glamour and hide her face from Cian or…"

"Or what?" She swallowed hard, both desperate to know the answer and fearful.

Sean returned his gaze to her. "Or she could be dead by now."

She shook her head. "No. I refuse to believe that. She's in there and we'll find her. We have to."

Despite everything that had happened between them, Aoife didn't want to give up on her mother. Not yet. Something deep inside her told her she could change her mind about this crazy quest in the past. That she could convince her otherwise and maybe they could make things right between them. It would take time, but maybe they could at least start down the path to reconcile.

A slow smile pulled at the corner of his mouth. "I hope so, my lady. I truly do. Let's head toward the camp and see what we can find out."

"How do we do that?" she asked.

He flashed a grin. "We listen. Stay behind me. Don't make eye contact with any of them and above all, don't speak to them."

"Why not?"

"Because you're a beautiful woman, Aoife, and they are men who need a place to put their lonely penises."

She swallowed hard, nodding understanding and moved closer to him. She had to remember this was a different world here and even though she'd been with Sean for most of her time in Faery, she knew it was still a dangerous place.

"Got it. I'll keep my mouth shut then."

He took her by the hand, lacing their fingers. "There's one more thing I want to ask you." He paused, his gaze searching hers. "Your magic. Can you tell if it's manifested yet?"

"My magic?"

"Do you feel any different? Don't answer right away. Think about it."

She considered. While she did feel somewhat different after their time together, she chalked that up to being on an emotional high and nothing more. But if she was being honest with herself, she would admit the feeling hadn't really dissipated at all. She still felt as though she were on that emotional high. Or buzzed as if she'd had too much caffeine.

"I don't..." She halted, bit her lip. "Yes, I do. A little. But I thought it was because...never mind. Why do you ask?"

His hands slipped up her arms, leaving gooseflesh in their wake. "Because I feel different, Aoife. I think when we were together...I think it recharged me somehow. It feels like my magic is back."

"What does that mean?"

"It means being in Faery and being with you has altered me." He cupped her face, held her gaze. "If it altered me, then it altered you."

She knew it would happen. That it would come to this. Things between them *had* changed and would continue to change. A lump formed in her throat and she swallowed hard. His gaze hadn't left hers and it was so intense, she shivered. Aoife recalled the story he'd told her about killing his family. About his wild magic. Wild, uncontrollable magic.

"But…you said they removed your magic," she said.

"I did say that," he replied with a nod. "But there's been a change. As though it was only dormant all this time and it took something…someone…to awaken it."

"And you think I'm that someone?"

"If it's back—and I think it is because I haven't felt this way in many years—then I can't stay with you, Aoife. You or Fiona. You'll both be in danger. I can't risk it."

Aoife was shaking her head before he even finished. "Don't talk like that. I won't let you."

"Aoife, I can't risk hurting you or your mother."

"And I can't stay in this world without you. I *won't* stay in this world without you. You don't know what's going to happen. Maybe something has changed inside you."

"Something *has* changed inside me. That's what I'm trying to tell you."

"Maybe it will be different this time."

"I have never been able to control it before."

She wrapped her arms around his waist, pulling him closer. "I won't let you leave me. I'll help you."

"How?"

Sean halted, not saying anymore but she could read it in his eyes. She knew he wanted to ask her how she expected to help him when she knew nothing of her own magic. She didn't know the answer to that but she was determined to find it. His thumb traced her cheekbone.

"The magic inside me has always been wild and unmanageable. I care about you too much to let anything happen to you, especially by my own hands."

Her heart skipped a beat. He cared about her. Was that as close to a confession of love as she was going to get? She could give him more time, but not if he intended to leave her.

He dropped his hands and reached into his pocket, bringing out the gold coin Niall had given him. "Take this. When we find Fiona, you two will go to Niall and he'll help you get home."

And just like that, her heart nearly stopped beating altogether. "What about you? How will you get home?"

"Don't worry about me." He reached for her hand and tried to press the coin into her palm but she refused.

"No, Sean. We stick together. I don't care what happens. We are all staying together."

"Aoife—"

"No. I mean it."

He sighed and pocketed the coin. "All right."

"Now. What about my magic? What do I do about that?"

"We have to find Fiona. She'll know how to help you." He kissed the tip of her nose. "Let's go get her."

Fiona woke with a horrible pain shooting through her upper body. She had no idea how long she'd been out but everything hurt. It took a lot of strength to lift her head and take in her surroundings. She had been moved to the dungeon once again. This time, her jailers had shackled her wrists to the wall over her head. Her hands were numb and yet she could feel the cold bite of metal—iron—against her wrists.

Iron rendered her magic useless. Iron meant she had lost her glamour. Her heart kicked into overdrive. By the gods, if she had no glamour, then Cian would recognize her. He would think he had the real Fiona of *this* time and then who knew what would happen to her. Would he kill her? Or keep her prisoner while he married her and took his marriage rights by force?

The very thought sickened her.

She jerked on her shackles, but it was no use. Without her magic, she was as good as dead.

Somewhere a door scraped open and closed with a slam and then footsteps followed. She lifted her head and faced the danger head on. She would not cower. If she was going to die here, in this time, so be it. But he wasn't going to get her without a fight.

Prince Cian and several guards halted outside her cell, peering in at her as though she were a caged animal at a zoo. She braced herself, waiting for him to recognize her. But he merely stood there not moving, his face impassive.

"Have you decided to confess?"

Her brows drew together in confusion. "What am I confessing?" Her voice cracked with her dry throat and lips.

"You don't recall?" He huffed out a breath. "That you had a hand in the death of my betrothed's family. That you also tried to stop me from taking what was mine."

Winnie. Oh, gods, he hurt Winnie. If she ever got out of here, she would make sure he paid for that. Her hands clenched, the burning tingling sensation pricking every finger. But something he said sparked a little hope inside her—he said *his betrothed*. Did that mean he *didn't* recognize her? And if not, how was that possible? She knew for sure her glamour couldn't be in place with the iron shackles around her wrists.

"I did not kill them," she said at last. "They were already dead when I found them. Save for the girl. The girl you viciously raped."

"She consented," he said. "She wanted me as much as I wanted her."

Fiona surged forward, her chains jangling. "Filthy liar!"

Cian gave a nod of his head and one of the guards unlocked the door. They poured in. One held a sword on her while two others unlocked her wrists. She pitched forward, unable to control her numb muscles and collapsed on the ground. Her arms and legs burned from being stationary for so long.

It was in that instant she understood why Cian didn't know who she was. In the flickering half-light of the dank dungeon, she could see her reflection in a pool of water on the stone floor. Her face had been beat almost to beyond her own recognition. She had two black eyes. Her cheekbone was swollen, red, with a large gash down the center. Her bottom lip was also cut and swollen. She remembered Cian kicking her in Winnie's chamber, but she did not recall such a brutal beating.

Had she been unconscious for that? She hoped so.

Cian grabbed a handful of hair and yanked her head up so she had no choice but to look at him.

"You call me a filthy liar when you're the one who has been lying all along. I'm done playing with you. You refuse to give me the truth so you will give me your life instead." He released her and stepped back. "Take her to the gallows. She hangs today."

For Cian, it wasn't enough she was beaten. Two of the guards hauled her to her feet and started for the open door. She reached for the silvery thread of magic that resided deep inside her, but she couldn't find it. It was as though it had been snuffed out.

Panic set in. She had to find a way out of this mess but what could she do? She had been so dependent on her magic she had no idea how to fight back. If she only had been able to get the Tears of the Dryad, she could have made it out of this wretched place.

They took her up the stairs and paraded her through the castle. Along the way, they collected more spectators who followed them toward the courtyard where the gallows awaited. They bound her hands in front of her, the rope biting through her already raw wrists, and positioned her on the platform over the trapdoor. A guard behind her placed the noose around her neck.

Prince Cian stood in front of her, the crowd cheering behind him as he looked at her with triumph written all over his face. Several people threw rotten vegetables, rocks, and whatever else they could get their hands on. All Fiona could do was stand there and take it.

At last Cian lifted his hand for silence and a hush fell over the mob.

"This prisoner is a threat to the crown and a traitor. She is single-handedly responsible for the death of my beloved's family."

The crowd shouted obscenities as she released a snort of derision that was lost in the noise. Cian waited for them to quiet again.

"Those who defy the crown are given a fair trial. A trial that will determine their guilt. This prisoner refused to cooperate time and time again. She has been punished, as you can see by her face. But she will also die today for her sins—for killing and for her traitorous actions."

As he spoke, Fiona scanned the crowd. The dirty faces of the commoners who lived within the castle's domain, the guards who stood with stoic expressions on their faces, the nobility who looked at her with a mix of pity or amusement. And then she saw them. The couple moving along the back of the crowd, the man's gaze fixed on Fiona. The girl standing behind him as though he were a shield. The girl with auburn hair and bright green eyes.

Hot tears clouded her vision and her eyes fluttered closed. Sean, by the gods, had come to find her. He must have the compass. She'd only just remembered the tracking tattoo on her shoulder. And Aoife—her daughter. Her beautiful, magical daughter who's skin had a hint of a glow. Fiona knew then her magic had manifested.

Her eyes flew open and she pinpointed Sean with her gaze and then glanced between him and Aoife. If her daughter's magic had manifested, then that could mean only one thing. The fight went out of her. At least she could leave this world knowing that Sean loved Aoife, that he would take care of her, that he would protect her.

Drums rolled, signaling her impending doom. She held her head up. If she had to die in front of her child, she would do it with dignity. She would die knowing she had failed in her quest to change history. And she would be glad of that.

She waited for her fateful drop with the noose around her neck, the beat of her heart matching the pounding of the execution drums. She kept her gaze on Sean and Aoife, wondering why they were there. Wondering if their appearance meant she would not die this day after all.

And then she had her answer. An explosion rocked the entire courtyard. The ground shook, the gallows vibrated and the next thing she knew she fell. The rope around her neck caught. She gasped as it choked her, her arms flailing. Her wrists still bound, she tried to pull the noose away from her throat.

A shriek from the crowd she thought belonged to Aoife. Shouts—Cian's voice. Other voices she couldn't pick out. Screaming. Another explosion. Pandemonium.

A second later the taut rope gave way and she was falling, falling, falling through the trap door and toward the ground. But the ground morphed from hard packed earth to a pile of soft hay. She landed, rolled and came to rest, coughing and retching and trying to catch her breath. Her eyes watered as she gasped.

Fiona had no clue what had just happened, other than she hadn't hanged that day. She'd lived and she was certain Sean and Aoife were responsible for her rescue.

They'd come to save her, not watch her die.

Another explosion rocked the area. She lifted her head to see half the inner bailey and some of the castle behind her on fire.

People scurried about. Some trying to put out the fire. Others trying to get out of the bailey. Someone skidded to a halt and crouched next to her.

"Mother."

Her voice, so quiet and full of anguish, made Fiona look into her daughter's clear green eyes. She blinked, sure what she saw was true. She had spotted the faint glow to Aoife's skin and knew she'd changed. A change Fiona recognized.

"Aoife. You're glowing."

"Mother, what happened to your face?" Aoife ignored her and grasped her, pulling her to her feet. "Come on. We have to get you out of here."

"Cian. He'll stop you. You'll never get by him."

"Don't worry about that. Sean is taking care of him."

"Sean. Where is he?" Fiona craned her neck to look for him, but didn't see him anywhere in the vicinity. Nor could she locate Prince Cian which was most troublesome. "Where's Cian?"

"Gone for now. Mother, come on. We have to *go.*" She pulled at her arm.

Fiona refused to move. There was someone else she needed to save. Someone else who needed her help more than anyone. "Winnie. I have to get Winnie out of here."

"Who's Winnie?"

"My handmaiden. At least, she was in the past. She's a prisoner in the castle. I have to get her out."

"You're in no shape to rescue anyone," Aoife said, her tone sharp and authoritative.

Aoife gave her a nudge away from the fires that burned hot. It had caused such chaos no one even noticed Fiona had made it away from the gallows. Sean ran toward them, a sword in his hand and his face covered in dirt.

"Why are you still here? I told you to take her and get out."

"I'm trying but she won't move." Aoife didn't hide the agitation in her voice.

Sean took up Fiona's other side and the three of them started to hurry out of the bailey.

"Your glamour spell has failed, Fiona. We have to get you out of here," he said.

"I know it has. I've lost my magic. What did you do, Sean? How did you get in here? Did *you* use magic?"

"I'll tell you later. Right now we have to get as far away from here as possible."

"Do you? I wouldn't count on that at all."

The three of them came to a halt and stared down the sword point of several guards and in the center of them all was Prince Cian.

They had been caught.

Chapter 20

Sean moved to stand in front of Aoife and her mother, as though he were still her protective shield. He pointed his drawn sword back at the others, unflinching and unyielding. It made her stupid heart flutter.

"Put down your sword," Cian ordered.

"No," Sean said. "We're walking out of here."

"Not with my prisoner you're not. And, thank you very much, you've made yourselves prisoners. Did you help her kill my betrothed's family on the road?"

"Your betrothed?" Sean's brows drew together.

Aoife knew then Prince Cian didn't have a clue that Fiona stood in front of him. She was so bloody and beaten in the face, he must not recognize her. Which also meant someone else did the beating. It was a blessing in disguise since Fiona's glamour spell had failed.

"I found her," Cian waved his sword toward Fiona, "amidst the massacre. My beloved's family was murdered in cold blood."

"Don't listen to him," Fiona said. "He planned to kill them all himself. Niall's men beat him to it."

"So you admit it was King Niall. I believe she had something to do with it. I also believe she buried the dead using magic," Cian said. "I have a strong distaste for magic users. A pity the gallows burned to the ground. There are other ways to execute you though."

"Your Highness!" A shout from a messenger interrupted them. The boy ran through the bailey, his threadbare cloak billowing behind him. "I come with an urgent message, Your Highness." He handed over a scroll sealed with red wax.

Cian snatched it out of his hand, opened it and scanned the contents. "Niall plans to marry Lady Fiona, the bloody son of a bitch. He's stealing my bride. But by the gods he will not steal my throne." He crumpled the parchment in a fist as he glanced up at the three of them. "A pity your execution will have to wait until my return. Take them to the dungeon and ready my horse. I depart at once. We all do."

Cian strode away as Sean squared off with the remaining guards and Aoife knew he wasn't going to let them take him without a fight.

"You can come with us willingly or you can die," said one of the guards.

Aoife placed a hand on his arm. "Sean, let's do as he says."

"The girl is right," Fiona said, her voice still raspy. "Better to live and fight another day than to die here."

Sean gave her a quizzical look Aoife didn't miss. She knew he didn't like surrendering so easily but it seemed they had no real choice. She also knew he could wipe them out with a thought. She gave him an imploring look. He dropped his sword, his face a grim mask of annoyance.

The guards escorted the three of them to the dungeons. Since her arrival in Faery, Aoife had spent more time in dungeons than she cared to admit. The guards shoved them all in a cell together and slammed the door. Fiona, battered and broken collapsed on the dirty floor as though all her energy had been zapped away.

As their footsteps faded, Sean spun from the bars and glared down at Fiona.

"Why did you do that? I could have taken them all."

"And had most of Cian's army down on our heads."

"Cian's army is headed to the Towers of Illyria unless you've forgotten," he snapped.

"I forget nothing." Fiona shoved to a sitting position and scooted against the wall.

"Sean, please. Hasn't she been through enough already?" Aoife dropped to her knees next to her and got a closer look at her wounds. "You need a doctor."

"No, what I need is here. We can't leave this place yet," Fiona said. And then coughed as she tried to catch her breath.

"Why not?"

"Because the Tears of the Dryad is here."

"The portal potion?" Aoife asked. She glanced up at Sean who still had murder in his eyes. He was pissed they'd been shoved in the dungeon and she couldn't blame him, but it did seem like a better option than death.

"That and my handmaiden, Winnie. She had the Tears. Cian took them from me and gave them to her. He called it faery dust."

"Where is it now?" Sean asked.

"I don't know. Cian took Winnie. He…" She pressed her lips together and looked away.

"He what, Mother?" Aoife asked. She placed a gentle hand on her shoulder to urge her. She knew there was something more there, something her mother was reluctant to say.

"He raped her. Like he raped me."

Aoife stared at her, wide-eyed as her heart twisted in her chest and her stomach cramped. Anger and maybe a little fear glittered there in her mother's eyes. Sean moved to kneel next to Aoife, peering intently at Fiona. He put a gentle hand under her chin and turned her face toward his.

"He did this to you?" he asked.

"His men beat me. The rape happened in the past. It happened before I managed to escape to the human realm."

Aoife sat back on her heels. Her heart broke for her mother and a dull ache of anguish passed through her. Thinking what her mother must have gone through, what she must have felt. She came through a portal, alone, terrified and trying to make sense of the new world around her. She must have been numb and in shock and yet she somehow managed to find the strength to get away. To survive.

Aoife understood her mother a little more.

"Mother…I had no idea."

"No one did." She glanced at Aoife. "You should know the truth. After Niall and I were married and after…well…after we were together, I still had it in my head I needed to warn Cian about Niall's impending attack on Anatolia. Even though I'd made him promise he wouldn't attack my realm, I didn't think he would keep that promise. I left him in the middle of the night, like a chicken.

"I went to Deaglan's workroom where he had taught me magic. I knew he had the Tears of the Dryad there. I'd seen it. I stole it and as I tipped the vial and a drop splashed on the floor, Deaglan came into his workroom. He tried to stop me but it was too late. How I wish I'd let him stop me."

She lapsed into silence, her voice a silent rasp and her face contorted in pain. It was heart-wrenching looking at her, seeing her distraught.

"I used the portal to get to Cian."

She paused again, licked her dry lips and leaned her head back against the wall. Aoife could see the tears watering in her eyes and reached for her, squeezing her hand.

"I warned him and then I told him I wanted to break off the betrothal. I thought he would accept it, so he could go on with his life. So he could marry whom he chose but it backfired. He attacked me. I used my magic to get away and the Tears to create another portal that sent me to the human realm."

Sean remained silent. Aoife didn't know what to say. Fiona closed her eyes, swallowed hard and composed herself.

"Mother…"

"I discovered I was pregnant not long after arriving in the human realm. I prayed the father was not Cian and was relieved to discover as you grew, Aoife, you were a lot like Niall." She brushed a hand down Aoife's cheek. "That man terrorizes women. I spent all my years in the human realm plotting my revenge. I wanted him dead and I wanted to be the one to kill him. Niall even took that from me."

"I don't understand. In our time, Prince Cian is dead?" Aoife asked.

She nodded. "When I disappeared to the human realm, Niall was beside himself with grief and rage. I know that now. He wiped out Anatolia because of me. Cian was presumed dead even though his body was never recovered."

"Is that why you came back in time?" Sean asked. "To stop him from wiping out Anatolia?"

"Partly." Again that small smile. She rested her head against the stone and closed her eyes as if remembering the past. "When I discovered the truth, I plotted a way to go back in time to change that. I resented Niall for what he did to me and my family. I resented him for destroying my homeland. I thought by killing him in the past it would give me the peace I wanted, and the revenge."

"This whole mess has been about vengeance?" Aoife asked. "Nothing more?"

"Revenge is a powerful emotion, Aoife. One I embraced for a long time. It gave me a dark hope. A way to cope with everything I'd lost—my home, my family and, yes, even the man I loved."

Despite the circumstances, it was nice for Aoife to hear her mother really did love Niall. It was clear to her Niall loved Fiona. Perhaps there was hope for them yet. Perhaps there was a way to get her parents back together.

But that didn't excuse the fact she wanted to wipe out Aoife from existence.

"What about Liam?" she asked.

"Liam took me in pregnant and I thought the three of us would be happy. He was kind at first. And then later things changed. Sunnie was unexpected. I let Liam raise you and Sunnie, Aoife. I was so hell-bent on finding a way back to Faery, I pushed you away. I knew I was going to return without you to save my family and do away with both Cian and Niall. I had to save Deaglan, too. I'm sorry I pushed you away." She reached for her hand, gripped it and squeezed.

Tears sprang to Aoife's eyes. She couldn't control that reaction no matter how hard she tried. After all these years, *this* is what it took to gain her mother's love and affection?

"I wanted only to protect you from Faery and Niall. I never intended for you to come here," Fiona continued without opening her eyes. "There is more about your father you don't know, Aoife. He intended to steal your magic with an Eradication Spell. I could never allow that to happen. I would kill Niall before I let him use that spell on you."

The blood drained from her head and Aoife pitched forward, pinpricks dancing in her vision. The same reaction she had when Niall told her how he'd used that spell and killed Deaglan and regretted it. She put her face in her hands and understood so much more about her mother now. She intended to use the very same spell on Niall.

"That's why I wanted you back in the human realm. It would shield you from the magic here," Fiona said.

"And you intended to use that spell on Niall," Aoife's voice was muffled against her hands. She lifted her head, met her gaze. "Didn't you?"

She squeezed her closed eyes as if trying to push out the memory. "I did." Her soft voice wavered and, like Niall had, rubbed the center of her chest. "I can't go through with it. Just as I can't give you back your childhood. I can't change the past. I know that now."

"There's still time to fix things," Sean said. "But we have to get out of here first and back to the Time Sphere."

"It's in Niall's library." Fiona's eyes popped open as she sat up. "We have a way out. But I'm not leaving without Winnie. Besides, she has the Tears of the Dryad. If we can get it, we can get out of here undetected. I know where we have to go, too. Fiona of the past is having doubts about marrying Niall. But she loves him…I love him…so we have to get to her—me—and convince her to marry him." Fiona gave a rueful smile. "It's all very confusing."

"It makes perfect sense," Sean said. "But first we have to get out of here." He stood at the bars, examining them.

"My magic is gone. But Aoife's isn't."

Aoife snapped her head in her mother's direction. "How do you know that?"

"I sense it in you. But you had a little help with its manifesting, didn't you?" Fiona glanced between her and Sean and then back again. "I approve."

"Mother…"

"Sean has it, too. Don't you? And all this time I thought this magic was merely dormant. But the two of you together…well, that's something."

"We can discuss family dynamics later." Sean ignored Fiona's question and reached his hand down to Aoife. "Come on, time to show off."

"But I don't know how to use magic." She gripped his hand and marveled at his warmth and strength as he helped her to her feet.

"It's easy," Fiona said from her seated position. "Close your eyes and look for the silvery thread of magic within you. You have it, Aoife, and it's finally come to life with Sean's help because the two of you—"

"I *know*, Mother." She huffed out an exasperated breath.

Aoife blushed to the roots of her hair. She'd never had the birds and the bees talk with her mother and she didn't want to start now. But Sean cocked a grin at her and waggled his eyebrows.

"Try it," Fiona urged.

Still holding Sean's hand, Aoife closed her eyes and concentrated. She wasn't sure what she was supposed to look for within her but she poked around in her brain. She almost mistook the flutter in her breast as nerves but then saw rather than felt the silvery thread her mother mentioned.

"I see it! Now what?"

"Good. Now, touch it. With your mind."

Aoife reached for it in her mind's eye, stretched out a hand and touched the silvery thread with the tip of her finger. A spark went through her, sharp and vivid, and she gasped.

"Aoife…open your eyes." Sean's voice was full of awe beside her.

She blinked them open and saw her body glowing so bright, she lit up the confines of the dank cell.

"I'm doing that?"

"You are." Fiona shoved her battered body off the floor and moved to stand next to her. "You glow because of the magic within you, Aoife. Deaglan believed a child of wizard and Fae blood would be more powerful than even me and Niall. You have that potential. You can do this."

"I don't know how to use it."

"Not yet. But you will. Give me your hand." Fiona held out her hand.

Aoife reached for her mother and they joined hands. She walked them closer to the cell door. "Point your forefinger. Now. Think about the lock. Channel that magic through you to the point of your finger."

"This is what you did in Niall's dungeon," Aoife said.

"It is. Feel the magic flow through you. When you do, touch the tip of your finger to the lock."

Aoife concentrated on the warmth cascading through her. She was surprised at how comforting it felt. When she was certain she had the magic directed the way she wanted, she pressed the tip of her finger against the cell lock. A snap and a sizzle and the lock melted. Fiona pulled open the door.

"That's my girl."

"You did it," Sean said, awestruck.

"I did it," Aoife repeated.

"Good work." Fiona turned to Sean. "It's better if you go alone, Sean. We don't want anyone to notice the empty cell and signal any alarms so Aoife and I will remain here. The prince's chamber is on the uppermost level in the north tower. That's where he's keeping Winnie, I think. She had the Tears of the Dryad on her when he took her. Hopefully she still has it. She thinks it's fairy dust. That's what he told her it was when he gave her the vial."

"I'll find her and the Tears."

"You have to. Once you have the Tears, use one drop no more to open a portal. Think of the place you want to go and then step through."

He nodded, then looked at Aoife. "I'll be back for you both."

"I hope so," she whispered.

He took a step toward the door and then halted, turning back. She knew he intended to kiss her and leaned in. Their lips met in a fiery kiss of passion and promise. When he broke, he brushed his fingertips over her cheek.

"Stay safe," he said.

"Hurry back."

Sean hurried away, the shadows eating up his form and all the while Aoife's heart beat a wicked tattoo. She said a little prayer for his safety and that he'd come back to her in one piece. They still had unfinished business.

"He'll be all right," Fiona said.

"I hope so."

"I know so. Aoife, come sit next to me."

She moved from the bars and slid down the wall to sit next to her mother. She drew up her knees, circling them with her arms and resting her chin on them.

"Why did you marry, Liam, Mother?" Aoife asked. It was one of the questions that had been burning inside her since she found out who her mother really was.

"Because he was kind and he took me in. You have to understand, Aoife, when I landed in the human realm, I knew nothing and no one. In a way, Liam was my knight in shining armor."

"How did you meet?" Aoife couldn't explain the need to know. Liam had been the only father she ever knew. The man who raised her. When she learned of his death, it was as though a little part of her died along with him.

"He was at his favorite fishing hole when I arrived, quite literally, out of thin air. He took me in, fed me and gave me a place to stay. It wasn't long after that I realized I was pregnant. He asked me to marry him, to give you a name. Names are very important to humans."

Aoife knew. In a small town like Brookdale, having the right last name mattered. That's why the popular girls were popular and the jocks were sports stars. Their parents may hail from the small town, but they also controlled it with their money and influence.

"We were happy for a while," Fiona continued. "At first I

feared the man who fathered you was Cian. I was relieved when I realized he hadn't. And then Sunnie came along and I knew that I had to change something or I would be stuck in the human realm pretending to be a human forever. I had never lost the taste for revenge. I wanted to destroy both Niall and Cian."

"That's why you would disappear. You were going back to Faery?"

She nodded.

"What about Niall?" She turned her head to look at her mother. Fiona resumed her position with her head back against the stones and eyes closed.

"It was complicated with Niall. Looking back, I know what motivated him. He had a deep hatred for his brother, Cian. I suppose you could say we have that in common here in this time."

"And Niall's plan to take my magic?" she asked.

"I wasn't supposed to know. I found Deaglan's journal outlining the plan. I felt betrayed by Niall. And I was hurt. I wanted to hurt him back," she said.

"I don't think he would hurt me," Aoife said, remembering their talk before going back in time. "He told me he intended to give up his quest to kill Cian and wipe Anatolia from the map. He regrets everything that's happened. I know he does. Just as I know he loves you."

"You believe he told you the truth?"

"Yes. He also mentioned the Eradication Spell and that he used it on his father and wished he hadn't." She glanced at her mother. Her eyes were still closed. "Do you still love him?" There. She'd asked the one question burning the most through her.

Fiona's eyes blinked open. "It doesn't matter now. I've ruined any chance I have with him."

"Maybe not. He still loves you. He sent us here to find you."

She smiled and patted her hand. "I thought as much. No one else would have the power to bring you here. I'm glad you're here, but I wish you hadn't come. You should have let me die."

"Mother, don't say that. We promised Niall we would bring you back. We couldn't let you die up there. Sean will find Winnie and be back with the Tears. I have no doubt."

A sort of sadness passed over her battered face. "I hope you're right." She reached for her hand, squeezed it. "I want you to know I can no longer go through with my plan to destroy Niall. I know we can't start over but I hope you forgive me. I'd like for us to start repairing our relationship. You have a great potential for magic. I can help you cultivate that."

Aoife wasn't sure about the magic part but she did like the idea of reconciling with her mother. She gave a slow nod. "I'd like that, too."

Now all they had to do was get out of this time alive.

It was relatively easy for Sean to slip out of the dungeon and into the halls of the castle. There were no guards at the door, which was odd. But he didn't question that. He headed through the corridors as though he belonged there. He only received a cursory glance here and there.

As he searched for the north tower, he was able to catch snippets of conversation. Prince Cian dispatched his army days ago to the Towers of Illyria to get back his betrothed. They waited there even now for his arrival. He'd left the moment he'd deposited Sean, Aoife and Fiona in the dungeon. Sean had no idea how far it was to the Towers of Illyria but the prince was definitely making haste.

That left the castle relatively unguarded and a prime time for him roam the halls. He eventually found the north tower and climbed the hundreds of stone stairs winding around the tower to the top floor. Two guards stood on either side of the prince's chamber with a less than friendly look on their stoic faces.

"What's your business here?" one of the guards asked.

"I'm a humble servant, milord. Here to fetch the bedding for washing."

The guard looked him up and down with a critical eye. "No one is allowed in or out. Prince's orders."

"The prince ordered me to fetch the bedding," Sean said, annoyed with the delay. "He wants his chamber polished and clean for his return."

"Sorry, man. No one goes in."

Sean wasn't going to give up, though. "Very well. Then I'll tell His Highness you wouldn't let me in and when he returns and sees his bedding still soiled and his chamber still dirty, I will make sure he understands who is responsible." He gave him a pointed look.

The two guards exchanged glances. Sean was banking on the fact that no one—not even his personal guards—would want to cross the prince. His reputation as a vile tempered man preceded him.

The guard reached for the door handle. "All right. If that's all you're doing. You best be quick about it."

"I plan to be."

The door opened and Sean stepped into the dimly lit room. He spotted the girl right away, sleeping curled on her side. Naked. She had bruises along her back and red welts on her backside.

"Winnie?" he called softly.

But she didn't move and he feared the worst. He stepped closer to see her wrists were bound together. A rope stretched from there to the bed post, keeping her in place. The prince had clearly had his fun with her. He'd broken her. He'd taken whatever he wanted from her. Sean's heart broke for the girl.

At the side of the bed, he placed a gentle hand on her shoulder. She started awake, her eyes popping open and she tried to scramble away from him.

"Don't," she said.

She curled into a tight ball, concealing as much of her nakedness as she could. Sean lifted his hands as if in surrender.

"I'm not going to hurt you. I'm here to help you. Fiona sent me."

"Fi-Fiona? Lady Fiona?"

"Yes. Are you Winnie?"

She nodded. Tears pooled in her eyes and streaked down her cheeks.

"I'm going to find something to cut away those ropes and get you out of here."

"He'll find you. He'll hunt you down if you take me out of here. He won't stop until he has me back again." Winnie's voice wavered as she spoke.

"You let me worry about that."

He searched a nearby table, but found nothing sharp he could use. There was a small hand-held mirror on the bureau. He picked it up, considering. A second later, he smashed it against the edge of the bureau and retrieved a shard of the mirrored glass. He returned to her as she held her wrists out to him. He quickly sliced through the ropes and removed them from her raw wrists.

"Where are your clothes?" he asked.

"He took them the first day."

He glanced around the room but saw nothing that might fit her. He grabbed a quilt from the floor and draped it over her. Then he scooped her up in his arms.

"We'll find you something later. Right now we have to get out of here."

"But…the guards…"

"You had a pink substance with you."

"The fairy dust? It was a gift from Cian."

Sean nodded. "Where is it now?"

"It was in the pocket of my gown when he brought me here. That was days ago. I don't know what's happened to it."

"I'm going to have to search for it." He laid her back on the bed as gently as he could.

"Why? There's no time for that. The prince will be coming back any time now."

"That fairy dust is our way out. I have to find it. And don't worry about the prince. He's left for the Towers of Illyria."

"He…left. And he left me here?"

He knew what she was thinking—that he left her tied up like some animal. He didn't know what to say as he continued to search through the room. He knew he was running out of time. The guards would wonder what was taking him so long. He pulled another blanket off the floor and tossed it on the bed. As he did, he heard a distinctive clink, as though something glass hit the floor.

Sean dropped to his hands and knees and peered under the bed. There, among the dust bunnies, was a small glass vial. He reached for it and pulled it out from under the bed. The pink substance winked back up at him.

"You found it." Her voice was soft and full of wonder.

He went back to Winnie and handed her the vial. "Hold this for me." She took the vial from him as he scooped her up into his arms. "Now, uncork it and spill one drop on the floor."

"But…are you sure?"

He nodded. "Do it."

She pulled the cork off and then turned it over. A drop splashed on the stone floor and a second later an opening appeared in the middle of the room.

"Take me to Fiona of the future."

He stepped through the portal.

Chapter 21

A black hole appeared in the center of the cell. Aoife jumped to her feet, her heart racing as she watched Sean step through cradling a girl to his chest. It took her moment to realize the girl was wrapped in a quilt and had been beaten. Fiona gasped as she struggled to stand. Aoife gave her a steadying hand.

As soon as Sean was through, the portal closed and disappeared as though it had never been there.

"By the gods, what did he do to her?" Fiona asked.

"She fainted when I stepped through the portal," Sean said. "I couldn't find her clothes but I did find the Tears of the Dryad."

"That bloody bastard. I'll get him for this." Fiona brushed gentle fingertips over the girl's forehead. "Poor Winnie. This is all my fault. When I saw him in the past, when he assaulted me in the tent at the foothills of the cliffs, he told me Winnie was safe back at Lambridge. He must have had her prisoner even then."

Aoife put a hand on her shoulder for comfort. "You can't blame yourself, Mother. What happened, happened and there's nothing you can do to change that."

"No but I can seek my vengeance and I intend to make sure he pays dearly for what he's done." She pried the vial from the girl's fingers. "Let's get out of here."

"Where are we going?"

"Back to the Towers of Illyria. We have to make sure the past Fiona marries Niall. I've never gone with more than one person through the portal so stay close."

Fiona held out the vial and then tipped it until one drop slid out and landed on the floor. Another portal appeared. Aoife stepped closer to Sean, wishing she could hold his hand but knowing she couldn't while he carried Winnie.

"Follow me." Fiona stepped through the portal.

Sean glanced down at Aoife, gave her a nod to go next. She stepped into the darkness and her senses were immediately assaulted by a bitterly cold wind that shot through her. It took her breath away. For a moment, she felt as though she was suspended in mid-air. She could see her mother's form ahead, but only an outline. She stepped out on the other side and a second later Sean came through.

The portal disappeared.

The chamber they were in was dark. Aoife could make out a few of shapes but couldn't really see much of anything. Her mother moved around the room, as though she knew exactly where everything was. She struck a match and lit a taper, then another and another. The small circle of light made the room glow.

They were surrounded by stone walls. An arched oak door was on one wall, a dark window on the other. A bookcase covered in dust and cobwebs stood at the far end of the room. There was a table, one chair and a narrow bed.

"Where are we?" he asked.

"It's an old chamber in the west tower not in use anymore. It's underneath Deaglan's chamber, Niall's father. Put Winnie there so she can rest. I'll find her some clothes." Fiona started for the door as Sean put Winnie on the bed.

As he did, he spun and took three large steps to move in front of the door. He'd moved so fast, he was almost a blur and Aoife had to blink to make sure she really saw what she saw.

"You're not going anywhere. It's too dangerous."

"I have to figure out what day it is. I need to know if we're close to the wedding day. Now step aside, Sean, and let me out."

"You can't go out there with your past self running around. I forbid it," Sean said.

Fiona's lips thinned and she put her hands on her hips. Even with her bloodied and swollen face, Aoife could see her defiant expression.

"Sean—"

"I'll go," Aoife said.

They both turned to look at her. Fiona's brows rose with her surprise. Sean shook his head but Aoife hurried on.

"I mean, I don't exist yet so there's no danger of me running into anyone I know or my past self. Right?"

"No," Sean and Fiona said together.

Aoife huffed out a breath. "I'm not a child. I can handle it."

"You don't know what this world is like, Aoife." Fiona reached for her, put her hands on her upper arms and squeezed. "It's not like the human realm."

"I know. I'm not an idiot, Mother. I'll just go, figure out what's going on and come right back."

"And how do you propose to do that?" she asked.

"I intend to start with the people who know what's going on—the servants," Aoife said. "I'll be fine, Mother. Don't worry. Besides, you can't go out looking like that. You'll scare people."

She scowled. "Gee, thanks."

Aoife kissed her mother on the cheek before stepping around her toward the door. The door Sean still blocked. He folded his arms across his chest.

"I don't like this idea, Aoife."

"I didn't ask you. You don't think I can do it?"

"It's not that at all. It's that…" He paused, clamped his mouth shut. "I don't like it. That's all."

Aoife reached up and patted his chest. She didn't want to notice the strong beat of his heart beneath her hand, but she did notice. She liked the way he felt under her fingertips, her palm.

"I'll be fine."

"Let her go, Sean," Fiona urged.

Reluctantly, he stepped to the side. Aoife reached for the door handle but before she could grab it, he snatched her wrist and pulled her into his arms. He held her against him, his breath trickling over her face.

"You be careful."

"I will."

She searched his eyes, could tell there was more he wanted to say but couldn't or wouldn't say it with her mother in the room. He kissed her quickly on the lips and then released her. She stumbled away from his arms and turned back to the door, disappointed he didn't say anything more. What did she expect, a profession of love? He hadn't said it even after they'd been intimate together and she poured her heart out to him.

"I'll be back."

"Aoife, one last thing. Deaglan's tower is the west tower. Niall's is the east. The servant's quarters are all on the south side of the lowest level. Find the cook she's a known gossip and will be able to tell you what you want to know."

Nodding, she opened the door and stepped into the hallway, closing it softly behind her. She stood there in the shadowy corridor for a long moment, getting her bearings. She would have to remember how to get back here once she discovered the information she needed. That and finding clothes for Winnie.

Taking a deep breath, she hurried down the hallway. She was not exactly good at north, south, east, west directions. She was somewhat directionally challenged when it came to things like that. She paused at the first intersection, wishing she knew the layout of the towers better. That was an advantage Fiona had over her.

She envisioned the compass in her head and surmised if she were in the west towers, then she would need to turn to her right to go south. She could hear talking and laughter as she went down the long hallway and knew she was getting closer to people. She hoped she could find the servants area quickly and then get back to her mother and Sean.

Aoife turned another corner toward the voices. She smelled food cooking and her stomach rumbled with a fierce growl. When was the last time she'd eaten? She couldn't remember. As she stumbled through the castle, she found the kitchen in the heart of the Towers and knew she'd at least gone the right direction. Thank God for small miracles.

The kitchen was a bustle of activity and no one even noticed her standing there gawking. There were dried herbs hanging from the rafters. She could see a pile of vegetables and fruit on one table waiting to be used. There was a large animal that looked like a deer on another table gutted and skinned and ready to be cooked. There were two large pots in a brick oven that were the size of cauldrons cooking something—maybe some type of stew. Bread came out of the oven steaming and smelling delicious. And again her stomach rumbled in response.

"You there. Why are you standing there? Get to work!" a man barked at her.

He was tall and robust with a thick mustache. He cleaned blood off a large knife and his apron was covered in dark blood. He must have finished cleaning the animal before her. His hands were dirty and his face was not the sort of face that welcomed anyone to cross him.

She jumped and scurried into the kitchen, snatching up an empty basket and trying to look busy.

"We've too much work to do for people to stand around doing nothing," he continued. "What with the wedding feast in only a few short hours."

Wedding feast. That meant Niall's and Fiona's wedding was *today*. Fiona would know when and where it was happening. All she had to do was get back to her mother and Sean and let them know. The man stared at her with narrowed eyes and she looked around frantically for something to do. Anything to do. Anything that would make her look useful.

"By the by, girl, don't you have a task?" He tossed the knife to the table and stomped over to her.

"I-I'm sorry. I'm new."

"New, huh?" He looked her over. "What's with the basket?"

"I'm not sure, sir."

He snorted. He snatched a bundle of herbs from the rafters and stuck it in her basket. "Take that to the cook. She needs it for the pheasant she's roasting."

Aoife dipped a curtsy and scurried away.

"Out back, you daft lass!" she heard the man call after her.

She had no clue where that was and didn't intend to waste time finding out. Now she was after something for Winnie to wear.

Where would she find the laundry? It would be somewhere in the south towers, wouldn't it? Should she find it, she would be able to swipe a gown and then make her way back. She roamed through the halls, blending in with the bustle of activity. She spotted a young girl carrying a basket overloaded with linens. Aoife made her way toward the girl and fell in step behind her, hoping she was heading to the laundry area.

She was so intent on following the girl, she never saw the man coming. She slammed right into him, bounced off him and then stumbled back a step or two. He reached out, grabbed her arms to steady her on her feet as she looked up at him.

He was a good head taller than her and elderly. She flushed to the tips of her ears, embarrassed she'd nearly run him over.

"I'm so sorry," she sputtered.

"'Tis quite all right, missy." He dropped his hands and looked her over with a contemplative look. He ran a hand over his smooth chin. "Do I know you?"

"I don't think so. I'm…new here. I…was looking for the laundry."

"The laundry?" He eyed her basket of herbs. "You certain you aren't lost?"

She didn't know what to do with the basket. She nodded,

though, trying to look convincing in her conviction she really did want the laundry. The man wrapped a hand around her upper arm and looked closer at her.

"You look familiar. I feel as though I know you."

"I assure you, I'm no one."

"Not no one." He shook his head. "I know a wizard when I see one."

A lump of fear formed in her throat and she swallowed hard, trying to dislodge it. How could he possibly know who she was?

"I'm not a wizard."

"Not fully, no. But there is wizard blood in you. I should know. I have it too and I feel it within you."

Oh, shit. She peered up at him again, trying to figure out who he was and how he'd know her. Was he a good wizard or a bad wizard?

"Why don't you come with me to my chamber and tell me who you really are." His voice held a no-negotiation edge.

Aoife shook her head, though, and tried to dislodge her arm. "I can't. I really have to go. It's important."

"I don't think so."

Still holding her, his grip tightening, he waved his free hand around them. A puff of blue smoke enveloped them and then her stomach dropped out as though she'd fallen off a cliff. A second later they were in another room. A chamber dimly lit with one window, a desk cluttered with scrolls and a half-burnt candle. A bookshelf resided on one side crammed full of old books and vials of colorful liquids.

"What happened? Where am I?"

"You're in my chamber." He turned to face her, his hands clasped behind his back. "I can't have someone with magic as strong as yours running around the castle unsupervised. Tell me who you are and what you're doing here. Are you working for Cian?"

"My God, no. That man is slime."

He lifted a brow. "Is he?"

"Yes, he is. He's a bad guy. He raped my mother and then he tried to kill her." She realized she said too much and clamped her mouth shut with a snap.

The man stiffened. "Who is your mother?"

Her heart sputtered, her nerves on a raw edge. "Never mind. It doesn't matter. She's all right. I saved her. Well, not alone. I had help." She huffed out a breath. Why couldn't she just shut up?

"You have a strange dialect. Something I've never heard. And I still have the distinct feeling I know you."

She shifted from one foot to the other under his scrutiny. "I am sure there is no way you know me." She took a step backward but he closed the gap between them.

"I sense magic in your blood. Wizard magic. No, Fae magic." He stroked his chin. "Perhaps both."

"Magic?" Maybe if she played dumb she could get out of this.

"What are you doing here, girl?"

"I-I came for the wedding."

"You know of the wedding?" Surprise edged his voice and his eyes narrowed to slits. "Only those residing within the Towers of Illyria know of the wedding today."

Well, shit. That didn't bode well for her.

"I have never seen you here before though I confess you do seem somewhat familiar."

Well, shit again. She took another step back, trying to put distance between her and the man.

"And the fact that I sense the wizard blood in you tells me I should be cautious of you."

The more he talked, the more she knew she was in deep trouble. Who was this guy?

"Mayhap if I give you my name, you will be so inclined to share yours. I am Deaglan."

Deaglan! Niall's father. Fiona's mentor. Holy crap, she definitely was in deep trouble. She stood across from the man who Niall would eventually kill for his power. The man who taught Fiona how to open portals and the man who was her grandfather.

"Deaglan." She said his name slowly, as though testing it out on her tongue.

"And you are?"

She didn't know what to do. If she told him, what would he do? Would he think she was mad and send her to the dungeon? She took a deep breath.

"My name is Aoife. I believe you're my grandfather."

Deaglan stumbled backward until he ran into his chair and sat down so hard on it, it nearly toppled. His face had drained of color as he stared at her as though she'd grown a second head.

"How can that be?" he asked, his voice a faint whisper.

"It's a long story but my mother, Fiona, came back in time and sent me make sure she married my father. I happened to run into you along the way."

His hands were limp on the table in front of him as he stared at her, wide-eyed as the silence stretched between them. Aoife shifted from one foot to the other trying to decide what to say next when he was spurred into sudden action. He shoved scrolls around on his desk and came to a pile of parchment, flipping through the pages until he paused, read it and then looked up at her, his face still white as a sheet.

"You're the one," he'd said.

"The one what?"

"You have Fae and wizard blood, my child. I knew I sensed it in you. That is something special." He gazed at her with something akin to awe and admiration. It did nothing but make her uncomfortable. "It was foretold a wizard of both Fae and Wizard blood would rule the realm."

Hot pinpricks went over Aoife and the words she had memorized resurfaced. *"A wizard of both Fae and Wizard blood will come into power and rule from a silver throne.* Isn't that what you meant?"

He stared at her in mute silence, his eyes wide and round. "My, my. You are full of surprises. How did you know that?"

"I read it somewhere. A page from a book, I think." She didn't tell him the letters on that page had rearranged into a language she could understand. Because she, herself, did not understand how that had happened. "What does it mean?"

"A silly prophecy that is likely not to come true. Nothing more." He waved it away as though it truly meant nothing but Aoife had her doubts. He glanced over her. "You don't know who you are, do you?"

She shook her head.

"Oh, gods." He heaved a heavy sigh. "Fiona has told you nothing."

"No. Nothing."

"Why is she here?" he asked, his gaze narrowing.

"She wanted to stop the wedding."

Deaglan blinked, determination coming into his eyes. "I find it difficult to believe she would want that. And at any rate she cannot. She cannot change the past no matter how much she wishes. The past is already set."

"But she said Niall accidentally killed you when he tried to take your power. She came back in time to save you."

He stared at her, blank and unemotional, and Aoife couldn't read him at all. Finally he gave a swift sake of his head. "Niall would never do that."

"But Fiona said he had an Eradication Spell. And now she has it."

His eyes widened. "How would she get that?'"

She shrugged. "I don't know but I saw it on her desk. Her desk of the future, that is. Not here in this world. Or realm. It was in the human realm."

"That spell is very dangerous. I've seen the spell scroll but I hid it away to make sure no one would ever find it. He wouldn't do such a thing," he snapped, closing the discussion.

Aoife pressed her lips together and started for the door. "I have to get back. My mother will be wondering where I am."

"Fiona is here with you? Now?" He didn't hide the incredulity in his voice. She nodded. Deaglan stood on shaky legs. "Take me to her."

Chapter 22

"She's been gone too long." Sean paced the length of the small room. "I don't like it. She should be back by now."

Fiona knew how difficult the Towers were to navigate. So it came as no surprise to her Aoife had not returned. Even so, she worried for her safety but masked it well. "She'll be fine. She probably got turned around and will be back before we know it. It's a big place."

"I shouldn't have let her go alone."

"You love her."

Sean halted his pacing and pinned her with his sharp eyes. Fiona stared right back, unflinching.

"I see it," Fiona continued.

"That's none of your concern."

"It is all of my concern. I'm her mother."

"Who wasn't there when she was growing up."

"I was there," Fiona insisted, trying to ignore the stabbing pain in her heart. "I was there for her and Sunnie. I made sure they were cared for."

"Oh, sure, in between visits to Faery. Aoife needed you and you abandoned her."

"Do not critique me on how I raised my child. Everything I did, I did to protect her."

"Everything including planning to wipe her out of existence."

Anger burned through Fiona. Anger and guilt. She regretted that now but it was something she would have to live with for the rest of her days. Still, she maintained her stance that Aoife would have been fine had she stayed where she belonged. "She would have been safe in the human realm. But *you* let her through to Faery."

"You don't know that for a fact. You don't know the magic wouldn't have touched her there. And yet it was a gamble you were willing to take, wasn't it?" Fury sparked in his eyes. "You were willing to erase everything she was and for your own agenda, your own vengeance."

"Don't you lecture me, Sean. I know what I did and why I was doing it and I don't need you to tell me I was wrong. I regret that now and I will spend eternity making it up to her. And if she's so precious to you, why don't you tell her the truth?"

"What truth?" He reared back from her, as though he had no idea what she was talking about.

"Oh, please. Like you don't know. Tell her you love her. Tell her the magic within her regenerated yours and helped manifest hers when you were together."

"Stop. That is not your business." He pointed at her, his finger right in her face.

"How does Aoife feel about you using magic to rescue me from Lambridge?" When his response was stony silence, she continued. "She's adored you since she was a girl. I know you've seen that. Even I have and as you say I abandoned her. I know my daughter and I know she loves you."

"I know that, too. It's why I can't be with her. My magic will kill her. It's too dangerous and uncontrollable."

"All magic can be controlled, Sean, with the right teachings. You can learn how."

Sean started to retort as the door opened and clamped his mouth shut. They both turned toward it, expectantly, as Aoife poked her head into the room. Her expression beamed joy as she closed the door.

"I found out today is your wedding day. The feast is being prepared even now. I saw it, too. It looked wonderful." Aoife pressed her hand against her stomach as it growled so loud even Fiona heard it.

"Then we haven't much time. We have to get the me of the past to marry Niall." Fiona put her hand in her pocket for the Tears of the Dryad.

"There's something else, Mother," Aoife said, stopping her. "Someone came with me to see you."

Fiona's throat constricted as Aoife opened the door and there stood Deaglan in the shadowy corridor. Seeing him there, alive and well, knowing what day it was made her burst into tears. She rushed toward him, flung herself into his arms and hugged him hard enough to make him expel a breath.

"By the gods, what Aoife said was true. You are from the future." Deaglan patted her back and hugged her hard. Then he held her at arm's length, looking her over. "What happened to your face?"

"That doesn't matter. All that matters is you're alive." Fiona sniffed, trying hard to regain her composure.

"Of course, I'm alive, dearie. Why wouldn't I be?"

Indecision flickered through her and she bit her lower lip. She wanted so much to tell him the truth—to tell him one of the reasons she'd come back to the past. She had intended to try to save his life, to make sure he understood Niall had been responsible for his death, now she wasn't so sure. Would her telling him alter too much of the future?

"It's nothing. I'm happy to see you." She stepped away from him and wiped the tears from her eyes.

"Aoife tells me you're from the future. Tell me truly, dearie, did you use the Time Sphere?"

He'd know about that, naturally. She nodded.

Deaglan blew out a breath. She could see the worry creasing his face.

"Why? What is it, Deaglan? What aren't you telling me?"

"The use of the Time Sphere is dangerous and only activated every five hundred years. I'm afraid you may be stuck here."

Aoife shook her head before he finished. "No. That can't be. We have to get back. My life isn't here. It's in the future. There has to be some way to get back."

"What about a portal, Deaglan?" Remembering the Tears, Fiona reached into her pocket and pulled it out. She held it up for him to see.

Deaglan smiled down at it, then her. "You stole that from me."

"Aye, many years ago. Now we need it to help us get out of here and back to our time."

"The Tears alone will not help you, dearie. I'd need something more. Another pink crystal with other ingredients to mix with it to open a portal across time and dimensions."

Aoife gasped and looked at Sean whose eyes had widened.

"I think we can help you with that," Sean said and gave her a nod.

Aoife pulled something out of her pocket and opened her hand. A pink crystal rested on her palm. "A pink crystal like this?"

"Where did you get that?" Deaglan asked.

"That's what I'd like to know," Fiona said.

"It's a long story," Sean said. "But suffice to say that it's being returned to its rightful owner."

Deaglan took it from Aoife and turned it over in his hand. "Aye, this will do." He held out his other hand for the vial.

Fiona shook her head and closed her fingers around it. "I can't give it up, Deaglan."

One dark brow rose in question. "You don't trust me?"

"No, it's not that. It's just that…I have one more thing to do before I return."

He dropped his hand. "Very well then. Use the Tears to make a portal to the foot of the cliffs one hour before dawn. Make sure you go to the south side of the cliffs to avoid Cian's army. I will see you there and get you home."

Anticipation tingled through her. She'd forgotten Cian and his army camped at the foot of the hills and knew this was her last chance to get to him before she returned to the future.

"We'll be there," Fiona said with a nod.

"Good. Now, if you'll excuse me. I have to see you to your wedding."

Deaglan ducked out of the room and Fiona knew it was time to put her plan into action. She uncorked the vial, as Sean's hand clamped around her wrist.

"What do you think you're doing?"

"If we're to make sure Aoife survives, then I have to make sure I marry Niall. I have to get to the Fiona of the past." Fiona knew it was a risk. She'd felt the cold breath of time rippling between her and her past self at the carriage site. But she had to go because if she didn't, it could alter the timeline.

"Looking like that?" Sean shook his head. "You'll scare the poor girl."

"Nonsense."

"Mother, I don't think that's a good idea," Aoife said.

Fiona noticed her daughter held a bundle of clothes and was grateful she'd managed to get something for Winnie to wear, though she suspected Deaglan must have had something to do with that.

"Why not?" Fiona asked.

"Because your face is bruised and swollen. Besides, I don't think it's a good idea for you to be in the same room as your past self."

"So? I can still walk and talk. Now release me, Sean, so I can open a portal."

"No," he said. "Aoife's right. You *shouldn't* be in the same room as your past self. Niall said as much."

"I don't care. I have to go."

"Why?"

She huffed. "Because on my wedding day, a woman appeared and came to me to convince me to marry Niall. It was a *woman* and now I'm certain it was me of the future."

"I'll go," Aoife said. "Let me go instead."

Hot pinpricks went over Fiona as she looked at her and remembered the sound of the woman's voice who had visited her in her chamber that day. It had been so long ago but she remembered it like it was yesterday. Her stomach clenched as she realized that it was not her future self as she'd always assumed but her future *daughter*. And that this moment would not be happening if Aoife wasn't standing there with imploring, desperate eyes.

"By the gods..." Fiona's voice was soft and trembled. "It was you."

"What?" Sean glanced between the two of them.

Fiona took a step toward Aoife, the uncorked vial still clenched tightly in her hand. "All this time I thought it was me. I thought the woman in the gold-edged hooded cloak was *me*. But it wasn't. It was you. My Aoife. My beautiful daughter."

Aoife's lower lip trembled. She took a deep breath and let it shudder out of her. Then she pulled the black cloak with gilt edges from the pile of clothes she held and let it unfold.

"Was it a cloak like this one?"

Fiona suppressed the hot tears that want to erupt and nodded. "Exactly like that."

"Then it's settled. I'm going."

"I don't like this," Sean snapped. "First, you run through the castle alone and now this. Stepping through a portal to your past mother's chamber is not a good idea."

"I'm doing this. I'm going," Aoife said, keeping her gaze pinned on Fiona.

"Aye, she does have to go. It's imperative she goes."

Sean took the gown from Aoife's hands. She put the cloak on and pulled up the hood. Fiona tugged it forward so it shadowed her face just enough to keep her identity hidden.

"Be careful," Fiona said.

"I will." Aoife nodded.

She pushed the vial of the Tears into her hand. "You know what to do?"

Again Aoife nodded.

"When it's safe, use the portal to return here, but only when it's safe." Then they'd get to the meeting place at the foot of the cliffs and wait for Deaglan.

Aoife took the Tears of the Dryad from her and then inhaled a deep breath. "Here goes nothing."

One drop hit the floor, opening the portal. Then Aoife stepped through and was gone.

The bitter cold of the portal sliced right through Aoife. She sucked in her breath as she stepped through to the other side and watched, amazed, as it closed behind her. The last thing she saw was Sean's face pinched with worry.

She could do this. She *would* do this. She had to prove to him and her mother she was not the wallflower they thought she was. Who was she kidding? She had to prove it to herself, too. She had always been the one to play it safe. To never take chances. Now was her time to shine. Now was her chance to show the world and herself she could do this.

Truth be told, she felt the change in her the second she made love with Sean. Like a light had been clicked on. Her confidence had soared. And when she stumbled upon Deaglan, she hadn't even been afraid. She'd been elated to meet her grandfather face to face.

Despite what Deaglan said about the past being set, she refused to believe it much like Fiona. And, much like Fiona, she understood now why her mother wanted to save the old man so much. Aoife wanted to save him, if only to restore more of her family line. A selfish reason, no doubt, but she knew she could learn so much from him.

A pop of light in the middle of the room interrupted her deep thoughts. A portal appeared. She pulled the hood down over her face and stepped backward into the shadows, watching and waiting as a younger version of her mother stepped through the portal and giggled, pressing her fingers against her lips as she smiled.

Aoife steeled her nerves and took that moment to step into the room, startling her.

"Who are you?"

"Who I am does not matter. I mean you no harm." God, did that ever sound cliché or what? But it was the only thing she could think of off the top of her head. Now she had to convince her mother to marry Niall.

Her mother narrowed her eyes. "Show yourself."

Aoife swallowed, her mouth dry as dirt. It was now or never. "I cannot. Lady Fiona, I came to tell you that you must marry King Niall. It is imperative you go through with the vows."

Her words came out in a rush, her voice wavering with the emotion she tried hard to suppress. In a way, she was begging for her life, ensuring her mother would go through with the wedding and consummate those vows.

"What? Why?"

Aoife didn't know what made her do it. But she reached for her, clamped her hand around Fiona's wrist. "You have doubts, I know, but he loves you. And somewhere, deep down, you love him. Marry him, Fiona. Say yes."

Her gaze searched Aoife's shadowed form, as though she could see the face underneath the hood. But Aoife made sure her face was concealed—all but her chin. There was no way the Fiona of this time would know who she was or how she got there.

"I-I do have doubts."

A sudden knock on the door made Fiona jump. "One minute!"

She turned toward it, allowing Aoife to release her and slip into the shadows. She pressed her back against the stone wall and covered her mouth to keep from making a sound. She had to let her mother believe she had disappeared.

Fiona ran to the window, peering out into the night. Aoife wondered what was going through her mind then. She must have thought the intruder had made it through the window, yet it was nigh impossible since the room was at the top of the tower.

The knock again. "Fiona, dearest, are you in there?"

Niall's muffled voice. Aoife's heart kicked into overdrive. Her father was here. Now. Just outside the room. She squeezed her eyes shut against the threat of burning tears.

Fiona smoothed her hair back and Aoife could see her hands

shaking. So, her words had affected her. She hoped it was enough. She went to the door, opened it and Niall stood on the other side. He was dressed in his finest in a royal blue jacket trimmed in gold with gold buttons, black pants, tall black boots polished to a high shine. A sword glinted in the candlelight at his side. He bowed to his bride, reaching for her hand and kissing it.

And Aoife's heart tumbled in her chest. How gallant, how chivalrous he was. How could Fiona *not* love him?

"Dearest, your hands are cold. Are you well?"

She pulled her hands free. "I'm fine. What brings you here?"

"May I?" She nodded and stepped aside. Aoife pushed back against the wall harder, as though that would make her disappear all the more. "Your fire is out. No wonder you're so chilled." He snapped his fingers and the fireplace came to life. "There. That's better."

"Did you want something, Niall?"

"Aye, I do." He moved to her, took her hands in his. "The time for our wedding has come. We cannot delay any longer. Have you decided?"

No one had prepared Aoife for that. She thought all this time Niall had come to escort her to their wedding. But no, he'd come to formally propose. She watched Fiona's face as the decision flashed through her eyes, how she looked him over with a contemplative look. Aoife glanced at Niall who waited, his face impassive, as though he already knew the answer to his question.

"I have decided. And I agree to marry you."

Aoife wanted to blow out a breath of relief. Instead, she pressed her hand harder against her mouth and squeezed her eyes shut. Her mother had agreed, thank goodness, but she was stuck there in her chamber. How was she going to be able to use to the Tears of the Dryad to get back without attracting attention?

She couldn't leave yet.

"That makes me happy to hear you say that, dearest." His smile was genuine as he kissed her hand once again. And once again Aoife's heart turned over.

Niall really did love Fiona. That much was obvious. But Fiona…she seemed as though she had a little more hesitation. As though she wanted to agree but something held her back.

"I only require one thing. A wedding present if you will."

"And what is that?"

"Cease your attack on Anatolia."

He released her, moved toward the fire. Closer to Aoife. He turned toward the warmth, his hands clasped behind his back as he peered down into the flames, the light flickering over his youthful handsome face.

"I cannot promise you that, my dear."

He glanced up and for a brief moment, Aoife thought for sure he looked right at her. She stopped breathing and if she could make her heart stop beating, too, she'd do that. Anything to not make a single noise. She knew her muscles quivered with the fear coursing through her and she tried her hardest to remain perfectly still.

"It is my condition for marrying you. Anatolia was my home. My family lived there for generations. There are innocent men, women and children who live there and are not a part of your fight with the prince. And despite whatever feud you have with Cian—"

"It is not for you to discuss with me. Anatolia is my concern. And mine only," he snapped, a sharp edge to his voice.

"Then I cannot marry you."

Oh, God, no. She couldn't change her mind. Not now. Not after what Aoife went through to get her to agree. Her father turned from the fire, his back to Aoife. She could no longer see his face. But she could hear his voice, tight and reedy and thin.

"It means so much to you?"

"It does."

He stepped toward her. "All right, then. It shall be done. You have my solemn vow the people of Anatolia will not be harmed." He took her hands again in his. "Does that satisfy you, dearest?"

"Aye, it does."

"Good. I'm glad to hear that. Then you'll marry me?"

"I will."

He cupped her face. "A kiss to seal the agreement?"

Fiona nodded. Aoife's eyes widened as she watched in wonder as the pad of his thumb brushed over her lower lip before his head dipped and their lips met. Fiona gave herself to the kiss, leaning into him as he wrapped his arms around her, pulled her close, and both of them sighed with mutual contentment.

When they broke, he said, "Preparations are already underway for our wedding. I hope you don't find that presumptuous."

She shook her head.

That explained the flurry of activity in the kitchen and why everyone else knew what was going on. Fiona hadn't. He'd prepared ahead of time in the hopes she'd say yes. What would have happened had she refused? Aside from the fact Aoife would have never been conceived, a situation that really messed with her brain.

Or would Niall have forced Fiona to marry him? He didn't seem like the type to force anyone to do anything against their will, but then she didn't know him all that well.

"I look forward to you being my wife, my lady."

When Niall kissed her again, it seemed rather intimate. It was a private moment meant to be shared with no one else but the two of them and yet there Aoife stood watching her parents fall in love. There was something voyeuristic about it. She wanted to turn away yet couldn't. These were her parents. They would marry this night. This was their true beginning and Aoife took comfort in having a hand in that, in making sure Fiona married her father. Her heart palpitated a painful beat.

"I would take you here, now, but I wish to wait until we are properly wed. I would never dishonor you."

Color warmed Aoife's cheeks hearing Niall confess his ardor.

"You would not dishonor me," Fiona replied.

The blush burned hotter through her with Fiona's admission that she not only welcomed him, but she wanted him.

He planted another kiss on her neck. "Only a little while longer to wait, my sweet. I will send servants to help you prepare."

And then he was gone.

Fiona turned and moved back to the window, leaning her forehead on the pane of glass. Aoife knew this was her last chance to get out before anything else happened. Still clutching the Tears, she tipped the vial and let one drop slide out and splash against the floor. The portal opened and she stepped through as quickly as she could, corking the vial. She saw the Fiona of the past turn toward the portal as it closed but she was through and to the other side. She didn't know if her mother saw her or not.

When she made it through, past the biting wind, she collapsed onto the floor, finally allowing her emotions to rush out of her. She couldn't stop the wracking sobs that shuddered through her even if she wanted to.

"Aoife!" Her mother's voice.

The next thing she knew, strong hands clasped her. Sean dragged her into his lap, wrapping his arms around her and holding her tight. He stroked her hair to soothe her while she buried her face in his chest and had her cry out and her mother paced alongside him, firing off questions. Question she couldn't even hear or comprehend.

"Shut up, Fiona," Sean growled. "Can't you see how emotional she is right now?"

"I need to know what happened." Her mother was back to her demanding, steely ways. "Where are the Tears of the Dryad? Does she still have the vial?"

Was that all she was concerned about? Aoife still had it clenched in her fist but she wasn't about to turn it over yet.

"She'll tell you in her own time." His arms tightened around her. "Give her a moment, for pity's sake."

It gave Aoife the comfort she so desperately needed. If only she could get her tears to stop flowing.

"She has to get herself under control before something happens." Fiona.

"She's fine. She'll be fine. Give her space." Sean.

"What's happening? Where am I?" Winnie, the girl Aoife didn't know. Her voice sounded strained and panicked.

Fiona's soothing voice took over and she spoke softly to the girl, but Aoife couldn't focus on her words. She clutched a fistful of Sean's shirt and blinked her tear-filled eyes open. It was then she realized what her mother meant. She glowed. Her whole body lit up the small room. It terrified her. She pushed out of Sean's arms and sat up, glancing around wildly.

"What'd I do?" A sob hitched out of her.

"It's your intense emotion, Aoife. You have to calm down."

"She's trying." Sean wrapped his arms around her again, pulling her to him. He whispered in her ear. "Let me help you."

She clutched his shirt again and buried her face in his chest. He had that musky masculine scent that reminded her of their night together. As she inhaled a deep breath and then blew it out, she did feel somewhat calmer, more at ease.

"There. That's my girl." He patted her back. Then he cupped her face and looked down at her. He wiped away the tears with the pads of his fingers. "All better now?"

Aoife nodded. "I'm sorry."

"Don't be." He granted her a smile. A genuine smile. "You're okay now."

"Tell me what happened," Fiona said.

"Back off, Fiona," he snapped.

"No, it's okay. I can tell her now. I'm okay."

Aoife patted his chest, taking comfort in the curve of muscle under her hand. Remembering how he felt when she was with him and wishing they could be together again. Wishing they could get out of this horrid place and get home.

"If you're sure."

She nodded. He helped her to her feet. She ran a hand through her tangled hair and pushed the cloak off her shoulders. She saw Winnie, then, sitting up on the edge of the narrow bed looking dazed and confused. She was dressed in the rough-spun gown Aoife had found. She handed her the cloak.

"Thank you," the girl said.

Aoife smiled and gave her a nod as she turned back to her mother.

"The Tears?" Fiona asked.

She unclasped her fingers and peered down at it, seeing it was nearly empty. She held it out to her mother, who snatched it and held it close to her heart. As if that was something she had been desperate to get back in her possession.

Aoife tried to ignore the annoyance tugging through her at the way her mother acted with the Tears of the Dryad. She took a deep breath and plunged ahead.

"I saw the past you, Mother. I convinced you to marry Niall."

Fiona bit her bottom lip and Aoife couldn't tell if she was happy about that news or not.

"I remember what you said. Back then, I had no idea who had come to me or why. Now I know." Fiona's voice wavered as she remembered.

"Niall…my father…came. You asked him to spare Anatolia as a wedding present. He agreed."

"But he didn't." Fiona didn't bother to hide the anger in her voice. Her fists clenched. "He destroyed my homeland. Wiped them all out."

Aoife ignored her outburst. "He asked you, formally, to marry him. You said yes. You said you'd marry him. And all the while he already had the preparations for the wedding underway. Did you know that? He loved you enough…he hoped enough…that you would agree to marry him that he went ahead and planned the wedding, knowing you had yet to agree."

Fiona was silent. She turned away, her shoulders slumping and her head in her hands. "That's enough."

Aoife knew, as Fiona, that Niall wanted—expected—her to say yes. Maybe her mother felt trapped or had another end game. It didn't matter. Her path was set.

"Then we know what happens. We know the rest of the story," Aoife said, still pressing on. "You married Niall, my father. And you consummated those wedding vows this night. And that's when I was conceived. Isn't that right?"

Sean placed a hand on her shoulder either to steady her or shut her up, she didn't know which. She didn't care either. She ignored him.

"You loved him but you couldn't tell him."

"He couldn't tell me," she said, her words muffled against her hands. "He never told me."

"He regrets that now. I'm sure of it," Aoife said.

She didn't know what she was doing or why. All she knew was she had to make one last ditch effort to get her parents back together. The way things should have been all along. What would her life be like had she been born here in Faery? Would she have been raised a princess? Would she have learned the ways of magic? Would she become a powerful wizard?

Would she be that prophesized ruler with Fae and Wizard blood sitting the silver throne?

Even Deaglan wouldn't reveal that to her, damn him.

"You can't change the past, Mother. You can only move forward. The only time you have the power to change is the present."

Fiona lifted her head and turned to her daughter, tears brimming in her eyes. "You're right. Let's go home."

Chapter 23

Relief spread through Aoife. Finally, they were getting out of this place. She didn't know how she would feel to get back to the present in Faery, when all she really wanted to do was get home to the present in her time, her world. Sleep in her bed.

But even as she thought it something didn't feel right about it. Sleep in her bed back at the dorm? Or home? After everything that had happened, could she really go back as though everything was 'situation normal'?

"But first," Fiona said and paused. Aoife could see the wheels turning in her mind.

"Mother, whatever you're thinking, no."

She held up the vial of the Tears of the Dryad. "We only have a few drops left. We need to make good use of them. I can get us out of the castle and to a place where we can use a portal to get to the bottom of the cliffs to meet Deaglan. We won't be able to meet him for a while. The wedding is about to start."

Aoife glanced at Sean who looked concerned. They were at her mother's mercy, though, and if she wouldn't open the portal, then they had to follow along with her plan. Fiona pressed a hand against her stomach.

"Besides, there will be a feast and I'm starved."

As soon as the words were out of her mouth, someone's stomach rumbled loudly. Winnie blushed.

"That was me. My apologies."

"When was the last time you ate?" Fiona asked.

She shrugged. "I don't remember."

"Bollocks. Then that's settled. We're getting to the wedding feast before we leave. We all could use the food I think." Fiona turned toward the door and pulled it open a crack. "Stay close to me and do not engage anyone."

"Mother…" Aoife began. "Won't someone recognize you?"

Even though her face was still beat up, Aoife suspected there were people here that would know her regardless. Her mother cursed under her breath again.

"I can't cast a glamour spell. My magic is nonexistent at the moment," Fiona said. She turned to her daughter. "But you have magic."

Aoife was already shaking her head. "No, I can't."

"A glamour spell is the easiest of all the magic," Fiona said. "I can teach you."

"Fiona, no." Sean stepped between them, acting like a shield for Aoife. "She's been through enough today. Leave her be."

Fiona huffed. "Fine. Come on."

Fiona motioned for Winnie to come with her as she opened the door and stepped into the hallway. She led the way, walking with a confident stride through the deserted hallways. Aoife fell in step with Sean and slipped her hand in his. He smiled down at her, making her heart flutter in response.

God, she loved that man. She could tell him she loved him again but the words didn't seem powerful enough, impactful enough, deep enough. How could she even begin to express her true feelings for him? She'd only scratched the surface at the inn the following morning after their night together.

A pulsing light flickered off the walls around them. Fiona halted and turned to look at her over her shoulder.

"Aoife, whatever you're thinking about, stop it."

She flushed, realizing her amorous emotions made her skin glow bright and light up the hallway. She tamped down those thoughts, but it took several minutes for her to get it under control.

"Sorry," she muttered.

Fiona resumed walking, Winnie beside her.

Sean squeezed her hand and whispered, "What were you thinking about?"

Her breath fluttered out of her as she glanced up at him. "You."

He looked dumbstruck as he focused his attention on the hallway in front of them. Maybe she shouldn't have said it. Maybe she should have kept it to herself but, damn it, she thought he needed to know. He *should* know.

Fiona came to a sudden halt as she peered around a corner. She waved for them to press against a wall. Winnie flattened next to Fiona. Sean and Aoife did the same. As they did, Aoife could hear the footsteps before the group came into view.

There were several guards leading the way, followed by Deaglan who escorted Fiona—the Fiona of the past. Aoife stared wide-eyed at her mother as she passed by, dressed in a beautiful pewter gown. As Past Fiona walked by them, something strange happened. A ripple wafted through the air and passed through them. Current Fiona shuddered and a breath escaped her, fogging in the air as though she stood in freezing temperatures. Even Aoife felt the cold air rush over and through her.

Deaglan sensed it, too. He turned his head and saw them, a horrified expression on his face as he shook his head.

"What it is?" Past Fiona asked.

Deaglan patted her hand resting in the crook of his shoulder. "Nothing, dearie. Nothing."

"I'm suddenly chilled," she said.

"Wedding jitters, I'm sure." He hurried her along, past the foursome standing in the shadowed hallway.

But the message was clear to all of them. Fiona standing in the presence of her past self caused the wave of icy air to go through them all.

"That was creepy," Aoife said.

"What was that?" Sean asked.

"My best guess is it was a ripple in time." Fiona's face had drained of color. "I've felt it before when I got too close to my past self."

"You're determined to go through with this?" Sean wanted to know.

"Aye."

Fiona charged ahead, unwilling to hear any further protests. Aoife exchanged a glance with Sean and she could see the uncertainty in his eyes. They arrived at the great hall in time to see Deaglan hand over the bride to King Niall. The four of them spread out, hovering close to the shadows and keeping to the back of the crowd. Aoife refused to release Sean's hand. She wanted to stay as close to him as possible.

As they stood there, they watched the cleric wrap the couple's hands together in a traditional handfasting ceremony. Emotion clotted Aoife's throat as she witnessed their union. Sean wrapped his arm around her shoulders and held her close.

"It's not every day you get to see the marriage ceremony of your own parents, aye?" Sean whispered it against her temple and then planted a kiss there.

She shook her head, not trusting her voice.

She stole a glance at her mother, who stood in the shadows, her expression stony. Aoife could tell seeing the ceremony from this angle did something to her. Niall and Fiona exchanged marriage vows and the cleric pronounced them married. As Niall leaned in for a kiss to seal the vows, the Fiona of the future turned away.

Something in her face in that moment gave Aoife all the information she needed—regret, guilt, despair. She wondered if her mother regretted leaving Niall on their wedding night. She couldn't bring herself to ask. She wondered if she wished she could change that aspect of the past—to have stayed with him instead of leaving. Instead of going to find Cian.

"The banquet is in the dining hall."

Fiona didn't wait for them to reply as she hurried away. Aoife and Sean fell in step together behind her mother and Winnie.

"You there."

The voice startled them. Fiona's head snapped up as she looked up at the guard approaching them. Aoife's heart jumped into her throat and fear washed over her. The guard held up a hand to halt them in the middle of the corridor. He peered at Fiona, but her face was still battered and bruised.

"What happened to your face? Are you all right? Do you need a healer?"

"Thank ye for the concern, milord." Fiona dipped a curtsey. "I'm quite all right."

His eyes narrowed. "Don't I know you?"

"I dinna think so," she said, responding with a thickened accent. "We're merely passing to the banquet hall for the feast."

"I know you. I'm certain of it. You resemble the queen."

The queen. Fiona stilled and inhaled sharply. Perhaps none of them realized the truth of it—that when Fiona married Niall she took his place by his side as his queen. Aoife looked up at Sean, imploring him to do something, but she could see the wheels already turning in his head. He stepped around Fiona and Winnie with a bright smile on his face.

"The bride's cousin," he said. "The resemblance is quite uncanny, really, when her face is…ah, normal."

"What happened to her?" He looked over Sean, his tone full of concern.

Sean took the guard by the arm and led him a step away, dropping his voice low enough to seem as though he whispered.

"Horse accident. Quite tragic, actually. The horse kicked her in the face. We had to put it down but the worst part…" He paused, glanced over at Fiona to dramatize his point. "I'm afraid she'll never be right in the head again." He tapped his temple then gave the universal signal for "crazy" by twirling his forefinger.

"Is that so?" The guard peered over at Fiona, who took a sudden interest in one of the torches braced along the stone wall.

"Aye, just so. She wanders, you see. She thought we were heading to the banquet hall, when in fact I'm taking her back to her chamber. It's not fitting for anyone to see her in this state. Do you agree?"

He nodded. "I'll escort you."

"That won't be necessary."

Before the guard could reply, Sean threw a mean punch. He hit him so hard, the man melted to the ground as though his legs had suddenly become boneless.

"I was beginning to wonder what your game plan was," Fiona said. "What took you so long?"

"I had to figure out if he was my size." Sean set about stripping the guard of his uniform. "Aoife, see if you can find a cloak or something for Fiona. We can't afford to get caught again. Especially if you're determined to go to the feast."

"I'll find one," Fiona said. "I know this place better than she does. Winnie, stay here with them."

She scurried away. Aoife stood, numb, in the hall trying to decide what she should be doing. She pressed her cold fingertips to her temples.

"This entire situation is crazy. All I want to do is go home."

"And we will, I promise." Sean had the man stripped down to this underwear. Once he had the uniform off and piled to the side, he took him under the arms and lifted his upper body. "Grab his legs."

"Where are we going with him?" Aoife asked.

"Anywhere out of sight," Sean said.

There was a doorway off to the side and he backed toward it. Winnie hurried around behind him and shoved it open for them. It was nothing more than a storage room. They deposited the guard and then Sean set about dressing. He pulled the jerkin on over his doublet and then strapped the sword to his side. The best thing about the jerkin was it was hooded and he could pull it up to conceal his features. Still, he looked about as out of place as a penguin in the desert.

"Found one!" Fiona announced as she came back into view wearing the cloak. She looked Sean up and down. "Nice work."

"Let's get this over with," he said. "I'm not happy about this situation and we should already be going to meet Deaglan."

"It's too early yet," she said.

They headed toward the banquet hall and blended in with the rest of the crowd. The king and queen had already arrived and sat at the high table, the place of honor. Servants passed through the cavernous room with steaming trays of food to place along the tables. Other servants had tankards of ale and filled the cups along the long tables. The foursome picked a table off to one side, away from Niall's and Fiona's direct line of vision. Aoife sat between Winnie and Fiona, trying to be as inconspicuous as possible, while Sean hovered behind them. He refused to sit, insisting on acting as a guard.

The food was served, but Aoife had suddenly lost her appetite. Winnie, however, went after her trencher with alacrity, hunching over it and scooping it into her mouth. The poor girl had been starving. Her mother patted her hand and leaned toward her.

"Eat, Aoife. It may be out last chance for food before we get home."

But where was home? The Fae future or the human realm future? She took up the wooden spoon and ate.

As Aoife finished her fourth course, King Niall rose from his seat and his bride followed, standing next to him with their hands still bound. A hush fell over the crowd and the room had gone still. All eyes were on the king and queen. All except for her mother's. She scanned the crowded room, though Aoife had no idea what or who she was trying to find.

"Honored guests, my queen and I bid you good night. Please stay as long as you like to enjoy more food and entertainments."

After Niall spoke, all went back to their feasting. Music played once more and the king and queen stepped down from the high table and left the banquet hall. The heated blush crept up Aoife's neck and into her cheeks. She knew what would happen next.

Seeing it was another matter altogether.

As soon as they were out of sight, her mother rose and stepped away from the table.

"That's it. Let's get out of here."

Aoife, Winnie and Sean followed Fiona away from the banquet hall and into the twisting and turning corridors of the towers.

"What's your plan?" he asked.

"My plan?"

"I know you have to open a portal, so where do you plan to do that?"

Fiona halted suddenly, her gaze fixed on something. Aoife followed her gaze and watched the king and queen walking together. They passed much too close. That same ripple went through the air and the temperature dropped around them. Fiona's breath came out in plumes, as though she were standing in the middle of winter.

"Did you feel that?" Past Fiona of the past shivered and moved closer to Niall.

"Feel what, my dear?"

"That sudden coldness in the air."

Sean clamped his hand around her upper arm and dragged her away, out of sight and around the corner. Before either of them noticed, Aoife and Winnie ducked down, too.

"The towers are cold this time of year. I'm sure we merely passed through a draft." Their voices faded as they left the area behind.

"Fiona?" Sean gave her a little shake to get her out of her trance.

"I'm all right. But there's something odd about seeing your past self walk by. At the time, I was so focused on what was to come, I noticed nothing else. Did you feel it? Did you feel the ripple in time?" She blinked, tore her gaze from the place where the couple had passed by and looked up at Sean.

He nodded. "I did. We all did. You shouldn't do that again."

She leaned against the wall and Aoife could sense the hesitation in her. "Mother, are you having second thoughts?"

"About what?" Her gaze flickered to her daughter.

"About any of this or…me?"

Her expression softened and she smiled. She reached for Aoife, patted her cheek. "No. Not at all." She turned to Sean. "You asked what my plan was. Let's get to the garden and open the portal. No one will see us there."

"All right then. Lead the way."

Fiona took them through the corridors of the Towers of Illyria. Most of the inhabitants were still in the banquet hall, blissfully happy with their feast, their music and their drink. It made navigating the hallways much easier. When they arrived at the gardens, Fiona took out the Tears of the Dryad.

"Deaglan said to meet him at the foot of the cliffs an hour before dawn. We have some time to kill before then." Fiona clutched the vial in her hand.

"Maybe we should get some rest, then," Sean suggested.

She nodded. "Probably a good idea. Come with me. I know a place where we can at least sit."

She led them deeper into the gardens until they came up on a greenhouse. She pushed open the door. Inside, the scent of fragrant plants burst around them. It was not a typical greenhouse. There were herbs hanging from the ceiling and potted plants lined up like soldiers along one long wooden bench on one side. On the other side, a row of what looked like lounge chairs. Her mother waved to them.

Winnie took a seat near the end. Fiona perched on the edge of hers and took her hand, talking to her in a soft voice Aoife couldn't hear. Sean moved to the end, out of earshot of her mother and took a seat. He motioned for Aoife to join him. When she started to take the chair next to him, he shook his head and patted his lap.

"Really?" Her pulse quickened. They hadn't been intimate since their night together at the inn.

"Really."

Aoife nestled between his legs and he wrapped his arms around her as she leaned back into his chest. He was warm and comforting like her favorite winter blanket. There was something peaceful and enchanting about the gardens, something that gave her a sense of calm in a world of strange chaos. Glancing up at the night sky through the panes of the glass ceiling, she could see the bright twinkling stars of constellations she didn't know.

"What happens when we get back?" she asked, her voice a quiet whisper in the darkness.

"We go on. We live. We figure things out." His voice rumbled in his chest against her back.

"Do we have things to figure out?"

"You know we do." His arms tightened around her. "Aoife, it's impossible for our relationship not to change after everything."

She flushed. "I know. I'm prepared for that." She turned her head so she could look at him over her shoulder. "All I ask is you don't shut me out."

"I didn't. I wouldn't. I couldn't. I've spent a lot of years protecting you. I don't plan to stop now."

A smile lifted the corners of her mouth. "I'm glad to hear that."

"Get some rest. I'm not going anywhere."

She took comfort in that and leaned her head back on his chest. It wasn't long before she dropped off to sleep. She hadn't realized how emotionally draining the last few days had been. It was nice knowing she was safe in Sean's arms for the moment and, for that brief moment, everything was going to be okay.

The next thing she knew, Sean shook her awake. It had seemed as though she'd only been asleep for a couple of minutes but in reality, a couple of hours past.

"Time to go," Sean said.

She struggled out of her chair, rubbing the sleep from her eyes as she got to her feet. Winnie and Fiona stood in the center of the greenhouse. Her mother held the Tears of the Dryad in one hand, ready to pull off the cork. But something about her demeanor told Aoife she hesitated.

"Mother? What is it?"

"I achieved nothing I set out to do when I came back in time. I couldn't stop my kidnapping. Both Niall and Cian still live. And...you, Aoife." Her gaze flickered to Aoife and their eyes met. "For that, I am grateful. I only wish I could have saved Deaglan."

"There may be a chance for that yet, Mother." Aoife gave her a reassuring, knowing smile.

"Let's do this," Sean said.

"Wait, my lady." It was the first time Aoife had heard Winnie speak up.

"Winnie? What is it?"

"Mayhap I should stay here." She shivered.

Fiona clutched the vial in her hand and wrapped an arm around her. "Why? Don't you want to go with me?"

"I do, my lady, I truly do. But...I...I'm afraid."

"There's nothing to fear," Fiona said. "I would never be able to forgive myself for leaving you here. Besides, the future is not so different from this past. Come back with us."

Winnie looked from Fiona to Aoife to Sean. Her gaze settled on him. "Before we go…I don't believe I thanked you properly for saving my life."

"No thanks are necessary," Sean said. "I'm glad I was able to get you away from there."

She smiled, nodded, and looked back at Fiona. "What happens when we get there?"

Fiona shrugged. "I don't know, honestly. But I do know you will be safe with me and Niall in the future. He will be happy to have you as part of his household."

"If you're certain."

"I am." Fiona gave her a squeeze and then stepped away. "Now, let's get out of here."

Aoife slipped her hand into Sean's. "I'm ready."

Fiona let one drop slide from the bottle and land on the floor with a silent splash. The portal opened and a second later, Fiona disappeared inside. Winnie followed, then Aoife and Sean. She hated the cold biting wind stinging her skin as she went through the portal and stepped on the other side. She was not prepared for the horrible biting wind ripping through her when she was out of the portal as it closed behind them.

They arrived at the foot of the snowcapped Cliffs of Mhothair. Snow drifted from the black sky and, much to their despair, they found themselves surrounded by men with swords. They had arrived in the middle of Cian's battle encampment and not where Deaglan had instructed them to go.

"Oh, shit," Fiona whispered.

When Niall and his new bride left the banquet hall to consummate their wedding vows, Deaglan knew it was time for him to leave as well. He only had a few hours before he had to meet the Future Fiona and his granddaughter at the bottom of the cliffs. And he had yet to make the potion to get them back home.

At least, he hoped he could make the potion. He had seen the recipe in one of his spell books long ago. He recalled which book, but he had never attempted to make it and he wasn't even sure it would work.

Once he returned to his workroom, he lit several tapers and set about his work. He found the spell book that had the recipe for the time portal and flipped open to the page he'd marked eons ago. He didn't know then why he would need this particular potion, but he understood it more now. He took the pink crystal Aoife had given him and ground it down into a fine dust. Then he pulled other magical herbs and crystals from his shelves and measured them according to the recipe. He ground them all together until it was nothing but a fine sparkling powder.

He only needed one more ingredient. He pulled down the Tears of the Dryad, uncorked the vial and then poured exactly one drop into the new vial he'd just made. A spark and a poof and then it was done. He replaced the Tears of the Dryad back on the shelf. He shook the new time potion, watching as it turned from pink to blue, shimmering like the Tears in a similar fashion. Satisfied, he placed it on the shelf next to the Tears with a wide yawn. He could get at least a couple hours sleep before he had to meet Future Fiona at the cliffs.

Chapter 24

It was nearly dawn. Deaglan awoke with a yawn and a stretch and then hurried back to his workroom to grab the new potion to find Fiona and the others and get them back home to the future.

As he opened the door to his chamber, though, he knew something was amiss. Standing in the middle of the room with an open portal was Fiona.

"Fiona, wait!"

She stepped through and the portal closed. It was too late. She had stolen the Tears of the Dryad and disappeared. But he knew that was the Fiona of the present. The Fiona of the future waited for him to show up at the bottom of the cliffs.

At least she hadn't stolen the wrong potion. She had taken only the Tears of the Dryad and left the time potion where it was. He would need to find where Fiona and the others at the base of the cliffs with the Time Sphere. Then he could use that and the potion to transport himself there.

Deaglan snatched the potion from the shelf and hurried down the winding steps through the now quiet castle to the library. He headed directly for the Time Sphere and, with a wave of his hand, activated it to show him Fiona, Aoife and the others.

He was horrified to discover they were on the wrong side of the cliffs. They had been captured by Cian and his men. They must have opened a portal in the middle of the encampment by mistake.

And the worst thing was they were all in trouble. Without turning off the Time Sphere, he cast a transportation spell to intercept Fiona and the others to save them from certain doom.

Aoife watched her mother prowl the prison tent, her hands tied behind her back and chewing on her lower lip. As if pacing back and forth would get them out of the tent faster. Outside, the tent was heavily guarded by several of Cian's men. Sean sat on the ground near the flap working his hands behind his back. Aoife took a spot next to him and leaned back to see he was working at the knots on his rope. His wrists were bleeding and raw and it shot pain right through her.

She met his gaze and started to ask him what exactly was his plan when he got free when he shook his head, a stern look on his face. It silenced her.

"Pacing a hole in the ground isn't helping, Fiona," Sean said.

"You don't understand. I have to get out of here. I have to get to Cian."

Sean went still and stiffened and Aoife was sure she could feel the sudden rage emanating off him.

"You damn fool. You brought us here on purpose," he said, his jaw tight.

Fiona stopped pacing long enough to peer at him. The evidence was written all over her face. "I thought I could get us closer."

"Your hatred for that man is going to get us all killed." There was razor sharp edge to Sean's voice, something Aoife had never heard before and was thankful it wasn't directed at her.

"I'm sorry all right," she snapped. "I intend to kill that man before we get out of here."

"No, Mother." Aoife was surprised at the total calm in her voice as was Fiona. Sean's head snapped over to her but she ignored him and peered at her mother with an unwavering gaze, her confidence swelling. "Your thirst for vengeance has gone on long enough. You're going to let Sean get us out of here and then we're going home."

Fiona visibly swallowed hard as she gave a nod of agreement. Her shoulders slumped with defeat. "All right. What's your plan? If you mean to use a portal, forget it. I only have a few of the Tears left and I intend to use them when Deaglan arrives to send us home."

When they were ambushed, Fiona had moved quickly to conceal the vial in one of her pockets and the guards hadn't thought to search them since they were all unarmed except for Sean. They confiscated his sword.

"My plan has nothing to do with the Tears," he said, his voice still terse.

That got Fiona's attention. "What *are* you doing?"

"Nothing." He glanced at the guard standing at the opening of the tent. The guard who seemed completely unconcerned with them.

Because they weren't a threat. They were merely four suspicious travelers who had stumbled upon the encampment and were tossed into a tent for interrogation. Prince Cian had been summoned and would soon arrive.

But what the guard didn't know and the rest of them did was Sean had magic. And so did Aoife, though she hadn't a clue as to how to use it. Her mother's magic was still strangely defunct. Sean gave one swift yank and then his hands were free.

But it wasn't without cost. Blood trickled down his wrists. He had worked the rope from his wrists but left raw, angry abrasions behind. Fiona's eyes lit with excitement when she realized he had managed to free himself. Aoife opened her mouth to ask a question but he placed a finger over her lips to shush her. Then he untied her wrists and pulled away the rope.

Fiona and Winnie gathered close. He unbound their wrists as well.

"What's the plan?" Fiona asked.

"I'm going to get us out of here, that's what."

"You're going to use magic," Fiona said, her voice quiet.

He cut her a glance as Aoife had a sharp intake of breath. She knew the risk.

"Sean, are you sure you should? After what happened at Lambridge…" Aoife placed a gentle hand on his arm, remembering the destruction he'd left behind.

Back at Lambridge, he knew he wouldn't be able to control his magic then so he'd sent Aoife to collect her mother. She knew he wanted her out of the way. It had quite possibly saved her life as well as Fiona's. Now he wanted to do more magic in such close quarters? How could he possibly contain it?

"It's the only way we're going to get out of here and meet Deaglan if we intend to get home." He turned to Aoife then and placed his hands on her shoulders. "I need you to help me. Can you do that?"

She nodded. "I'll do whatever you need me to do."

"What I'm about to do is dangerous. And I don't want you to get hurt."

Hot pinpricks of fear went over her. She knew he meant his magic. He didn't know if he could control it once he released it. She recalled the story he told her before when they were at the inn, how his wild magic had killed his family. How he had been turned into a weapon. She was also there at Lambridge when he nearly destroyed the entire castle with this power. It had left behind charred earth and shattered walls and a lot of dead.

"What must I do?" She whispered it so only he could hear.

"Remember how you felt earlier? When you returned from talking to your mother?"

She nodded, biting her lip.

"And how your emotions were running high and it made you glow."

"Yes."

"And when I took you into my arms and held you, it calmed you. Soothed you."

She swallowed the lump in her throat that had suddenly formed. "Yes." The word came out like ice.

"Then I need you to do that for me, if I can't get myself under control."

"Aye." Fiona stepped closer to them. "That's the way of it. You finally get it."

"Stay out of this, Fiona. This is between me and Aoife." He practically snarled the words.

"No, I will not." She shoved them apart and turned to him, her hands on his upper arms. "You listen now. Aoife's magic reawakened yours. Your magic manifested hers. You two are tethered to each other now. You harness each other. She can help you as you can help her."

Aoife's heart skipped a beat. "How? How did that happen?"

"When you were intimate," her mother said.

Aoife knew things would change between them. She did not know how much, though, or even that they were tied to one another now. No wonder she had felt so different, so vibrant, so alive. It went beyond her love for Sean and burned somewhere deep in her core where her magic lived.

"It wouldn't have happened with just anyone," her mother continued. "It only happens when there is a shared bond between the two. Between *you* two."

Aoife's mouth went bone dry. "What…are you saying?"

Sean shoved away Fiona and stepped around her. His eyes were intense and burned bright with passion and love, stark and vivid. She had never seen it before. It scared her and she took a step backward. But he took a step forward, keeping her close.

"She's saying I'm in love with you, Aoife."

Her breath caught in her throat as she gasped. Her stomach dropped to the bottom of her shoes. She had hoped for this moment all her life, yet she never expected he would tell her in the middle of a tent with her mother and another stranger standing by to hear. She had never expected she would be standing in the past in Faery after fighting for her very life. She had never expected him to tell her when they were so far from home, so far from everything she knew.

She'd expected him to tell her over a romantic dinner.

He reached for her, took her hand in his, lacing their fingers. Fiona moved in, hoping to hear what he had to say next. Sean turned toward her and barked, "Give us some space, damn it."

Fiona put her hands up in surrender and stepped away. She wrapped an arm around Winnie and turned around, putting their backs to them.

Sean took a deep breath and pulled Aoife closer.

"Sean, are you…sure?"

"I've never been more sure about anything in my life. As much as I hate to admit it, your mother is right. When we were together, the magic between us came alive. Yours. Mine. It scared me. I don't want to hurt you."

She knew something was wrong between them, but she couldn't pinpoint it. Now she knew. She understood so much more about him.

"You could never hurt me, Sean." She was sure of it even as she said it, her voice calm as she gazed up at him. She only wanted to drink in the moment, to relish the way he looked at her now—as though she meant more to him than anything else in the world.

"But I could. I would never forgive myself if anything happened to you."

Her hands slipped up his chest, over the curve of muscle. She rested her hands there and was all too aware of the strong, steady thump of his rapidly beating heart. "I trust you. I always have."

He released her hand and cupped her face. "I'm glad it was you who awoke the magic within me once again."

"Me, too." She could barely force the words out. "I love you."

He kissed her then, his lips warm and soft and sweet on hers. It was nothing more than a whisper at first and then he deepened the kiss into something slow and thoughtful and intimate. She wanted to imprint this memory into her mind for the rest of her life, to savor this moment. And though it wasn't the perfect time to tell her or the best of circumstances, she had never experienced such happiness as she did then.

When he broke from her, he leaned his forehead against hers and dropped his voice so only she could hear. "You're glowing."

"I can't help it. You make me glow."

He dropped a kiss on her forehead. "When we get home, I intend to show you how much you mean to me."

Her heart fluttered as he released her and turned away. He cracked his knuckles.

"Are you sure you should do this?" she asked.

"I have to. It's the only way we'll get out of here alive." He dropped his voice lower. "Cian won't like that we infiltrated his camp, so we have to get out of here as soon as we can. The only way we can do that is if I make that happen."

Fiona turned from her seclusion. She and Winnie moved to stand next to Aoife behind Sean. He took a deep breath.

"You can do this, Sean," Fiona said.

He lifted one hand toward the opening of the tent, took a deep breath and released the magic. It was nothing more than a brilliant white light that trickled from his fingertips in lazy curls as though it were smoke curling from a chimney in the dead of winter. Aoife watched, holding her breath, as the tendrils of white magic enveloped the guard standing outside. A moment later, he fell to the ground.

"Wait here." Sean stepped outside the tent and a second later poked his head back in. "He's dead. Let's go."

They followed him out of the tent and into the cold early morning before dawn. The temperature had dropped even more since their arrival and snow collected around the edges of the tents. Aoife shivered, trying to ignore the bone-chilling cold, and kept close to Sean as they made their way through the encampment. It wasn't long before their presence was noticed. Guards appeared in front of them.

"Turn around," Sean said

When they turned to head back the other way, more guards closed in. They were trapped.

"This isn't good," Fiona said.

"Use the Tears," Sean suggested.

"No. There isn't much left. Besides, we can't risk one of them following us and I'm not sure where we'd go anyway. Use your magic again, Sean. You can fight them with ease."

Aoife glanced up at him and could see the indecision flicker across his face. She knew he was leery of trying his magic again. She placed her hand on his arm in reassurance.

"You can do it." Her voice was soft and full of encouragement.

He lifted his hand again but this time, the tendrils of magic fired off as though he had fired a gun. The blast from his hand was so powerful it sent him back a few steps. The puff of white magic hit the first guard square in the chest. He turned to a pile of smoldering ash.

Behind them, one of the other guards shouted for their arrest. Sean spun around and fired off another round of magic at the men coming from the other direction. He killed two more. They, too, turned into a pile of ash.

Now there were others stepping out of tents and more reinforcements coming from both directions. They were definitely outnumbered. Aoife turned to Sean for ideas but she drew up short. He had a look of severe concentration but it was more than that. It was terrifying. The color had drained from his face. Sweat beaded his forehead.

"He's lost in his magic," Fiona said. "You have to bring him back, Aoife. Do something."

Panic rose in her throat. "I don't know what to do."

Sean's hands had become dangerous weapons. He fired off round after round of his deadly magic, killing one right after the other. One guard had a shield he put up and discovered the magic glossed right over him. The others quickly caught on.

"Aoife! Do something!"

"What am I supposed to do?" She was frozen in a state of panic.

"Bollocks," Fiona said. "We have no choice then. I'll make a portal."

She pulled out the Tears of the Dryad. As she uncorked it, one of the guards lunged toward Aoife. She dodged and the guy collided with her mother. The hit was so violent the vial was knocked from her hand. Aoife regained her footing in time to see it tumble end over end, as if in slow motion, until it finally hit the ground.

And shattered.

The remaining Tears poured onto the ground and a sudden wailing erupted as a black portal exploded in front of them. There wasn't any time to react as a fierce black wind kicked up, sucking in anything and anyone in its path. Fiona grabbed Winnie and shoved her out of the way.

Aoife turned to Sean to try and get his attention when suddenly the magic bursting from his hands went wild. It hit a nearby tent, engulfing it in blue-white flames. The brutal wind from the portal blew through her, cutting her right to the bone. The white fire spread through the tents, eating up the canvas walls as though it were nothing more than dry timber.

"Sean!"

He seemed not to hear or notice her. In a last ditch effort, she put her head down and charged toward him like a linebacker ready to tackle a quarterback. She smacked into him, head first, wrapping her arms around his waist. It shoved him off his feet and he tumbled to the ground. She fell with him, landing on top of him while fire raged around them and snow drifted to the ground from a blackened sky.

"Sean, can you hear me?"

He blinked several times. His eyes cleared and she could tell he had come back to himself.

"What happened?" He took a deep breath and then coughed. "There's a portal?"

"It was an accident."

"The fire?"

"That was an accident, too."

She scrambled off him, helped him to his feet and hurried over to Fiona and Winnie.

"Close the portal," Fiona shouted over the wind to Sean.

"I don't know how."

Fiona turned her hopeful gaze on Aoife. She already knew she was going to ask her to do it and she hadn't the first clue as to how to close a portal. Before her mother asked, Aoife stepped away from the group to focus. Maybe she could do it.

Remembering how she unlocked the cell door back in the dungeon, she reached down inside her and found that glittery silvery thread of magic. It was warm and wonderful and decadent and when she touched it with her mind, it seemed to light up with joy. As though it was happy she had returned to use it.

Despite the circumstances, she smiled.

The wind whipped through her hair as she took another step toward the portal. She latched onto the magic inside her and held it, letting it fill her.

"Aoife, what are you doing?"

It was Sean yelling at her. And then her mother's terse reply, "Let her try."

The only person Aoife had seen perform magic was Sean and when he did it, he held his hand up as though reaching for something or someone. So she did the same and recalled, too, that's how she did it when she broke them out of the cell.

She pointed her hand toward the open portal that still sucked in Cian's unsuspecting men, horses, tents and whatever else was in its path. The icy wind continued to slice through her but she couldn't tell if that was from the weather or the portal.

It didn't matter.

As Aoife reached her hand toward the portal, she closed her eyes and imagined what it would look like if she could close the portal with the magic. Warm tendrils burst from her fingertips, there was a flash of light behind her closed eyes and then she heard a gasp behind her. She could only assume that was her mother.

The wind halted. She cracked her eyes open and saw the portal was gone. She had also managed to douse the flames that were spreading through the camp.

Sean moved to stand next to her. "You did it."

Her heart pounded an erratic beat as she realized she had really done it. And she wasn't even sure how.

"That's my girl."

Before Aoife could reply, a puff of smoke appeared in front of her. When the smoke cleared, Deaglan appeared looking more than unhappy.

"What happened? There was an open portal here moments ago."

"Aoife closed it," Fiona said, sounding like a proud mother.

His scrutinizing gaze landed on her and she shifted from one foot to the other. "*You* closed it?"

She nodded. "Yes, I did."

One dark brow lifted either in disbelief or astonishment, Aoife wasn't sure which. And she didn't care. She had closed the portal.

"How did it get open in the first place?" he wanted to know. He looked at Fiona when he asked.

"There was an accident," she said. "The vial was bumped out of my hand. It shattered and spilled the rest of the Tears."

He closed his eyes and shook his head. "Do you have any idea what damage that has caused?"

"A few of Cian's men were sucked inside," Fiona continued. "I don't see that as bad thing."

"Do you even know where the portal led to?" he demanded.

"Well…no."

Across the camp, shouts could be heard and then they could see blue-white flames rising higher and higher into the night sky. Fiona turned toward it.

"That fire. That was my doing. That means I've already gone through the portal to the human realm." She spun toward Deaglan. "You have to send us back."

"I can't. Not without the Tears of the Dryad."

Color drained from Fiona's face. Aoife moved closer to Sean, trying hard to maintain her hopes even as they seeped away.

"The spell I intended to use would only work with the Tears of the Dryad. The second potion I made will only work with a few drops of the Tears." Deaglan held it up and they could all see the bluish shimmer in the vial. Fiona eyed it closely before he put it back into his pocket out of sight.

"Surely there must be something you can do. You're a *wizard*," Fiona said. "You have the Time Sphere. We can use that."

He shook his head before she even finished. "I can't use that."

"Why not?"

Even Aoife could hear the high-pitched desperation in her mother's voice.

"The Time Sphere is a dangerous tool, Fiona. I thought you understood that. I thought you also understood it can only be activated every five hundred years and now is not that time."

"What about the second one?" Aoife asked, finally finding her voice.

"What second one?" Deaglan's forehead creased in confusion.

Fiona's eyes widened in surprise. "Aye, the second Time Sphere in the Ivory Wood. We could try that one."

"There is only one Time Sphere and that's in Niall's library.

There's not a second one in the Ivory Wood." Deaglan looked at them as if they were all crazy.

"No, there is. I was there. I used it to come back in time," Fiona said.

"I'm telling you that's not bloody possible because it doesn't exist," Deaglan said.

"Maybe not in this time." Everyone turned to Sean. "I'm just saying that it's possible it doesn't exist yet."

"We should go to the Ivory Wood to find out, then," Fiona suggested. She turned back to Deaglan. "You can get us there with your magic."

Consideration flickered over his haggard features. Aoife noticed for the first time how tired he looked. He nodded finally. "All right. I'll take us."

"No one is going anywhere."

King Niall stepped around Deaglan and he looked far from happy to see them.

Chapter 25

A gasp escaped Fiona as she saw the man she married so long ago. If she hadn't been such a fool back then, she would have realized she had been in love with him and stayed.

"Niall."

His gaze flickered to her and scrutinized her, much the way he had when she had first come to him. She remembered that look well. It took a moment, but recognition passed over his face and then anger and rage. He stomped toward her, took her by the arms and gave her a little shake.

"Who did this to your face? If it was Cian, I'll kill him." He glanced over her. "And why are you dressed this way?"

"Let her go, son. She's not who you think." Deaglan's calm voice wafted over both of them. She'd forgotten he was there along with Winnie, Aoife and Sean.

Aoife. She couldn't allow Niall to know who she was for fear it could alter things in the future. Or mayhap being here anyway altered things. She didn't know and it was too confusing to try to sort out.

Niall's head snapped toward Deaglan. "What do you mean by that?" When he looked back at Fiona, his gaze went over her from head to toe. "Are you telling me this Fiona is an imposter?"

"No, Niall. I'm not an imposter." Fiona wasn't sure why tears filled her eyes and threatened to spill. "He's trying to tell you something else. I'm not the Fiona of this time you know."

Color drained from his face as he dropped his arms and stepped back. She knew he would understand and guess what had happened. "You used the Time Sphere, didn't you? When? How?"

She could no more stop the tears from falling than she could stop loving Niall. She bit her lip and nodded. "I'm so sorry. I should never have come here."

"How did you get here?" he wanted to know. "And what happened to your face?"

"It's a long story. One that will take a while to tell."

He glanced around, saw the others behind her. "Who are they?"

Winnie kept her eyes downcast. In her world, he was still a king. But in Fiona's, he was her husband, her lover and the father of her child. The others peered at him as though they were equals.

"They're all friends," she said before anyone else could answer. "They came to help me. Nothing more. We're all trying to get back where we belong. I'm trying to get back to you."

He squared his shoulders, his expression turning stony. "But you left me."

"I did. I'm sorry. I should have stayed. I wish now I *had* stayed." She placed her hands on his chest. "Forgive me."

He seemed to soften. "Where did you go?"

"I-I can't tell you."

"He knew," Aoife said. "He knew all that time when he told us the story but he didn't tell us *this*."

Niall ignored Aoife's outburst and narrowed his eyes at Fiona. "How do I know you're telling the truth?"

"I can prove it." Sean stepped forward, pausing next to Fiona. He reached into his pocket and brought out a smooth gold coin. He held it out to Niall.

The king's gaze landed on the coin in his palm and he stared at it for a long moment. "Where did you get that?"

"You gave it to me. In the future."

His eyes narrowed. "Who are you?"

"Who he is doesn't matter," Fiona said before he could answer. She didn't want Sean giving away any pertinent details about the future. "What does matter is that you can help us get home."

"That's what you told me, too," Sean said.

Niall took the coin, turned it over in his hand as he gazed at it. "This is one of the coins of the old empire. Before I came here and conquered this realm."

"Can you help us?" Fiona whisked away the tears, wishing she hadn't allowed them to shed. But she'd been overcome with emotion at seeing Niall she couldn't stop herself. "Can you get us to the second Time Sphere?"

His brows creased. "There is no second Time Sphere. Only the one in my library. Father, do you know of a second one?"

"No, but they insist it resides in the Ivory Wood."

Niall shook his head. "I know of no such thing in the Ivory Wood."

"Nor I," Deaglan agreed.

"It's the one I used to come back in time," Fiona said.

"Well, there's only one way to find out, isn't there?"

Niall did a wave of his hand and a second later they were whisked through the realm to the Ivory Wood. He'd sifted them. Aoife groaned, holding her stomach and leaning against Sean. Winnie pinched the bridge of her nose between her thumb and forefinger. Deaglan looked unaffected—he wouldn't be since he was used to that sort of thing. Nor was Fiona affected.

The white bark trees soared upward toward the sky, the leaves and branches creating a canopy overhead that blotted out morning light. The ground was still covered with a thick carpet of yellow, orange and red leaves—an oddity as the leaves overhead were stark white. They had made it to the place where the Time Sphere had been and Deaglan and Niall were correct. There was no Time Sphere.

"I don't understand," Fiona said. "It was here before."

"In the future," Sean added. "But this is a different time in Faery. And, as we all know, time in Faery moves at a different pace."

"Aye," Deaglan agreed with a nod. "It is not a constant either in the past or the future. Returning you to the exact moment in time you left will be tricky." He paused, smiled, and pulled the shimmering blue vial from his pocket. "But I believe I can accomplish that."

"I don't have any more Tears of the Dryad," Fiona said.

"But you have me. And you, Fiona, you have your magic as well," Deaglan said.

"I'm afraid I don't. Somewhere along the way, my magic fizzled out. I can't reach it anymore like you taught me. It's gone."

"Then my father and I will get you home." Niall took Fiona's hand between his. "Fiona, tell me what happened to your face."

She swallowed the hard lump that formed. She'd not seen him look at her like that in so many years it made her want to melt into a puddle. She could tell by the look in his eyes, he was truly interested in what happened to her and why. If she knew him, he wanted to fix it, to make sure it would never happen to her again.

"I was captured by Cian's forces. They beat me and tried to hang me as a traitor to the realm of Anatolia."

His jaw clenched. "Then I will make sure he pays dearly for hurting you. I'm sorry I couldn't protect you."

"It's not your fault. It's mine. I should never have left." She didn't want to cry again, damn it, but she felt the threat of tears.

"There's only one thing left for me to do. Let's get you home."

Fiona wanted to weep for joy as Niall released her hand and turned to Deaglan. "How do we do this, Father?"

"I do hope you remember all I taught you, my son. For you will need all your power now. I once showed you how to open a portal with magic. Do you recall?"

Niall nodded.

"Good, then. Come with me." Fiona started to follow when Niall turned and motioned for her to stay. "No. Stay back. The spells we are about to cast are powerful. Should anything go awry…well, it would be best if you waited here."

She glanced over at Sean, Aoife and Winnie who looked at her with expectant faces. Clearly she was in charge now. "All right. We'll wait here."

She watched Deaglan and Niall take several steps away to a clearing. She recalled the Time Sphere in the Ivory Wood sat on a pedestal in a clearing much like the one in which they now stood. Her breath caught in her throat and she thought she knew what was about to transpire. She moved closer to stand next to Aoife and took her hand.

"I hope this works," Sean said, sounding doubtful.

"As do I," Fiona said with a nod.

Deaglan uncorked the vial and held the bottle at the ready. He gave the go-ahead nod to Niall, who lifted his arms, his hands out ready to cast a spell. His hands glowed bright white, as though a static energy was about to be emitted from them. Fiona could see Deaglan take a deep cleansing breath and then he jerked the vial in one violent shake. The shimmering blue substance spilled outward from the bottle and Niall caught it in his white magic.

A pop sounded followed by a flash of light so bright, it blinded her. Her ears started to ring. She couldn't see or hear anything.

"What's happening?" Aoife said next to her, but it sounded like she shouted.

Another blast and this time, she felt the magic go through her. It pushed her off her feet and she lost her grip on Aoife and then everything turned black.

She didn't know how long she was out but she heard Niall's voice in her ear calling her name. She pried her eyes open as he helped her to a sitting position.

"Are you all right?" he asked.

"Where's Aoife?"

"She's fine. Everyone is fine."

Fiona struggled to stand. He gripped her arm to steady her. As she stood to her full height, she saw the glowing ball on the pedestal.

"By the gods…" she breathed. "Is that a Time Sphere?"

"It is. We created it." Even Niall sounded awestruck at their handiwork.

Aoife, Winnie, Sean and Deaglan stood around it. All of them looked on with wide-eyed amazement.

"You did it," Fiona said.

"It's a dangerous thing to have two of these." Sean walked around it looking at it with a critical eye. "Are you sure it will get us back?"

Deaglan nodded. "I'm sure. And you're right. It's dangerous. That's why I intend to put a protection spell over it. One that can't be broken by anyone."

Fiona bit her lip. She looked at Sean and Aoife who gave her a knowing glance. They knew, as she did, that she had been the one to break the protection spell in the future to come back in time. Odd they had come full circle, that Niall and Deaglan had created the very Time Sphere she had used to go back in time to destroy the king. But that was in her past now and something she couldn't change, even if she wanted to.

Neither Aoife nor Sean seemed ready to tell Deaglan the truth and for that she was grateful.

"Aye, Deaglan, a protection spell. Make sure it's a strong one. Make sure that not even a wizard can break the spell. Or a powerful Fae." He lifted a brow in question but she didn't want to elaborate. She moved closer to the sphere. "Can you get us home now?"

"I can with Niall's help. If you're ready."

They all added, echoing Fiona's own thoughts. "We're ready."

"I cannot, however, promise I can return you to the moment you left."

"I don't care as long as we get back," Aoife said.

Fiona could see the look of despair on Winnie's face and put a comforting hand on her arm. The girl had been different since waking up in Deaglan's tower. She had taken the news well that Fiona was from the future. She'd never taken the idea well of going forward in time. Now she looked distraught.

"Everything will be all right, Winnie." Fiona wanted to do everything she could to reassure her.

"I'm scared," she whispered. "I've never been so far from home as I am now. And I'm worried about my mum."

Fiona could have kicked herself. She should have known the girl would still have family here and would be worried about them. But she hadn't thought of it. She mentally slapped her forehead. Fiona wrapped an arm around her shoulders.

"Your mum would want you to be safe. You weren't safe at Lambridge. Not with Cian."

She nodded agreement. "I know. I just thought…I thought I would be able to go home."

Oh, gods. She hadn't even given the girl that option, had she? She expected her to go along with the ride as though it were natural and Winnie would *want* to return in time with them. Fiona didn't know what to do then. She'd been completely absorbed with her own problems, she hadn't even considered poor Winnie. And hadn't the girl been through enough?

"She can return with me," Niall said. "I'll take her back to the towers with me and we'll find her mum."

Winnie's eyes lit up. "Oh, aye, I'd like that."

Fiona was grateful for Niall for his quick thinking and his kindness. She smiled at him, her heart fluttering and wondering why she ever left him in the first place. She reminded herself she was a different person then, much younger and naïve than she was now.

"Thank you, Niall." Then she hugged Winnie and whispered in her hair so only she could hear. "I shall miss you. I'm terribly sorry for everything that's happened but I'm happy you're going home."

"Thank you," the girl whispered back.

"You should wait over there," Niall said, nodding toward the edge of the clearing.

She released her and Winnie moved out of the way of the Time Sphere. She paused at the edge of the clearing, her hand on one of the trees as if to hold on to it to make sure she didn't go with them.

Niall turned to Fiona then, taking her hands in his. "Come back to me?" His voice went so soft, she wasn't sure she heard him. But when she met his gaze, she knew she *had* heard him.

"Aye, I will. I promise."

He kissed her. It was only a brush of the lips and much like that first kiss he'd given her so long ago in his library. But it was still a kiss and a promise of things to come. When she returned to the future, when she was home again where she belonged she would never leave him again.

A lump formed in her throat and again she felt the stinging threat of tears. All her life, she had been strong and had barely shed a tear. Now it seemed she couldn't stop shedding them. But she bit her lip and she nodded.

"Aye, I will."

He leaned in, his lips whispering against her cheek. "See you soon." Niall turned to his father, her daughter and Sean. "It's time."

The three travelers gathered around the Time Sphere and clasped hands with Aoife in the middle.

"Safe journey to you," Deaglan said.

He raised his arms, palms up, and closed his eyes. The orb came to life and a mist trickled outward from it, surrounding them in its cool dampness. Niall mimicked Deaglan's movements and together the two chanted a spell of the old tongue, something that even Fiona didn't know or understand. In all the time she had spent in the towers, they had never done magic together. It was surreal watching the two of them work together.

Slowly the world around them began to spin. It gained momentum, going faster and faster until their surroundings was nothing more than a blur. Next to her Aoife stiffened. Something cold and hard punched her in the lungs and she exhaled, then realized she couldn't breathe so well.

"Don't let go of each other."

Deaglan's last words pounded through her. The ground fell away and they were suddenly floating and then there was nothing. Next to her, Aoife's body went limp. She gripped her hand tighter and realized Sean, too, had lost consciousness.

Fiona's muscles ached but she managed to move to wrap an arm around Sean while still gripping Aoife's hand. Holding the two of them was difficult but she was too afraid to let go of them for fear she would lose them in whatever place they happened to be floating.

A second later there was a flash of light and then she was out.

Chapter 26

Aoife heard a voice calling her name in the distance. It was as though she climbed upward from a dark place, clawing her way to the light. Her limbs were heavy like she swam underwater against the current. And for a moment she thought she *was* underwater by the sound of the distant voice. When she finally came to and blinked her eyes open she was greeted with a bright flash of light that quickly dimmed to normal. As her eyes adjusted, her head pounded from the base of her skull to the bridge of her nose.

"Aoife, thank the gods. Are you all right?" It was Niall's voice near her ear.

"Niall?" She forced his name out through cracked lips and a dry mouth.

"I'm here."

She turned her head as he knelt beside her, worry etched along his forehead. He took her by the arm and helped her to a sitting position. Even that little movement made her hurt all over and she groaned. She pressed fingertips into her forehead to stop the throbbing.

"Where's Sean?"

"He's here. He's all right. He hasn't come to yet. Neither has your mother."

She craned her neck to look around but the blinding pain was too much to bear. She put her head in her hands and groaned again.

"My father assures me the pain will pass."

She sucked in a sharp breath and tried to lift her head but couldn't. "Deaglan? He's here?"

"Why wouldn't he be?"

Before she could respond a moan sounded next to her. She managed to turn her head to see Sean struggling to sit up. Niall moved to help him.

"Easy, there."

"What happened?" Sean sounded groggy, like he'd just woken up from a deep sleep.

"You all returned via the Time Sphere. It was quite a thing to witness, to be sure," Niall said.

"Aoife? Fiona?"

"I'm here," Aoife said. She crawled toward him. He reached for her, wrapped his arm around her and hugged her tight.

"You okay?" he whispered into her hair.

She could hear the steady beat of his heart under her ear. "I have a headache, but yes, I seem to be fine."

"Fiona?"

"She's still out cold," Niall said. "I'm afraid to move her. She hit her head fairly hard when she landed. Who beat her?"

"It's a long story but it was Cian's men," Sean said. "What happened to us exactly?"

His arm tightened around Aoife when she started to move out of his embrace.

"The Time Sphere came alive so suddenly it was startling. A blinding light lit up the entire library and then a mist swirled inside it," Niall said. His voice held a awe and wonder as he explained. "It hummed. A loud hum I have never heard before. It was so strange. I approached the Time Sphere, stretched out my hand..." His voice trailed as he mimicked the motions.

Aoife could see then the seared skin along the tips of his fingers.

"It burned you?" she asked.

He nodded, glancing down at his fingers. "It was something akin to lightning. A brilliant flash of light. I stumbled backward. There was a sizzle and as I looked up, the three of you appeared."

"You need to see a healer," Sean said.

"I'll be fine. Staying here with all of you was more important."

"I'm so tired." Aoife was acutely aware of her low energy. All she could think about was crawling into bed and sleeping off her headache. "I feel as though I've run a marathon and been hit by a Mack truck."

"Me, too," Sean agreed.

"Let me get you to a room. You'll want to rest."

Niall helped Aoife to her feet, then Sean. Before they could take a step, though, the doors to the library banged open and a man entered in a hurry. His hair was mussed, his eyes wild with first fear then surprise then joy. Sean's face broke into a large grin as he left Aoife's side and stumbled toward him. They clasped hands and gave each other a manly hug.

"I didn't think I'd ever see the likes of you again," the man said.

"How did you get here?" Sean asked. "Through the portal in the warehouse?"

"Yes." The man's gaze flickered to Aoife and then Fiona. "You found them I see. About time."

Aoife joined them, her expectant gaze on Sean as she waited for an introduction. It was clear the two of them knew each other and well.

"Aoife, this is Caleb. We worked together at the agency."

She shook his hand, peering at him intently. "You seem somewhat familiar to me. Do I know you?"

"We haven't officially met," Caleb said, smiling. "I was assigned to your mother so I know all about her and you." He looked back at Sean. "We have much to discuss. You've been gone a long time."

"How long is a long time?" Sean asked, sounding wary.

Caleb and Niall exchanged looks. Her father gave him a go-ahead nod. Caleb took a deep breath. "Six human years."

"Six years?" Aoife's breath rushed out of her and her knees started to buckle. Sean wrapped an arm around her and held her upright. "How is that possible?"

"Mayhap you should sit down and explain it to them, Caleb." Niall waved toward the nearby chairs. "I will stay with Fiona."

Her gaze flew to Niall. She hadn't realized it when she first came to but he had a full-grown beard. Even though he didn't age as humans, he *had* aged. His face had worry lines etched along his eyes and mouth. It must have been harrowing for him waiting for their return.

Aoife was beyond stunned. She had never imagined being in Faery in either time period would have robbed her of so many years and yet she still felt as though she hadn't aged at all. What had become of her friends back in Austin? Had they forgotten her? Packed up her stuff and sent it…where? Because no one lived in her childhood home anymore. She stole a glance at Fiona who was still out cold on the floor while Niall hovered over her.

Sean led her to the chair by the fire. They sat together while Caleb took the seat opposite them.

"What happened?" Sean asked, getting right to the point.

"I told you I'd give you forty-eight hours and then I'd follow,"

Caleb said. "You never showed up and I had a feeling something had gone wrong. By the time I made it to Faery and to Niall's towers, it was too late. You had already gone back in time to get Fiona. Why did you do something so insane?"

"Because I had to."

Sean glanced at Aoife as she looked up at him. Their eyes met. She could see all the emotion in that one glance and knew it was all the information he was willing to give Caleb. She didn't know why. Maybe he wanted to keep their relationship—whatever it was— close to him.

"Bryant still wants the women returned to the human realm," Caleb said.

Aoife stiffened. It was something she hadn't truly considered. Go back to her life as it was before? Could she? Did she even want to? She couldn't help but wonder what had happened to her college life in Austin. Likely it was gone now. She couldn't go back to that. Her friends were gone, her classmates graduated. And she was nothing more than a ghost to them.

Sean was shaking his head before he even finished. "No."

"No?" His browed winged upward.

"At least not yet." He hugged her tight.

"He'll also want a debrief."

"In time," Sean said. "I'll tell him everything. Just not yet."

"Then when?" he persisted.

"When I'm ready." Sean's voice was thin with a hint of annoyance and anger.

Aoife didn't know what motivated him to want to stay away from Bryant—she assumed that was his superior—and she really didn't care what the reason was. She had bigger things to worry about. Like her mother and Niall and the fact Deaglan was alive. Neither Sean nor Caleb seemed to realize the timeline had been altered.

"Bryant will want an answer soon and he'll want them back in the human realm." Caleb's tone was less friendly and more persistent.

"I'm not going back." It was an impulsive decision and one she hadn't intended to voice aloud. Both their heads snapped in her direction. She swallowed hard. "It's just that…I don't belong there. Not anymore."

"She's right," Sean said with a nod and a smile. He never took his eyes off her as she spoke. "She doesn't. She's Fae and a wizard. She belongs in Faery."

"Bryant won't be happy," Caleb said.

Anger flared inside her. "I don't give a crap what this Bryant person thinks or wants. He's not in charge of me. I'm the daughter of the king of Illyria. I'm staying."

Caleb lifted his hands in surrender while Sean gave her a grin that said he was on her side.

"We'll talk more later, then," Caleb said. "There is more I need to catch you up on, Sean."

"Later," Sean agreed. "Right now I have a raging headache."

"Me, too," Aoife said.

"I'll take you to your rooms." Niall rejoined the conversation, pretending that he hadn't overhead when everyone knew he had.

They rose and started to follow him toward the door but then he turned back. He reached for Aoife, wrapped her in his arms and hugged her so tight she could scarce breathe.

"I'm glad you're staying," he whispered so only she could hear. Then he released her and motioned for the rest of them to follow. "Come."

As she followed him out of the library, Aoife knew she'd made the right decision.

There was a high-pitched squeal ringing in Fiona's ears. It was so loud she flinched when she finally came awake and whimpered with the pain. And then she realized there was someone hovering over her, shaking her. Opening her eyes, she peered right into the crystal clear blue eyes of Niall. But this was not the Niall she had left only moments before. He was older, with fine lines along his forehead and around his eyes. This Niall sported a full dark blond beard and was graying at the temples.

"Niall?"

"Thank the gods. You're all right. I was so worried."

He took her hand in his, kissed her knuckles as though it had been years since he'd seen her. And mayhap it had. For her, it had only seemed like a few minutes ago. For him…clearly, it had been longer than a few minutes. How much time had passed since she'd come back?

"Where is Aoife? And Sean? Are they all right?"

"They're safe. Resting comfortably in their chamber."

She wanted to sit up, but her head refused to let that happen. Pain exploded through her skull, making a blinding white flash behind her eyes. She winced and remained where she was. "Where am I?"

"The library. Let me help you."

He wrapped an arm under her shoulders and the backs of her knees and lifted her from the floor as though she weighed nothing. It was only then she realized he carried her. She saw the flash of the Time Sphere in his library as they walked by. It was still lit up with a pale blue shimmer that reminded her of the one back in the Ivory Wood. The one Niall and Deaglan had created to return them to their future. He passed through the tall shelves into the main area of the library where there was a small seating area and a fireplace blazing with a bright cheery fire.

She had always loved this library. Even when she was here against her will. It had given her comfort in a time of discord. He gently lowered her to the chaise near the fire, then poured a cup of mulled wine and handed it to her. She shivered, and hadn't realized until that moment how chilled she was. He noticed and covered her with a quilt. She was grateful for the wine as she took it from his hand and sipped. It warmed her right to the tips of her toes.

"How long was I out?"

"Several hours." He stood near the mantle, his hands clasped behind his back in that old mannerism with which she was familiar. The one that also reminded her of Deaglan. "I didn't want to move you until you came awake. You have a lump on your head. You must have hit it when you landed. And your face. What happened to it?"

That explained the pain. She ran her hand over her forehead and felt the faint lump near the hairline. It was tender and she winced when she touched it.

"It's nothing to worry over. I'm fine. Did we land here?"

"You did."

Fiona sipped the wine again, it relaxed her. She extended the cup to him and he took it, placing it on a nearby table as she leaned her head back, her eyes closed. Everything hurt. The ache went bone deep. She recalled struggling to hold on to Aoife and Sean and how heavy they had been. That was moments before she blacked out.

"I'm so tired."

"You need rest. When you're up to it, I'll take you to your chamber."

Her chamber? Her eyes blinked open. What had transpired since her disappearance? What had changed? Was Deaglan alive? Had she, at least, managed to save his life? And where was Winnie? And her father? She had rescued him from certain death on the trail after the attack from Niall's mercenaries. What had become of him? She'd lost track of him when Cian had kidnapped her and taken her to Lambridge and, truthfully, she hadn't thought of her father again. Guilt swarmed her.

She had to be the worst person ever.

She flung off the quilt and tried to stand, but the room dipped and spun and she pitched forward. Niall was there in a second, catching her and putting her back onto the chaise.

"Whoa. You're not going anywhere, love."

"I've got to find out…" Her voice trailed off. She didn't even know where to begin.

"Find out what?"

Fiona looked up at Niall. His tall lithe form hovered over her. She reached for his hand, grasped it.

"Tell me true, Niall. How long were we gone?"

His jaw clenched. She could see the muscles flexing and she knew he didn't want to answer. He took a deep breath.

"Six human years."

Six human years. It didn't seem possible. Six years? But in Faery, that was double, mayhap triple. Time was odd in Faery and couldn't be measured like that in the human realm. Days were longer, sometimes shorter. Months didn't exist and the seasons came and went as they pleased. The only constant about Faery was that it wasn't constant.

She didn't know what to say. She didn't know what to feel. Instead she pointed out the obvious.

"You grew a beard."

He ran his free hand over the facial hair, the scruff rasping against his palm. "Do you like it?"

"Not really. No."

"Me either. I vowed I wouldn't shave until your return. I was starting to feel rather desperate."

He waved a hand over his face and just like that, the beard was gone and he was the clean-shaven man she remembered with the cleft in his chin. And yet the gray remained at his temples as though her disappearance had aged him.

The thought stabbed her in the heart. She had missed him, too, if truth be told. She never realized it until that moment how much she had longed to be with him again. He had been her one true love. The one who could see right into her and know what she was thinking, feeling. He knew her better than anyone and she marveled at that. He was the man with which she'd spent the least amount of time. Yet something about him put her at ease, made her calm, made her realize he was her one and only.

"I'm sure you have a lot of questions," he said.

"Do you have answers to them?"

He pinpointed her with that striking blue gaze that always seemed to see right into her soul. "My father lives."

Fiona couldn't help it. She burst into tears.

Niall moved to her side in a lightning quick move, his arms wrapping around her as he held her close. She buried her face in his shoulder and let the tears flows. Tears for a thousand different emotions she'd felt since she'd time traveled back in time. She had managed to do one thing on her list—save Deaglan.

"You saved him from me, love. You saved me from myself. I can never thank you enough for that."

"How…d-do you know about that?"

"Something strange happened when you returned." His voice was full of wonder and awe as he held her, stroking her hair, calming her. "When you came through the Time Sphere I could see the two different timelines. It was as though they split in half. And I had a choice. Follow one and we would end up right back where we were. Follow the other and allow the changes made in the past."

"I don't understand. You saw us come through the Time Sphere?"

He patted her hand. "After I sent Aoife and Sean back in time, I spent every waking hour here in this library waiting for the Time Sphere to activate. I worried I might have killed them by sending them back in time. I realized, though, as things changed, that I hadn't killed them and I hoped they'd found you."

Fiona craned her neck to look up at Niall. "What things? What changed?"

He took a deep cleansing breath. "This is difficult to explain. When you left me all those years ago after we married, I was enraged. I wanted revenge. I stole my father's magic to make myself more powerful and yet I had no idea at the time it would kill him. Even that wasn't enough to assuage the pain I was in from losing you. I destroyed Anatolia. In the process, I thought I had killed Prince Cian but his body was never found."

Fiona's heart kicked into a wild beat. She gripped a handful of his tunic and remained silent, waiting for him to continue.

"Every day when I awoke, I noticed little things had changed. Like a rose bush that had previously never flowered, now had fully bloomed. There were strangers in my castle, servants I didn't know. A girl named Winnie, for instance."

"Winnie?" Fiona pushed off from him and sat up. "Tell me. Where is she? Is she here?"

"Do you know her?"

She nodded. "Please. Tell me."

He had a distant look in his eyes. "She said she knew you. That she was your lady's maid. I had no reason not to believe her but I didn't know how she ended up here in the towers. She told me I brought her here, but I had no memory of it at all."

"Is she…still here?"

"Oh, aye, she is. She'd been through some sort of trauma, but she would never tell me. So I let her be and allowed her to have the run of the castle. She took to polishing the silver and then cleaning the balustrades and…well, when I tried to discourage her of that she refused me. She told me she had nothing else to do and so she went about her business. She runs my household and quite well."

Fiona pressed cold fingertips against her lips and tried not to cry again. "Thank you. Oh, thank you, Niall. What you did for her was…more than a kindness. I will be forever grateful."

"You sent her back with me, didn't you?" he asked.

She nodded. "She didn't want to come forward in time. She wanted to find her mother."

Sadness creased his forehead then. "Ah, that. Aye, she asked me about that. I tried to find her but her village had been decimated by Prince Cian. Her mother was killed in the raid. She had nowhere else to go, so I told her she could stay here."

Fiona hated to hear such a thing and it made her hate Cian all the more. "What else happened? Tell me."

"Not long after Sean and Aoife left, a man showed up here. Said his name was Caleb and he worked for the Inter-Dimensional Portal Protection Agency and he knew Sean O'Connell."

"Caleb is *here?*" Fiona asked, blinking with surprise.

"You know him, too?"

"I knew him in the human realm," she said.

"Well, then, he's here, too. There's something I don't like about that fellow. I'm not sure I trust him," Niall said. "I also have no idea what this Inter-Dimensional Portal Protection Agency is or does."

"It doesn't matter. None of that matters anymore."

Fiona waved away the thought. She knew Caleb had found a portal to get to Faery from the human realm just as she knew he and Sean were assigned to keep her in the human realm. A lot of good that did them. She managed to get through anyway. But she wasn't interested in him or how or why he was in Faery. She wanted to know more about the Time Sphere.

"Tell me more about this split in the timeline."

He turned serious, took her hands in his. "My father told me I should be present when—if—you ever made it back. He felt certain you would. So I waited and then it happened. The Time Sphere came alive. I helped pull you through time, but when I did…" Niall paused, staring down at their entwined hands and the burned tips of his fingers. "I could see what a terrible person I was. The way I destroyed Anatolia after promising you I wouldn't. The way I killed my father for his magic. I hated myself for that and I didn't want to be that person anymore. The other timeline showed me something else in a different world where Anatolia was still on the map and my father still lived."

She hiccupped a breath, a lump of emotion in her throat. She squeezed his hands.

"I chose the second timeline, Fiona. I chose it because I knew you would come back to me."

"That's what you said to me," she whispered as she looked up at him, met his gaze. "You said, 'Come back to me.'"

"And you did." He kissed her fingertips. "This time I'm never letting you go."

"I never want you to let me go. I love you. I have always loved you. I was a fool to leave you in the first place. I'm sorry. I'm so sorry, Niall. I altered time and shouldn't have. I should have let things be as they were. I thought changing my past would change my future. I thought Aoife would be safe in the human realm while I did it. But she wasn't ever safe. And my stupid acts cost me. I lost my family all over again. I'm responsible for the horrible things that happened to Winnie. I also lost my magic."

"I don't think you are responsible for what happened to Winnie. Some things cannot be changed. Mayhap what happened to her was part of her fate. She's stronger than you think and she survived. She survived because of you. And about your magic…well…I'm sure there's a way to get it back." He gave her a lopsided grin.

Warmth spread through her, knowing what he implied and what he wanted. She wanted that, too. "Can you ever forgive me?"

"I can. If you can forgive me." He tipped her chin up and cupped her face.

"Aye, I can."

"I'm glad. I've loved you since that first day you walked into my life."

He kissed her, their lips meeting for what seemed like the first time in centuries. It was not the chaste kiss he had given her on her cheek before sending her through time. It was the kiss of passion and longing, desire and need. The kiss of a starving man. It was a kiss Fiona was all too willing to return.

"What do you say we go back to my chamber and I show you how much I missed you?" A grin pulled at the corner of his mouth.

"I say that's a wonderful idea."

It had been so long since she'd been with him, her body tingled with anticipation. He took her by the hand and helped her to her feet. They left the library behind and walked through the towers toward his chamber and it reminded her of not so long ago when she walked with him the night they married. Her feelings now were not so unlike her feelings then. But this time she knew without a doubt she loved him and would stay with him.

The Towers of Illyria had largely remained the same since she had been here last, which, oddly, was in her past. Even Niall's chambers had not changed much. The same desk with the high-backed cushioned chair and the thick luxurious rugs running along the stone floors. Even the diaphanous curtains billowing at the open windows had not changed. With a wave of his hand, he lit the candles to create a warm inviting glow. She still loved the wide terrace that overlooked the cliffs. Though she had never spent much time there to enjoy the view, she hoped she would be able to, now that she had decided to remain in Faery.

The thought struck her. She hadn't made a conscious decision to stay in Faery, though she knew, deep down, it was where she belonged. Not the human realm. She would decide what to do about Sunnie later when her mind was more focused, when she was not thinking only of Niall.

No words passed between them as he led her to his bed, as he slowly undressed her. He peeled away layer after layer of clothing until she stood before him naked. He kissed every inch of her flesh as though he paid homage to her, as though he had all the time in the world to explore every inch of her. To caress her. To love her.

When he laid her down on his bed—the bed they'd shared so long ago—she opened to him. He slid on top of her, inside her and loved her. Everything about the moment was perfect. In the long years she spent in the human realm, she never thought she would come back to him this way. She had long harbored her rage and hatred inside her, wanting nothing but revenge.

Now she wanted nothing but an eternity.

Her climax came with his and together they peaked. It was in that moment, the magic inside her reignited. Almost as though the flame had merely been snuffed out and was now lit once again. The golden glow burst from her body to light up their small cocoon.

Niall kissed her forehead then leaned his against hers. "I think you have your magic back, love."

Fiona placed her hands on either side of his face. "I do thanks to you."

His fiery mouth met hers as he gathered her to him and rolled to his back, holding her close. And she knew she would never leave his side again.

Chapter 27

Aoife yawned and stretched then pushed up in the big bed to look around the chamber. Late morning light slashed across the stone floor through the window. She'd managed to sleep late and felt rested for the first time in days. She had insisted on leaving the draperies open so the sunrise would wake her, though it hadn't this morning.

It seemed quite normal to be living in the tower of her wizard king father. Not at all odd as she had first thought. She settled into life with ease, in the towers with Sean. In a way, he had become her anchor, giving her a sense of the familiarity in a new world full of discovery and wonder.

She shoved off the coverlet and padded across to the window. Her view from the tower was nothing but a big blue expanse of sky. Not even a cloud dotted the heavens. Far below, she could see the craggy rocks of the Cliffs of Mhothair, which were an impenetrable fortress. No wonder Prince Cian could not breach the walls when he tried to attack.

It had been two days since their return. Her mother had finally awoken and she and Niall had reconciled. Her mother's magic was back. Her parents were reunited and she couldn't be happier.

A soft knock sounded on the door before it opened. Sean entered and then stood there gazing at her with a sexy smile on his face. Happiness filled her knowing he was there with her sleeping in the same bed, sharing the same chamber.

"You're up finally. And still glowing, I see."

"I'd say I'm sorry but I'm really not. I've grown to like it. Do you think it will ever, not be so obvious?" She didn't exactly want the whole world to know she was getting it on with Sean. Every time they were together, it recharged her and she glowed brighter.

He shrugged as he walked toward her, taking her in his arms and kissing her. "I don't know. Does it matter so much?"

"It's rather noticeable *why* I'm glowing, don't you think?"

He dropped a kiss on the tip of her nose, mirth twinkling in his eyes. "Embarrassed by me?"

"Of course not. Did you talk to Caleb?" She used the abrupt change in subject to avoid any innuendo.

Despite being back in Faery, Sean still had a job to do. He still had to report into his agency but he had expressed his feelings that he wanted to remain with her as long as he could. She took that as a good sign.

"What did he say about you staying in Faery?" she asked, trying not to sound too curious or probing or hopeful.

"He thinks the agency will grant me a leave of absence," Sean said.

Hot pinpricks of desire, excitement and anticipation went through her. "Do you mean to stay then?"

He nodded. "For as long as I can. Bryant is interested in how the Time Sphere works and wants to debrief me on everything that happened. I have to visit him soon for a full report."

She didn't like the thought of being separated from him. "When do you have to go?"

"Not for a while." He laced their fingers together. "I want to stay here, talk to Niall and Deaglan about the Time Sphere."

Deaglan and Niall had placed another protection spell on the one in the Ivory Wood. This time a spell that couldn't be broken.

"Do you think they'll tell you anything?"

He gave her that wicked lopsided grin again. "No. But it's worth a shot. Niall has no idea what the agency is or does. I need to talk to him about what we do. I think he can help us. Cal has returned to the human realm to make sure the portal in your house is closed and sealed for good."

"What about my sister?"

"What about her?"

"Won't she wonder why he's in our house?"

Consternation passed across his face. "Aoife, there's something I have to tell you about Sunnie. Maybe you should sit down."

She didn't like the way that sounded, as though something grave had happened. "No. Tell me."

"Cal came for another reason other than trying to find me. After I followed you to Faery, Sunnie started asking questions about Liam's death. She believed Fiona had something to do with it. She...well, she found the portal, Aoife. She's here."

Aoife's mouth went dry as she took a step back from Sean. "How? How did she get here?"

"He didn't know. All he did know for sure was she somehow managed to activate the portal in the trunk. He tracked her through Illyria but he lost her trail. He's not sure where she went."

"Any guesses as to why she's here?" she wanted to know.

"Maybe to find Fiona?"

Her stomach cramped and she didn't even know why. She and Sunnie had never really gotten along but that was no reason to fear her, was it? "If she's here, then she has to know she's part Fae. Don't you think?"

"It's a good bet that's true, yes."

"How would she have found out?"

He shook his head. "I don't know."

"We have to find her. Does my mother know?"

"Not yet."

"I have to tell her." She started for the door, her feet pounding along the stone floor with her hurried steps.

Sean caught her arm and spun her to face him. "Not yet. Let's not tell her yet."

"Why not?"

"Something about this doesn't feel right to me. I need to figure it out first."

"So we just don't tell her? Don't you think she has a right to know her other daughter is here?"

"Yes, of course. I'm simply asking you to wait a little while. Let me handle it. I'll find her and see what she's up to. I don't trust her." He spread his hands, imploring her.

The truth was, Aoife didn't trust her either. There was something about her sister that struck a nerve deep down. They had grown up together with a healthy dose of sibling rivalry. She had been Liam's favorite, though, that much was clear, while he mostly ignored her and Fiona began to disappear to Faery more and more. She understood Fiona's reasons now but she never understood why Liam treated her that way. Perhaps the reason was that Aoife wasn't his biological daughter.

At any rate, it didn't matter now since he was dead and she was in Faery.

"All right. I'll wait." Even though she agreed to wait, that didn't mean she would agree to sit on the sidelines. She would help Sean whether he wanted her to or not.

"Good." He kissed her cheek.

A knock sounded. Sean opened the door and Winnie waited on the other side, her hands clasped in front of her.

"Good morrow." She dipped a curtsy. "I've come to help my lady bathe and dress for the ball tonight."

Aoife's ears perked up. "There's a ball tonight? Sean, you didn't tell me."

"I didn't have a chance." He motioned Winnie inside. Several servant girls followed with clothing and a copper tub. "We'll talk more later."

She blew him a kiss as he walked out the door and closed it behind him. Winnie used her authority to direct the girls to prepare the copper tub. It was clear she had grown out of her meek demeanor and was stronger than she had been when they left her back in time. The girls placed the copper tub next to the fireplace. A young Fae learning to use magic waved her hand over the tub and it filled with steaming water.

Pleased with the results, Winnie turned to Aoife. "Now then. Let's get you ready."

Several hours later, Aoife's auburn hair had been washed and combed and plaited. Winnie dressed her in a gown of emerald trimmed in gold to bring out the green of her eyes. She and the servants left while she waited for Sean to return and escort her to the ball. She couldn't help but feel like a fairy princess. Technically, she *was* a princess since her parents were the king and queen of Illyria.

Sean knocked before opening the door and poking his head inside. He saw she was dressed and ready so he pushed the door wide, standing in the entry with a look of awe on his handsome features.

"Aoife, you look magnificent."

"Winnie picked it." She waved at the gown.

"She did a marvelous job." He stepped into the room, taking her hand.

It gave her a chance to look him over and admire him. He was dressed in a dark blue tunic, black pants and black knee-high boots polished to a high shine. His black hair was combed to perfection, a twinkle in his dark brown eyes. It was a change from seeing him in street clothes or even the peasant clothes he wore in the past. She had a hard time not staring.

"Shall we go, my lady?"

She laughed. "Oh, aye, we shall."

"Before we go." He paused and took a step back. "There's something I want to give you."

Her heart fluttered as she waited while he slipped his hand into his pocket and pulled out something clasped in his fist.

"I spent a lifetime waiting for you to grow up, Aoife. I don't want to waste another lifetime waiting for the right moment."

Oh, her heart pounded a wicked tattoo. "The right moment for what?"

"I know you love me. You took a chance and told me when you knew I wasn't ready to hear it. I regret that now, not telling you then." He turned his hand over and opened his fingers. A delicate silver bracelet rested in his palm. "It's not a ring. But it *is* a promise."

As he slipped the bracelet around her wrist, a warm blissful glow flickered through her.

"I love it," she whispered.

"I wanted you to have this, so you know whatever happens between us I will always come for you. It's all I have left of my mother."

She admired the way the candlelight caught the metal and winked back at her. She was touched by the gesture.

"Thank you." She put her hands on either side of his face and kissed him.

"We better get to the ball before people start wondering what's taking us so long." His grin was irresistible and devastating all at once.

He placed her hand in the crook of his elbow and led her from their chamber, down the long corridor and the winding stairs to the great hall where the place had a festive air about it. It reminded her much of the day Niall and Fiona married. There were long tables set up throughout and on one side a small quartet played cheerful music. At the front of the room, a high table with five empty chairs.

Inside the great hall, Fiona and Niall stood together, inseparable. They mingled through the room, greeting their subjects. Her mother noticed their entrance first and leaned toward

Niall to whisper something in his ear. He extracted himself from the couple he and Fiona had been talking with to head toward Sean and Aoife. Deaglan fell in step with them. He seemed genuinely happy to see them.

"Allow me to be the first to welcome the princess to Illyria." Deaglan kissed her on the cheek.

"Thank you, Deaglan. I mean Grandfather." She grinned and he looked well-pleased with the new title.

"There's my lovely daughter." Niall approached, the happiness at having her there clearly written on his face. "I want to give you something before we present you to the realm."

"Present me to the realm? No one said anything about presenting me." She looked at Sean who merely shrugged as if to say he had no idea. Aoife, though, could see the truth in his eyes. He must have known and wanted it to be a surprise.

"You are the crown princess. The future of Illyria. The people know you're here and have been waiting to meet you. They're also happy with the return of their queen. This ball is in honor of both of you. Now, give me your hand."

She obliged by extending her right hand to him. He reached into his pocket and pulled out a ring, slipping it on her middle finger. It was a silver band with a large red stone set in it. The fiery color caught the light, making it shimmer.

"It's beautiful," she breathed.

"It belonged to my grandmother," he said, sounding well-pleased. "And it's magical."

"It is? What does it do?"

He laughed. "You'll learn all in good time, my daughter. I will teach you all that I know." He extended his elbow for her to grasp. "Shall we?"

Aoife couldn't halt the sick feeling in the pit of her stomach as she took her father's arm. He led her and her mother to the front of the room. Sean remained behind, though she wanted to turn to him and beg him to come with her. Niall halted, turning to the gathering crowd who had suddenly fallen silent and looked to their king with eager expressions.

"Tonight we celebrate the homecoming of our queen, Fiona. After many long years, she has finally returned to the realm to rule by my side." He gave her a loving glance and she smiled, looking regal and the perfect queen. "But tonight is not only about the return of the queen. It is my greatest pleasure to introduce you to my daughter…your princess…Aoife."

All eyes turned to Aoife as they gazed at her with wonder and awe. She had not been prepared for this moment and had no idea what to do. So she did the only thing she could think to do and did a deep curtsy. As she did so, they erupted into applause and cheered her.

It did not escape Aoife's attention that Niall and Deaglan both had called her princess.

Nor did it escape her notice that she was led to the high table to take her place of honor next to her father. Fiona took the seat on the other side of him. Deaglan took the end chair on the other side of Fiona. Which left one seat vacant next to Aoife. As they sat at the table, servants circulated the room with trays full of succulent food and flasks of wine and mead.

"Are you all right, Aoife? You look pale," Fiona said.

"I had no idea this was going to happen."

"We thought it best you came unprepared," Niall said. "Your mother thought you would…how did she put it? Chicken out."

"She would have, too," Fiona agreed even as she gave Aoife a good-natured grin. "Welcome home to Faery, my daughter."

Home. Yes, it was home to her even in the short time she'd been there.

"Tomorrow, Deaglan will begin teaching you how to use all that magic you've stored up. It will do a bit of good for you, I should think, and calm that constant glow of yours," Niall said.

"Aye. Your mother was an adept student. I expect you to be the same. Mayhap a little less inquisitive and more patient." Deaglan leaned over Fiona to talk to her.

"I was a wonderful student." Fiona sniffed derisively but she grinned the whole time, knowing Deaglan poked fun at her. Aoife, though, blushed to the roots of her plaited hair at the hint of the reason behind her shimmering skin. Thankfully, Sean approached the table then, saving her from more embarrassment from her parents.

"May I join you, Your Highness?" He bowed and motioned toward the empty seat next to her.

It took her a minute to realize he addressed her. "Ahh…"

"The empty seat is for Sean, Aoife, dear," Fiona said. "He is your consort, after all."

"Thanks, Mom," she said through gritted teeth.

Sean laughed and took the seat next to her. He slipped his hand into hers under the table and gave her a quick squeeze. "They love you already, you know."

"Who?" she asked.

Two servants placed a roasted pheasant on a silver platter on the table in front of them and started to carve it. Another servant came by and filled their goblets with wine.

"The people of Illyria," Niall said. "They're pleased to know there is an heir. I'm sure they'd given up on me all these long years."

For the first time in her life, contentment flooded through her. She sank back in her seat and eyed the silver bracelet sparkling in the candlelight of the great room. She ran a fingertip over the links and felt a hum of magic running through it. Sean had given her a magical bracelet. As she looked closer, she realized she recognized the links. They were Celtic triskelions—three interlocking spirals. There was no clasp to hold the bracelet together. It merely slipped over her hand and onto her wrist. No beginning. No end. Infinity.

And Sean had given it to her as a promise. A magical promise of forever.

"It's a beautiful piece, isn't it?" Sean asked, his voice low so only she could hear.

"Yes."

"I'm glad you like it."

When all the cups were filled around the room, Niall took his and got to his feet. "A toast to our lovely royal ladies. Céad Míle Fáilte! Sláinte!"

"Sláinte!" the crowd repeated and everyone quaffed their wine or ale.

"What does it mean?" Aoife whispered out of the corner of her mouth.

"A hundred thousand welcomes! To your health!" Sean tipped his cup to her. "Sláinte, Aoife."

As they drank, the doors to the great hall burst open and a man sauntered inside. He was dressed in black from head to toe. His eyes were dark as midnight, his hair the same shade. There was something distressing and menacing about him that presented a foreboding air. Something that didn't seem quite right. As he neared, she could see he had a wicked scar down the left side of his face making him look even more imposing. And yet something about him was oddly familiar. As she watched him approach, recognition hit like a fist to the gut.

Sean's expression stilled and grew serious. She glanced at her father and saw the surprise lining his features. Fiona unfolded her body from the chair in a slow fluid motion, as though she were moving against a heavy current. She'd gone pale. White. Almost as though she'd seen a ghost. They all had.

Liam Burke was supposed to be dead.

But he was alive and well and halting in front of the high table, scrutinizing them all. His gaze started with Sean long enough to acknowledge his presence. He passed over Aoife with disinterest, looked over Niall as though he peered at a long-time enemy and then finally fixed his lethal gaze on her mother. He stared at her for the longest time, a look of loathing and hate and abhorrence. Fiona peered right back, unwavering, unflinching, unswerving.

"Well, well. What a surprise to find you all here in Faery."

"You were dead. I saw the men kill you," Fiona said.

"And I identified the body," Sean added. "When I last saw you, Liam, you were lying on a metal slab in the morgue."

He nodded agreement. "It's true. I was dead on that slab but something happened to me there. Something brought me back."

Aoife sucked in a sharp breath as she realized the calamity of their actions. Things that happened before had not happened again.

"The Time Sph—"

"No," Niall snapped, cutting her off.

He gave her a sharp glance and she clamped her mouth closed. He glanced at his father and they exchanged a silent communication. Deaglan waved his hand and they were all whisked away from the party and into the library to the seating area in front of the fireplace. Not far from where the Time Sphere was silent.

"How did you survive?" Fiona demanded. "There must have been something—"

"I am Fae," Liam announced and straightened as though proud to finally acknowledge it.

Fiona clamped her mouth closed with a snap, her face draining of more color as she slowly sank to a nearby chair. "I don't understand."

"When I awoke in the morgue, I was surrounded by others who were determined to help me. Eventually I learned the truth. That as a babe I was taken from my Fae home and switched for a human child," Liam said.

"A Changeling," Aoife said on a gasp.

He glanced her way and gave her a smile. "Once I learned the truth, there were so many things I understood that I had not before. Things about you, Fiona, my dear." He took a step toward her but Niall moved in front of him, blocking him. "And things about Aoife."

"Me?" she squeaked.

"There was a distinct difference between you and Sunnie, though I never really understood why. Fiona put you both under a glamour spell to hide your true appearance. I know that now though at the time I didn't quite grasp why you both seemed to shimmer," Liam said. "And Sunnie. She's Fae, too, isn't she?"

Fiona swallowed hard. "She is."

But not a Halfling as they had all thought. Sunnie was a full-blooded Fae, likely with magic as well. And she was in Faery looking for them all and no one but Aoife and Sean knew it. She looked at him, questions on her mind and he shook his head. Now was not the time to tell anyone Sunnie was somewhere in Faery.

"Which means she, too, has magic," Niall said. "We should find her."

"*We* will do no such thing," Liam said. "You'll all stay away from her. She's *my* daughter."

Fiona looked as though she wanted to protest when Niall waved her off. "We won't harm her."

"You'll stay away," he warned, his words hard.

"How did you get here?" Sean asked, returning to the subject at hand.

Liam granted him a smile as he looked him over. "I followed your old friend Caleb. He showed me how to get into the realm through a portal."

"Caleb would never do that," Sean said.

"He would because he's one of my best operatives."

Aoife sensed the anger radiating off Sean as he stiffened. "He doesn't work for you. He works for Bryant at the Inter-Dimensional Portal Protection Agency."

"Everyone works for someone, Sean, and Bryant works for me."

"It was you." Fiona's voice wavered when she spoke. "You

wanted to keep me out of Faery."

"I tried my hardest, yes. That is true. I knew you were dangerous and with your wizard husband's help you had the ability to change things. To alter the past. I'd been following you for some time, watching you. I knew you were planning something. I knew you had some way to time travel and I intended to keep you in the human realm for as long as possible."

She pressed her fingertips against her lips. "But you were dead. I don't understand how this is happening."

"Altering the timeline changed more than we thought," Niall said.

"Yes, and I intend to alter it further."

Before anyone could move, Liam sifted away and was gone. Niall sucked in a sharp breath as though he'd realized something horrible had happened. He sprinted through the library. A moment later he returned, his face horror stricken.

"He took the Time Sphere."

Sean stalked to the fireplace. He leaned against the mantle, his head in his hands. Aoife didn't know what to do, other than remain rooted to her spot. She wanted to go to him, to comfort him but she wasn't sure how to do that. It seemed as though everything had suddenly spun out of control. What would happen now?

"This is all my fault. All of it," Fiona said. "If I had never used that portal to begin with none of this would be happening."

"It doesn't matter now. I need to get my Time Sphere back and I need answers," Niall said. "What does this portal protection agency do exactly?"

"It was created to ensure the safety and security of Faery portals to keep humans from entering the realm and to keep unauthorized Fae from leaving Faery," Sean said. "I was assigned Fiona's case when Aoife was small. What I don't understand is how Liam came to be a part of it."

"Neither do I," Fiona said.

"That's something we'll have to figure out. Fiona, what happened the day he died? Tell me everything," Niall said.

She sank into the cushion of the chair. "I had planned to leave the human realm and return to Faery. Liam and I weren't on speaking terms exactly. I was by the creek as I prepared to open the portal when he came to stop me. He wanted me to stay. As we argued, the soldiers arrived. I knew who they were." She glanced at

Niall who nodded.

"My men. Go on."

"They tried to capture me but I ran, intending to use the Tears. One of them tried to stop me with his magic. The next thing I knew, Liam was on the ground. I thought he was dead."

"But maybe he wasn't," Sean suggested.

"I used a portal to escape and find Sean. I knew I had to entrust the house to him. That he would keep it safe," she continued.

"From Aoife," Niall added. "Then what happened?"

"I called the girls to tell them and then I used the trunk in the attic to make my escape. I thought I could keep that portal open for a hasty return should I need it," she said.

"That doesn't explain how he survived," Sean said. "Only that he did. And I saw him in the morgue. I identified the body. How did he come to the IDPP?"

"Does it matter?" Niall asked.

"It does if we want to right the timeline," Sean said.

"How do we do that?" Aoife asked.

"Liam has to die in the past in the human realm," Fiona said, her voice grim.

"Any suggestions?" Niall wanted to know.

"We'll figure it out. I have to go back to the human realm to find Caleb. I need to know if what Liam said about him was true," Sean said. "I don't believe he's a traitor."

Niall looked thoughtful for a long moment. He ran his hand over his chin and glanced at his father. More silent communication passed between them and Deaglan gave him a nod of agreement.

"I'll help you find him," Niall said. "He has the Time Sphere. That thing has too much power to be left in the hands of someone who knows nothing about it."

"And so will I," Fiona added. "This is all my doing so I should at least help."

"Your Majesties should remain here." Deaglan moved to stand near them, his hands clasped behind his back. "I do not think the realm could survive if it suffered a loss of all the royals."

Niall looked defeated. "You are right, of course, Father. You should go."

"Me? I'm an old man. I cannot—"

"You are more powerful than me and you can help them in ways I cannot. You also know how the Time Sphere works."

Reluctantly, Deaglan nodded agreement.

Sean looked to Aoife. She was unsure how she felt about everything that had happened. The thought of Sean leaving her again made her heart palpitate. He reached for her, ran his hands up her arms.

"I'm sorry, Aoife. But I have to do this."

"I understand." The magic flared bright inside her and the bracelet on her wrist whispered encouragement. "But I can't let you go without me."

A slow smile spread on his face. "You intend to go with me then?"

"I do. You'll not stop me either, Sean. I'm coming whether you like it or not."

"Are you certain?"

"I've never been more certain about anything in my life."

"Then it's settled," Niall said. "Father and I will consult his spell books and scrolls to see what we can use to fix this. Then you will be well-prepared to track down Liam."

Niall ushered his father and Deaglan out of the library and Fiona followed but Sean remained. Aoife hesitated before taking a step toward the door. He caught her by the arm, stopped her.

"Aoife, this thing we're about to embark on. It's not going to be easy. And it will be dangerous. I will never forgive myself if something happens to you."

She placed her hand on the side of his face. "Don't worry, Sean. You gave me the bracelet. Everything is going to be fine. We'll find Liam and the Time Sphere."

"I hope so."

She hoped so, too. She kissed him in an effort to comfort both herself and him. As their lips met, though, the rippling current went through them. A flash of light and suddenly, they stood together in the ruins that was once Niall's library in the Towers of Illyria. They were surrounded by crumbling walls. The roof was partially missing and overhead was a stormy winter sky. Snowflakes drifted to the cracked floor littered with books. A bone-chilling wind whipped through them. She fell against him as he wrapped his arms around her.

"Sean, what just happened?" Her breath plumed white.

"Liam must have used the Time Sphere. He altered time."

Acknowledgements

First and foremost I have to thank Holly Lisle and her writing courses for helping me find my way back to writing. I don't know that I would still be writing today without her workshops. Special thanks to content editor Deb Nemeth for her wonderful suggestions on improving the book. Special thanks, too, to Patricia Essex for her excellent line editing and proofreading skills. These ladies are the bomb and I could not have done this book without them.

Another shout out to my long-time friend, Janice, who beta read this and asked (demanded? *grin*) more chapters as I was writing them. Her enthusiasm for the story helped me get to the end.

I also have to thank my husband, Robert, who always supports me no matter what and listens to me whenever I'm down, working out plot holes or trying to figure out how to navigate the industry. He's my rock.

And finally special thanks to my Plotting Princesses who make writing worthwhile.

Praise for *On the Hunt for the Wizard King*

On the Hunt for the Wizard King, Book 2

"We really got to watch all of the characters grow and change throughout the book. No one was what you expected. Miles did a great job of keeping you guess and wondering what was around the next corner." —5 stars, Amazon Reviewer

"Wow! This story is so full of magic with action and adventure I could not put it down. The land of fae is an exciting magical world where anything can happen, and I definitely was not expecting some of the twist and turns that transpired." —5 stars, Amazon Reviewer

Also by Michelle Miles

Dream Walker
Call of the Dark
Blood and Bone
Flame and Fury
Smoke and Ashes
Light of the World

Dream Walker: Origins
Provenance

Age of Wizards
In the Tower of the Wizard King
On the Hunt for the Wizard King

A Ransom & Fortune Adventure
Highland Fling, Vol 1
Dead of Winter, Vol 2
The Citadel, Vol 3
Lord of the Underworld, Vol 4

Dragon Protectors
Desiring the Dragon Lord
Seducing the Dragon Knight
Tempting Her Dragon Bodyguard

Guardians of Atlantis
Tempting Eden
Seducing Eve
Ravishing Helene
Guardians of Atlantis Box Set

Realm of Honor
One Knight Only
Only for a Knight

A Knight to Remember
A Knight Like No Other
Shadows of the Knight

Shorts and Anthologies
A Dance Among the Faeries, Short Story
Eorwulf, Short Story
The Soul of Sharah, Short Story
Sinfully Sweet, Short Story
Flights of Fantasy: A Collection of Short Stories

Available in Audiobook
In the Tower of the Wizard King
On the Hunt for the Wizard King
One Knight Only
Only for a Knight
A Knight to Remember
Call of the Dark

Watch for more at www.michellemiles.net

starlet returns home determined to find the truth about her parents, he's desperate to keep her from the portal leading into Faery. Sunnie's untapped Fae magic surfaces with wildness she cannot control, and when her sudden sifting leads her right to the portal in the trunk, Caleb has no choice but to follow her. He quickly discovers he can't protect her from the dark magic in the enchanted staff, no more than he can control his own dark magic swirling inside him forcing him to face his cryptic past.

Now in the land of Fae, the two are at the mercy of a cruel sorceress whose malevolent machinations threaten the lives of the only people Sunnie ever truly loved—her family. The longer her dark magic consumes her, the more it puts all their lives in peril and the more Sunnie's true self dissolves. An ancient prophecy holds the key—only one person can break the spell and release her. Caleb is determined to find that person…even if it means sacrificing everything Sunnie holds dear.

Read more at www.michellemiles.net

About the Author

Michelle Miles believes in fairy tales, true love and magic. She writes heart-stopping urban fantasy, epic fantasy and paranormal romance with an action/adventure twist that will leave you breathless. She is the author of numerous series that includes everything from angels and demons to fairies, dragons and elves.

A native Texan, in her spare time she loves reading, listening to music, watching movies, hiking, and drinking wine. She can be found online at Facebook, Twitter, Instagram, Pinterest and Goodreads.

Your Adventure Awaits.